A DAUGHTER'S SECRET

Anne Bennett was born in a back-to-back house in the Horsefair district of Birmingham. The daughter of Roman Catholic, Irish immigrants, she grew up in a tight-knit community where she was taught to be proud of her heritage. She considers herself to be an Irish Brummie and feels therefore that she has a foot in both cultures. She has four children and four grandchildren. For many years she taught in schools to the north of Birmingham. An accident put paid to her teaching career and, after moving to North Wales, Anne turned to the other great love of her life and began to write seriously. In 2006, after sixteen years in a wheelchair, she miraculously regained her ability to walk.

Visit www.annebennett.co.uk and www.Author Tracker.co.uk for exclusive updates on Anne Bennett.

By the same author

A Little Learning
Love Me Tender
A Strong Hand to Hold
Pack Up Your Troubles
Walking Back to Happiness
Till the Sun Shines Through
Danny Boy
Daughter of Mine
Mother's Only Child
To Have and to Hold
A Sister's Promise

ANNE BENNETT

A Daughter's Secret

HARPER

Harper
HarperCollins*Publishers*
77–85 Fulham Palace Road,
Hammersmith, London W6 8JB

www.harpercollins.co.uk

This paperback edition 2008
1

First published in Great Britain by
HarperCollins*Publishers* in 1986

Copyright © Anne Bennett 2007

Anne Bennett asserts the moral right to
be identified as the author of this work

A catalogue record for this book is
available from the British Library

ISBN 978-0-00-787486-6

Set in Sabon by Palimpsest Book Production Limited,
Grangemouth, Stirlingshire

Printed and bound Great Britain by Clays Ltd, St Ives plc

Mixed Sources
Product group from well-managed
forests and other controlled sources
www.fsc.org   Cert no. SW-COC-001806
© 1996 Forest Stewardship Council

FSC

To my grandson Jake, the eldest Bennett boy,
with all my love

ONE

As Thomas John Sullivan drove the horse and cart past St Mary's Catholic church on the way home from Buncrana, the nearest market town, the noon Angelus bell was tolling.

'Dear Lord, but it's perishing cold,' his wife, Biddy, commented from the seat beside him. 'The fields and hedgerows are still as heavily rimed with frost as they were this morning, for the sun hasn't put in an appearance all day.'

'Aye,' Thomas John agreed, 'it's mighty cold, right enough. That's Donegal for you. Sure, don't we have the coldest of winters here at times?'

'We do indeed. Is the child all right, Aggie?'

In the back of the cart, Aggie nursed her little brother, Finn, holding his body tight against her own, her warmest shawl wrapped around the two of them, and yet still he shivered.

'He is all right,' she said. 'Just cold, like the rest of us.'

To divert him, Aggie said, 'We'll be home in no

1

time now, and it's meant to be cold, Finn, for it is nearly Christmas.' She knew that Finn would know little of Christmas, or Santa Claus either, for he was only just turned eighteen months old. She saw a slight frown pucker his brow as she went on, 'You'll like Santa Claus, Finn. He brings good boys and girls presents.'

The child would, she knew, barely know the word 'present' either, for the Sullivan children had few of them. There was no money for such frivolities. But for Finn, the youngest, it would be different. Much had been made of him by all the family when he arrived. Aggie knew her mother had bought a few wee things in Buncrana that morning to fill his stocking on Christmas morning and she was looking forward to seeing his face.

'Aye, nearly Christmas,' Biddy said. 'And then the turn of the year – 1898, I wonder what that will bring.'

Thomas John chuckled. 'What would it bring, woman, but more of the same? Life seldom changes much, except we all get older.'

Aggie thought her father was right, and she was glad. She liked the familiarity of one day following the other predictable and safe. She had been twelve in June, so she had left school and now helped her mother in the home full time. She always looked forward to Saturday morning when she would go to Buncrana with her parents, leaving her brothers Tom and Joe to mind the farm. Her mother would sell their surplus produce in the market, like many

2

other farmers, while Aggie went with her father to buy things needed for the farm. Since Finn's birth, however, her primary task was to look after him while her parents were busy.

She didn't mind this in the slightest, for it gave her a chance to meet up with her former classmates, and especially her best friend, Cissie Coghlan.

That day, though, it had been so cold that she had been glad to go home, and she was looking forward to getting into the warm house and out of the wind. When they passed the church she breathed a sigh of relief that they were not that far from home.

Tom and Joe were waiting for them in the yard, having heard the rumble of the cart. Thomas John brought it to a halt in the cobbled yard before the squat whitewashed cottage, scattering the pecking hens as he did so, and alerting the two dogs, who came from the barn barking a greeting.

Tom went forward to take the horse, saying as he did so, 'I have the water on to boil and the potatoes are in a bucket on the stool inside.'

Biddy nodded and said to Aggie, who was climbing out of the cart with Finn in her arms, 'Take the wee one inside. This intense cold is too much for him.'

The warmth hit Aggie as she opened the door. The room was dimly lit from the one small window at the end, though the sky looked grey and cloud-laden. But the fire burned brightly in the hearth and she saw that one of the boys, likely Tom, had banked it up with peat. There was a further stack of it the other side of the fireplace. The heavy black pot was heating the water over the fire, held up by one of the hooks of the crane that folded out from the wall.

She carried Finn across the stone-flagged floor and sat him near the warmth on a creepie, a low seat made of bog oak.

'You sit there, my wee man, and get warm while I start dinner for us all,' she said, and she was rewarded by a broad smile from Finn as he felt the heat from the fire.

Aggie ladled water from the pot above the fire into a basin, which she then placed on the table, the bucket of potatoes beside her ready for scrubbing. Her mother came in, followed by Joe, carrying parcels. One of these newspaper-wrapped bundles Biddy placed beside Aggie: she knew what was in it and that was fish that her father had bought from the fleet at Buncrana harbour.

Later, with the scrubbed potatoes boiling in their jackets in the big pot, and the plates taken from the dresser and put on to the side of the hearth to warm, Aggie helped her mother prepare the fish for frying, first, chopping off their heads and then slicing through each one expertly to remove the bone, as she had been taught from a child.

It was as the family was halfway through the meal and their hunger somewhat eased that Aggie said, 'Me and Cissie were talking to Mr McAllister today.'

Biddy looked at her daughter. She knew McAllister was newly arrived in the town and there had been great curiosity about the family as there would be about anyone new. Biddy said, 'Isn't he the husband of Philomena, who was left the grocery store?'

Aggie nodded.

Thomas John frowned slightly. 'And what business had a man like that with two young girls?'

'He was nice, Daddy,' Aggie protested. 'I'm sure he was just being neighbourly. He asked our names, and when I said mine was Aggie Sullivan he said he could take a bet that wasn't my given name and that Agnes had a much better sound to it.'

'Stuff and nonsense,' snapped her mother. 'You are called Aggie and that's all there is to it.'

'Whisht,' Thomas John cautioned his wife. 'Let the girl get on with her tale. What else did he say?'

'Then he asked would we like to learn to do the Irish dances properly and I said yes but there was no one now to teach us,' Aggie continued.

'Seems a strange thing to ask a body,' Biddy said. 'Why would he ask you a question like that?'

Tom, two years younger than Aggie, kept his head down so that his mother wouldn't see his smile. He knew Aggie would have liked to dance all the day long if she had been let. He could take a bet she and Cissie had been jigging about and this McAllister had seen them. No wonder he asked them such a question.

Aggie didn't answer her mother. Instead she went on, 'Mr McAllister said it was shameful for us to lose our heritage this way and that he came from the West where such things were prized highly.'

'Not just now he didn't,' Biddy said. 'His wife was only after telling me this morning that they had been living in Birmingham, England this long while when news came of her aunt's death. She was really surprised that she had been left the grocer's shop in the town.'

'Anyway,' Aggie said, fearing that they had gone off the track a little, 'he has offered to teach us to dance, and he said he can also play tin whistle and fiddle, and he can teach any who want to learn those too.'

'I dare say he would have the time right enough,' Biddy recounted wryly, 'for he is more this side of the counter than the other side. He seems to prefer talking with the customers to serving them. His wife has her work cut out with four wee ones to see to as well, for he doesn't seem to be great in that department either.'

'Talk sense, woman,' Thomas John said. 'What man has a great hand in rearing weans? Sure, that's a woman's job.'

'I know that,' Biddy said. 'I just think it a shame that that Philomena McAllister has such a hard time of it. She told me herself her husband is too fond of sitting in Grant's Bar. In fact, he is there so often she wonders if he has shares in the place.'

'That's between them, surely,' Thomas John replied, 'and not our business at all, at all. From what I see of McAllister, he's a personable-looking fellow and he is right, the children shouldn't forget their heritage. But there has been no one bothered since Matty Phelan died a few years ago.'

'There's nothing like a spot of Irish dancing right enough,' Biddy conceded. 'I could fling my heels up with the best of them when I was a girl.'

'So I can go?' Aggie burst in, almost breathless with excitement.

'We will make enquiries,' her father said. 'That is all I am offering to do at this point. And you can take that smirk from your face, Tom, for I have a mind to ask the man if he could teach you a few tunes on the tin whistle.'

Tom looked at his father in amazement. He was not averse to learning the tin whistle. In fact, if his opinion had been asked, he'd have said that he was quite pleased, but he did wonder when he might get time to practise anything he learned because he and Aggie, being the eldest, were kept hard at it.

His doubt was reinforced when his mother said to Aggie, 'And don't you look so pleased with yourself. If we allow you to go to this dancing it will be on top of your duties, not instead of them, and the same goes for you, Tom, and the tunes you learn.'

'Don't you be giving out to Aggie and Tom before they have done anything wrong, Biddy,'

Thomas John chided. 'Neither are slackers, but there is no point in Aggie learning the dancing and Tom the tunes if they are not given time to practise. Haven't I Joe to help me – and we mustn't forget Finn, of course,' he added, ruffling the hair of his youngest son.

Biddy said nothing more. Really, she expected she would have a houseful of sons by now – not that she was keen on children herself, not even her own, but she knew sons were essential on a farm. But she had gone six barren years after the birth of Joe before she produced Finn. She had really thought her childbearing days were over.

Thomas John couldn't understand why she worried over the lack of sons. 'What is the problem?' he would ask, in genuine bewilderment. 'You have a daughter to help in the house, a wee one to dandle on your knee and gladden your heart with his smile, while I have two fine, strapping sons to help me about the farm. Many would be satisfied with far less.'

Biddy never answered this, but both Tom and Aggie could have told their father that their mother was easily dissatisfied and discontented. The two of them, and to a lesser extent Joe, had borne the brunt of her ill humour time and enough, meted out by the stick that she kept hanging up to one side of the hearth.

In the New Year the dancing lessons were held each Saturday afternoon in St Mary's church hall, the older ones going to the later class. The church had had to be put at least a mile outside the town, as decreed by the British, who had controlled Ireland at the time it was built. It was in a district called Cockhill. The Sullivans' farm was also in Cockhill and a little over a mile away from the church so it was no problem for Aggie to get there.

McAllister owned a gramophone, a magnificent thing with a big golden horn. It was his pride and joy, and when he put records on it and lifted the needle over, tunes came out of it. Aggie and the other girls were enchanted, for they had never seen anything like it before in the whole of their lives.

'I thought he would play the tunes on the fiddle for you,' her father said when she told her parents about the gramophone, 'or, indeed, the tin whistle, for he has a fine hand with them both.'

'He said he couldn't play and teach us properly, and using the gramophone is better,' Aggie said.

'And you enjoy it?'

'Oh, yes.' But much of Aggie's enjoyment was down to the fact that she had been attending the classes only a little time when she fancied herself in love with McAllister.

'I can't understand why his wife complains about him so much,' she said to Tom one day, after she had just come from a lesson. 'She should be grateful to be married to such a handsome man and one that seems to be in good humour all of the time.'

'Maybe that good humour is Guinness- or

poteen-induced?' Tom suggested with a grin, and added, 'That's what Daddy said, anyway.'

'Tom,' Aggie said angrily, 'how can you say such a thing? Isn't he doing a grand job with you and the tin whistle? And what's wrong with a man taking the odd pint of Guinness or nip of poteen anyway? Our own daddy does the same thing now and again.'

'I was only repeating what Daddy said.'

'Well, don't!' Aggie retorted. 'Isn't the man giving up his time freely?'

It wasn't exactly freely, though no money changed hands. However, as he taught Irish dancing to the butcher's daughter he got his payment in kind, and he had similar treatment from the newsagent for teaching his daughter so that he had all the tobacco he needed. The various farms around provided him with other produce and so, with their own grocery store as well, his wife was well enough pleased.

The teaching of the tunes was done in the children's own homes and the payment for this was usually in the shape of a bottle of poteen, which was distilled in the hills of Donegal. It never seemed to affect McAllister's ability to teach, however much he drank, and he rode from farm to farm on the horse that was also used to pull the cart for the shop.

Philomena once said to Biddy that half the time she didn't know how he made it home and it was a good thing his horse knew the way. She wouldn't be at all surprised to find him fallen into a ditch somewhere one day, having slid from the horse's back.

Biddy knew exactly what Philomena meant, for the man had often been well away when he left their house. If she ever complained about this, however, Thomas John would always maintain there was no harm in the man, that he just had a terrible thirst on him.

Aggie thought there was no harm in him either. In fact she thought him wonderful and strove in all ways to please him. With her love of dancing she soon progressed, and after she had been at it a year McAllister declared her a gifted little dancer. Soon after this, he asked her and Cissie to go for extra lessons on Wednesday evenings, to which Thomas John readily agreed.

He was delighted with McAllister. Tom had got on so well with the tin whistle that Joe had asked to learn too, and Tom had begun to learn the fiddle. Each week, McAllister would listen to them playing the tune he had taught them the previous week, which he expected them to master before he would teach them another. They soon had a fair collection of material and would often entertain their parents in the long winter evenings. They would play for Aggie too, and she would roll back the rugs and dance on the flagged floor of the cottage, her brown eyes flashing, her dark brown plaits bouncing to each side and her feet fair flying along. Afterwards her cheeks would be flushed and pink, and Tom realised with some surprise one day that Aggie was very pretty.

Afterwards, those pictures would often come back to haunt Tom. They were a time of innocent pleasure that would never return – before his life and Aggie's were touched by evil.

As Aggie began to develop, her infatuation for McAllister grew stronger. In her own home, as he taught her brothers, she was able to study everything about him, like his fine head of hair, so black it sometimes shone blue in the lamplight. He had wonderful masculine hands too, with a dusting of hairs on the backs of them, and long and very flexible fingers with square nails. She watched the movement of his mouth, with his fine, full lips, listening to the lilting timbre of his voice and the way he threw his head back when he laughed, as he did often.

Tom wondered if Aggie knew that her eyes went all dopey and dreamy in this scrutiny of McAllister. It worried him slightly, though he barely knew why, and he hoped that the man himself had never noticed.

But, of course he had, and it pleased him greatly to have a young, nubile girl lusting after him. As yet she was but a child, anxious to please him and do things for him. When she was a little older, maybe he would see just how far she would go in pleasing him, for she was turning out to be a very fetching little thing.

* * *

Not long after Aggie had passed her fourteenth birthday, Biddy announced to the family that she was having another baby. She was unaccountably excited about this pregnancy, different from the way she had felt about the others. At first she said Aggie had to give up the dancing for she would need her full help in the house. It was Thomas John who said she needn't do that.

'Sure, it is the only place she goes, unless you count Mass. It doesn't take her out of the house much all told, and the girl needs some distraction.'

Biddy never argued with Thomas John, the only person that she ever listened to and took heed of. Aggie knew that, and she gave a sigh of relief at her father's words and hugged herself with delight.

Her little sister was born on a blustery day in February 1900 when the wind howled so fiercely around the cottage, it sounded like a creature in torment. It rattled the windows and caused the fire to splutter and smoke. All that ceased to matter to Aggie as she held in her arms the little sister that she had helped the midwife bring into the world. She felt a special bond with her. She was overwhelmed when Biddy asked her if she would like to be the child's godmother, and the baby was christened Nuala Mary when she was less than two weeks old.

The whole family was charmed by that one small baby – even wee Finn, who would spend hours just gazing at her.

'Don't you try lifting her out of there,' Biddy

said to her small son one day, catching him by the side of the crib.

Finn looked quite astonished that his mother might think he had such a notion. 'I wouldn't,' he said. 'I might hurt her.'

'You could well,' Biddy said grimly. 'And that goes for you too, Tom and Joe. Don't you two be thinking of playing with her, for you are too big and too rough altogether.'

Tom thought his mother didn't need to say that to him. He had left school now and was at work full time alongside his father. With his hands chapped and callused he wouldn't touch the child at all, and as for holding her, she was so petite and delicate-looking, he would be afraid that she would break.

'They are stronger than you think,' Aggie told him one day when he said this.

She was lifting the child as she spoke and Tom marvelled at the easy way she did this. She laughed, but gently, at the look on his face. 'It's easier for a woman,' she said. 'And that's how it must be, of course, for I will probably have my own weans one day.'

'Aye, and meanwhile you are mooning after him, McAllister . . .'

Aggie flushed with embarrassment and guilt but she denied the accusation vehemently. 'I am not.'

'Yes you are,' Tom maintained. 'You just be glad that Mammy hasn't noticed.'

'There's nothing to notice,' Aggie said heatedly. 'This is all in your imagination.'

'No it isn't,' Tom said. 'And for the life of me I don't see what the attraction is. He is an old man and a well-married one too.'

'You don't understand,' Aggie said, and as Tom shook his head at her, Aggie hid a smile. At home she was just good old Aggie to her father and brothers, and an extra pair of hands to her mother, especially now, and her life one of boring drudgery.

Twice a week she was Agnes Sullivan, talked and listened to as if she wasn't a child any more, especially when she attended the special Wednesday evening dancing classes with Cissie. And that was all down to McAllister. He wasn't exactly old either – not like her daddy was old, anyway – but he was mature. The lines on his face just added to his character, and he had the darkest brown eyes. But what was the point of saying any of that to her brother? He'd laugh himself silly if she tried.

Of course, when he was in the farmhouse, teaching her brothers or drinking with her father, he had to be far more proper towards her, seeming to know without her having to say anything that her parents wouldn't like any sort of familiarity. If he addressed her at all, he called her 'Aggie' and she called him 'Mr McAllister', but on Saturday, after the younger children had left, and especially on Wednesday evening, she was Agnes and he was

Bernie. He also kissed her and Cissie on the cheek when the class was over, making them blush at first, before they began to enjoy it, but the two girls were sensible enough to say nothing about this at home.

Aggie did daydream about Bernie McAllister sometimes, and her nights too were punctuated with fantasies about him. Sometimes, she would imagine that he would hold her in his arms and kiss her properly. She had no idea what a proper kiss was; she just knew people seemed to hold great store by it, as a sign that one person liked another. She never allowed herself to go further than that kiss, though, and yet in the morning she would be ashamed of herself. She never even whispered these thoughts and dreams to Cissie, fearing she would be shocked.

It was more than three weeks before Christmas when Aggie got to the church hall one Wednesday evening to find that Cissie hadn't arrived. That was strange, as she was always there before Aggie. Usually, as Aggie was going out the door, her mother would find another job for her to do, for though she wouldn't openly defy Thomas John and forbid Aggie to go dancing, she resented it bitterly. She particularly disliked the Wednesday evening sessions and so would deliberately make Aggie late, and she would arrive red and out of breath, having run every step of the way.

That night was no exception. As she stood framed in the doorway, McAllister's breath caught in his throat. She was truly beautiful, with her flushed cheeks, heaving bosom and dancing eyes. Cissie was a bonny enough girl, but she didn't hold a candle to Agnes, and the girl was totally unaware of it too.

'Where's Cissie?' Aggie asked, scanning the room.

'Cissie isn't coming tonight,' McAllister said, crossing to stand beside her. 'She has the measles. Her mother caught me in the town and told me, but I came on here to wait for you.'

'How awful for her,' Aggie said. 'Poor Cissie.' And then disappointment trickled through her body as she said uncertainly, 'Well, I had better go then.'

'Why?' McAllister said, drawing her into the room and closing the door with his foot. 'Do you want to go?'

McAllister's face was very close, and Aggie said, 'No, not really but—'

'You are very lovely, you know, Agnes,' McAllister said, cutting across her.

No one had ever mentioned loveliness to Agnes and her eyes opened wide. 'Am I?'

'You are,' McAllister said emphatically. 'Did no one ever tell you that before?' he asked, knowing just how unlikely that was.

'No, never.'

'Anyone ever tell you how your eyes sparkle

brighter than the stars in the sky?' McAllister asked. As Aggie's face flushed further with embarrassment he added, 'And that you look so enchanting when you blush.'

'Oh, Bernie, really,' Aggie said, flustered. 'Please don't say such things.'

'Why?' McAllister asked. 'Don't you wish to hear them?'

'No, not really. I'm sure it is wrong to make a person think too much of themselves, especially when the things said are not true.'

'Who said they were not true?'

'Exaggerated then . . .'

'Not a bit of it,' McAllister cried. 'Look into a mirror, Agnes, my darling girl, and you will see it all for yourself.'

'You have me all of a dither.'

McAllister caught up her hand and said, 'Don't be ashamed or embarrassed, for as you grow up you'll hear many such comments. And you must learn to accept them gracefully and thank the person applauding you so.'

'Oh, I do thank you, Bernie,' Aggie said earnestly. 'It was just that it was so unexpected. I am not at all used to hearing people say such things about me.'

'That's all right,' McAllister smiled. 'And now to show you that I really mean the things I said, I will give you a wee kiss!'

Aggie returned the smile and, expecting the type of kiss that he gave both her and Cissie when they were leaving each Wednesday evening, she said, 'All right.'

McAllister caught Aggie's face up between his hands and kissed her mouth gently and then, as if Aggie's arms had a life of their own, they encircled his neck. His kiss became more ardent and demanding, and Aggie's whole being began to shake, and she knew she wanted that kiss to go on and on for ever.

When they broke apart at last, both were breathless. Aggie dropped her arms and pulled herself from McAllister's embrace before allowing herself to look into his eyes. She saw the yearning there and though she didn't understand it, she was a little alarmed by it. But what was more worrying by far were the strange longings she had coursing through her own body, feelings the like of which she had never had before and wasn't sure they weren't downright sinful.

'Oh, Agnes,' McAllister said, 'that was truly wonderful.'

'I know. But I don't think we should have done it.'

'And why not? Don't say you didn't enjoy it, for I shall not believe it. It wasn't a stranger's arms that came about my neck, or a stranger's lips kissing me so hard.'

'I know,' Aggie admitted, her face flaming again, but this time with shame. 'I'm sorry. I don't know what came over me.'

19

'Don't be sorry. Did I push you away?'

'No, but . . .'

'For two pins I would repeat the experience,' McAllister said, reaching out for Aggie, but she twirled out of his grasp.

'No, no!' she cried. 'We mustn't.'

'We mustn't,' McAllister mimicked, but gently. 'Mustn't touch, mustn't kiss, and mustn't have fun in any shape or form.'

'I'm sorry.'

'Stop being sorry. Stop saying you're sorry,' he snapped. He seemed to think for a moment and then suddenly said, 'Well, if a kiss and cuddle is out, then we must dance. Take off your shawl and boots and we'll make a start.'

Aggie looked at him and knew that while one part of her wanted to go into his arms willingly, the other part was urging her to bid the man goodnight and go home. She did neither, and as she removed her shawl she said, 'I can't dance without Cissie,' because the two girls had been practising a duet they were to perform in the Christmas concert put on by the Church.

'Aren't you the girl for finding problems where there are none?' McAllister said. 'We will do dances that need not include Cissie.'

'We will?'

'Yes, we will. They are called polkas. They're fun to do and a chance for me to hold you in my arms legitimately. What do you say?'

'I say maybe I should go home.'

'You disappoint me, Agnes.' McAllister shook his head sadly. 'Really you do.'

Aggie thought of her home and knew she wouldn't be right in the door before her mother would be roaring at her for something and there would be a list of jobs waiting for her. And if she went, she would upset the man she admired before all others. Anyway, she wanted to stay in the church hall, lit softly by the paraffin lamps, and she knew too she would be warmed further by McAllister's arms around her as they moved to the music.

'I'll stay,' she decided, facing him, and he beamed in approval.

'Good girl.' And he took her in his arms.

Aggie loved the polkas, the tantalising and evocative music, and dancing in McAllister's arms was just heavenly. They danced for ages, stopping only when the gramophone needed cranking up. Eventually they were completely out of breath.

'Sit down and recover before you attempt the walk home,' McAllister invited. 'And tell me about yourself.'

Aggie couldn't remember opening her soul as she did that night with McAllister. The man listened to the child – she was little more – who was at it from dawn till dusk just because she had the misfortune to be the elder girl in the family.

'That's why I love dancing, you see,' she said. 'It is a chance to get out. Mammy would have

21

stopped me ages ago if Daddy hadn't put his foot down.'

'I'm glad he did then.'

'Mm, so am I. Have you any family? Brothers, sisters?'

'I have three brothers older than me who high-tailed it to the States, and an older sister, Gwen, living in Birmingham,' McAllister told her, taking a hip flask of poteen out of his pocket as he spoke and taking a long drink. 'I was the baby.'

'And spoiled, no doubt,' Aggie smiled. 'Like Nuala will probably be. She is just ten months old and she rules the roost already.'

'But Nuala might not be the youngest always,' McAllister said, and laughed at the blush forming on Aggie's cheeks. 'Now what's embarrassed you?' he asked.

'It's just . . . well, the thought of my parents doing that sort of thing.'

'What sort of thing?' McAllister teased. 'Sex?'

Aggie gave a gasp. 'I don't think we should say that word.'

'What word? Sex? Let me tell you, girl, the world would be a very peculiar place without it. You do know what it is all about, don't you?'

Aggie nodded. 'Of course I do.' She lived on a farm and had seen the bull brought in to service the cows, the ram for the ewes, the boar for the sow, and the baby animals born afterwards.

McAllister, guessing a lot of the thoughts tumbling around in Aggie's head, said, 'You have seen the animals at it, I imagine, but for humans there is pleasure to be had too.'

Aggie's face was a picture, for she had never heard that before. She looked at McAllister incredulously and he laughed as he pulled her to her feet.

'Come on,' he said. 'Get your boots and your shawl. It's time to go home.'

Aggie was loath to bring the evening to an end. It had been a special time with just the two of them, which would probably never happen again.

At the door McAllister took another hefty drink from the flask and offered it to Aggie. 'Care for a drop?'

Aggie smiled as she shook her head. 'Daddy gave me a wee sip just the other day and it burned my mouth and my throat, and afterwards it was as if my stomach was on fire. I have no liking for it at all.'

'You don't know what you are missing, girl,' McAllister told her. 'Still, your loss, sweetheart. Now, I will see you home.'

'Oh, but really there is no need.'

'Agnes, the wind would near cut a body in two and the night air is raw and bone-chillingly cold,' McAllister said firmly. 'If you will not have a wee drop of poteen to help you cope with that, then you need my arms around you to keep you from freezing altogether.'

Aggie did not protest. She could think of few

things nicer than walking home wrapped in her warmest shawl and cuddled into Bernie McAllister, and she nodded her head happily.

'I'd like that,' she said, and they stepped into the night together.

TWO

Aggie recalled that walk home many times. She remembered how secure and protected she had felt. McAllister had his arm tight around her so that, despite the bleakness of the night, she felt glowingly warm inside.

He had been telling himself since they'd set out to go easy and have a bit of common sense, but the very nearness of Aggie was making him harden. He knew to touch her was madness. Hadn't his wife threatened what she would do if ever she found him at it again, after that last time?

And he knew that if they hadn't had the offer of the grocery store, and been able to flee to Ireland when they had, he'd have more than likely been laid out in a hospital bed, if not on a mortuary slab, as soon as the pregnancy of their neighbour's daughter had become obvious. He remembered how she had pleaded with him for help and he had promised to think of something, even as they were making plans to leave. He had blamed the girl for her condition, though, claiming that she had teased him and flirted with him outrageously and that a man was only flesh and blood after all.

He had seen the telltale flush of shame steal over the girl's face and she had even apologised for leading him on so. He had patted her hand and said she wasn't to worry her wee head about it any longer; that he would deal with it.

How Philomena found out he never knew, but she had and she was not best pleased. Yet she made plans to leave at once and in the early morning before many were astir. McAllister had a fleeting flash of pity for the young girl left alone to cope, but it was gone in an instant and he had to admit he was relieved to be away out of it.

When Philomena saw this, however, she had snapped, 'This isn't being done to save your skin, so never think it. What you did to that young girl was disgusting and my heart goes out to her and the life she will likely have because of you. But I have my own weans to see to. It would not help them if you were dead or crippled, and I know you would be one or the other if we stopped here one moment longer than necessary.'

He knew she was right. He was also well aware that the girl would name him as the father, because if she wouldn't tell willingly, her father was the sort to beat it out of her. Then he and the son would have come for him. Fear had crawled all through McAllister at that thought. His salvation, in the shape of a grocery shop in a remote part of Ireland, hadn't come a moment too soon.

'I appreciate it,' McAllister had said to his wife. 'And I'm sorry.'

'You're always sorry,' Philomena had replied scathingly. 'And in the end it makes no odds. But I am telling you now, Bernie, I know that that girl was not the first, but she will be the last, for if this ever happens again, that will be the finish of us.'

'It won't, I promise.'

'You've promised more times than I have had hot dinners,' Philomena snapped, 'but this time think on, because I mean it. Keep your hands to yourself and your prick in your trousers, and we will get along well enough.'

Philomena had meant every word. He remembered that she had kicked up shocking when he had suggested the dancing and music lessons.

'They have no one to teach them,' he had told her. 'Surely you are not for them forgetting their heritage.'

'It may surprise you to learn that we have a business to run, Bernie McAllister,' Philomena had said. 'If you have time and energy enough for this, then I suggest those energies would be better employed the other side of the counter.'

'It would stifle me, woman,' McAllister had protested. 'A man has to have some outlet.'

'Are you sure you are not up to your old tricks?'

'For God's sake, woman, are you crazy or

what? Don't you think I've learned my lesson this time?'

'I certainly hope so.'

'Look, I teach the music at the children's own homes and the dances at the church hall in a group.'

'Well, yes, I know,' Philomena conceded.

'Then trust me.'

And Philomena tried. She knew that Bernie was no model husband. He said the grocery shop bored him, and certainly he was seldom seen behind the counter. He also drank far too much, but all that Philomena could put up with. As the months and then years passed she even told herself that the flight to Ireland had at last seemed to cure him of his taste for young girls, so that when he told her he was selecting two of the older and better dancers for special tuition one evening a week, she had dampened down the suspicion that arose in her. When he said to her, 'Look, Philomena, I know how you feel, and with reason, but I promise that I will never see either of the girls alone,' Philomena's fears abated somewhat.

Then why hadn't he allowed Aggie to go home that night; even sent word to the house and told her not to bother coming out? He knew why full well. The madness was coming over him again and the blood was coursing through his veins at the nearness of the girl tucked in beside him so tightly he could hear her heartbeat.

When she gave a sigh, snuggled closer and said,

'I love being here with you like this and I am so grateful for you leaving me home,' he knew he had lost any shred of reason that might have been attached to him. Overpowering lust had taken its place.

'How grateful are you?' he asked Aggie huskily, as he pulled her to a stop and turned her to face him.

She smiled as she said, 'Lots.'

'Grateful enough to give me a kiss?'

Aggie hesitated. 'I'm not sure . . .'

'I thought you were grateful,' McAllister said reprovingly. 'Fine way to show it. What harm is a kiss between two people who like each other?'

'Nothing, I suppose,' Aggie had to admit.

'Well, then?' McAllister said, opening his arms wide.

Aggie couldn't remember the arguments for feeling it wrong to kiss McAllister, especially when she wanted to so much. She went into his arms willingly. This time, though, McAllister prised her mouth open with his tongue while his other hand fumbled underneath her shawl. Aggie was totally startled and a little afraid. She struggled, but even with one arm McAllister held her fast with ease, and the groan she gave of dismay and distaste he thought was one of pleasure.

Then the shawl fell from her shoulders and McAllister's hand began to caress her breasts.

'Please, please stop,' she said when she eventually pulled her mouth away from him and struggled to free herself. 'Let me go, Bernie. Please, for God's sake.'

McAllister took no notice. There would be no stopping him now. His whole body was on fire to taste the delights of Aggie and he was also impatient. When he couldn't work out how to unfasten her dress, he took hold of the neck and ripped it down the front.

Aggie felt the night air hit her bare skin. She gave a yelp of terror and tried to twist from McAllister's arms as she cried, 'Please, Bernie. We can't do this, really we can't.' She felt the tension running all through him and she was desperately frightened. 'What's come over you?'

'You, my darling girl,' McAllister said. 'God Almighty, you have bewitched me totally.'

'Let me go, Bernie. Please! I am begging you,' Aggie cried.

'Let you go? No, my darling girl. I am going to show you a good time.'

'I don't want it. Really I don't. I just want to go home.'

'Don't give me that,' McAllister said almost harshly. 'You want it as much as I do. Why else were you snuggling in so close?'

Aggie was mortified by shame. Had she brought this on herself? 'I didn't mean . . . not this . . . I meant it just as a friend.'

'Don't play the innocent with me,' McAllister said. 'You were ripe for it right enough. Almost begging for it, you were.'

Aggie was so frightened she had trouble drawing breath to speak, but she knew she had to make McAllister see he had made a mistake, and with a supreme effort she pulled herself away from him, panting as she faced him. 'If I did show you that I was willing and all,' she gasped, 'then I am heart sorry. I didn't mean you to think that, but I see that I probably am at fault as well, so shall we say no more about it and I will go on home by myself from here?'

'Just who are you trying to kid?' McAllister said. 'You stand there half naked and say words your whole body is denying. You are so craven with desire you can barely speak.'

'No,' Aggie said. 'I can't speak because I am so feared.'

McAllister shook his head as he might at a naughty child. 'It's not fear you are displaying, but pure carnal lechery, which I am going to satisfy before you and I are much older.'

'No, Bernie,' Aggie said, backing away.

'Ah yes, Bernie, yes,' McAllister said. He made a grab for her, grasping her so tight she was unable to break free. 'That is what you will be saying before the night is done.'

He pulled Aggie down to her knees, still clasped tight in his arms, and then pushed her with such force that her head hit the ground with a resounding crack. For a moment or two her senses reeled and McAllister took advantage of that. His hands shot beneath her clothes and he pulled off her

31

knickers and stockings in one swift movement, and so roughly his fingernails scored deep scratches down her legs.

This brought Aggie to her senses and, though whimpering with fear, she began to fight like a wildcat.

'So that is the way you want to play, is it?' McAllister asked almost in amusement, catching hold of Aggie's flailing arms and pinning them down across her body with one hand.

'If you don't let me go, I'll scream,' Aggie said fiercely, though even as she said it she wondered what good it would do. The wind would snatch away the sound of any scream, and who would be around to hear it anyway? There were no houses near and few would be abroad at that time of night.

McAllister threw himself on top of her. 'Scream away then, though I might have something that will take away any desire to struggle at all.'

Aggie looked at him in terror. In all her fifteen years she had never seen a naked man, but she had seen the mating of the animals and so she knew what she was feeling between her legs. 'Please don't do this,' she begged again. 'Let me go now and I swear on my mother's life that I will not mention this to a soul.' Then seeing that had no effect, she said, 'What of Philomena and the children?'

'What the bloody hell is it to do with them?' McAllister asked. 'Come on, we have prevaricated more than enough,' he went on irritably. 'My bloody cock is ready to explode, I can tell you.'

He drew a fresh hip flask of poteen from his pocket as he spoke.

'I'm not having any of that,' Aggie said, 'so don't think it.'

'Oh, but you are, bonny girl.' McAllister lifted the flask to her lips. But Aggie threw her head from side to side so that the dribbles of poteen spilled from her mouth and ran down her neck.

McAllister was furious. He gave Aggie a punch in the face, causing her eyes to go out of focus and her nose to pour with blood, and she cried out in pain and terror.

'Now look what you have made me do,' McAllister said. 'Just because you weren't being a good girl and doing as you were told. Now open your mouth and swallow this nice and easy, or I will make you swallow it.'

Too frightened not to obey, Aggie opened her mouth a little and McAllister put the flask to her lips again. To make sure she would swallow this time, he held on to her bruised and smarting nose. Aggie gulped at the fiery liquid, feeling it burning her throat as it went down and then hit her stomach like a ball of fire. But far more worrying, the more of the stuff she drank, the less she wanted to fight off the man lying on top of her.

When Aggie's useless arms fell to the sides of her body and stayed there, McAllister smiled, knowing that now she would be unable to prevent him doing what he wanted. He took the drained bottle away and let his hands trail over her body.

Part of Aggie knew she should protest at this, but she didn't seem able to. It was as if it was happening to someone else and she was out of her body, looking down on herself. The moan took her by surprise. McAllister heard it and knew she was drunk enough to pose no resistance at all.

When he slipped his hands between her legs and began to caress her, she burned with shame for what she was allowing him to do to her, and she knew she should at least try to protest. She opened her mouth, but what came out made no sense at all and McAllister looked at her and laughed.

'You are spouting nonsense, bonny girl,' he said. 'Just lie back and enjoy it.'

Aggie stared at him. She knew she was wicked because she should be pushing McAllister off and at least attempting to fight, but she seemed unable to, and she was too frightened to enjoy anything.

He entered her forcefully and she gasped as he whispered in her ear, 'Now, my little wanton, are you not gagging for it?'

Aggie didn't even try to answer as a sudden, stabbing pain shot through her and she cried out in alarm, but McAllister took no notice and continued to pound into her. Each thrust caused her such discomfort that she bit her lips to prevent herself crying out, afraid of inflaming McAllister's anger and giving him cause to hurt her further.

When it was all over McAllister said, 'Jesus Christ, Aggie, but you are wonderful. In fact you are absolutely bloody marvellous and we'll take care to repeat that experience very soon.'

The words seeped into Aggie's addled brain and so did the realisation of what she had done. She knew it was the very worst sin a girl could commit, and she didn't know how in the world she had allowed it to happen.

She tried to tell McAllister how she felt, but it was as if her brain and her mouth were unconnected, and he just laughed. She beat at him with her fists, but there was no power in the blows and he laughed again. But at least he rolled from on top of her and left Aggie shivering in abject fear and helplessness.

'Cover yourself up, for Christ's sake,' he said almost harshly, pulling her to her feet. 'Put your shawl around you at least.'

But Aggie seemed incapable of anything. She staggered and would have fallen had he not caught hold of her.

'For Christ's sake, get a grip on yourself.'

Aggie said nothing, but stood swaying and staring at McAllister until he picked up the shawl from the ground, saying as he did so, 'Don't look at me that way. You wanted it as much as I did and you can't deny that now, can you?'

Aggie shook her head but it seemed to be filled with cotton wool and she couldn't form any words. She could remember the sexual act, though. It seemed etched in sharp relief on her brain and she imagined it always would be.

'And whatever you think now, it was bloody marvellous,' McAllister said, 'in fact so good that if you don't get dressed soon, I may begin all over again.'

Those words sent Aggie scrambling for her torn dress, though McAllister had to help her put it on. She was able to put on her own knickers but the stockings befuddled her altogether until she gave up on them and, holding them in her hand, pushed her bare feet into her boots.

McAllister tucked the shawl around Aggie's shivering frame and said, 'Will you be all right from here?'

Aggie looked at him wordlessly. She was having trouble standing and didn't know if she would be able to put one foot before the other, but McAllister seemed interested only in himself.

'Philomena will be wondering,' he said, as if he had just remembered that he had a wife.

Aggie wanted to beg him not to leave her drunk and alone, and to give her some idea how she was going to get into the house unseen, or tell her what tale she could tell her mother to explain any of this, but she knew she could never manage to say any these things.

She could hardly believe it when McAllister just melted into the night and left her totally alone and so drunk she had trouble standing up. She wanted to call to him to come back and not abandon her in this way, and she actually tried to follow him, but her legs buckled, she fell to her knees and wept.

When McAllister reached home, Philomena, worn out by four weans to see to and a grocery store to run, had taken herself off to bed. She had left the lamp on low and, as McAllister turned the wick up to throw more light into the room, she woke from her semi-doze and watched him undress through narrowed eyes.

He had a look on his face that she had seen before, like a cat that has had the cream. As he nipped out the lamp and slipped in beside her she smelled the sex on him, even overriding the ever-present smell of poteen.

She felt her heart plummet to her boots and wondered who had had his attention that night. She knew it was his night for taking the two older girls and hoped to God it wasn't one of those he had taken down. Dear Christ, they were little more than children, and neighbours into the bargain.

She would confront him – ask him outright. But what would that achieve? She knew he would deny it and she would get angry and so would he, and the shouts and roars of them might waken and frighten the weans and resolve nothing . . .

However, McAllister had noted her slight movements. 'You awake, Phil?'

'No.'

'Ah, now don't be like that,' he said coaxingly. 'Isn't this your darling husband, come to give you a bit of loving before we both settle down for the night?'

Philomena gave a shiver of distaste, knowing

her 'darling husband' had just come from a sexual encounter with another. 'Not tonight, Bernie. I am tired, so I am,' she said.

'Tired be damned, woman,' McAllister snapped angrily, grabbing for her. 'You are my wife.'

'Aye, poor foolish sod that I am,' Philomena might have said. But she didn't. She knew him well and felt his tension like a coiled spring that night. If she were to inflame him in that state she might well come off the worst for it. Instead, with a sigh, she submitted to him and, after pawing and groping at her, he had his way, as she had known he would.

Fully satisfied, he had fallen asleep almost immediately. Philomena listened to his even breathing and felt so degraded that she cried herself to sleep.

Tom was concerned. Aggie was usually home long before this and he wondered if some accident had befallen her. He couldn't go and look for her because he was alone in the house, apart from Nuala and Finn, in their beds and fast asleep, and he couldn't leave them unattended.

His father had left just after evening milking. He had closed a deal on a bull that afternoon and had gone off to Buncrana to seal the sale over a few pints, as was the custom. Tom knew from experience he wouldn't be back for hours yet.

His mother, though, could be in at any time, for she had gone to help a neighbour who was having a baby. Aggie wasn't long out of the house when the Lannigans' eldest boy came over and said his mammy was took bad and had been like it all the day. Biddy knew she was expecting but the baby wasn't due for a few weeks yet.

'I must go up and see what's what,' she had said to Tom, 'for all I'd like to seek my own fireside this night. Sadie's man is away in England working and she has three weans to see to. I'll take Joe with me in case I have to send for the doctor. You wait here with the wee ones until Aggie comes home.'

But Aggie hadn't come home and if she didn't return before her mother, she would probably feel the sting of the bamboo cane kept by the side of the fireplace.

Tom crossed to the window and looked out. He was almost certain he saw a shape at the head of the lane and it certainly wasn't his mother, who would in all probability come across the fields anyway as that had been the way she had gone. It must be Aggie. Then why didn't she just come on down to the house?

Sudden apprehension that something was very wrong caused the hairs on the back of Tom's neck to rise. He took his jacket from behind the door and left the house.

Aggie had eventually pulled herself up by holding on to the hedges. She ached all over and the pain between her legs was almost unbearable. Shambling and unsteady, she slowly made her way forward by holding on to the bushes, though she fell to her knees more than once.

At last she stood unsteadily at the head of the lane, looking down on the cottage where the lamp shone brightly in the window. She didn't know what to do next. Only one thing was certain and that was that her mother would beat the living daylights out of her when she saw the state of her. Her insides crawled with fear of going home and of not going home, and tears seeped from her eyes and ran down her cheeks.

When Aggie saw Tom appear before her it was as if her last vestige of strength oozed out of her and she sank to the ground with an anguished cry.

'Oh, Tom!'

'What is it, Aggie?' Tom cried, going forward, and then he was nearly knocked back by the smell of poteen. He recoiled and gasped almost in disbelief, 'Aggie, have you been drinking?'

Aggie nodded and, concentrating hard, she said, 'Lots.'

Her words were slurred and indistinct, but Tom understood and he was shocked to the core that his elder sister was in such a state. She clutched at him and began to cry.

'Hush, Aggie. Come on now,' he said almost impatiently.

'But he took me down, Tom.'

'Ssh,' said Tom, looking about anxiously. Words carried in the night air and those were not words to be said where any might overhear. He hoped to God it wasn't true, that it was the ramblings of a girl in the throes of drink, but a dead weight

40

seemed to settle in his stomach. 'Come on, let's get you up to the house,' he said.

'I can't, Tom. Mammy will—'

'Mammy isn't there,' Tom said and, in an attempt at light-heartedness added, 'You have chosen the right evening to go on a bender. There is only me and the wee ones home because Mammy is at Sadie Lannigan's, as she was took bad, and she took Joe along with her. So let's away in before they are back and you can tell me all. Can you walk if I support you?'

Tom almost carried Aggie, and was very glad to reach the cottage and lower her gently into a chair. There he surveyed his sister properly and gasped with horror. He noted the slack mouth and vacant eyes of the very drunk, but he also saw that the eyes had been blacked – by someone's fist, by the look of things – and tear trails were visible on her cheeks, mixed with dried blood smeared across her face. Her shawl was earth-stained, her dress ripped so that it was almost indecent. He saw too that her legs were bare and that her knees were grazed and had been bleeding. There were two deep scratches the length of her legs and she held her stockings screwed up in her hand.

He could barely speak he was so angry, but he was also not quite sure what to do. He knew before all else he had to try to sober her up so that she could tell him who had hurt her, but he was terri-fied that any minute his mother would burst through the door. If she saw Aggie in this state she would surely kill her.

He brought Aggie a drink of water from the bucket by the door and gave it to her because it was all he could think of. She drained it thankfully and he brought her another. Again Aggie took the cup and drained it.

Then Tom said, 'Who did this to you?'

There was no point in lying. Aggie looked at her brother steadily. 'Bernie McAllister.'

Her words were indistinct and little above a whisper, but Tom understood her and felt himself burn inside. He was just a boy and so he said to Aggie, 'Daddy will trounce him when he hears this.'

'Tom, Daddy is to know nothing,' Aggie said, clutching his arm. All the way home, the one coherent thought in her head was that she had to keep silent about the whole thing. She knew McAllister would say she was willing and then she would be the one being trounced.

'He has to know,' Tom insisted. 'Didn't he bash your face up and all?'

Aggie nodded. 'He made me drink. He held my nose.'

'Well, then. If you tell Daddy that . . .'

Aggie's heart began to jump about in panic. She knew she had to make Tom see the reason for secrecy. She concentrated and said, 'McAllister will say I took the drink of my own free will, and that I was more than willing for sex, and they will believe him,' she said sadly. 'You know they will.'

42

Aggie didn't understand herself why a stranger was believed over a family's own flesh and blood, but that's how it was. It always seemed to be the woman's fault. She knew the cruelty of McAllister now. A man who could make her drunk so she was incapable of preventing him violating her, and then abandon her in the dark and freezing cold when she had been barely able to stand, would have no qualms in telling everyone the wanton that Aggie had become that night.

She could almost hear him say that she had become addled with the drink she had begged from him and had offered her body for sex and enjoyed it as much as he had. She knew once he told this tale, faster than the speed of light she would be locked up in one of the convents for bad girls that she was supposed to know nothing about.

Tom was still shaking his head. He couldn't understand this. In his book, you did wrong and you were punished. That was how things worked.

'It's wrong that he should get away scot-free,' he said.

'I am not prepared to run the risk of telling our parents, are you?' Aggie asked bitterly.

Tom looked into Aggie's eyes and saw the fear there, and even understood some of it. He shook his head; he felt completely helpless. He said, 'Shall I make you a cup of tea, Aggie? I have the water boiling and people say it's good for shock.'

Aggie gave a sigh. 'That would be good,' she

said. 'And then I need a bowl of warm water. I need to wash all over.'

'I will fetch your nightdress from the room,' Tom said, 'and then sit in there until you are done. But be quick. Mammy may be in any minute.'

With Tom out of the way, Aggie began to wash herself as fast as she could from head to foot, dabbing at the bruises on her face and legs but being more fierce altogether with the dried blood on the inside of her legs. Once ensconced in her nightdress, and with a cup of tea inside her, Aggie felt a little calmer though she could still feel her heart thumping.

She said to Tom, 'I think it will be better if I am in bed when they all come back, don't you?'

'I do,' Tom said fervently. 'I'll say you were feeling badly and you pretend to be asleep whether you are or not, and face the wall so Mammy won't catch sight of your face.'

'What about tomorrow?'

'Jesus, haven't we enough to worry about today?' Tom said. 'Let tomorrow look after itself.' And then as Aggie still hovered, he urged, 'Go on, get yourself away. I'll clear up here.'

'All right,' Aggie agreed, getting to her feet. 'Thank you, Tom, for all you have done. There is just one more favour I must ask of you.' She lifted her ruined dress from the floor as she spoke. 'Will you burn this? It wouldn't do for Mammy to catch sight of it.'

Later, before Tom thrust the dress into the fire,

he examined it and gave a low whistle. He imagined a lust-driven Bernie McAllister tearing it from his sister and was angry that he would go unpunished. He shook his head, for hadn't they already been down that road? To protect Aggie they both had to stay silent. He pushed the dress into the fire, poking at it almost savagely until the flames had devoured every vestige of it.

THREE

Biddy came in with Joe about an hour after Aggie had gone into the room, bringing in the cold of the night and declaring that Sadie Lannigan had given birth to a baby girl and though the new-born was small, both she and her mother were thriving.

'Sadie roared so loud I was sure all those in the six counties would have heard her,' Biddy said. 'And in the end nothing would do her but she had the doctor, and I sent Joe to fetch him. I hope her man earns well, wherever he is, because the doctor doesn't come cheap. Anyway, when the doctor came, I sent Joe to Buncrana to fetch up the woman's mother-in-law to see to her. Sadie doesn't care for the woman, I know that, but as I said to her, the woman is family after all and I have my own bed to go home to.' She looked around the room at this point and said, 'Where's Aggie? Don't say she's not in yet?'

'Oh, aye, Mammy,' Tom said. 'She has been in

this long while, but said she was feeling badly and she went to bed.'

Biddy's lips curled in annoyance. She was quite astounded that Aggie had taken herself off to bed without waiting to see if her mother might have need of her. She took one of the lamps and went into the room, intending to give the girl a telling-off at least, and possibly rouse her from the bed altogether.

However, Aggie, worn out by the events of that night and the unaccustomed alcohol, was in a deep sleep, her body just a hump in the bed, so little of her was visible. Biddy cast her eyes around the room and they softened as they lighted on her youngest child slumbering peacefully in the crib beside her sister's bed. Biddy knew Nuala would be the last. She had told Thomas John there was to be no more of that carry-on now.

When she had held her baby daughter in her arms that blustery day in February, she had felt a rush of maternal love that she had never felt before. She didn't understand it herself, for she was no great lover of children, but she knew at that moment she would have laid down her life for that child.

She felt her to be a true gift from God and vowed that this child would not be worked to death either, or have her childhood over before it had begun. That was Aggie's lot in life, but it was not for this perfect little being.

However, it had been the presence of Nuala in

her room that saved Aggie that night, because Biddy would not risk disturbing the baby by trying to wake her sister and decided that she would leave any upbraiding till the morning. She came from the room, saying as she did so, 'She is fast off. By, she will get the length of my tongue tomorrow.'

Tom let out the breath he had been holding. It was audible only to Joe, and Tom saw his brother's eyes narrow quizzically, but he knew he would say nothing in front of his mother. Once in the bedroom he would give him some tale to satisfy.

He turned to his mother and said, 'Shall I make you a cup of tea, Mammy? You must be perished.'

Aggie woke up in a lather of sweat, the bedclothes in a tangle around her and a thousand hammers thumping in her head. Her throat felt raw and she opened her bleary eyes as Tom came into the room on his way to the byre to milk the cows. Aggie was usually up by then too.

'What's up?' Tom said, but quietly, mindful of the sleeping baby, and Joe still dressing in the other room.

'I feel awful, Tom,' Aggie said, her voice a mere croak.

Tom lifted the lamp he was holding and looked at his sister. She did look bad. Her bloodshot eyes were screwed up against the light and Tom saw the blackening underneath them was less noticeable as her face was brick red and glistening with sweat.

'My head aches terribly and my throat is so sore,' Aggie told him.

'You likely have a hangover,' Tom whispered. 'I have never experienced one myself, but I hear tell you often feel powerfully bad the next day and everyone speaks of the aching head. Even Daddy has had it a time or two, I know.'

'Does it get better?'

'Oh, aye,' Tom said confidently. 'You'll be as right as rain by and by.'

'Well, that's as may be, but I can't get up just now,' Aggie moaned. 'I would be sick if I tried it. Could . . . could you get me a drink of water, Tom?'

'Aye,' Tom agreed sympathetically. 'I'll tell Mammy too, shall I?'

Aggie shuddered. Facing her mother was what she feared, but she knew she would have to cope with that eventually so she said, 'Aye, Tom, if you will.'

Tom had no need to tell his mother. She put her head round the bed curtain, saw Tom dipping a cup into the pail of water by the door and demanded to know what he was doing.

'It's for Aggie, she's badly,' he said.

'What nonsense is this?' Biddy snapped, struggling from the bed. 'Leave down the cup. Be away you and help your father, and I will see to Aggie.'

Biddy saw, as Tom had, that Aggie was far from well, though she put the discolouring under her eyes down to lack of sleep when Aggie professed that she had tossed and turned half the night. She

49

gave her the water and Aggie gulped at it eagerly, but almost immediately brought it back up again, though fortunately Biddy had seen it coming and had whipped the chamber pot from under the bed just in time.

That was just one of many times that Aggie was sick that day, though she ate nothing at all. By evening, despite Tom predicting she would feel better, she felt worse.

'Maybe we should have the doctor in?' Thomas John said.

'I don't think we need to bother the doctor yet,' Biddy answered. 'I will bathe her down just now with cool water and likely she'll be better by morning.'

Aggie was not better, though – much worse in fact. She had developed a racking cough and was semidelirious. Tom, who had never heard of anyone who had had a hangover for two days, was worried for his sister, and so was his mother when he called her in. There was no question now but that the doctor had to be called.

'Measles,' he declared, after examining Aggie. 'And a bad case, I'd say. Mind you, half the town has been coming down with it and they will likely infect the rest. It spreads like wildfire and so it will probably go round the whole family now. Might as well get it all over with, anyway. The older they are when they get it, usually the worse they are. As for Aggie, keep bathing her in tepid water to get the temperature down. I can make up something at the surgery to help there, and something for the cough too if Tom or Joe will come and fetch it. She probably won't eat much, but give her plenty of fluids and keep the lamps turned low and the curtains drawn.'

By the next day, despite the doctor's medication and Biddy bathing her down, Aggie was raving. The sheets were damp with sweat, the coughing shook her whole body and the rash had broken out that day too. Aggie was ill for over three weeks. Christmas had come and gone by the time she was in any way recovered. By then, the clothes hung on her frame gaunt from lack of food, and her legs were shaky and slightly wasted. Finn and Nuala had succumbed and she helped nurse them, though both recovered much quicker than she had.

The little ones weren't right over it when Tom and then his father caught it. Aggie was run off her feet tending to them and helping Joe with the jobs around the farm, until he too was taken sick. With the whole family ill, Aggie had no time to reflect for any length of time on the night she was raped, although she was relieved not to have to see Bernie McAllister, not sure at all how she would treat him when they did eventually meet.

She made one important decision, however: she was finished with the dancing. She would tell her mother she was tired of it. She knew Biddy wouldn't mind. She had said more than once that Aggie was too old to be prancing about the place when she could be such a help at home.

When her mother too became ill, Aggie's life grew harder still and she didn't know whether she was coming or going. Tom and her father were nowhere near better, but at the very least the cows had to be milked twice a day. Then there was the house to tend, the others to nurse, and Finn and wee Nuala to see to as well.

All in all, January had drawn to a close and February begun before the house regained a sense of normality. It was the middle of the month, just after Nuala's first birthday when Aggie realised she hadn't seen her monthlies for some time. She had been due the middle of December, a week after the incident with Bernie McAllister, and when it didn't happen, if she had thought of it at all, she put the absence down to how ill she had been. In January she had been too busy to give any mind to it at all. But now, in February, she faced the dread possibility that she was carrying Bernie McAllister's child and she was filled with horror and shame.

Only a few days later, Biddy now up and about, at last missed the dress Aggie had asked Tom to destroy. Aggie knew her mother would miss it – she hadn't that many clothes that she could lose any of them – and she had no option but to tell her that she had torn the dress so badly that she had burned it.

Biddy could hardly believe her ears. 'You took it upon yourself to destroy a dress?'

Aggie knew she was for it whatever she said or did, but she tried. 'It was so badly torn, Mammy. I couldn't have worn it.'

'It was for me to be the judge of that, surely,' Biddy said. 'Tears can be mended and if it had really been beyond redemption then it could have been made up into a dress or two for wee Nuala. Did you not think of that?'

'No, Mammy,' Aggie said softly.

'Then maybe the bamboo cane will help you remember in future.'

Aggie had expected the beating to be a severe one. Finn was so unnerved by the flailing cane that he ran out into the yard, crying for his father. Thomas John came in and took the cane from his wife's hand.

'Whatever the child has done,' he said, 'she has had enough punishment.'

Aggie slumped to the floor and Thomas John helped her to her feet. 'What was all that over?' he demanded of his wife.

'Oh, madam here ripped her dress,' Biddy said, 'the good one that she wore to her dancing class. And instead of telling me and letting me fix it, or use the material to make up something for Nuala, she put it in the fire and burned it. She has admitted it so.'

Thomas John rubbed his chin, for that was indeed puzzling behaviour from his daughter. 'Well,' he said, 'I will own that you would be annoyed but there was no need to beat her so badly. Anyway, she has even less clothes now for you have that dress almost whipped from her.'

Biddy, now that she was calmer, saw that Thomas John was right. There were huge rips in the material. She looked at her daughter, trying to remain standing with her father's support, then said to Aggie grudgingly, 'All right, maybe I did go a bit too far. Go on into the room and take off your dress. I will put some goose fat on your back and you will then do well enough.'

Aggie did as her mother said, glad to lie down for she was in extreme pain. She had been beaten before many times, as all her brothers had, but seldom so severely. Later, when Biddy saw her daughter's back, crisscrossed with open stripes, blood squeezing from them, she felt sorry for her. It had been a bold thing to do right enough, but she was a grand help to her and had never given her a minute's bother till now.

'Stay in bed for now,' she said as she rubbed the fat well in. 'After that we'll see.'

Aggie sighed in relief and yet she still said, 'Are you sure, Mammy?'

'I'm sure.'

'I'm sorry, Mammy.'

'So am I, child dear,' Biddy said. 'It was such an odd thing to do. I mean, what possessed you to burn a dress? You've never done such a thing before.'

'I've never had it near ripped from my back and then been raped,' Aggie might have said. She didn't, of course. What she did say was, 'I don't really know why I did it. I was so annoyed with myself because I really liked that dress.'

'So, what happened?'

Aggie decided to stick to a semblance of the truth. 'It was the day you went to the Lannigans' and I was coming home from dancing when I fell on the road in the dark and tumbled over the remains of a rusty iron fence and into a thick briar bush in the bottom of a ditch. I'd heard the dress tear on the fence, and then it was ripped to bits on the briar bush before I managed to get myself free. When I got home and looked at all the jagged rips and all, I just threw it into the fire, I was so cross.'

'But didn't you have your shawl on?' Biddy asked.

Aggie had to think fast. 'Yes, but it fell off as I tipped forward. Anyway, after that I was ill and sort of forgot all about the dress.'

'All right,' Biddy said. 'We'll say no more about it now. You'll not do such a thing again, sure you won't.'

'No, Mammy,' Aggie said fervently. 'I think I can promise you, hand on heart, that I will never do such a thing again.'

Biddy was satisfied but Aggie breathed a sigh of relief, glad that she wasn't expected to move anywhere because she didn't think she could have done so. As it was, she had to lie on her stomach to sleep, and despite the cold couldn't bear even her nightdress or the bedclothes to touch her skin.

Sometime during the night she was woken with drawing pains in her stomach, similar to those she had each month. 'Oh, praise God,' she breathed in thankfulness. She would endure any amount of beatings if it would also beat out the child she knew she was carrying. However, after a time the pains in her stomach eased and on checking herself, she saw that there was no blood and she lay in the bed and thought of what she was to do, her mind in a wild panic.

She knew that Biddy would soon tumble to what was wrong, for there would be no pads left to soak in the bucket. She was also aware that she had got away with it so far only because first her mother had been so busy with them all so ill and then was taken bad herself, but time was against her now. That last beating would be nothing to the beating she would have to endure if her mother tumbled to the fact that she was having a child, and her unmarried. She would kill her altogether then. Aggie shuddered in fear, for her mother's true rages were absolutely terrifying.

Worry drove away all thought of sleep, but by morning she was no further forward. She seriously thought of throwing herself in the river, but that was a mortal sin and she would roast in Hell's flames. No, she decided, she had to see Bernie McAllister, though her insides crawled at the thought, and tell him what he had done to her. There was no help for it. Maybe he would think of something. He *had* to think of something, and quickly too, Aggie told herself, because it was more than half his fault. She would have to wangle it so that she had a quiet word with him after Mass on Sunday.

The next day, Biddy let her stay in bed again and put goose grease on her back three times. When Aggie woke the second day after the beating she knew that, although she was stiff and sore, she would be better up and occupied because the worry was driving her demented and there was far too much time to think just lying there. She rose gingerly and was immediately assailed by nausea and vomited into the chamber pot she'd grabbed from beneath the bed.

The following day, Tom said as he crossed through her room from his and his brothers' beyond, 'You all right, Aggie?'

Aggie turned to look at her brother and even in the dim light of the lamp Tom held, he could see the bleached pallor of her face and the way her eyes seemed to stand out in her head, but her voice at least was firm enough and quite sharp.

'Why wouldn't I be?'

'Well, it's just that I heard you being sick this morning, and yesterday as well.'

Oh God! Aggie thought. How hard she had tried to stop the nausea rising to her throat, but had been unable to. When the bout was over she had climbed out of the window to throw the vomit into the gutter before swilling the pot itself with water from the rain barrel beside the door. But now Tom knew something was up, and if he or Joe were to get one hint of what ailed her and said something about it before she could snatch a word with Bernie, the whole thing would blow up around her.

So she faced Tom and said, 'I had something that disagreed with me, that's all.'

'What? Two days running?'

'Yes,' Aggie snapped. 'Don't fuss, Tom.'

Tom shrugged and went on out before his father would give out to him, like he did every morning to Joe, who liked his bed too much to be up and at it.

With Tom gone, Aggie sat down on the bed again. She knew she should have been raking up the fire and putting on the kettle, but she felt so tired and drained.

She knew if she lingered any longer her mother would give out to her, and with a sigh she got to her feet. Joe, his hair still tousled from sleep, clattered through the room, pulling on a jacket as he went, the untied laces of his boots dangling, threatening to send him flying.

'Ssh,' Aggie said warningly. 'You'll have Finn and Nuala awake with your carry-on.'

'Sorry, Aggie,' Joe said. 'Only I'm late, see.'

'As ever. You should get up when Tom calls you,' Aggie smiled.

'I'm still tired then.'

'Aren't we all?' Aggie said with feeling. 'But get you away now before Daddy bites the head off you.'

Joe shrugged. Nearly every morning his father was cross with him and he was used to it now. Daddy said he would never make a farmer and Joe wasn't sure he wanted to be. It was a grind of a life, though Tom seemed to like it well enough.

And Tom did. Usually milking was one of his most favourite occupations, finding it soothing to lean his head against the velvet flank of the cow and see the bucket between his legs fill with the creamy milk.

However, that morning his thoughts were far away and Aggie was at the forefront of them. He knew she wasn't right, whatever she said, and he knew his father was worried about her too. Only the previous evening, watching Aggie pick at the meal before her, he had said to their mother, 'Aggie's never really perked up after that dose of measles she had, I'm thinking, and not eating enough to feed a bird. Maybe we should ask the doctor for a tonic.'

Aggie had said she was all right, that she was just not hungry, but she had a sort of hunted look on her face.

Thomas John was far from satisfied but Aggie got so agitated that he said he would leave it so for now, but if she didn't pick up in a day or two he would ask the doctor to take a look at her.

Tom was the only one to notice the horrified and frightened expression on Aggie's face as she began to collect up the plates. Did she think he was some sort of idiot to think he would believe that something had disagreed with her to make her so sick?

Nuala had just passed her first birthday and he remembered that when her mother was carrying her, she had been sick every morning. So was Aggie having a baby? She could well be, though it was the very worst thing that could happen to a young unmarried girl and something that couldn't be hidden either. He wondered what in God's name she intended to do about it if she was.

In the bedroom Aggie was having similar thoughts, and she hoped that Bernie McAllister might have some sort of plan up his sleeve, or she was done for: her life would be over before it had really begun. She felt tears sting the back of her eyes and brushed them away impatiently.

The time for crying was long gone. She mentally braced her shoulders and opened the door into the kitchen to start the day.

The next Sunday, Aggie inveigled herself close to McAllister as she left the church, and once outside she whispered, 'I need to speak to you.'

McAllister's eyes widened salaciously. 'Can't wait for another session, is that it?'

'Ssh,' Aggie cautioned, looking anxiously around at the people streaming out of the church to see if anyone was in earshot. 'Not here. Come a little way in amongst the gravestones.'

Tom had seen her talking with McAllister and he skirted the back of the church and secreted himself behind another gravestone, not far from where they had stopped. He could plainly see that Aggie was angry with what McAllister had said and he heard her say sharply, 'You disgust me. It gives me no pleasure to have to seek you out this way, but I needed to see you as soon as possible.'

'What about?' Bernie asked suspiciously.

'Shh, I can't tell you anything here,' Aggie said. 'We daren't risk being overheard. I can't get away easily in the day, and certainly not without permission being granted and a load of questions asked. Anyway, there are too many people about in the day, but the house is quiet before half-past ten most nights, so could you meet me at the head of the lane tomorrow night about that time?'

Bernie's eyes narrowed. 'Dare say I could,' he said. 'But I wish you would stop all this secrecy and tell me what it is all about.'

'You'll know all tomorrow.'

'Not a little hint?'

'None,' Aggie retorted. 'I need to go. My mother is looking for me.' And catching sight of Biddy standing at the gate gesturing to her impatiently, she scurried towards her.

Bernie watched her go with a lewd smile on his lips.

This was noticed by his wife, who followed the direction of his gaze and her eyes came to light on Aggie Sullivan. Surely to God he hadn't designs in that direction. Thomas John would tear him apart if he thought he was messing with his daughter. Well then, let him, she suddenly thought and, God forgive me, I would even help him, for Bernie is little use to me either in the shop or out of it. It would make no odds to me if he was to meet a sticky end. In fact, it would be one less thing to worry about.

As Philomena turned away, Tom emerged from behind the tombstone. He had listened to the whole conversation and he was more worried than ever. He knew for certain now what Aggie wanted to see McAllister about because every morning she was sick. She was expecting the man's child, and the shame and disgrace of it would destroy them all.

He did wonder what Aggie expected McAllister to do about it, but he knew he needed to be told. However, Tom decided, after what McAllister had done to her before, there was no way he was going to let her meet him alone and in the pitch-black. He wouldn't tell her, though. He would just go after her and try to keep her safe.

FOUR

The clock beside Aggie's bed said twenty past ten when she began to dress. Tom, in the room beyond, listening intently, heard Aggie, and slid out of bed carefully so as not to wake Joe or Finn. When he had followed his two brothers to bed an hour before, he had thought to get undressed was a waste of time, but if Finn or Joe were to wake, they might be very interested as to why he had got into bed with all his clothes on and the least people knew about this the better for Aggie. He eased the window up and the blast of cold air caused Finn to mumble in his sleep and turn over. He didn't wake, though, and Tom was through the window in seconds, pausing only to close it again because the night air was piercingly cold.

The sky was clear, the stars twinkling silver while the moon, like a golden orb, lighted the way up the lane enabling Tom to see to keep a sensible distance between him and his sister.

Aggie, unaware of this, reached the road and

looked about her anxiously. What if the man didn't come? She bit her lip in agitation and the next minute felt strong arms encircle her as Bernie stepped out of the shadows.

'Leave go of me,' Aggie said, twisting out of his grasp.

'What's up with you?' McAllister demanded. 'Last time you couldn't get enough of it, so don't come the innocent with me.'

'Stop it, Bernie,' Aggie said. 'You know that just isn't true. Anyway, you had me filled with poteen. When you left me, I could barely make it home.'

'The poteen was just to release your natural desires,' McAllister maintained.

Aggie shook her head. 'I was filled with shame afterwards.'

'That was afterwards and the way the Church has you,' McAllister said.

'And what purpose was the punch in the face?' Aggie said bitterly.

'Without the poteen you were too hidebound by the Church to enjoy it at all,' McAllister said. 'And you wouldn't listen, wouldn't do as you were told. Admit it. After you drank plenty, you put up no resistance at all.'

Every word McAllister spoke hammered into Aggie's heart. She knew she hadn't struggled enough. Some girls would rather die than give in to a man the way she had.

By the light of the moon, McAllister watched Aggie's face, saw the shame and recognised the guilt that she hadn't struggled enough. 'You probably wouldn't admit it in a million years,' he said, 'but you enjoyed it as much as me.'

His words inflamed Aggie. She wasn't going to take all the blame. All right, maybe there was a flaw in her make-up, but there was a great, damaged slash in his.

'Are you mad?' she cried. 'Dear God, you must be some sort of deranged creature if you think that I enjoyed one minute of that rape. And that is what it was, Bernie, rape. You forced me to have sex with you and when I would not submit to you willingly, you got me so drunk that I didn't know whether I was coming or going. Did you not wonder what my parents would do when I arrived at their door as drunk as a lord, with the dress almost ripped from me and my stockings in my hand? Did you not worry that my father would come up to the house and beat you to pulp?'

'I knew the likelihood was that your father wouldn't be there,' McAllister said. 'I popped into Grant's Bar before I went over to the church hall and your father was there celebrating the sale of a bull, and to all intents and purposes set to make a night of it.'

'There was always my mother.'

'You are a resourceful girl,' McAllister said. 'I was sure you would think of something. If you hadn't I would have had to tell your mother the brazen hussy you had become.'

'She . . . she wouldn't have believed you.'

'Oh, yes, she would,' McAllister insisted confidently. 'The way I would tell it she would believe it. But in the end that wasn't necessary. She told Philomena the following Saturday that she had been at some neighbour's house that night helping with a birth till nearly eleven. She said you had the measles too and wouldn't be at any Christmas concert. So, you see, you got away with your waywardness.'

Aggie opened her mouth to say there was no waywardness on her part, but she shut it again, for what did it matter what he thought? They had to deal with the consequences of that night. She said, 'I haven't come to bandy words with you. How I behaved that night is neither here nor there, but what is important is the fact that I am carrying your child.'

She let the words sink in and though she could see little of his face she saw his eyes flash in the moonlight and heard his sudden intake of breath.

'And now I want to know what you are going to do about it,' Aggie added.

'What d'you want me to do?' McAllister demanded harshly. 'Surely, this is your problem?'

'It takes two, Bernie,' Aggie cried. 'I didn't do it on my own.'

'You offered it on a plate,' McAllister said. 'A man cannot be blamed for taking what is offered so willingly.'

'Stop that talk,' Aggie said. 'It's solutions I need now.'

'What do you expect me to do? You're pregnant and that's that.'

'Isn't there some way of having it taken away?'

'There are some places but it is illegal and dangerous.'

'I don't care how dangerous it is,' Aggie declared. 'You must help me, Bernie.'

McAllister shook his head. 'I don't have to do anything,' he said. 'When it becomes apparent, I could easily tell your father how you begged for it and how I tried to fight you off and eventually could hold off no longer. He will believe me. He would know how a man has no defence against a wanton woman so determined. He will wonder what sort of girl he has reared and then send for the priest.'

'I wouldn't be so sure about how my father would react,' Aggie said stoutly. 'He has great feeling for me, and after fifteen years surely he knows the kind of daughter he has? I should be careful, if I were you, for he might come for you some fine night.'

'I don't think so,' McAllister said almost mockingly. 'And whatever feeling he has for you, would it extend to rearing your bastard child? You would drag your family through the mud with you. They would never be able to hold up their heads again.'

Aggie knew McAllister was right. She imagined her father's face filled with shock and reproach and then disgust, and she knew she could not do that to him. The disgrace of it all would surely kill him.

'And then of course there's your mother,' McAllister said, and, despite the darkness, saw the shudder that ran all through Aggie's body as he added, 'There are places you can be sent to, run by the nuns.'

'Aye, and I would rather die than enter such a place,' Aggie said fiercely and desperately. 'Listen to me, for every word I speak is the truth: the river is where I will end my life if you refuse to help me.'

'A little melodramatic, don't you think?' McAllister replied superciliously.

Aggie wondered why she had ever thought the man in any way attractive. When he reached out and tried to pull her closer, she shook him off. 'Don't even try to touch me! I am not being melodramatic. Far from it. I mean every word I say.'

'So, what do you want me to do?' McAllister cried. 'I can't work miracles even if I wanted to.'

'Do you know someone who would get rid of it for me?'

'Do you know what you are asking? You could be locked up if the police got wind of this. And as for such places themselves . . . you could die, Aggie.'

'I'm prepared to take that risk,' Aggie said. 'Any risk at all, in fact.'

'That's as may be, but I don't know anyone in the whole of Ireland that would even contemplate doing this.'

'Then where?'

'What makes you sure I know anyone at all?'

'Don't play games with me, Bernie. You either do or you don't. Put me out of my misery, for God's sake.'

McAllister heard the despair in her voice and sighed. 'There was someone I knew would help you in Birmingham, England. It'll cost you, though.'

'How much?' Aggie asked. 'But then what does the price matter? If it was tuppence I couldn't afford it. I never have a penny piece to call my own and the only money I see is the two farthings I get before Mass each Sunday morning to put in the collection.'

'That then is no good at all,' McAllister said. 'You best put that idea out of your head altogether. Anyway, it would mean travelling to Birmingham. You'd hardly want to do that, even if the money could be raised.'

'Are you mad?' Aggie demanded. 'I tell you, Bernie, though I have never left Buncrana in the whole of my life, I would go to Timbuktu if I had to.'

'So, what will you do for money?'

'That's your department.'

'And just why would I give you money, even I had any to give?'

'Because this child is half yours,' Aggie said. 'And if you refuse to help me, then tomorrow morning early I shall tell your wife the same. I know you are right in what you say about the men here, my father apart; perhaps they will all blame me, but what of your wife? If you refuse to help me before I end my life, I will tell her that, in the guise of taking me home, you raped me one bleak night in December. You will have my death on your conscience for the rest of your life,' Aggie went on. 'And when you do die you will roast in the flames of Hell.'

The flames of Hell didn't unnerve McAllister as much as the thought of his wife getting to know, and he didn't doubt for one minute that Aggie would do as she threatened. After all, what did she have to lose?

'You will have cooked your goose right and proper then,' he said.

'Bernie, my goose was well and truly cooked that night in December,' Aggie said softly. 'And, anyway, I think Philomena should know the type of man she is married to.'

But Philomena did know. That was the very devil of it. She had given him an ultimatum and he knew her well enough to know that the threats she had made, should he stray again, were not idle ones. One hint of this and he would be out on his ear. The scandal would stick to him too. In fact he might even be forced to leave town.

Better by far to find some way of sending the troublesome Aggie to Birmingham to his sister, Gwen. There was always money in the till that he could lay his hands on. He had done it many times before when he had been short, and though

Philomena gave out to him, she put up with it. His sister would know what to do with Aggie and where the 'little problem' could be dealt with. He had no doubt that Gwen would be agreeable to this; she had never refused to do anything he asked.

'Say something, for God's sake,' Aggie pleaded.

McAllister realised the silence had stretched out between them. 'All right,' he said. 'Say I can get some money together and got you away, sent you to my sister, Gwen, in Birmingham – what would happen afterwards? Would you come back?'

Aggie let out a sigh of pure and blessed relief, but she said, 'Huh, you know my parents and can ask that question? I'll not be let back, never fear. And if you do this thing for me, then I will never breathe a word to Philomena, or indeed anyone else. As I said, I am ashamed of my part in it and I have no desire to broadcast it unless I have to.'

'I would have to take you as far as Derry in the shop cart,' Bernie said, 'and in the early hours of the morning too, for you could hardly walk into the station in Buncrana in broad daylight and buy a ticket like any other body.'

Aggie knew she couldn't, but she hadn't thought as far as making arrangements. She was just thankful that he had thought of this, or in fact that he had agreed to do anything at all. She hadn't been sure he would.

She was further gratified when he said, 'I will write a note to my sister, to give you so that she knows all about it. She lives not far from the city centre and she will sort you out.'

Part of Aggie recoiled from being beholden to a relative of Bernie McAllister, who had got her into this mess in the first place, but then she had no idea what life was like outside her own small town. Maybe it was as well, certainly in the early days, to be with someone who knew what was what. So she said, 'Thank you, Bernie. I really appreciate this.'

'I should think so,' McAllister said. 'I am putting myself out a great deal to help you.'

'I know you have put yourself out, but it is as much to protect your own skin as mine,' Aggie retorted. 'I am no fool.'

McAllister shrugged. 'What is the good of arguing about it now?' he said. 'We need to deal with practicalities, like when you intend to go.'

Aggie swallowed deeply. She was scared rigid of leaving all that was familiar, of stepping into the unknown, but it had to be faced and there was no point in putting it off. 'I suppose that it had better be done as soon as possible,' she said.

'I couldn't agree more. How about the early hours of Wednesday morning?'

'As soon as that?'

'The sooner the better. And it is safer, so people say. Anyway, what is the purpose of delaying?'

He was right and Aggie knew that. She nodded. 'All right then.'

'I will be at the head of the lane with the shop's

cart at three o'clock,' McAllister said. 'You be ready because we have to be out of here as quickly as possible. We cannot take the risk of anyone seeing us.'

'I will be there,' Aggie promised, and she watched him move away until the darkness swallowed him.

Minutes later Aggie passed right by Tom, who had melted into the shadow of the hedge. His senses were reeling with what he had overheard, and he waited only until McAllister's footsteps faded down the road before catching up with his sister.

'Aggie.'

The girl nearly jumped out of her skin. 'Tom, what are you doing here?'

'What do you think?' Tom said. 'I am trying to look after you, and I tell you, Aggie, if I was fully grown I would take McAllister apart with my bare hands.'

'That wouldn't help the situation at all.'

'Neither will this,' Tom said desperately. 'Aggie, you can't just go to England. It's madness.'

'It's the only thing I can do,' Aggie said. 'Look, Tom, there is no alternative. You do know what ails me, I suppose?'

'I guessed, and then I heard you talking with McAllister after Mass. I was behind a tombstone and decided to follow you in case McAllister should try punching you again.'

'I'm grateful, Tom, really I am,' Aggie said. 'But

73

if you know it all then you will see that I cannot just bide here as if there is nothing the matter, though I will be heartsore to leave and I will miss you all greatly.'

'But, Aggie, I might never see you again,' Tom said plaintively.

Aggie swallowed deeply because she loved Tom dearly and would probably miss him the most of anyone.

'That is a cross both of us must bear.'

'Aye, because of bloody McAllister.'

'And me, Tom.'

'Don't give me that,' Tom said. 'I saw you when you came in that night and you wouldn't have known what you were doing. This is all McAllister's fault, and because of him I will lose my sister.'

Aggie heard the break in Tom's voice. She swallowed the lump threatening to choke her and put her arms around him. Generally they weren't a family that hugged and kissed, and such displays of affection would have embarrassed Tom in the normal way of things. That night, however, it seemed right. Tom hugged his sister back. He would always miss her. Hatred for McAllister burned in his soul.

Twice the next day, Thomas John asked his daughter if she was all right because she couldn't shift the melancholy that seemed to have settled around her, and each time she said she was fine.

'You seem out of sorts,' he had said the first time and she had assured him she felt all right.

The second time he said, 'Is there anything on your mind, Aggie? You look sad.'

Aggie managed a watery smile for her father. 'I can't go round with a great grin plastered over my face all and every day,' she said as light-heartedly as she could.

Thomas John, however, mentioned his concerns to Biddy. She didn't see Aggie as a person very often, just as an extra pair of hands, but when her husband brought it to her attention, she could see that something was amiss. 'What's up with you, girl?'

Knowing her mother wasn't the sort to fob off, Aggie muttered that she felt under the weather.

'In what way?'

'It's hard to explain,' Aggie said. 'All at sixes and sevens.'

Biddy looked at her daughter and saw her pinched white face, the blue bags beneath her eyes, and the fact that there was so little flesh on her bones. 'Maybe your daddy was right and you needed a tonic after the measles, for you had it worse than any of the others. Must be that that has affected your monthlies too.'

'Yes, that must be it,' Aggie said in little more than a whisper.

'Yes, well, that can make a person feel sluggish, I always think,' Biddy said. 'If you don't pick up in the next few days I will get your daddy to take you into Buncrana to see the doctor.'

75

Tom came in the door just as Biddy said this and heard her. His eyes met Aggie's sorrow-laden ones across the table and he felt pity for her wash over him. Yet he knew that if she was determined to leave, then it was best to go as soon as she could. To delay at all would open a can of worms that would be much better left sealed.

Aggie tried to lift her spirits for the rest of that day for the sake of her parents, but she knew she wasn't very successful. Each passing moment meant she was one step nearer to leaving this house and her family for ever. She was glad to seek the solitude of her bedroom away from the watchful and concerned eyes of her father.

She didn't feel the slightest bit tired. Sitting down on the bed, she wished she could have embraced her father that night as she had Finn, until the child had complained that she was holding him too tight. She didn't try it with Joe, or Tom either, for that would have certainly brought comment, and while Tom might have understood, Joe certainly would have been horrified at her girlish sloppiness. For her parents too there had been just the usual peck on the cheek, but she knew her disappearance would be a grievous blow for her father, for he had a soft spot for her.

She would always miss them, not just her father but her mother too, though she could be sharp and unfair at times; the darling baby, Nuala; cheeky wee Finn, and Joe, who was always telling them the exotic places he would visit when he was a grown man; and her favourite and special brother, Tom.

Everything was familiar: the cottage where she had been born and reared, where the hens pecked at the grit in the cobbled yard before the door. She would even miss the indolent, smelly pig in the sty beside the house, too fat to move easily and too lazy to care. Farmland stretched on every side, some fields filled with cows, with their big eyes and swollen udders as they placidly chewed the cud, while others were cultivated, and the hillsides were dotted with sheep.

She had looked on the farm so many times without really appreciating the beauty of it as she did now. She knew that she was doing the only thing she could do to save her family's disgrace, but it was hard and she was bloody scared stiff.

She got up and took a turn around the room, which suddenly seemed very dear to her, and she touched each item in turn until she came to the crib. Then she looked down at her little sister's podgy hands either side of her head in the total abandonment of sleep and traced her finger gently around one until the baby gave a sigh and her hand closed in a fist. Aggie leaned over the crib and gently kissed Nuala's little pink cheek as the tears began. She tried to stifle them, but Tom, lying awake too, heard. He wished he could go in, but knew Aggie would probably be embarrassed.

Eventually, awash with tears, she threw herself on the bed and closed her eyes.

She awoke stiff and shivering with cold, and saw with horror the clock said the time was half-past two. She roused herself quickly and began to gather the things that she was taking with her. She decided to travel in her clothes for Mass as they were the smartest she had: woollen plaid dress, black stockings and button boots, a proper coat and matching bonnet. She had taken her mother's large bag that she took when she went into Buncrana on Saturday, because she didn't have anything else, and into it she put underwear and nightwear, her two everyday dresses and cardigan and her warmest thickest shawl.

She had one last look around the room and then eased the window up gently and climbed through it. But, as quiet as she tried to be, Tom heard as he was lying wide-eyed on the bed, worry for his sister driving sleep from him, though he was aching with tiredness. He pulled the curtain aside and saw her walk by the window. Hurriedly he dressed and followed her.

Aggie was glad when Tom fell into step beside her. She hadn't expected it when he had to be up at five for the milking anyway, but she valued his company. They didn't talk much. They had said all that needed to be said, but Aggie thought for her brother to be there walking by her side was comforting. Tom wished with all his heart that he was older, that he could care for Aggie, and if her parents wouldn't let her stay at home then he would take her some other place and see to her. It seemed abhorrent to him that a young girl should travel so far completely alone and all because a man had taken advantage of her.

McAllister was there waiting for her and impatient. 'Where have you been?' he hissed. 'For this to work I must be back in Buncrana with the horse stabled before the place is awake. Come on now, get up and be quick about it.'

Aggie handed McAllister her bag and turned to Tom. 'Goodbye, then.'

'Goodbye, Aggie,' Tom said. 'Look after yourself.'

'I'll try,' Aggie said, putting her arms rather awkwardly around her brother.

'We haven't time for this,' McAllister snarled.

Aggie turned on him. 'Listen here, you,' she said. 'Your life will not change in any way, shape or form because of that one night. I am leaving behind my home and all in it that I hold dear. I know that I will see none of them ever again and you dare complain because I spend a few minutes saying goodbye to my brother?'

McAllister said no more, for he knew that Aggie had a point. She kissed Tom on the cheek before climbing in beside McAllister. The cart rolled down the road almost silently and Tom saw with surprise that the horse's hoofs had been wrapped in cloths so that they would make little noise. He had to admit that that was a wise move, for the sound of hoofs on the road could be heard for miles in the still and quiet of the early hours.

He yawned, weariness suddenly hitting him, and with the cart lost in the darkness he turned back to the farmhouse.

FIVE

'Have you anything to wrap around yourself?' McAllister asked Aggie when they had gone a little way down the road. 'You are shivering like a leaf.'

'It isn't with cold, or at least not that alone,' Aggie said. 'It's mainly fear.'

'Well, I can do nothing about the fear; you must combat that on your own,' McAllister answered. 'But if you have brought a shawl or anything, I would put it around you, that's all I'm saying.'

Aggie did then delve in the bag and pull out the shawl, but even wrapped tight around her, it did nothing for the icy dread that seemed to be seeping all through her body.

'Are you sure your sister won't mind me just landing on her?' she asked at last.

'No,' McAllister said confidently. 'I have explained it all in a letter that I will give you to show her. Big sister Gwen refuses me nothing.'

'You might be a better man if she had a time

81

or two,' Aggie was tempted to say, but she bit back the retort. There was little point in annoying McAllister at this late stage, particularly when she needed information. So instead she said, 'And what about getting rid of the baby and all? Will she know someone?'

'Course she will,' McAllister said. 'You won't be the first person she has helped, not by a long chalk. Everyone in the area knows her. Her name isn't McAllister but Halliday, Gwen Halliday, for she was married. She lives in Varna Road now in a place called Edgbaston. That's not far at all from New Street Station in Birmingham city centre.'

'Her husband might have something to say about me just turning up,' Aggie said, 'however lax Gwen seems to be.'

'Oh, the old man is dead and gone now,' McAllister said. 'She was left with the one son to rear but he's grown up too. See, Gwen is twelve years older than me and was more of a mother to me than my own ever was. She won't let me down, never fear.'

'Won't she be shocked that this is your child that I am having to get rid of?'

'Why should she be?' McAllister said. 'She knows what men and woman get up to. The prostitutes working the area were forever seeking her out. Can't work if they have kids hanging on to them, can they now?'

Aggie had never been so shocked in the whole of her life. 'Does she know prostitutes?' she said.

In Buncrana such things just didn't go on, but everyone knew that prostitutes were the very dregs of society.

McAllister laughed. 'Time for you to grow up, little girl,' he sneered. 'When our father died, Gwen was fifteen and there were six mouths to feed. With my mother gone to pieces altogether, Gwen went on the streets to prevent us all starving to death. She eventually married one of the punters. Our mother had died by then too, and as I was the youngest she took me in to live with her and her husband. Then when she was widowed, she went back out on the streets again to provide for her son. That's how it is.'

Aggie mouth dropped open. She had never been so shaken in the whole of her life. Surely that wasn't really how things were, not in normal, respectable society.

'What price is virtue, Agnes?' McAllister went on. 'Especially if the alternative is starving to death?' He gave a wry laugh and added, 'Not that Philomena knows any of this. She would react very much as you did, shocked to the core of her Roman Catholic soul. She doesn't know much about my earlier life at all. She met Gwen just the once, at our wedding, and they never really hit it off. I used to visit Gwen on my own after that.'

'I am not surprised they didn't hit it off,' Aggie said, her lip curling in distaste. 'Your wife is an honest and decent woman. You talk about women

83

choosing to go with men for money as if it is just a job like any other.'

'So it is.'

'How can you say that? Aren't there normal jobs for people?'

'Jobs are often few and far between,' McAllister said. 'And if you should get one, it will usually be backbreaking work for long hours, and all you pick up at the end of the week is a pittance of a wage. Gwen didn't want that sort of life and I don't blame her.'

Aggie was silent. She wondered what sort of place she was going to at all where things totally alien to her seemed almost commonplace. What sort of woman was this Gwen, whom she would be forced to rely on? The apprehension in her increased. However, it was too late now for doubts and second thoughts. The die was cast.

McAllister delivered Aggie to Derry Station, but could not take time to stay with her because he had to get the horse back to Buncrana before the place was astir. Aggie understood his concern, even shared it, and yet it was hard to see him disappear into the darkness. The waiting room was open so there was shelter from the wind at least, but inside the dark was so intense Aggie thought a person could almost touch it. She was so cold her teeth chattered and she couldn't remember being as scared in the whole of her life.

For a time she sat on the wooden bench

running around the walls, aching with cold and fear, but eventually, worn down by weariness, she lay down on the bench, drew her legs under her, and with her shawl wrapped about her she closed her eyes.

She woke stiff and colder than ever, and noticed straight away that the darkness was not so deep. She pulled herself to her feet and began to walk briskly around the small room, slapping herself with her arms to get the blood flowing as she watched light steal into the day. Already she would have been missed at home, but her parents would know no more than that, because Tom would never betray her.

She wondered what they would think, for she'd spoken the truth when she'd told McAllister that she hadn't a penny piece to bless herself with. She wondered how long it would be until her mother noticed the missing clothes and would guess that she had run away. Mammy would be perplexed for she would know that Aggie had nowhere to run to.

Would McAllister betray her? She doubted that. There was one other person, though, that would, at the very least, be aware that McAllister hadn't slept in his bed that night and that was Philomena. When the news that she had run away from home became common knowledge, would she put two and two together? Would she challenge him or, heaven forbid, tell her parents of her suspicions?

Would they call out the Garda and could they make her return home if they found her? She imagined they probably could, and that thought made her feel colder than ever. She wouldn't feel totally safe until a stretch of water separated her from her parents.

It seemed an age until other people began arriving at the station and the ticket office opened. Aggie was then able to spend some of McAllister's money and make her way to the platform where the train lay waiting. There were few travelling that February morning, but those on the train were curious about such a young girl travelling alone.

Aggie knew they would be and she had her story ready. She told them she was to take up service in one of the big houses near Birmingham in England. As she told the lies she thought that in the end that might be the truth because when this was all over – provided she survived, of course – she had to have a job and place to live. Being in service seemed as good as any other employment.

'Why Birmingham?' one woman asked, while another commented that she was young to travel so far alone.

There again Aggie had her answer. Her brother worked in Birmingham, she said, and would be meeting her off the train at the other end and taking her to her place of work. The women were only slightly mollified, but Aggie knew how delighted she would be if the tale she had delivered had been the truth.

She was glad of the women's concern for her, though, when they reached the mail boat straining against the ropes that secured it to the dock side for she was scared as well as a little excited to be boarding it. But the excitement fled when the boat was on the move, tossed from side to side by the turbulent waves, making Aggie feel so sick she vomited over and over till her stomach ached and her throat felt raw.

'You'll likely get used to it,' one of the women told her.

'Aye,' said another. 'Sure, wasn't I just the same when I went over first? Now I take it in my stride as you will, cutie dear.'

Aggie gazed at her through bleary eyes. She could not remember feeling this ill since she had had the measles, and she had the feeling she could never get used to the crossing. Anyway, she told herself, she wouldn't have to get used to it; the chances were that she would never see the shores of Ireland again. Maybe some day she might regret that, but at that moment all she could feel was relief.

'Come on away inside,' the first woman urged. 'The wind would cut you in two and it's cold enough to even freeze a penguin's chuff, as my old man would say.'

It was cold, and the sight of the huge, relentless waves crashing in cascades of foam against the sides of the rolling boat did little to stop the churning of Aggie's stomach, so she gave a brief nod and followed the woman as she led the way into one of the saloons. The smell of cigarette smoke and Guinness was mixed with slight body odour and vomit from those who hadn't made it outside. Aggie only managed a minute or so of breathing it in before she was making for the deck again.

And that was where she stayed until the boat docked in Liverpool. Even when the sleety rain began she stayed put, so by the time she was ready to disembark, she was wet to the skin. The women tutted over the state of her and said she would catch a chill if she wasn't careful. Aggie hid her wry smile. Dear God, if that was all she had to worry about.

She continued to feel sick even when she had left the boat far behind and was in the train travelling down to Birmingham. She hadn't thought to bring anything to eat, but didn't feel like anything either, and when her companions offered to share their food with her she shook her head.

'Thank you, but my stomach isn't right yet.'

'Might feel better with something in it.'

'I don't think so yet,' Aggie said. 'Maybe when we get to that place called Crewe. You say that we have to change trains there?'

'Aye,' one of the women told her. 'It's a regular stopping place. Nearly everyone has to change at Crewe and it has got a café on the station. And you're right, you may well feel like something there.'

The only thing that Aggie really felt like, though, when she sat in the slightly smoky café at Crewe Station was a cup of hot sweet tea. She gulped at that gratefully as she gazed out on to the platform through grimy windows that were slightly misted over because of the teeming rain outside, and waited for the train to take her on the last leg of her journey.

She knew in her heart of hearts that the nausea and weakness she felt was more a sickness of the soul. With this behind her she would soon be fine and healthy once more. Then all she would have to cope with was the fact that she was alone in the world, and she'd not be the only one. They had foundlings enough at their own workhouse who had never known the love of a family and growing up among brothers and sisters. She imagined in a large city like Birmingham there would be plenty more and so she told herself firmly to stop feeling sorry for herself.

When she arrived at New Street Station, however, the sheer size and noise of the place unnerved her totally. The train pulled to a stop with a squeal of brakes and hiss of steam, and people spilled from the carriages onto the platform.

Everyone seemed to know where they were going, Aggie thought, sniffing at the damp and sooty air, surrounded by more people than she had ever seen in the whole of her life. The place was full of sound. Apart from the clatter of the trains and the ear-splitting screech of the hooter, there was the tramp of feet and the noise of raucous voices raised in laughter or greeting.

Porters' voices warning everyone to 'Mind your backs, please' rose above it all as they pushed laden trolleys through the milling crowds. Through this cacophony, a news vendor with a strident, though slightly nasal-sounding voice, shouted out in an attempt, Aggie supposed, to sell the newspapers spread before him, but she had to guess this because she couldn't understand a single word that he said.

'So where is your brother, dear?' said one of her travelling companions. 'We'll stay with you till we see that you are all right.'

Aggie was filled with panic. They intended to wait with her till the brother she had invented should put in an appearance, and she looked around anxiously. There were still plenty of people around and, knowing that there was nothing else for it, she picked up her bag and said, 'There he is, over by the steps. Thank you so much for looking after me.' She was away before they could think to detain her, to insist they meet the fictitious brother and ascertain that Aggie was all right.

Aggie was soon hidden from their view by the crowds of people and she secreted herself behind a pillar and watched her travelling companions who were scrutinising the crowds going up the stairs closely. Then one gave a shrug and they turned their attention to their luggage scattered around them on the platform. Aggie didn't breathe easy, however, till they had left the platform altogether. Even then, she stayed where she was a little longer and the crowds had thinned out considerably when she slid out of her hiding place and made her way towards the exit as resolutely as she could.

If the station had unnerved Aggie slightly that was nothing to the way she felt when she stepped into the street outside. Rain was falling so heavily it was like a wall of water and turned the late afternoon to dusk. Lights were lit on many of the vehicles, which gleamed onto streets glistening with water.

Aggie stared, for she had never seen so many vehicles all packed together on the roads, even some of the new petrol-driven motor cars that she had heard tell of, but never seen. There were horse-drawn vans and carts thronging the streets, and hackney cabs were ringing the station, waiting for customers. The smell was incredible: acrid, sour and sooty. It lodged in the back of Aggie's throat and made her cough. The noise was relentless: a constant drone mixed with the chattering and shouts of the people, the sound of boots and the clopping of horses' hoofs on the cobbled streets.

And then Aggie saw a clattering, swaying monster coming towards her. It both repelled and fascinated her. She drew nearer for a better look

91

and saw that it ran on rails laid all along the road, while steam puffed from its funnel in front. It tore along at a furious rate, using its hooter constantly to warn people to get out of the way.

Aggie had drawn closer to the hackney cab drivers too, and one of the drivers, from the shelter of his seat, had watched her with slight amusement, noting that she seemed not to notice her soaking hair plastered to her head or her sodden clothes. Eventually he leaped from his seat and said to her, 'You seem very interested in the trams, miss.'

'Trams. Is that what they are?'

'They are, miss,' the cab driver said. 'Run by steam and, if you believe what people say, they can travel at fifteen miles an hour.' Here he gave a rueful smile. 'People always seem to be in a hurry these days. Those blessed trams could easily put me out of business. I mean, Bessie is a good horse and no slouch either, but going full out on a flat stretch of road she can only manage half that speed. Maybe I will have to invest in one of those petrol engines for my next cab, but tell you the truth they scare the life out of me.'

'And me,' Aggie agreed. 'And as for those trams, I don't think I will ever have the courage to get on one. I have never seen anything like them before. There were none where I came from.' She thought for a moment and went on, 'When I was at school there was a girl come up to live in Buncrana from a place just outside Dublin and she said something about steam trams and the electric ones around Dublin. We weren't at all sure that she was telling the truth, to be honest, and anyway, it was hard to visualise. They may have something similar in Derry or Belfast, I suppose, but it was too dark to see much.'

'You have just come over on the boat then?'

'Aye.'

'May I say, miss, that you have chosen a fine time to come visiting?'

Aggie looked at him and in the lights from his lamps he was moved by the sadness in her eyes as she said, 'It wasn't by choice that I came now.'

The cab driver longed to ask why she was here then and whose choice it was, but he stopped himself. His wife was always telling him not to get so involved in the lives of the people he carried in his cab. His job, she said, was to get people from A to B, and if he didn't spend so long talking to each one then he would probably earn a damned sight more than he did.

She was probably right, but he was interested in people. He couldn't help it and he reckoned he couldn't do the job as effectively if he didn't like people.

As for the young Irish girl, she looked so vulnerable and naïve she aroused the paternal instinct in him. So he said, 'You are very wet, miss, if you don't mind me saying so. You should get on to where you are going quickly and then out of those sopping clothes or you will be ill.'

Aggie felt ill, chilled to the marrow, but that wasn't solely due to the weather, as she well knew. She wasn't at all sure either, now she was here in the city, what she should do next. McAllister said that his sister lived no distance from the centre in a place called Edgbaston, but in the deepening dusk, how far was far, and in what direction? She shivered with apprehension more than cold, because she guessed that once she left the city centre there would be few abroad that rain-sodden night to advise her.

'I know I should,' she said to the man, 'but I am not at all sure what to do now.'

'Well, where are you making for?'

'Varna Road,' Aggie said. 'My aunt lives there.'

The cab driver thought of his young daughter at home. She was only six, but he hoped that she would never have to travel to some strange city alone, and he said angrily, 'Fine aunt then, if she hasn't even come to meet you.'

'I don't know her that well,' Aggie admitted. 'And I was delayed and unable to let her know. I was told it wasn't far from here. If you just give me directions . . . ?'

'And have you die of pneumonia?' the cab driver said with a rueful grin. 'Come on, I'll have you there in a jiffy. It is no distance really, just off Belgrave Road.'

'Oh,' said Aggie taken aback. 'Will it cost very much?'

'Not to you, and not tonight,' the cab driver

said, picking up Aggie's bag with ease. He knew if his wife ever got to hear about this she would give out to him, but the girl was affecting him strangely. 'Let's just say that I am feeling in a generous mood.'

To Aggie this was all a little unreal, but she was so very tired, cold and unnerved at the thought of what lay ahead of her. So she let this man, this perfect stranger, take her hand, help her into the cab and drive her into the night.

Varna Road was a depressing street, one of many of back-to-back housing that was so prevalent in the city. It was Aggie's first experience of such a neighbourhood and she was shocked to the core. Had she but known it, the cab driver hesitated to leave her there. He knew the profession her aunt was probably involved in if she lived in that street. Surely she hadn't invited this untouched and beautiful young girl to join her?

'It's none of your business if she has,' he could almost hear his wife's voice in his ear. 'Needs must when all is said and done.' And so he said to Aggie, 'You all right then? You did say this one.'

In the light of the guttering gaslamps Aggie could see the whole place was shabby, much of the paint was off the door, and flimsy grey nets hung at the grimy windows. She noted with shock that one of the panes of glass was out altogether and replaced by a piece of card. She hated the cab driver to think that she was related to someone who lived in such a dingy, unkempt house, and yet this was the address that McAllister had written.

As she lifted out her bag she said, 'Yes, this is it. Thank you so much. You have been very kind.'

'You're sure now that you will be all right?'

'Aye,' Aggie said, wondering if she would ever be all right again. 'Honestly, I will be grand now.'

The cab driver would rather have waited until he saw the girl safe inside the house at least, but he had earned little money that night and couldn't go home yet awhile, and so he waited only until he saw the girl lift the knocker before he jiggled Bessie's reins, the horse gave a toss of her head and the cab rattled over the cobbles.

While she waited for someone to open the door, Aggie watched the cab driver go, heard the clip-clop of the horse's hoofs and the rumble of the cab grow softer, and still no one came in answer to her knock. She lifted the knocker again, but before she let it drop, the woman next door came out.

'Ain't no good you knocking there, ducks. Her's done a moonlight. Heard tell the bums were coming to put her out, like.'

Aggie stared at the woman in stupefaction. She hadn't the least idea what she was talking about.

The woman realised that by the look on her face and it annoyed her. 'You deaf or just plain stupid?' she barked.

'I'm sorry,' Aggie said, trying to collect her scattered wits. 'I am looking for a Mrs Halliday, a Mrs Gwen Halliday.'

'Ain't you listened to a bleeding word I said?' the woman snapped. 'She ain't here, like I already told you.'

'Not here?' Aggie repeated. 'But where is she?'

'How the bleeding hell do I know?' the woman said. 'Look, you come over on the banana boat or what?' And then at the terrified look on Aggie's face, she relented and said, 'Look, ducks. Her was took bad and got behind with the rent, like, and she heard that the bums was coming. If they throw you out they take your things to sell them, so Gwen took off, like, in the middle of the night. She dain't leave no forwarding address neither. People who have to do a moonlight don't usually, in case them bums get hold of it.'

'So no one knows where she is?' Aggie asked in horrified tones.

'That's about the shape of it,' the woman said. 'What do you want with her anyroad? You in trouble? Up the duff, like?'

'Up the duff?'

'Lord give me strength,' the woman cried in exasperation. 'You got a babby in your belly, 'cos that's the main reason people come seeking Gwen?'

Aggie nodded miserably.

'Do you know of anyone else?' the woman asked.

'I don't,' Aggie said. 'Not a soul.'

'You poor sod,' the woman said. 'Then it will be the workhouse for you.' She saw the shiver that ran through Aggie and cried, 'OK, so it ain't the Ritz, but it's better than the streets. And talking of streets, I better get out there and earn my crust, though I doubt there will be many punters out in this filthy night.'

Aggie suddenly realised what line of work the woman was talking of. In case there should be any doubt, she went on, 'I think I'll go and hang around the gentlemen's clubs in the town. They often take you to a nice warm room. Course, a lot of them want the kinky stuff, but I don't mind that if they pay enough.' The woman wrapped her shawl tighter around herself as she spoke. 'Well, tar-rah a bit, duck, and if I was you I would get myself inside somewhere pronto. Even the workhouse is better than freezing to death.'

Aggie didn't speak. She couldn't, for despair and desperation were blocking her throat. Then, as she watched the woman tripping down the street, sudden nausea overcame her and she turned and vomited into the gutter.

Aggie had always been a practical child, an attitude fostered by her mother, but now she walked through the backstreets of Birmingham aimlessly and in despair. The rain continued to trickle from skies that now were almost black as the night began to close around her. She had never ever been so petrified with fear. She hadn't a clue what was going to happen to her because she knew not one person in that teeming city.

She had money and could probably get lodgings, but that would only help for that one night, and there was still the problem of getting rid of the child she carried. She had little hope of finding this Gwen Halliday if she didn't want to be found, and so her life was effectively over, though her whole body recoiled from knocking at the door of the workhouse.

She wasn't sure afterwards how long she had walked, or why. She just felt she couldn't stand still. She was light-headed with worry and lack of food. It had been hours since she had eaten. Hunger pangs began in her stomach so severe that she wrapped her arms tight around herself and groaned in pain.

As the night really took hold, the temperature dropped and Aggie began to shiver violently, for her sodden coat offered little protection against it. She felt suddenly weary too. She stumbled as she walked, and longed to lie down and rest somewhere, so that a little later, when she tripped over the kerb and fell to the ground, hitting her head on the cobbles, she made no effort to get up.

Lethargy so affected her that to move was too much effort. She suddenly had no pain, just a numbness affecting her whole body. A tiny part of her urged herself to get to her feet, to keep walking, but she ignored it. She lay as still as the death that would soon claim her, while the night deepened and settled around her and the rain continued to fall, and she was so tired that her eyes closed of their own volition.

SIX

Lily Henderson was making her way home. Usually she didn't return until much later, but the rain had kept the punters away that night. In the end, she was so chilled she had gone into a public house for a few gins to chase the cold away. As she swayed her way home, she almost laid her length on the cobbles when she stumbled over Aggie. At first she thought it was just a pile of rags, and complained loudly at the stupidity of people throwing old clothes into the street to trip up inno-cent people going about their business.

Her strident voice semiroused Aggie, and she groaned. Immediately Lily stopped her complaining, not entirely sure if she had really heard a sound or not. But then it came again. Lily fell to her knees and whistled in astonishment when she felt Aggie's saturated coat. She worked her way up her body until she reached the face, and assuming by the bonnet that the figure was a woman, she tapped her cheek lightly.

'Come on, ducks,' she said, and when there was no response, the smack was a little harder. This was followed by a shake, but the woman continued to lie so still and silent that Lily was alarmed. If they didn't get her indoors soon, the girl or woman, whatever she was, would die. She set off for home to get help, hoping and praying that there was someone in who had also returned early.

The houses in Belgrave Road were large terraces. Lily shared one of these with other 'ladies of the night'. Each had her own room, and there was a larger room downstairs that they used as a sort of sitting room. They got on well enough, for each had her patch and none impinged on the others.

Susie Wainwright, who was much younger than Lily, had just got in. She had changed out of her wet clothes and was drinking a cup of tea in the sitting room. Her feet were bare and she had a towel wrapped turban-style around her black curls. She had no intention of stepping out again that night and wasn't a bit impressed with the tale that Lily was telling.

'So,' she said, 'why are you telling me this?'

'She'll die if we don't bring her in, like.'

'Oh, Lily, for God's sake!' Susie exclaimed. 'She's probably just some old drunk and no loss if she does peg it.'

'There weren't no smell of booze off her.'

'And just how could you be so sure of that?' Susie said sarcastically. 'Your breath is so gin-laden it is nearly knocking me back.'

'All right, but this isn't about me.'

'All the same . . .'

'For Christ's sake, just come and look, will you?' Lily cried. 'It won't take you a minute. It's no distance from here.'

'You're a bloody nuisance, do you know that?' Susie grumbled, getting up and shoving her feet into her still-damp boots. 'Pass me my coat, you old nuisance, and if this is some wild-goose chase—'

'It isn't. I just know it isn't.'

A few minutes later, Susie knew it wasn't either. 'She's just a bit of a kid,' she said, looking at Aggie in the light of the matches she had thought to bring with her. 'Let's get her inside quick. Your room would be best, as it's on the ground floor.'

'Yes, I suppose,' Lily said. 'She can have my bed as well for now at least.'

'Can't put her on the bed yet, though, Lil,' Susie said, as between them they lifted Aggie's inert body. 'Her's wringing wet.'

'Can't leave her on the bare boards either,' Lily said. 'Do her no bloody good at all, that.'

They manhandled her as gently as they could into the house and then into Lily's fairly spartan bedroom.

'Leave her down on the floor a minute while I get a blanket off the bed to lay her on,' Lily said to Susie. Lily set light to the fire that she had laid before she left the house that evening.

'I should take off her coat first,' Susie advised. 'It's that wet, the blanket will be sodden in minutes.'

Lily saw the sense of that and it was as they eased Aggie's coat off they realised that the moisture was not just water; some of it was blood running from her in a scarlet stream and covering her dress.

'Almighty Christ!'

'Where's it coming from?'

'God alone knows,' Lily said grimly, 'but we need to find out.'

'Come on, then,' Susie urged. 'And quick. This young girl looks in a bad way to me.'

When they removed the last of Aggie's soaked and bloodstained underclothes they realised the blood was pumping from inside her and the two women looked at one another.

'God blimey, she's miscarrying!' Susie cried.

'Aye, poor sod,' Lily said sadly. 'And if we're not careful we'll lose her as well as her babby.'

'You're right there, Lil. I'll get some towels.'

They used the towels to pack around Aggie and then Susie rubbed at her shivering body, trying to bring life to it. Aggie's eyes never opened, though she stopped shivering, and Lily wrapped her in the second dry blanket she had ready and moved her nearer to the fire. 'Now, we've made her as comfortable as we can,' she said. 'I reckon that babby will come away before long.'

The two women sat on into the night, talking quietly together, near the crackling fire. Aggie was hot now, very hot, and Lily knew she had a fever. She sponged her down constantly, listening to her laboured breathing and watching the grimaces of pain flit across her face.

It was two in the morning before Aggie expelled the tiny foetus from her body and by that time both Lily and Susie were very tired. Lily washed Aggie down with warmed water she had ready and then put one of her own nightdresses on her. With Susie's help she lifted her onto the bed. She packed her with fresh towels and then raised the bottom of the bed with bricks that Susie had found in the yard to try to prevent her haemorrhaging. Aggie didn't regain consciousness.

By the morning the sweating had eased and Aggie's face had returned to a more normal colour. The fever had broken and Lily breathed a sigh of relief.

'Come on,' Susie said. 'I'm fair jiggered, but I will give you a hand hauling down one of the mattresses from the attic because you will never manage it alone.'

Lily was glad of Susie's offer, for she had thought to just curl up on a rug. It wouldn't really matter where she lay, she thought, as they struggled to bring the mattress down the stairs, because she was so tired she could have gone to sleep on a clothesline.

'Where d'you want it?' Susie asked as they pulled it into the room.

'Right beside the bed,' Lily said, 'so I will be on

hand if I am needed. And you best seek your bed before you fall to the floor in sheer weariness.'

Susie went thankfully. Lily turned to the girl on the bed. She noted her face was as white as the sheets Lily had pulled up to her chin, and her dark brown hair, released from her plaits, was fanned out on the pillow.

'Who are you, bab?' Lily murmured almost to herself. 'And what man did the dirty on you, eh? Susie is right, you are very young.'

She didn't expect an answer – the girl was still unconscious – and with another sigh she got to her feet, made up the mattress and undressed before slipping between the covers and falling into a deep sleep.

In a small cottage in Ireland the previous morning Tom rose to help with the milking with a heavy heart. He had been in his bed just about an hour and a half and he had no enthusiasm to face the day, for concern for Aggie was like a large knot of worry inside him. Added to this, he had to pretend he knew nothing about her disappearance in the night.

Biddy was annoyed that Aggie had not done her jobs that morning. Thinking that she had over-slept, she told Joe, pounding through the house to join his brother and father in the cowshed, to rouse Aggie.

'I can't. Aggie isn't there, Mammy,' Joe said.

'Not there?' Biddy echoed, going in to see for

herself. Aggie's bed was empty. Biddy could only presume that she had risen early and gone off on pursuits of her own. She herself had to complete the jobs Aggie usually did and she remarked to Thomas John that the girl would get the rough edge of her tongue when she did return. Thomas John, however, remembered his daughter's strange behaviour the previous day and warned her not to be too harsh on the girl.

'Maybe she wasn't feeling too well this morning and needed to walk in the fresh air a wee while,' Thomas John went on. 'Generally, you must admit she has never given you any bother.'

'No,' Biddy conceded. 'In the main, she is a good girl.'

'Well, then,' Thomas John said, 'let her have a few minutes to herself and I'm sure she will be full of apology and explanation when she does come home.'

She didn't come home, though, that was the problem, and with the milking over Tom and Joe were sent to scour the farm lest Aggie had fallen and hurt herself. By the time they returned, Biddy had checked her room, found her things missing and knew she had run away.

'But where would she run to and why?' Thomas John asked.

'The why we can go into when she is brought back,' Biddy commented grimly. 'As for where, well sure there is nowhere but Buncrana, for the girl knows no one beyond, and has no money.

Tom, as soon as dinner is eaten I want you to go into Buncrana and ask around her friends and all. Be discreet. I don't want the Garda alerted yet. I am sure she will be found in no time at all.'

Tom knew she wouldn't be. If all had gone to plan she would now be on her way to Birmingham. Hatred for McAllister, who had forced this course of action on his sister, deepened still further. Though he knew it was fruitless Tom played the part and asked around. When he returned Thomas John insisted on informing the Garda and two officers came to the cottage that evening.

They were grim-faced but reassuring. 'You'd not be up on what the young are at at all, at all,' the older man said, 'but as she has no money and no place to go, we'll soon pick her up, never fear.'

'There were gypsies camping not that far away for a few days,' the younger garda said.

'I hope you are not suggesting that my daughter has run away to gypsies?' Biddy asked, affronted.

'I'm not saying she has, missus,' the garda went on, though he knew she wouldn't be the first one to do that. 'It's just that gypsies get about and hear things.'

But the gypsy camp had been disbanded and there was not a sign of them when the garda investigated. The news that Aggie had run away with the gypsies spread like wildfire, as such things do. Tom could see that the garda believed that as well.

That first Sunday, after Mass, many came to talk to Biddy and she knew that while some offered support, others were there to gloat a little that their daughters hadn't done such a thing. Tom, though, could not believe his ears when he heard McAllister commiserate with his father as he shook him by the hand.

He said that he had known Aggie well through the dancing and she was the last person he thought would disappear from her home and worry her parents so. 'All goes to show that no one person knows the heart of another,' he went on. 'But this is one heart anyway you can be sure of, and if you need anything you only have to ask.'

'Thank you, Bernie,' Thomas John said. 'You are very good. Tell you the truth, this has knocked me for six. I would never have said that Aggie was a bold girl, but this is as bold as it gets.'

McAllister nodded sagely in agreement and heat flowed through Tom at the unfairness of it all. One person noted Tom's discomfort and his cheeks flushed crimson, and that was McAllister's wife, Philomena. She remembered that the night that Aggie was reputed to have gone missing was the night that Bernie hadn't sought his bed until the early hours. The following day she had found a large amount of money missing from the till.

It didn't take much to put two and two together and her heart ached for she knew she was partly to blame. If she had left Bernie to his just deserts in Birmingham that time and come to Buncrana alone, she could bet that Aggie Sullivan would not have felt the need to flee the way she did, and her heart went out to the boy who so obviously missed his sister.

All morning, Tom festered over what McAllister had done and what he had said to his father. And then at dinner his mother referred to Aggie as 'a viper in the nest', and said that she was no longer a child of hers and no one was to mention her name in the house ever again.

'Mammy, what are you saying?' Tom gasped.

'Is there a problem with your ears, Tom?'

'No, but Mammy—'

'It's the only thing to do, caddie. This is the only way that I can cope with it.'

Tom noted the deep lines on his mother's face, her eyes puzzled and confused, while his father's was just a mask of sadness. He felt for both of them. 'I know, Mammy,' he nodded. 'I am not blaming you, but it will be hard for me to forget Aggie ever existed.'

'Well, you must try, lad,' Biddy said sharply. 'And that goes for all of you,' she added, glaring at her family as they sat staring at her. 'She has run away from this family to God knows where, so therefore she no longer deserves to be part of it. Her name is never to be mentioned again and it's no good looking over our shoulders all the days of our lives expecting her to come in at the door.'

Tom knew she would never do that, but he could hardly bear it. The sister he had known all his life was gone forever. He knew if he allowed himself to dwell on that thought, the tears would start in his eyes and that would never do. No one said a word, not even his father. They sat in stunned silence, even little Finn, who had picked up the charged atmosphere. But then, in God's truth, knowing as little as they did, what was there to say?

Suddenly, the Sunday dinner that Tom looked forward to all week tasted like sawdust, and he pushed his plate away, leaving the food half eaten. His mother hated waste and, normally, would have given out to him, but that day she took his plate away without a word.

'Daddy, would you mind if I took a wee walk out?'

It was an unusual request. Tom had scant free time and even on Sunday there were jobs aplenty for him to do. However, Thomas John knew that the knot of worry he had for his daughter was shared by Tom and so he said gently, 'Aye, Tom. See if the fresh air can help you any.'

Outside, the day was overcast and there was a hint of moisture in the air. Tom saw not another soul out and about like himself, though he went nearly as far as the town.

Philomena saw him standing on the hill above the shop. Her heart went out to him and she suddenly thought she had to talk to the dejected boy, try to help him in some way. Calling to her elder two children to mind the others for a while, she followed him.

Tom was glad he met no one because he knew he would be poor company that day. What McAllister had done filled his mind. As if abusing and raping his sister and causing her to flee from her home were not enough, he had had the bare-faced cheek to commiserate with his father that morning. 'One heart you can be sure of,' he'd said. That man's heart would be as black as pitch, Tom thought.

And then, as if his thought had conjured him up, he saw McAllister riding down the country lane below him. He knew he was bound for the O'Learys' cottage, whose farm abutted the Sullivans'. Tim O'Leary told him that morning at Mass that he had a fiddle lesson with McAllister that afternoon. Tom had thought at the time that he was glad he had given up the music.

After the attack on Aggie and the house laid low with measles, McAllister wasn't that keen on visiting. When everyone was better, Tom had declared that he didn't want to continue with the music lessons. Thomas John, weakened by the measles, was quite glad of this at the time and Joe gave up too, but then he had never been as keen, or as good at it as Tom.

Tom was just glad that the man had no occasion to come to the house any more. He couldn't have borne it. But others, being unaware of what McAllister was capable of, treated him as they always had. Tom imagined him being fêted and praised at the O'Leary house, for the O'Learys, like most people in the town, thought McAllister a grand chap.

No really knowing why, Tom descended to the lane and walked the route McAllister had taken, with no plan in his head until he came to trees on either side of the road followed almost immediately by a left-hand fork. An idea began to take shape. If he were to stretch a rope of some sort between the trees, McAllister wouldn't see it until he was virtually on top of it and neither would the horse. Tom felt that he would have struck a blow for Aggie if he were to injure the man in some way. He tore home as fast as he could, to find a suitable line.

Philomena watched him go and wondered what had sent him home in such haste. She hadn't long to find out, for the Sullivans' place was no distance across the fields. Though Tom proceeded stealthily, once he got near the farm all was quiet. He knew the bale of metal twine they used for mending fences was in the barn and he chopped a sizeable bit from the bale with the axe before heading back.

Philomena saw immediately what Tom was about and went down to stop him. She reached him as he was tying the last knot to the second tree. He was startled and frightened when he saw Philomena but she set out to reassure him.

'Don't worry, Tom. I know what you are trying to do and why, and though I understand, this isn't the way.'

'You don't know what he has done.'

'I can have a good guess,' Philomena said. 'Is this something to do with your sister's disappearance?'

Tom stared at her, his mouth agape, more unnerved than ever. Then in a horrified voice, little more than a whisper, he said, 'How did you know?'

'I didn't,' Philomena said. 'That is, well, I knew he had a fancy for her, but I didn't think, never dreamed . . . Tom, is she expecting his baby?'

Tom nodded miserably, knowing there was no longer any need to deny it, to Philomena at least.

'And do you know where she has gone?'

'To Birmingham, to his sister.'

'Where she will get rid of it?'

'That was the plan,' Tom said. 'None of this was Aggie's fault, you know. He had her filled full of poteen. She could barely stand when she came home. God knows how she had got so far. She was in a state and he had the dress near ripped from her back.'

'Was that the night your mother was helping out at Sadie Lannigan's?' Philomena asked.

'Aye, and my father was in Buncrana,' Tom said. 'You may be sure that this would have come out long ago if either or both of them had been in. It's a wonder he didn't think of that.'

'He thinks of nothing but satisfying his desires when he is that way inclined, if you know what I mean,' Philomena commented glumly. 'I know that to my own cost. He never thinks of the consequences of his actions.'

'Aggie would have done all in her power to keep what happened that night a secret, anyway,' Tom said, 'if she could have. I mean, if she hadn't been expecting.'

'Aye,' Philomena agreed with a grim smile, 'pregnancy is one thing that no one can hide for long.'

'He told her he would say she came on to him, offering it on a plate, as it were. Aggie thought everyone, even possibly our own parents, would believe him over her.'

'Poor girl,' Philomena said with feeling. 'And the devil of it is she is right. The man is usually believed first in any case, and Bernie can be charming when he wants. I mean, I fell for his charm and I am not a stupid woman. He has this ability to make people think he's just such a grand man altogether.'

'I know,' Tom said. 'And it's all bloody false. You should see how he went on to my father this morning.'

'I did, and I saw your reaction. Then I knew my earlier misgivings were right,' Philomena said. 'And that is why I followed you and came to try and stop you.'

'Why?' Tom demanded. 'He is worth nothing.'

'You're right,' Philomena said, 'and I tell you now that he if was on fire in the gutter I wouldn't spit on him. I do agree that he needs teaching a lesson, but not by you. I don't want you getting into trouble.'

'I won't unless I'm caught. Or you tell on me.'

'Haven't you listened to a word I've said?' Philomena replied. 'I would never tell on you. I hate the man and wish to God he was not the father of my children and that I was not married to him for the rest of my life, but I am and that's that. But honest to God, Tom, haven't your family suffered enough?'

'Aye, but—'

'Think,' Philomena reasoned. 'If it is found that you did this in a bid to hurt my husband, questions will be asked and then you risk exposing your sister. He will delight in dragging her name and that of your whole family through the mud. I know just how vindictive he can be and I know he would see to it that you would never be able to lift your heads up again.'

Tom realised that he hadn't thought the whole thing through enough. He was starting to untie the first knot when he heard the drumming of horse's hoofs approaching fast up the lane.

'Come on,' said Philomena. 'We'll just have to hope for the best. I pray to God it is Bernie galloping this way and not some other poor innocent soul going about their lawful business.'

Oh Almighty Christ, thought Tom. That was another thing he hadn't considered. He allowed Philomena to draw him into the shelter of the trees and his sigh of relief was audible when it was McAllister who came into view seconds later.

The overcast skies had turned the afternoon to dusk and it had begun to rain. Visibility was bad and McAllister was riding far too fast. He had his head down as he careered round the corner, thumping his legs into the horse's sides to make him go faster still. The horse ran into the wire at speed. It hit it above the knees and with a scream it stopped dead and dropped to the floor. McAllister didn't have a chance to save himself. He sailed through the air over the horse's head and landed heavily. Both woman and boy heard the thud as he hit his head on the knoll of a tree and then lay still.

Tom's heart was in his mouth. He had no intention of seriously injuring McAllister. He would have run to see if the man was all right, but Philomena forestalled him.

'Leave him to me,' she said. 'Untie the rope and hide it. It wouldn't do for anyone to think this is anything other than an accident.'

Before Philomena went to her husband, though, she caught the horse, who had struggled to its feet, and examined its bruised and battered knees.

'Poor feller,' she said. 'I'll see to those when I get you home,' and she tied the horse loosely to a tree before turning to her husband. There was no need to rush, because she knew by the strange angle of his neck that the man was dead.

She knew she was wicked but all she could feel at that moment was relief – relief and thankfulness. Oh, she'd play the part of the grieving widow, all right, for the benefit of the townsfolk, and pray for the repose of her husband's blackened soul, for if anyone needed prayers he did. But she was free of him and she could have danced a jig.

However, paramount in her mind at that time was protecting the young boy from the consequences of what he had done, and that meant clearing up all the evidence.

'How is he?' Tom asked then, coming towards her as he wrapped the twine around his arm.

'I'm afraid, Tom, he is dead.'

The blood in Tom's veins suddenly ran like ice and his teeth chattered with fear as he stared from the prone figure to Philomena. 'Are you sure? Maybe he is just knocked out.'

'Tom, his neck is broken.'

'Oh Jesus, Philomena, I never meant that.'

'I know, but if we are both to get away with this then we must keep our heads.'

Tom could hardly believe his ears. 'You mean you're not going to call the Garda and tell them what I did?'

'Not a bit of it. What purpose would that serve? As I see it, you have done me a favour. Bernie had it coming to him. He couldn't have gone on the way he was and not expected some retribution to fall his way eventually. Aggie is not the first to have her life damaged and destroyed by my husband and, God help me, I can't feel sorry for the death of a man like that.'

'D'you think it will be believed that he died by accident?'

'Yes, if we are clever about this,' Philomena said.

'I will say the horse made his way back to the stable without the rider and with bruised and bloodied knees. Fortunately, the knees are damaged enough so that the mark of the twine won't even be seen.'

'I'm sorry about the horse.'

'So am I,' Philomena said, 'but I'll see to him and he'll be grand. But make sure you hide that twine well.'

'I will.'

'Now be off,' Philomena said. 'It would never do for someone to be along the road and catch sight of Bernie, and me not even home with the horse.'

Tom needed no further bidding and he scampered off, stopping only to throw the twine to the bottom of the well. He didn't care either that his parents both gave out to him for being so long away and getting his good Sunday clothes so wet because that was familiar and safe. He went into the room, changed to his everyday things and followed his father to the cowshed without a word.

Philomena also took care to change her clothes and footwear, and recoiled her dampened hair into a tighter bun before informing the Garda that her husband was missing. There was no need for them to be suspicious, or to disbelieve anything Philomena McAllister told them. She was known as a respectable woman of the parish and community. When she showed them the damaged knees of the horse, they were very worried indeed and set up a search of the area immediately.

The body was soon found. The priest was sent for and the whole town alerted to the fate of Bernie McAllister, who died when he was thrown from his horse.

120

SEVEN

Aggie drifted in and out of consciousness, though this was helped by the laudanum that Lily was dosing her with. She saw no harm in this. She took tincture of opium herself, as all the women in the house did. It gave her a warm and delicious feeling of euphoria, especially when mixed with gin, which they all drank in copious amounts. Laudanum was also the usual remedy for fever and ensured that Aggie would sleep till Lily's return.

'Wouldn't do for her to come to, like, and find me gone, would it now?' she said to Susie on Monday evening as they sallied forth to work. 'Might frighten her half to death.'

'Mm,' Susie said in agreement. 'Has she said owt yet?'

'No,' Lily said. 'She's not with it half the time. She's still a really sick girl, Susie.'

'I know and it's lucky for her that you came upon her when you did.'

Aggie didn't know where she was and who the

woman was with the gentle hands and the soft voice, who would wash her so tenderly, for Lily was very kind.

She was honest too, in her way. She had found the money in Aggie's possessions, which she had rifled through in an effort to find out who she was. She had discovered from the travel ticket on her bag that her name was Agnes Sullivan and she was from Ireland. Lily had left the money alone. While she might lift a gold watch or a wallet from a well-heeled gentleman, even one of the punters, without the slightest pang of conscience, she wouldn't steal from one of her own. Despite the money, she knew from Agnes's clothes that she was a long way off being rich and she guessed that money had been to pay for an abortion she no longer needed.

It was Tuesday evening when Aggie opened her bleary eyes as Lily was bathing her face and said, 'Who are you? Please, I have to know.'

'Course you do, ducks, and there ain't no secret of that either,' said Lily. 'I'm known as Lily, Lily Henderson, and a few days ago I found you collapsed on the road and the rain teeming down on you. So I came for my friend Susie Wainwright, and we carried you in here.'

She let this knowledge settle in and then went on, 'And I know your name is Agnes Sullivan.' At Aggie's startled look she explained, 'It was on the ticket attached to your bag.'

Aggie sighed in relief. And then, because in her

life so far only one person had called her Agnes and that was Bernie McAllister, she said, 'I am never called Agnes. I am known as Aggie. And I don't really understand. When was this?'

'Wednesday night.'

'And what day is it now?'

'Tuesday.'

'And you have cared for me all this time!' Aggie exclaimed. 'How kind you must be.' And then Aggie remembered what she was doing in Birmingham and her one hand touched her stomach. The movement was barely perceptible and yet Lily not only saw it, she also understood it.

'The babby's come away, ducks,' she said gently. 'You lost it that first night.'

She saw relief flood the girl's face and so wasn't surprised when she said fervently, 'Oh, thanks be to God!' As soon as the words had left her lips, though, she realised what they must have sounded like to Lily, and she flushed with shame. 'You must think me awful, but you see I didn't . . . It wasn't . . . I mean I never . . .'

Lily covered Aggie's shaking hands and said, 'You don't have to justify yourself to me or anyone else either, and you just remember that. You'll tell me or not in your own time and in your own words.'

Aggie sighed in relief that this woman would never force her to tell anything she didn't feel happy about.

Because of Lily's innate kindness, her soft

speaking voice and the tender way she had cared for Aggie, even giving up her bed, Aggie thought her some kind of saint. Lily's age would be about forty, and she had a kind and open face, with rosy cheeks and beautiful soft brown eyes, so full of expression that they lit up her face when she smiled. Her hair, Aggie guessed, had once been the same colour as her own, but now it was liberally laced with grey and yet it suited her somehow.

She looked homely and wholesome, and so later that night, when she said she was going to work, Aggie looked at her with amazement. 'I could make you up a dose of laudanum before I go, if you like,' Lily said. 'I make it into a sort of cordial. That's what I gave you to bring down the fever and ensure that you slept until I returned when you were really sick.'

'What was in it?'

'Opium, mainly, and gin, of course, a bit of water and sugar.'

'Opium?' Aggie repeated. 'Isn't that a drug?'

'Course it is, ducks,' Lily said, 'and you takes enough, it makes you feel just wonderful. Bloody marvellous, in fact.'

'I have never taken drugs in my life.'

'You have, love, since you come here,' Lily said. 'I had to get the fever down somehow.'

'I'm not blaming you at all, Lily,' Aggie said hastily, wary of offending.

'Point is,' Lily said, 'if you don't sleep what are

you going to do with yourself, because I will likely not be back till the early hours?'

'What do you do till then?' Aggie asked innocently.

Lily looked at her as if she couldn't believe what she had just heard. 'I know you came over from Ireland, but surely you are not that naïve,' she said. 'I am a prostitute, Aggie, and the streets are where I work.'

Aggie's eyes opened wide with astonishment and Lily smiled. 'Shocked you, have I?'

Shocked was an understatement. The only prostitute she had ever seen had been Gwen Halliday's next-door neighbour. In Aggie's world, prostitutes were a subclass that respectable people didn't associate with.

There was nothing to prepare her for Lily Henderson, who worked in that profession and yet had lifted a vagrant and desperately ill girl from the cobbles and given up her own bed while she nursed her back to life and dealt with the child she had aborted. Aggie owed her a huge debt, one that she might take a lifetime to repay because she knew but for Lily's intervention she would have died. Now she told herself firmly that how Lily wished to live her life was her business.

She wouldn't risk upsetting this woman to whom she owed so much, and the only one who had shown her such compassion and understanding, and so when Lily said, 'Right, now, if you have got over your amazement, I am making up a tincture and you are going to drink it,' she nodded her head.

'I'll do whatever you think is right, Lily.'

Two days later Aggie insisted on getting up, though Lily thought she was still not well enough. In fact, Aggie was surprised how weak she felt, and her legs shook so much she managed to cross the room only with difficulty and collapse with a sigh of relief into a chair Lily had placed before the fire.

'What on earth is the rush anyway?' Lily said. 'You'll get better in time.'

'Aye, I know that,' Aggie said. 'But until then you are supporting me and that is not right.'

'Have I complained?'

'No, and in a way that makes it worse,' Aggie said. 'I have money for now that you can use, and gladly.'

She stopped. Despite what Lily had said about not having to tell her anything she didn't want to, she felt she owed her rescuer some explanation for how she came to be in Birmingham, so she went on, 'I had it to give to the woman who was going to take my baby away, though maybe you guessed that already. Anyway, that money isn't needed for that any more.'

'I found money when I was looking through your things to find out who you were,' Lily said. 'And yes, I had a fair idea what it was for. I haven't touched a penny piece of it, don't worry. By, it must have taken some saving.'

'I didn't save it,' Aggie said. 'I couldn't have if I had wanted to. The only money I ever had placed into my hand was two farthings my mother would give me for Mass on Sunday morning. No, that money came from the father of the child I was having.'

'You were lucky then,' Lily commented. 'Not many cough up.'

'Doubt he would have done either,' Aggie said, 'if I hadn't sort of blackmailed him. I was desperate, you see, and so I threatened to tell his wife everything. He said he would claim that I led him on, offered myself to him, and while most people in the town might believe him rather than me it would at least sow the seeds of doubt in his wife's mind. Anyway, whichever way it was, he seemed more bothered about his wife knowing than anything else, so he gave me the money. They have a grocery shop in the town – at least his wife has – and he probably took the money from the till or something. I didn't want to know really, because I felt bad enough about Philomena as it was.'

'None of this is your fault, you know,' Lily said. 'I suppose he forced himself on you?'

'Well, aye, he did right enough,' Aggie said. 'But I didn't struggle much. I have thought about it over and over since, and sort of blamed myself, but he had me full of poteen, you see. It's this really powerful drink. They distil it in the hills. It's made from potatoes and—'

'You don't need to tell me,' Lily said. 'One of

the girls was given a bottle of it by a punter, and when she had a few glasses of it she nearly went off her head. I'm not that fussy, as a rule – I mean, I drink anything going – but I couldn't take that stuff. Just the smell was enough. I said to her that it was like something you would use to strip paint. I'm surprised that you developed a taste for it.'

'I didn't,' Aggie said. 'I hate the stuff, but he held my nose and I had to swallow it in the end.'

'Oh, you poor cow!'

The sympathy in Lily's voice brought a lump to Aggie's throat. Lily saw the sheen of unshed tears in her eyes and heard the anguish in her voice as she went on, 'When I found I was expecting, God, there aren't words to tell you how scared I was. I was in despair. You have no idea what it is like over there. To have a child out of wedlock is a desperate thing altogether, and a mortal sin too. The shame of it, not just for me but for the whole family, is immense.'

'They don't exactly clap their hands with joy here either, you know,' Lily commented.

'I suppose not. It's just that there . . . well, I know my parents couldn't have borne it.'

'What I can't get over, though,' Lily said, 'is when you had the money and all, why you came all the way to Birmingham to get the job done.'

'There wasn't anyone in Buncrana that would do such a thing,' Aggie explained. 'Anyway, McAllister, the man who raped me, had come from here a few years before and he told me to contact his sister and she would sort me out.'

'And who's that?'

'A woman called Gwen Halliday.'

'Oh Christ!' Lily exclaimed. 'So this man that violated you was her little brother Bernie?'

'Aye. Did you know him?'

'Well, her more than him really. He used to live with his sister, see, and not that far away either. People say that he couldn't keep it in his trousers from when he was in his early teens. Course, she was on the game as well, so he saw it all round him, and then too she spoiled him rotten. Felt bad about him being orphaned when he was just a nipper, likely. Anyroad, she always seemed to care more about him than her own boy. People say that it wasn't entirely natural either; that she made a man of him when he was just twelve.'

'Surely not?'

Lily shrugged. 'Who knows, or cares really? It's just what people say. I was surprised, though, when she told he was marrying someone. Didn't seem the marrying sort, if you know what I mean. I saw his wife-to-be too, and she looked a respectable woman. Her and Gwen never hit it off, but then Gwen would think no one would be good enough for her brother. Anyway, despite this fixation with her brother she is all right, is Gwen, and soon has our girls organised when it happens to them.'

'Pregnancy, you mean?'

'Of course, what else? Can't work when you

have a baby, can you, and even if you could, how can anyone bring a kid up in a place like this? No, any that find themselves up the Swanee goes to Gwen and she fixes them up.'

'Well, they will have to find her first,' Aggie said, 'because her house is empty – saw it myself – and a woman there said something about her doing a flit and the bums coming. I didn't really know what she was talking about at first.'

Lily smiled. 'The bums are the landlord's men, and they put you out if you don't pay your rent. Gwen was in the hospital a few weeks back and she obviously couldn't work and so got into arrears. She'll pop up again somewhere or other before long. After all, she has got to eat.'

'And so have we,' Aggie said. 'I insist you take that money and use it for now. By the time it's gone, I hope I will be strong enough to look for a job somewhere and pay you back.'

Lily looked at her. She was a very beautiful girl, she realised, now that she was rested and less fearful and had had good food inside her. Maybe Alan Levingstone would have an opening for such a comely girl in his club, for Lily would like to keep her off the streets as long as she possibly could, though that's where she would probably end up eventually.

She knew that Aggie would have no idea of what the future held, but she couldn't see any other job she might be offered without references of any kind. She decided not to tell her just yet, not until she had sounded out Levingstone, at least.

It was Levingstone – Mr Levingstone to any other than Lily – who provided the house the girls lived in. It was a large house, three-storeyed and terraced, and housed six. Each room was fairly basic, though some of the girls had put up ornaments or pictures to make it more homely.

Lily hadn't done anything more than cover the oilcloth on the floor with a few rugs. Apart from that she had a bed and a chest of drawers, a wardrobe and a large ottoman for spare linen. She was content.

As well as the sitting room, the girls shared a kitchen and a bathroom off it. They were very lucky: few prostitutes had such good accommodation. It wasn't the only house that Levingstone managed, though; they were dotted around the city.

He also ran a club for selected male clients. The only girls in the place, apart from the maids in his own private quarters, had to be both young and beautiful, and the men could choose who was to entertain them for a few hours. Upstairs were the plush bedrooms, and Lily knew that working that way was much safer than being on the streets night after night.

Lily had been with Levingstone longer than most. They had grown up on the same street and so she had a little influence and she was sure she could convince him that Aggie could be an asset.

*   *   *

Tom often felt overwhelmed by what he had done. Whatever type of man McAllister was, he had killed him just as surely as if he had hit him with a lump of wood. It was all right Philomena saying that McAllister was no loss, she hadn't done the deed, and she'd actually tried to stop him. What in God's name had he been thinking about even to consider such a thing anyway? Hatred for McAllister had got in the way of reason and justice, and he really thought he should pay the price for that.

At home, if he had done anything wrong then he would be punished for it, sometimes severely. He had never protested because that was the way it was, but now he had done this very wrong thing, almost the worst thing one person can do to another, and nothing was going to happen to him.

Worse still, he was unable to confess it. The priest couldn't speak of what was said in confession but he would know who Tom was and could seek him out later and maybe urge him to confess all to the police. Then everything would come out about Aggie and McAllister, and Philomena's part in it. It would also be the end of his life, for if he wasn't hanged he would probably be transported, and then how would his parents cope? They would be destroyed with shame by the actions of their children.

He shouldn't attend Mass or take Communion while this mortal sin nestled in his soul, yet he knew full well he would never be excused Mass. Then if he didn't go to the rails for Communion, it would be noted, and back at home the inquisition would start. He would have to go on as he was for years and years, every Sunday compounding that sin till his soul would be as black as coal. He tossed and turned in bed at night, unable to sleep, though his body was often weary and his eyes smarted with tiredness, until Joe would growl at him to keep still.

Small wonder he had nightmares. They were so bad that he was almost afraid to go to sleep at night and was sluggish throughout the rest of the day. Thomas John would often lose patience with him, and Tom could only hope that he would feel better when the man was buried.

However, on the day of the funeral, the whole town turned out to pay tribute to this 'fine man'. Tom had hoped that the sister McAllister had spoken about would be there, and maybe, if the opportunity presented itself and he didn't lose courage, he could ask her about Aggie. Philomena, though, told him Gwen would not be coming.

'For myself I can't stand the woman,' she told Tom. 'But I asked her for Bernie's sake. The letter was returned marked "Not known at this address", and I have no other way of letting her know about the funeral.'

'Yes, but what does that mean for Aggie?' Tom said. 'I mean, was she moved someplace else when Aggie got there?'

'I don't know,' Philomena said. 'But you can do nothing about it so try not to worry. Believe me, the funeral will be enough of a strain for the two of us to go through.'

And it was, particularly in the room at the back of Grant's Bar where the funeral party went after the Requiem Mass and the prayers intoned at the graveside. Tom listened in amazement to the varied tales the men told about McAllister's exploits and the women who shed tears over the grand figure of a man taken in his prime like that. Tom realised that once a person dies, he becomes a saint.

He found it all very hard to stomach. When they began to commiserate with Philomena on her tragic loss and go on about what a good husband and father he was, Tom reckoned that he had heard enough and he slipped outside.

Philomena saw him go and went out after him as soon as she was able to.

'All right?' she asked.

Instead of answering, Tom burst out, 'How do you stand it, Philomena?'

'Stand what?'

'Look,' Tom said, 'you may as well know that there is seldom an hour goes by when I don't feel guilty at the death of your husband. Yes, I meant to harm him, but not kill him, and I wish it hadn't happened to him. But the way they go on in there is just sickening. He was not the great man they are describing and lamenting the loss of.'

'You're right, he wasn't,' Philomena agreed

placidly. 'No great shakes at being a good husband and father either.'

'So doesn't it make you feel mad inside when they go on and on, talking about a man neither of us recognises?'

'People are people the world over,' Philomena said. 'Many are nervous about speaking ill of the dead, thinking – oh, I don't know – that they may come back and haunt them or something, I suppose. It's easy for people like that to remember only the good times, and Bernie could be the life and soul of any gathering.'

'I know that, but—'

'Words are easy to speak, Tom,' Philomena said. 'I know the real Bernie McAllister, but that man's body is lying in a coffin in a graveyard and cannot hurt me or bring disgrace on me or mine ever again, so I will keep my own counsel. In a while, I'll sell the shop and move away from here, and start afresh where no one knows us. I'll bring my children up on my own, which I have been doing since the day they were born anyway. And you, Tom, must forget that day Bernie died and forget you had a hand in it.'

'I can't!' Tom cried. 'I took a man's life, whichever way you look at it.'

'Aye, you did,' Philomena said. 'And thank God for it, for he wrecked so many young girls' lives and would have gone on and on doing that if he had lived. I tell you, Tom, you did the world a favour. Now you think on that and then put all this behind you, for you have your whole life to live yet. I must go back in now before I am missed.'

Tom watched Philomena go back to join the party and thought about the things she had said to him. He knew she had spoken wisely. He accepted that he had helped kill a man, and yet all the regret in the world would not alter that fact. So, he had to either do his damnedest to put it all behind him now, or let it eat away inside him till he was destroyed too. He mentally squared his shoulders and followed Philomena.

Ten days after Aggie first felt well enough to get up, Mr Levingstone agreed to take a look at her and was even more interested when Lily told him she could do Irish dancing. She had found out by accident as Aggie let it slip to her one night and she had gone on to tell the five girls that she shared the house with. They, of course, wanted to see this for themselves and as one of them had a gramophone, as soon as Lily deemed Aggie strong enough, they sallied forth to buy the records with the dance tunes that she knew.

Aggie herself wasn't too keen on this. Every time she thought of that night in December, she felt sick and she knew that it was her love of the Irish dancing that had led in the end to the attack. If she had never been to classes to learn, then she would, in all likelihood, be still be at home now with her parents and her brothers and baby sister. She agreed to demonstrate her dancing only to please Lily, yet when she heard the familiar strains of the jigs and reels fill the air, she felt her toes curling with anticipation.

And when she began to dance a skip jig in the bare feet that she was used to, all nervousness left her. It was as if she was an extension of the music. The girls sat spellbound watching her, and the applause at the end was spontaneous and heartfelt. Aggie was pleased though she flushed with embarrassment.

'My God, girl, Levingstone will snap you up,' Lily said when they went back into the room for Lily to change to take to the streets again. 'He would be mad not to. He would be sitting on a bleeding gold mine.'

Aggie made a face and Lily rapped out, 'Don't look like that. Let me tell you, girl, it will be a sight more respectable than what I do.'

Aggie remembered asking McAllister, rather primly, if there had been no ordinary jobs that people could do. She had known nothing then, and it had been Lily that had put her right to the true situation when she had suggested looking for a job.

'Where was you thinking of looking, ducks?'

'I thought of work in service somewhere,' Aggie had said. 'It's all I know really.'

'Listen, bab,' Lily replied, 'you won't be taken into service or any other place respectable without references.'

Aggie could see that now – see that and understand it as well – but still she asked, 'What am I to do?' The silence spoke volumes. 'I . . . c-couldn't do what you do,' she stammered.

'That surely would depend on how hungry you get,' Lily snapped.

'Don't be offended.'

'Why shouldn't I be?' Lily said. 'I bring you in and look after you, put food on the table and get coal for the fire to prevent us freezing to death, and you look down on me. The money you brought is almost gone, so what're you going to live on then, fresh air?'

'No,' Aggie said. 'I'm sorry.'

'Time you grew up, girl,' Lily said. 'Think I chose this life? You think when I was a nipper at school I thought, when I grow up I'm going to be a prostitute? Tell you why I did it, girl. I lost my parents to typhoid and there was just me and my little brothers. I was thirteen, and it was either me go onto the streets, the only thing that would pay enough to keep us, or throw ourselves on the mercy of them at the workhouse. Course, I didn't know the least thing about how to go about it then, and I was terribly frightened. The first man I propositioned was Levingstone.'

'Did you do anything with him?'

'Yeah, I did,' Lily said almost defiantly. 'He was kind, though, and gentle, and yet I felt dirty – filthy, in fact. When he had gone, I vomited into the gutter. But he paid well. He came again the next night and the next, and each time I vomited. Then he asked if I wanted to work for him, but he didn't have management of the clubs then. As a sort of extra payment, and because we had been neighbours, he looked after my brothers too, saw them through school and that, and later paid their passage to America. And I became one of his whores. There weren't no choice really, and that was it. I stopped being sick in the end, though I never liked it and don't now. That's why I drink so much. We all do. And we take the opium 'cos it blurs the edges a bit.'

'Was the letter that came yesterday from one of your brothers?' Aggie asked.

'Yeah,' Lily said. 'I have only the one now, because the youngest died on the trip out, but the eldest is doing well. Point is, Levingstone didn't have to do the half of what he did. Course, he was one hell of a lot younger then, not so hard-boiled and cynical, and he said he felt sorry for me. When he took over the management of this house, I was the first one he moved in, and there ain't any other line of work I could take up now.'

'Did you never have a baby?'

'Ain't allowed no babies,' Lily said. 'Levingstone is adamant about that.' Her voice suddenly sounded sad and Aggie saw the tears in her eyes as she went on, 'I fell pregnant four times. The first time I was only fourteen. But they was all taken away – aborted, like. After the last time, the woman damaged summat and I never fell pregnant after that. Just as well, really.'

'I'm sorry, Lily,' Aggie said. 'Who am I to judge anyone?'

'I'm sorry too,' Lily admitted. 'I was just like everyone else, you know. I wanted a husband and kids, and a little house with roses round the door, but the dice didn't roll that way for me. But don't look down on me, Aggie, because it hasn't for you either and we just have to make the best of it.'

Then, seeing that Aggie still looked scared to death, she continued, 'Look, Levingstone is just about as decent as they come in this business and yes, the blokes he has there have the pick of the girls, you included, but he don't allow no funny stuff. Some of the whorehouses have rooms like bleeding torture chambers, and you'd scarcely believe what they put some of them girls through.'

'Ooh, don't. That's horrible.'

'So better the devil you know, eh?' Lily said. 'When he comes to see you dance tomorrow morning, you put on your best performance. Be nice to him and do what he tells you and he will treat you right.'

Aggie was hardly reassured by that. All this was like a nightmare coming true.

EIGHT

Aggie wasn't really that keen on Levingstone when she met him the following morning. He was a fairly tall man with very black hair and deep-set dark eyes, and he was clean shaven, which emphasised his large and rather bulbous nose and his wide mouth. But what was really off-putting was the way his eyes were narrowed in scrutiny and his mouth turned down as she began to dance.

They didn't stay that way, though, for within minutes of watching Aggie, Levingstone saw she was a gifted dancer. There was soon a twinkle in his eyes, his mouth turned up in approval and his foot was tapping along to the music. She was a beautiful girl, almost a child still, and when he spoke to her afterwards, he found her lilting accent so endearing. Despite what had happened to her – for Lily had told him how she had found Aggie collapsed in the street, and later she had miscarried a child – there was an air of vulnerability about her. He knew his club members would pay dearly to see this little girl dance and he was totally enchanted by her.

Had the child been born to affluent parents maybe she could have gone to a school of dance, for she was extremely talented, but what was the point of wishing things were different? He wanted her in his club as soon as possible. That would keep her off the streets for now, which was really all she could hope for in the circumstances.

'Pack your things,' he said. 'I want you in my place from tonight. I will send a hansom cab for you this evening at eight o'clock and you will not be returning. Don't look so scared; you will not go down in the club until I see fit. I want you for myself.'

Aggie gasped. The man's words hadn't made her feel any better. Risking his wrath, she said, 'I've never done things with a man but the once, and then I was forced.'

'I will not force you,' Levingstone said. 'I have never had to force any woman, but if you refuse to do this, what will you do instead?'

Aggie knew there wasn't any 'instead'. She had to agree to do what he wanted or be thrown out onto the street, and yet her insides quailed at the thought and she had flushed with embarrassment as she said, 'I'm sorry. I might not be very good, but I will do my very best to please you.'

'Good girl,' Levingstone said, beaming his approval at her. 'I promise that you won't regret it. Till tonight then, sweetheart.' He drew her towards him and kissed her gently on the lips. Aggie willed herself not to pull back.

Lily, who had been shopping, came in just a few minutes after Levingstone had left. She was delighted for Aggie and said if she played her cards right she would be set up for years. The other girls in the house agreed, and were pleased that things were finally going right for Aggie.

'Do you think so really?' Aggie asked Lily on the quiet. 'See, in my wildest dreams I never thought of this sort of life for myself.'

'Lots of us was the same, ducks,' Lily said. 'Life dictates what we do, and that. If I was you, I would forget the life you come from and the family you come from.'

'They would probably not want to know me after this anyway.'

'Best way,' Lily said. 'They would barely recognise you and wouldn't want to acknowledge you. You know I went on the streets to put food in my brothers' mouths and give them a start in life, yet my brother doesn't want me to be part of his life in America. He is married and has a couple of kids, but I wasn't invited to the wedding and have never been asked over since either.'

'Doesn't that hurt you terribly?'

'Bab, it's life,' Lily told her. 'The gin and drugs helps when life gets up and kicks you in the teeth. But you, ducks, should be happy. The club is for the real nobs, you know. You have to be rich and have a certain status to go there. It's still in

Edgbaston and yet it might be a million miles away. Levingstone has rooms above the club, so they say. Plush rooms, I mean, a proper apartment and with maids and all. If he wants you for himself, then, girl, you have it made. And it is one hell of a lot safer for you there, bab. Levingstone will look after you and it's better you keep off the streets as long as you possibly can.'

'Won't I be able to stay at the club for always?'

'Always is a long time,' Lily told her. 'Like most blokes, Levingstone likes to surround himself with young and pretty girls. Don't do anything to annoy or offend him, and you might last longer than most.'

It didn't sound very promising, but the girls thought it the best possible news and decided to throw an impromptu leaving party for Aggie that lunchtime.

Aggie liked all the girls because they had been kind to her, especially Susie. She was much younger than Lily, no bigger than Aggie, and full of fun. She confessed that she was twenty-five. She had an arresting appearance with her mop of black curls she was constantly trying to tame, skin light as alabaster and a rosebud mouth.

'You're a lucky little cow,' she said good-naturedly to Aggie, after they had all toasted her health. 'Tell you, I would have given anything to go in such a place, but my wonky eye put paid to that.'

Aggie felt sorry for Susie, for though her eyes were so dark they were almost black and very alluring, there was a cast in one of them. 'Is that all Levingstone rejected her for?' Aggie asked Lily quietly when Susie had moved away and was joking with one of the other girls.

Lily nodded. 'It's sad, I know, but when you pay as much as the punters do that Levingstone pulls in, I suppose they demand perfection.'

'That's horrible!'

'So it is, bab,' Lily said, 'but it ain't your fault. Now hand me up a glass and I'll fill it for you.'

Aggie, still apprehensive of the future and mindful of Lily's advice on dealing with it, drank the gin in a few minutes and was ready for another. She liked the taste of it, for it was nothing remotely like poteen, and Lily was right: after her third glass it made her feel as if nothing mattered and all was right in her world. In the end, though, she drank so much she was unable to stand, and Lily had to help her to bed.

Four hours later Aggie opened her eyes and thought she had dropped into Hell. She felt sick, had a raging thirst, a thumping head and the room refused to stay still. Suddenly into her mind, which seemed filled with cotton wool, came the memory of her dancing for Levingstone that morning.

By screwing her eyes up she could focus on the clock across the room and saw that it was already six o'clock. Levingstone's cab would be here in two hours and she felt like death warmed up. That was what she told Lily when she came in just a few minutes later.

'You just got a hangover, bab, that's all,' Lily said to her. 'Bet it is your first.'

Aggie thought back to how she had felt when she woke up the morning after the rape, but that was all mixed up with her sickening for the measles as well.

Lily laughed gently at her. 'Won't be your last, Aggie, not in this business. Where you are heading, drinking and encouraging the punters to drink is part of the culture – what Levingstone will expect you to do.'

'I really don't think I will be able to stand it,' Aggie said.

'You'll get used to it in the end,' Lily said. 'And you will stand it all right, because you are not stupid and you know what the alternative is. Now I am going to get you a big drink of water, and when you have drunk it I want you on your feet, washed and changed, and ready to please and charm Levingstone.'

Aggie knew Lily was right: how she behaved in the next few hours could shape the next few years of her life. She couldn't look further than that, and so she took the glass from Lily, downed it immediately and then gingerly got to her feet and tried to ignore her pounding head.

Despite the water and the wash, Aggie wasn't quite sober when the cab arrived to take her to Levingstone's club. It was a beautiful cab, she could see even in the dim light from the hall. The horse was dark, though his mane was coffee-coloured and she saw with surprise it was plaited.

The driver was dressed in a dark green uniform, and was extremely smart. He called her 'miss' very correctly and doffed his cap to her. Aggie wanted to laugh at the absurdity of it. She was going to a club where she would be expected to sleep with a man who was almost a stranger to her and this cabman was treating her with the utmost respect.

Aggie would have enjoyed the drive more if she hadn't been so scared about what awaited her at the journey's end. She did note though that the area they were travelling through was nothing like the area she had come from. Lily was right, it might have been a million miles away, for they had left behind the mean streets and the houses squashed together. The street they were travelling down was wide and lined with trees, and they shared it with other vehicles, some pulled by horses, some powered by the noisy, smelly engines. Aggie saw too that there were the rails of the tram track at the edge of the road. And the houses were large and set in their own grounds. In fact, some couldn't be seen at all from the road, and that increased Aggie's apprehension still further.

After about twenty minutes they approached the club from the back. A young maid answered the coachman's knock and Aggie was taken up the carpeted stairs and into a hall of sorts, where the maid helped her off with her coat and bonnet. She then led the way to a dining room where a table was beautifully laid for dinner. Aggie's feet sank into the dark red carpet and as she approached the table she felt her heart thudding in nervousness. She had never seen so many knives and forks in all of her life, nor so many glasses, which sparkled in the light of the two glass chandeliers set in the sculptured ceiling. The room itself had gold-varnished wood halfway up its walls, another thing Aggie had never seen before. Above the wood the walls were covered with pretty paper with a gold leaf design.

Then Levingstone came in, took Aggie's trembling hand and led her to a seat at the table, while he sat opposite. The maid Levingstone addressed as Mary, dressed in a black dress and a white apron, served them delicious food, which Aggie was almost too overawed to eat. She was also worried about using the wrong knife and fork, and copied Levingstone meticulously, but was far too agitated even to make a stab at any sort of conversation. Levingstone seemed to know that, however, and chatted away to her instead.

He served her wine with the meal. He said it was white and fairly sweet because wine was an acquired taste, but Aggie found she liked it and had quite a few glasses of it. Soon she was feeling pleasantly woozy. Then Levingstone took her hand and led her to a chair beside the cosy fire blazing in the grate.

She didn't like the brandy that he insisted she have with the coffee, which she found quite bitter.

'It will help you relax,' he said. 'You're still incredibly nervous, aren't you?'

Aggie didn't trust herself to speak because she was having trouble stopping her teeth from chattering. When Levingstone saw that the brandy, which she'd downed with a grimace, had made little difference, he rang the bell and told Mary to prepare a tincture for the young lady.

It was the sort of drink Lily would mix for her, but slightly stronger. Aggie drank it gratefully, knowing the numbing effect it would soon have on her.

So, when she had drained every last drop of the drink and Levingstone extended his hand, she took it without hesitation, though she staggered so much when she was on her feet that he put an arm about her instead and helped her into the bedroom, which he said he kept for guests.

Again the room was carpeted and softly lit with lamps. Aggie saw with surprise the sheets were silk and the colour of the midnight sky, and turned down ready. Lily had packed her prettiest nightdress for Aggie to wear, but she suddenly sensed that she would never have the occasion to put it on.

She knew she had to block out what McAllister had done to her, so that she could truly submit to Levingstone, for her very survival rested on her pleasing him. Anyway, a pleasant lethargy was seeping through her body so that now she worried about nothing. Though her head was spinning slightly, it was not an unpleasant sensation, and she felt no shame as Levingstone undressed her.

He was a skilled lover and not an impatient one, and he was very attracted to the slight and beautiful little Irish girl. He really liked virgins, but Lily had told him that Aggie's only experience had been forced upon her and therefore was hardly enjoyable. He intended to show her a different side of sex, because when he deemed she was ready and she was introduced to the clients, he imagined that she would be in great demand. He wanted to make sure that she knew what was expected of her and would give the men good value.

So that night, he gave himself up to pleasing Aggie. The drugs and drink had successfully dampened down any embarrassment she might have felt as the last of her garments fell to the floor and she lay totally naked before a man for the first time in her life.

When that man fondled her breasts, gently at first and then more vigorously rolling her nipples between his fingers, she couldn't have held back the moan of desire that escaped from her any more than she could have prevented the sun from shining.

Many times that night Aggie groaned and moaned in an agony of lust that Levingstone induced in her until, when there was no area of her body that he hadn't explored, and often followed with his lips, and when he eventually entered her, she cried out in thankfulness.

The joy and rapture of it went on and on, wave

after wave rising higher and higher, and Levingstone felt her responding to him and knew he had a gem in Aggie. She was a sensual woman and, with her inhibitions loosened, one who would enjoy sex and in time endeavour to please him as much as he pleased her. She would remain his and only his until he tired of her.

Aggie knew none of Levingstone's thoughts, of course. She just knew that when he kissed her gently, tucking the sheets around her as he slipped from the bed, for he had a club to run, she turned over with a sigh of satisfaction and remembered nothing more.

When Mary came in the next morning to open the curtains, Aggie groaned, for even the light of the grey day stabbed at her eyes. Levingstone had given instructions that Aggie was to have anything she required and so when the maid asked her if she would like any breakfast and Aggie said that she could eat nothing but she would like a large tincture, the maid just bobbed her head in acquiescence. And if she thought a mixture of gin and opium was not a terribly good way to start the day, she kept those thoughts and feelings to herself.

Aggie badly needed the drink because, as the memories returned, the shame crept in and she didn't know how she would be able to look Levingstone in the eyes. She felt so degraded and dirty, and she needed to make those memories hazy so that they could be pushed to the back of her mind. The tincture also got rid of the pounding headache and she had to fight the desire to ask for another. After a few minutes she felt well enough to get up. Mary brought her a jug of hot water to pour into the basin already there and with the most beautifully scented soap, Aggie lost no time in washing herself and drying herself on the soft fluffy towels, amazed at how much better she felt after that.

When Levingstone came in a little later, she was glowing from the invigorating wash, but he knew from her slightly glazed eyes that she had taken opium. He wasn't surprised. He knew that the previous night had been her first true sexual encounter and maybe she had needed some help coping with that when she remembered it this morning. And yet when he held his arms out, she went straight into them and snuggled against him.

He so desired her at that moment that he almost took her again, there and then, as she had shown him plainly that she was willing, but he had further delights in store for her first and so he dampened down his ardour and whispered his plans for the morning in her ear.

'Clothes!' she cried in delight. 'You are going to buy me clothes?'

'Yes, pretty things for you to wear in the club.'

Aggie eyes clouded. 'Am I to go down to the club then?'

'Not yet,' Levingstone told her. 'For the moment I want you to please just me. Think you can do that?'

'I will do my best,' Aggie said, mightily relieved that the ordeal of meeting other men who would take her to bed and do unmentionable things to her was to be deferred.

'Can't ask for fairer than that,' Levingstone said, and Aggie smiled at him.

He had been so considerate of her nervousness and so gentle the previous night that any memory of McAllister's clumsy fumbling and savagery in his haste to satisfy his own need had fled from her mind. If she was honest she had enjoyed sex with Levingstone very much. She knew, though, it wouldn't be like that with every man and if some encounters reminded her of the rape, then that was a problem she would have to deal with on her own.

'But I can't be selfish indefinitely,' Levingstone said. 'Later, when you are ready and I am agreeable, after you have danced for the men's entertainment, they will want you to change and join them for drinks. You will need the right clothes for that, and we must get you the proper clothes for dancing too. I have been making enquiries and there is a dressmaker in Wellington Road who makes dancing dresses.'

'I have never had the right clothes,' Aggie said. 'We wore what we had. There was no spare money for anything else.'

'Well, money is no object to me, so as soon as you are ready we will set off.'

*　　*　　*

Aggie could scarcely believe the type of clothes that Levingstone bought her.

He considered her one of the most bewitching girls he had ever met – and he had been involved with a fair few – so it pleased him to see her decently clad. He bought her such beautiful soft undergarments, as well as nightgowns of silk trimmed with lace and satin ribbons, that she was speechless with pleasure. Seeing her open-mouthed amazement amused Levingstone, and he only waited until the shop assistant was wrapping the nightclothes before whispering in her ear, 'Those are a bit of a waste really, I suppose. I like my women naked in bed. Clothes get in the way of real honest-to-goodness sex, and I don't like anything to get in the way of sex.'

Aggie felt mortified with shame for Levingstone using such words, and in a public place too. She was glad the assistant was not yet back with the parcels. But when she did return, 'Aren't you the lucky girl then?' she said to Aggie with a knowing, almost sneering look.

Aggie didn't answer and when they were in the carriage she said to Levingstone, 'Does that shop assistant know who I am, or is it what I am?'

'What are you?'

'Well, I suppose I am a prostitute.'

'Not yet you're not,' Levingstone said. 'You are my fancy piece, if you like – my kept woman.'

'And she would know that?'

'I'd say she would have a fair idea.'

'How would she know just by looking at me?' Aggie demanded. 'I mean, I haven't got it stamped on my forehead.'

'My dear,' Levingstone said, 'the woman knows me and knows the business I am in.'

'I am not the first girl you have taken there, am I?' Aggie asked.

Levingstone laughed. 'Of course not, my dear. I am not a monk.'

Aggie was unaccountably disturbed about this, although she told herself she had no right to be.

The droop of her mouth irritated Levingstone and he said testily, 'Why the long face? Be careful, my dear, for I can't bear a woman who sulks. And when you consider what I have bought you this morning, you have no need to feel hard done by.'

'I know, I'm sorry,' Aggie said, truly contrite that she had upset Levingstone, who had been so kind to her.

'I should think so,' Levingstone said. 'I have taken a great many young women to that shop and others like it, and bought them clothes, as I have you today. You don't need to know this, but I will tell you anyway: I have never bought so many for one person, or taken so much pleasure from it, but that is as far as it goes.'

Aggie knew then Levingstone was saying she was perhaps special to him at the moment, but there would be no permanence there; that she was just one in a long line of many. She could have felt unhappy about this, but she reminded herself that Levingstone didn't like to see sad faces and so she thought of all the nice clothes and that brought a smile to her face. 'I do understand,' she said, 'and I am so grateful for all you have bought me today.'

Levingstone gave a grunt of satisfaction and then said, 'And it is not over for now we are off to the dressmaker for dance dresses for you.'

'I know,' Aggie said. 'I can't tell you how excited I am about that.'

Levingstone's good humour was fully restored and he said, 'Your eyes speak for you, my dear. You are incredibly beautiful, you know, and when you blush like that you are lovelier than ever. Get used to compliments, for you will get many as you get older.'

'I think I might need some time to do that,' Aggie said, 'because for fifteen years I was not encouraged to think of my appearance at all. It will probably take me time to adjust so totally. If my mother ever caught me looking in the mirror she said I was vain.'

Levingstone smiled. 'You have something to be vain about,' he said. 'When I do take you down to the club I will have to take great care of you, or they will be at you like devouring wolves and, for the time being, you belong totally to me.'

'And that,' said Aggie, 'is how I like it.'

She did mean that. If she had to live this kind of life, she would rather live with Levingstone and let him have sex with her whenever he wanted than be forced to lie with any Tom, Dick or Harry at the club.

'Good,' Levingstone said with a broad smile as the cab drew to a halt in front of a house in a tree-lined road. 'Now let's see about the making of these dresses . . .'

The woman who answered the door was dumpy, with a heavily lined face and grey hair scraped back in a bun. However, her blue eyes were as bright as buttons and her smile was so welcoming it nearly split her face in two. She introduced herself as Eileen Flaherty, originally from County Mayo. Aggie felt herself relax and let the familiar accent wash over her. Levingstone introduced her as his ward, Agnes, who had just come over from Ireland, and Aggie let out her breath in a silent sigh of relief.

'The dresses are all made to measure,' Eileen said, 'and I have the bolts of cloth in the other room, if you would like to follow me.'

They did, and Aggie looked around the sewing room with interest. Rolls of cloth stood against one wall and a treadle sewing machine against another, and on the shelf under the window there were boxes full of pins, buttons, brooches, ribbon strips, needles and sewing cottons and silks, while a tailor's dummy stood in the middle of the room.

'We do three colours for Irish dance dresses,' Eileen said, 'and that is the saffron here, or the green or the white.' She crossed the room and pointed to the rolls.

'What do you think, Agnes?' Levingstone asked.

His use of her full name made Aggie feel uneasy, as it was the name McAllister had used. She didn't know what to say. Her opinion had seldom been asked, and certainly not concerning clothes. Even the new things Levingstone had bought earlier that day he had selected, and so she said, 'Um, I don't know really.'

'Well, the white is very nice, don't you think?' Levingstone asked Mrs Flaherty. 'Don't you think it will go nicely with Agnes's colouring?'

'I do indeed,' Mrs Flaherty agreed. Then, turning to Aggie, she added, 'Suit you a treat, dear. White is very popular amongst the young ladies.'

'On the other hand, white can be a bit wishy-washy,' Levingstone went on. 'Saffron, now, is a vibrant colour.'

'Yes, and just as suitable with the young lady's dark hair.'

'Tell you what,' Levingstone said suddenly. 'Make up two, one in yellow and one white.'

Eileen Flaherty had never heard of such a thing before and she stared at him. 'Two, sir? Are you sure?'

'Quite sure,' Levingstone said. 'Now is there any decoration on these dresses?'

'Oh, yes, sir,' Mrs Flaherty said. 'The dresses are made up with a shawl fastened with a brooch on the shoulder. I have a selection of brooches here and each one is decorated with designs from the Book of Kells, which is a very old Bible, illustrated beautifully by the monks. When the young miss has chosen what design she wants I will embroider the dresses to match either around the neckline, or the hem, or both if she wishes it.'

'That sounds very satisfactory.'

'Now while Agnes is choosing her designs and she is being measured, can I interest you in a glass of wine in the other room?' Mrs Flaherty said. Levingstone agreed, and Aggie busied herself searching through the brooches.

Eileen Flaherty had a healthy interest in people, and was terribly curious about Levingstone and Aggie. As she was laying out the brooches she asked the girl, 'Is he very rich, your guardian?'

Aggie knew she had to be careful what she said, but she couldn't not answer. 'Think so,' she replied. I think he owns clubs and things like that. I don't know that much about him. As he said, I have only recently come over from Ireland.'

'Did you lose your parents, dear?'

Aggie remembered what Lily had told her about her own parents. 'Yes, they had typhoid,' she said.

'I am so sorry, dear,' Mrs Flaherty said sympathetically. 'Such a tragedy for you. What good fortune you have such a well-to-do guardian.'

Aggie hid her smile as she agreed and wondered what this respectable woman would do if she were to blurt the truth out to her.

She didn't, of course, and with the brooches chosen she removed her dress and the shift beneath it so that Mrs Flaherty could measure her. She was surprised to be measured only to the knee.

'That's where the hem is,' Mrs Flaherty said when Aggie queried this.

Aggie was surprised. She trusted that Mrs Flaherty knew what she was talking about and yet she had never worn anything so short. Her own skirts reached the top of the ugly boots she had arrived in from Ireland. Thinking about that, though, as she dressed herself again, put her in mind of the beautiful boots Levingstone had bought her a little earlier. They were black, of the softest leather and fastened with little buttons – quite the nicest footwear she had ever owned.

As if she knew she was thinking of footwear, Mrs Flaherty said, 'If you are ready, we will talk about dancing shoes.'

'I never owned dancing shoes of any description,' Aggie was saying as Mrs Flaherty showed her into the other room.

'So what did you dance in?'

'Bare feet mainly.'

'So what about the dances that need hard shoes?'

'Well, that was mainly hornpipes,' Aggie said, 'and we tended not to do many of them because we used our ordinary shoes or boots and it just wasn't the same without the tap. For most of the jigs and reels, soft shoes are needed anyway and bare feet sufficed there.'

'So there is a whole area of Irish dance that you haven't explored?' Levingstone said.

Aggie shrugged. 'Well, yes, but all the girls in my home town were in the same boat.'

'Well, it isn't the case now,' Levingstone said. 'I want Aggie to have the works, hard shoes and soft shoes and anything else she needs.'

'Well, I have a collection of shoes here, and going by the size of her boots I am certain that I can get her fitted up with all she requires,' Mrs Flaherty said. 'Then at least she can keep practising while she is waiting for the dresses to be made up.' She turned to Aggie. 'Are you thinking of entering for competitions, my dear?'

Aggie didn't know how to answer this and was glad Levingstone jumped in before her slight hesitation could be noticed. 'That's the sort of thing we had in mind,' he said. 'And she has to look the part.'

'Oh, yes, indeed she does.'

It was as they were going home in the cab, Aggie clutching the bag containing the shoes and the regulation black stockings, that Levingstone struck terror into her heart when he said, 'I am going to arrange a dancing teacher for you.'

Unbidden, there came into Aggie's mind McAllister's lust-filled face that night the previous December as he thrust himself inside her time after time. She felt suddenly sick and so, without thinking, she looked Levingstone full in the face and said, 'Oh no you're not.'

Levingstone was amazed, and he said with a grim and humourless laugh, 'You, my dear, are in no position to tell me what to do.'

Aggie was flustered. 'Oh, I know, and I am sorry but I really don't want a dancing teacher.'

161

'Aggie, by your own admission you have done virtually no work on the dances requiring hard shoes. People are going to pay good money to see you dance and your repertoire has to be as extensive as possible.'

'But I really can't have a dancing teacher,' Aggie said. 'Please don't ask it of me. I will teach myself, dance my feet off, do anything else you want . . .'

Aggie had been unaware that she was wringing her hands until Levingstone enfolded them with his and said quite gently, 'What's this all about, Aggie?'

She turned to look at him and even Levingstone was moved by the depth of sadness there as she whispered, 'It was the dancing teacher in Ireland that raped me and made me pregnant. He forced me to flee here, to leave my home and family behind for ever. I want no truck with any dancing teacher.'

Levingstone gave Aggie's hands a little shake. 'I can't fix what happened to you,' he said, 'but any impropriety will not be tolerated in any dancing teacher I engage.'

'How do you know? How can you be sure?'

'Aggie, you are under my protection,' Levingstone said. 'No one will touch you, never fear.'

Aggie had dropped her head and he lifted it and looked into her eyes.

'Do you trust me, Aggie?'

'Yes, of course,' Aggie said without hesitation.

'Then we will have no more silliness about the dancing teacher.'

Behind the gentleness in Levingstone's tone, Aggie heard the steel and she knew in all things this man would have his way. She also knew she couldn't make any more fuss because then he might be really angry with her.

NINE

'I have found you a dancing teacher,' Levingstone announced to Aggie. It was just over a week since she had been measured for the clothes and so Aggie was surprised. She had thought and hoped it would take him longer to find someone who knew much about Irish dancing in Birmingham.

Levingstone smiled at her surprised look. 'That gave you a shock, I see,' he said. 'I don't believe in letting the grass grow under my feet when I have decided something. Anyway, this man goes by the name of Colm Donahue. In fact, I didn't have to go that far to look for he is the cook, Bessie's, nephew and he works with a fiddler called Tim Furey. Bessie said Colm was in competitions all over Ireland and set to win all before him,' Levingstone went on, 'but he crocked his ankle up, and that was that as far as competition-level dancing went. So now he teaches it instead and he vouches for the fiddler. According to Bessie, he says it is better to have live music than a gramophone record. Then if you are teaching something new you can go over the same movement again and again to get it right.' He gave Aggie a rueful glance. 'I should say he is a hard taskmaster, but that shouldn't bother you too much, should it?'

'I have never been afraid of hard work,' Aggie said. 'I have been about it since I was a child.' She stopped as her words brought a flash of memory of her home in Ireland, dancing to the music of Tom's fiddle, and she felt pangs of homesickness stab at her heart.

Levingstone watched her with narrowed eyes and knew, from the wistful look on her face, she was remembering her earlier life. He knew a little of her background, but as far as he was concerned, the girls' lives started when they came to work for him and what went before was irrelevant.

So he said to Aggie, 'It does no good looking back, you know?'

'Do you think I don't know that?' Aggie said sharply. 'The memories come unbidden and they sadden me, for my life here is so different.'

But then she was changed too. Every night she welcomed a man who wasn't her husband into her bed. And that was the word too: welcomed. He had said he would not force her to have sex, that he had never had to force a woman, and he was right. She had been on fire for him and still was. Surely that made her a disgusting and depraved creature?

'Is it a bad life?' Levingstone asked. 'Are you happy, Aggie?'

She considered the question and answered honestly, 'I don't mind my life at all. I have never had such an easy time of it. In fact, when I first came here, I was overawed with the opulence of this apartment and you having servants and all. It still feels odd to have people doing things for me as if I was some big important person. Mary and Bessie are very patient with me, though, and so kind, and I am getting better at treating them as they expect, but I would be very hard to please if I didn't like living with you, and I know my life would have been vastly different if I'd had to trawl the streets looking for perfect strangers to have sex with.'

'Don't worry about it,' Levingstone said. 'That sort of life is years away from you at the moment.'

Levingstone hadn't said she'd never have that sort of life. She remembered Lily saying something similar and warning her that Levingstone liked young, pretty girls around him – Susie had been disregarded because of her wonky eye – and she suddenly went cold inside.

She knew it was no good badgering Levingstone about it and so instead of going down that road she said, 'If you are determined to engage this dancing teacher for me, I suppose I had better know something about him.'

'Don't know that I can tell you that much,' Levingstone said. 'I have only met him the once myself.'

'Well, how old is he?'

'Youngish, I believe,' Levingstone said. 'Well,

that is, he's not a boy or anything. Early thirties, I'd say.' He glanced at Aggie. 'At your age I suppose you think that old?'

'Not old exactly,' Aggie said. 'But not young either.'

'Oh, very nice,' Levingstone said sarcastically. 'What does that make me then?'

'You, Alan, are timeless,' Aggie told him. 'It's just with the dancing teacher . . . oh, I don't know.'

'Now what's the matter?'

'Nothing.'

'Come on, Aggie, I know you better than that,' Levingstone said. 'Out with it.'

Well, I know you will think it's silly and maybe will be cross with me,' Aggie began, 'but he is coming here to teach me, and being the nephew of your cook and all, he'll know what I am.'

Levingstone shrugged. 'So? What of it?'

'He won't think that I'm fair game?'

'I can't tell you what he might think,' Levingstone said. 'A man's thoughts are his own affair, but I can't seem to stress this enough for you. This man will not lay one hand on you, and what's more, he will treat you with respect or he will have to answer to me.'

Aggie doubted that until she met the two men. Tim Furey was younger than Colm and far more handsome. He had a fine head of black curly hair atop a round, open face with merry eyes, and a wide mouth that turned up slightly so that it looked as though he was constantly smiling.

Colm, on the other hand, was just beginning to go bald, and his face and nose were slightly on the long side. His mouth tended to be thin, which gave his face a mournful look. His saving grace, however, was his deep, dark brown eyes that could light up his face when something pleased him.

And Aggie pleased him because when he saw her dance he knew that she had a rare and very beautiful talent. He thought it a crying shame that she was going to dance to a crowd of leering men, who wouldn't care about the dance at all and would just want to maul and abuse her young body. In fact, he thought it somewhat obscene. He portrayed none of this in his manner to her, but Aggie saw his speculative eyes on her more than once.

As far as Tim was concerned, Aggie was the most beautiful girl he had ever seen and still had a naïvety and vulnerability about her, which was strange when he considered the future that was mapped out for her.

When he said some of this to Colm, though, he was quite sharp with him for his own thoughts about Aggie were in turmoil.

'We are here to teach young Aggie dancing, and that is all. The rest is none of our business. Never say these things to Aggie either, for if she was to repeat them to Levingstone, we would soon be out on our ear. Anyway, you were glad enough to take the job on when I offered it to you.'

'I hadn't met the girl then, nor seen her dance.'

'That shouldn't make any difference.'

'It's the thought of all those men ogling her and worse,' Tim said. 'She is so young and I know it's daft, given what she does, but she looks sort of untouched.'

'Strangely, I know just what you mean,' Colm said. 'She isn't going down to the club yet, though. My aunt told me that much. She said the master is keeping her for himself. He does that sometimes with a girl that takes his fancy, and then, when he tires of her, she joins the others.'

'That's monstrous!' Tim exclaimed. 'And the man is old enough to be her father, at least.'

'That's life,' Colm said with a shrug. 'And however old he is, at the moment the love of his life is Aggie and she shares his bed every night. Now tell me, does the girl look unhappy?'

'Well, no, she doesn't,' Tim had to admit.

'Levingstone is caring for her in one way,' Colm said. 'What sort of life would she have on the streets?'

'Has she no parents? No one at all to care for her?'

'What do you think?' Colm said. 'Would she be here if she had?'

'I suppose not.'

'Right, so you just stick to the job you're paid to do and whatever way we feel about it, for both our sakes we will keep our mouths shut.'

At first when Tim played his fiddle, Aggie couldn't help remembering an earlier, simpler time when she would dance to the sound of Tom's fiddle and sometimes Joe's tin whistle for their parents' amusement. Colm wondered what she was thinking about because she often looked a little forlorn. He didn't ask, but stuck to the job he was there to do.

Aggie would probably not have told him anyway. She acknowledged that Colm bore not the slightest resemblance to McAllister, which in turn made her relax more, and so Colm saw her improving week by week. When the memories threatened to overwhelm her, she used the tinctures of opium, which helped chase them away.

They had decided from the first to use the foyer of the club as a dance floor. It was deserted when they practised in the morning, for none of the girls was an early riser and the foyer was far enough away from the bedrooms so that no one was disturbed.

Colm would keep Aggie hard at it, often making her go over the same movement again and again until her muscles ached and her toes throbbed. She never complained, though, and only when Colm was satisfied would he release her. Aggie would always be starving, for Colm didn't allow her to eat before that first practice and so she would tuck gratefully into the breakfast she shared with Levingstone and tell him how the dancing had gone.

After they had eaten, Aggie was allowed to rest until the afternoon, when she would have another gruelling practice. The other girls were awake by this time and many would drift along to watch. Aggie was intrigued by the girls who worked in the club, knowing that eventually, when Levingstone decreed, she would be joining them.

They were impressed by her dancing ability and told her so candidly, though some were envious that Levingstone thought so much of her. Many of them had shared his bed, maybe for a few days or a few weeks, and since Aggie's arrival he had taken little notice of any of them.

One old hand at the club, Rita, still felt resentful about this, and she lost no time in warning Aggie, 'Don't think you are set for life with him. You'll do till something better comes along. He was all over me like a rash for a few months, and then one day I found myself down here. Now it is your turn, and in a couple of weeks it will be someone else's. You are just one in a long line and don't you forget it.'

When Aggie said nothing, another girl, Brenda, said with a grin, 'You don't believe her, do you? She is right, though. Just enjoy it while you can, I say.'

'Yes,' said another, called Patsy, 'and while he thinks you are the tops, screw as much money as you can out of the old bugger.' And the girls laughed together.

A month after the order was placed, the completed Irish costumes were delivered and Levingstone demanded that Aggie put them on and model them

171

for him. For the white costume, Aggie had chosen a simple design of spirals and coils on the brooch that fastened the cloak, and this design was embroidered around the neck and hemline of the dress. She wore it with the black stockings and soft shoes. For the yellow dress she had chosen a more intricate design on the brooch of six intertwined serpents, which Mrs Flaherty had told her was a detail from the opening text from St Mark's Gospel in the Book of Kells. Here again the design had been embroidered on to the dress and with that dress she wore shiny black shoes.

Aggie had tied her hair back with one of the ribbons that Levingstone had bought her on their shopping trip and he thought he had seldom seen anyone lovelier. He knew with a pang that he wouldn't have her totally to himself for much longer. He had been promising the punters a surprise for some time now.

When they saw her and watched her dance, he knew they would want her for themselves, and there were some people he really couldn't afford to offend. He tried to tell himself that that was life and she was just another girl, but he knew that she wasn't. She had got under his skin in a way that none of the others had, and was even sharing his bed in his apartment. No girl had done that before. He valued his privacy in his own rooms and any girls that he had had living with him before had used the guest room.

Aggie didn't know this, of course, but she hadn't been there a week when he had asked her into his bed.

Aggie knew that she had pleased him with her dancing and so she asked for something that had been in her head for some time, waiting for the right opportunity to broach it.

'Alan, could I possibly see Lily and the others sometimes?'

Levingstone's face darkened. 'Haven't you everything you would ever want here?' he asked. 'I have done everything to make you happy.'

'You are kindness itself to me,' Aggie said, quick to reassure him. 'I am happy and I have everything here for my comfort.'

'Look at the beautiful and classy clothes you have to wear.'

'I am grateful to you for buying me such things,' Aggie said, choosing her words with care, 'but you see, no one but you sees them. I go nowhere and see no one but you. Mary and I might exchange the odd word and I talk to the girls downstairs sometimes, after I have finished practising. But you must admit, Alan, that apart from going out with you to choose the clothes and be fitted for the Irish costumes, I haven't once left this place since I moved into it in mid-March and sometimes I am lonely.'

'I don't know that I want you to be too friendly with those old lags,' Levingstone said. 'You're more than a cut above them.'

'Don't talk about them like that,' Aggie answered reprovingly. 'They are surely what society has made them. Anyway, am I any better?'

'Of course you are,' Levingstone said. 'You are my woman, that's the difference.'

'Lily and Susie saved my life,' Aggie reminded him, 'and then Lily nursed me for weeks; gave up her bed and everything. Without them, Lily in particular, I wouldn't be here. Doesn't something like that deserve a bit of loyalty? Anyway, they are the only people I know in the whole of Birmingham and the ones who befriended me when I was desperate and destitute.'

'Well, I agree you might owe Lily at least some sort of debt,' Levingstone conceded at last, 'and she is all right, is Lily – best of the bunch – but I don't want you walking about the streets alone because they are not safe, particularly around there. So when I collect the rents this Saturday you can come with me. Will that suit?'

It wasn't exactly what Aggie wanted and she hoped that Levingstone wasn't going to stay with her for the duration of the visit because she could hardly be completely natural with Lily and the others if he did. However, she knew that that concession was all she was going to get – this time, anyway. So she wound her arms around him and kissed him slowly and lingeringly on the lips, and when he pushed her gently away moments later he was smiling.

'You, my dear, are a minx,' he said. 'I have to

174

admit that no woman has ever got around me the way you are able to.'

'Well, aren't you the sight for sore eyes?' Lily said in delight at finding Aggie on the doorstep with Levingstone.

'She was fretting and so I brought her to see you all,' Levingstone said.

'And why not?' Lily flung the door wide. 'Come in, come in.'

'No, I won't,' Levingstone said. 'I have some business in town. No rest for some of us, even on a Saturday.'

'You must have been very wicked in a previous life,' Lily pointed out.

Levingstone laughed. 'That must have been it. Now,' he said, turning to Aggie, 'this won't take all day. An hour, two at the most. That all right?'

Aggie turned to Lily, grinning. 'Can you put up with me for so long?'

'As long as you like, ducks,' Lily said. 'You can stay all bleeding day if you like. I've nothing spoiling.'

'Right, I will be off then,' Levingstone said. Before setting off down the street he drew Aggie into his arms and kissed her gently. The action wasn't lost on Lily, and she smiled inwardly. Obviously the girl had played her cards well and had the man fair besotted with her, so far anyway.

She barely waited until the door had shut behind Levingstone before catching up Aggie's arms. 'Will you look at the cut of you,' she said. 'That coat must have cost a pretty penny.'

'It did,' Aggie said, 'and the hat,' and she spun around so that the skirt billowed out and then settled again, just touching the tops of her button boots. 'And that isn't all. I have three silk blouses of the prettiest colours and two skirts to wear with them. I have two day dresses too, and three for evening, and underwear galore, the softest and prettiest imaginable.'

She removed her hat and, handing it to Lily, said, 'I have one of the blouses on now, in peach, see?' removing her coat as she spoke. Lily saw the beautiful, shimmering silk blouse with ruffled lace neck, fastened with mother-of-pearl buttons, which was complemented so well by the navy skirt in heavy velvet.

'Oh, girl,' she breathed, 'you look the business, really you do. I am that glad for you and I know the others will be. He is kind to you, then?'

'Oh, yes.'

'In all ways, I mean,' Lily said, and Aggie met her gaze levelly.

'Yes, in all ways, Lily.'

'Come away in and see the others,' Lily said, leading the way. 'We often talk of you and wonder how you are getting on.'

'I'm getting on just grand,' Aggie said.

Susie, and a girl called Janey, who were in the sitting room, seemed to agree with that sentiment. Susie declared they seldom had someone so grandly dressed knocking on their door, and she made Aggie parade up and down and give them all a twirl to show the full effect of the clothes.

'Soon you will be too grand to visit the likes of us,' Susie said, but Aggie shook her head emphatically.

'I'll never be that. I know how much I owe you all – you and Lily particularly, of course, but all of you for being my friends, the only ones I have. I told Alan the same and that is why he brought me. I know he will do it again.'

'You are very sure of yourself.'

'I'm very sure of Alan Levingstone,' Aggie said. 'Let me tell you what he has done about having Irish costumes made and all, and the Irish dance teacher and fiddler engaged.'

'Soon have you down the club then, I'd say,' Lily remarked.

'I think so,' Aggie agreed but added, 'He doesn't want me to go with any of the men yet, though. He said he wants me for himself.' She saw the women exchange glances. 'What is it?'

'Look, bab,' Lily said, 'look but don't touch will only work for a bit. The people going to that club pay big money to touch. And they are important people, influential, like. You remember I told you this before?'

'Aye, I remember.'

'It's as well to be prepared, that's all,' Susie told Aggie.

'I know that that day will come, followed by

years of the same, and that is the one thing that scares me,' Aggie admitted. 'Levingstone is gentle and kind, but the man who raped me in Ireland was anything but.'

'I know just what you mean,' Janey said. 'I had this awful old bugger yesterday and, Christ, I thought that he was going to rip me in two.'

'That's what McAllister was like,' Aggie said. 'It's one of the things I am afraid of when I do go down to the club and I know too that I will be filled with shame.'

'Now you listen to me,' Lily said. 'Don't you think we all haven't had these feelings from time to time? I'll tell you now these fine principles are all very well when you have a full belly and a roof over your head.'

'We provide a service,' Susie said.

'Do you really think that?'

'Course I do,' Susie maintained.

'There wouldn't be any need for prostitutes if there weren't men that needed them and used them,' Janey added.

'Yeah,' Lily agreed. 'Can you see us walking the streets for the fun of it? I'd stick to me own fireside if there weren't blokes out there out for a bit of slap and tickle, or a bit of the other, and prepared to pay for the privilege. This keeps me out the workhouse, Aggie. Think on that.'

'Anyroad,' Janey said, 'this is neither here nor there. Whatever the fellers are like, you will have to cover your distaste and disgust and hide any pain or discomfort inflicted. If you don't please them and they complain to Levingstone, your fine life could come to an end in no time at all.'

'I know,' Aggie said. 'It scares me that I won't be able to do that.'

'Course you will,' Lily said. 'The opium will help, especially mixed with plenty of gin. Nothing will bother you if you have enough.'

'And talking about gin,' Susie said, 'we could all have a drop now, couldn't we?'

'Yeah,' Lily agreed. 'Get the glasses out and we will toast Aggie's future.'

'Aggie's future,' they chorused a few minutes later as the glasses chinked, and Lily added, 'And long may fate continue to shine on her.'

'Amen,' Aggie said, but silently to herself.

TEN

Three weeks after the costumes were delivered, and on a Friday afternoon, Levingstone came to watch Aggie practising. He had known that she was good the first time she had danced for him, but he plainly saw how much she had improved.

He had insisted she wore the proper costumes and the shoes, and performed a variety of dances for him. She seemed to fly as she danced the jigs and reels in her soft shoes. The intricate footwork left him spellbound, and she leaped and twirled and turned until he was dizzy. As for the hornpipes and some of the polkas, the click of her shiny hard shoes emphasised the foot movements and engendered excitement in him that seeped all through his body.

When Colm eventually drew Aggie to a halt, she was breathless, her cheeks dusted pink with the exertion, and yet her eyes sparkled as she faced Levingstone and asked with a smile, 'Was that all right?'

The man gazed at her, mesmerised by both her beauty and her ability as he said, 'Oh, my darling girl, you were much, much more than all right.' He glanced over to Colm. 'You have done well.'

Colm shrugged. 'It's easy to work on good material,' he said. 'Aggie has a talent seldom seen.'

He nearly added, 'Far too good for this place,' but he stopped himself in time. What bloody good would it do if he was to spout that out? He knew that Tim felt the same – his face often gave him away – and when Levingstone said to Aggie, 'I want you down the club tomorrow,' and he saw the colour drain from her face, he heard the sharp intake of breath from Tim.

Thankfully, Levingstone did not hear Tim's reaction, because he had eyes only for Aggie. But he could almost feel the apprehension running through her, and it annoyed him. 'Come, come, Agnes,' he said. 'Don't look like that. You knew what you were working towards from the beginning. Isn't that so?'

Aggie nodded. Levingstone's use of her full name showed the level of his irritation with her and she bit her lips to try to prevent the tears that she could feel gathering behind her eyes from trickling down her cheeks, for she knew that might truly anger the man.

But with the acquiescent nod, Levingstone was satisfied. He turned to Colm and Tim. 'So your work is almost at an end and you will both be well rewarded for this. I have hired a band for tonight to play the tunes for Aggie, and I would like you to put together a programme for her for two spots lasting at least an hour and a half each. If you can meet the band sometime tomorrow afternoon to go over the tempo I would be grateful.'

'That will be no problem,' Colm said, knowing that it would be easier for Aggie to dance to the best of her ability if they were to do this for her, but personally he thought it far too gruelling a programme. For all he worked Aggie hard, he would call a halt and let her rest if he really thought she was tiring, but he knew that there would be no let-up here. But what was the point of him saying any of this? Levingstone was the boss and what he said went, as far as Aggie was concerned. There was no doubt that he was fond of her – in fact you would be a hard man to please if your heart didn't quicken when you caught sight of Aggie – but he also saw her as a commodity, a hook to get the punters in. He also knew that Aggie accepted the fact that Levingstone owned her body and soul, because her own survival depended on pleasing him. For Aggie, her fate was already sealed.

As Levingstone predicted, that Saturday night Aggie caused a storm. He just announced her as 'The little Irish girl with the golden feet'. The band struck up the introduction to 'The Star of the County Down' and Aggie danced on to the stage. She looking stunning in her shimmering white costume, her hair tied back from her face with a white silken ribbon and she circled the stage before stopping in front of the punters with a curtsy. There was a roar of approval.

All afternoon, Aggie had practised with the band, but then Tim and Colm had been present too, and though the band members had all been nice enough, it was unnerving to be up on stage on her own. Leering ogling men stared at her and she wished her costume were longer.

She had felt it was almost indecent to wear something so short when she had first put the dresses on, but then she had asked herself what she was thinking about. Who was she to worry about the length of her skirt as if she were a normal, respectable girl?

With a slight sigh she gave a small nod to the band and, as they began to play the first skip reel, all nervousness dropped away from her.

In the club, everyone stopped what they were doing to watch. Levingstone smiled to himself. He saw many lecherous and lascivious looks cast Aggie's way and he knew most had undressed her in their mind's eye and would be wanting to sample her other delights later. But that was his pleasure and his alone for a little while longer.

The other girls too watched Aggie, some jeal-ously, for none of the men seemed a bit interested in them now. They had eyes only for the girl on the stage.

'The word is none of the men are to go with

183

her,' Hattie said to the others. 'Not tonight, anyroad.'

'Are you kidding?' Maggie replied. 'What's she doing down here then, tantalising them and everything?'

'Men are bloody easily tantalised, if you ask me,' Brenda said with a grim smile.

'Yeah, minds like sewers, most of them,' Patsy agreed. 'Only thinking about the one thing.'

'Good job for us they do,' Rita replied. 'Wouldn't we all be out of a job if men wasn't like that?' And the girls murmured in agreement.

To rapturous applause, Aggie thankfully left the stage for her break. Men were falling over themselves to buy her a drink or even just talk to her and commend her on her performance. They knew it was all they were going to get for now – Levinstone had made that abundantly clear – but that state of affairs couldn't go on for ever. When he released Agnes to 'entertain', as the other girls did, most were aware they would have to form an orderly queue for there would be many who would want to see what the little Irish girl had to offer.

Levingstone guarded her almost jealously that night and saw many looking at him enviously. He knew Aggie would feel better with his arm wrapped around her as it was her first time in the club and she might be a little nervous.

Aggie was more than nervous. She hated the men ogling her with eyes full of lewdness, which reminded her of McAllister, and yet she knew without being told that she had to smile and be polite to them, however rude she thought them. The longer she was kept out of their clutches the better she would like it, even if she had to dance her feet off.

She was almost relieved when her break time was over. At least, on the stage she was away from them all.

The second round of dancing got even more acclaim than the first, and Levingstone watched her proudly.

Eventually Aggie came to the end and curtsied to the audience, to thunderous applause and calls for more.

Levingstone shook his head as he went forward to claim her. 'You will have to wait till tomorrow,' he told his clients. 'Agnes is tired.'

She was more than tired, she was exhausted, and so, though Levingstone took her around and introduced her to people she hadn't met before, he steered her to the back stairs to their quarters as some of the other girls were taking clients to the upstairs rooms.

'Did I do all right?' Aggie asked as she faced him across the bedroom.

'Darling, you were marvellous, sensational,' Levingstone said, taking her into his arms. 'Later I will show you how grateful I am. Wait for me.'

'I will, Alan.'

However, when Levingstone returned to the

bedroom, it was to find Aggie in a deep sleep, so deep that he hesitated to rouse her and he buried his frustration as he slid in beside her.

The next afternoon, Aggie was resting and Levingstone was in the sitting room when there was a knock at the door downstairs. A few moments later Mary came in to tell him that Mr Donahue and Mr Furey would like a little word with him.

'Show them in,' Levingstone said.

He wondered what they wanted to see him about, but shook hands warmly with them both and offered them a drink.

'Whisky your tipple?' he asked.

'When I can afford it, sir,' Colm said with a smile, taking the glass from him.

'I don't know why you are here,' Levingstone said handing a glass to Tim, 'though you are both very welcome. But maybe it isn't me you have come to see at all, but Aggie. She is resting but I could always rouse her if you wish.'

'No, sir,' Colm said. 'It is you we need to see, but it concerns Aggie.'

'I am intrigued,' Levingstone said. 'Do go on.'

'Would you mind if I spoke with you candidly, Mr Levingstone?'

'Please do, Colm.'

'Can I ask you how many nights a week you will require Aggie to dance?'

'I hadn't thought,' Levingstone said. 'She went down so well last night that I have engaged the band for this evening too. Why do you want to know?'

'It's just . . . well, to dance for three hours every night would be a tiring enough programme for anyone,' Colm said. 'Wouldn't you agree, Tim?'

'I would. Especially for Aggie, for she always gives it everything. She dances with her whole body.'

'That's it,' Colm said. 'And on top of that she will have to practise every day as well.'

'If you wouldn't mind me also saying, sir,' Tim said, 'the ability and talent Aggie has is one that is seldom seen. She really is a superb little dancer and having her perform every day, as well as wearing her out, sort of cheapens what she does.'

'What do you mean?'

'Well, I know it is a little presumptuous of me because it is your club and you know the clientele and all, but if you made it that Aggie would just dance at the weekends, she would be the star turn, as it were.'

Levingstone nodded. 'Yes, I can see that. What you mean is, if Aggie was to perform every day then it would become commonplace?'

'That is it exactly,' Tim said. 'Though commonplace is never a word anyone could use to describe what Aggie does.'

'There is also the danger that she would become stale doing the same thing day after day,' Colm said. 'I used to see it myself in the competition world when people were over-rehearsed and the performance they gave then was often technically brilliant, but wooden. Aggie would always dance well – she is at one with the music – but if she were to lose her special sparkle, then that would be a tragedy.'

'It would indeed,' Levingstone agreed.

'You don't mind us speaking out this way?'

'Not at all,' Levingstone said. 'In fact, I am gratified that Aggie has such champions in the pair of you. You have also given me some food for thought and I will rethink the whole issue of Aggie dancing, I promise.'

When the two men had left, Levingstone thought long and hard about what they had said and knew the points they had made were valid ones. But if Aggie was not to dance so frequently, he didn't know how he could justify keeping her out of the punters' hands.

Aggie was not told of the visit of Colm and Tim, and when Levingstone told her that she was not to dance on weekdays, she was part relieved and part alarmed. 'What are you expecting me to do then instead?'

'To be a charming companion on my arm,' Levingstone said. 'And go around talking to the punters.'

'Talking?' Aggie said surprised. 'Is that all you want me to do?'

'For now, yes.'

'They will expect more, surely?'

'Yes, well, what they expect and what they get are two entirely different things,' Levingstone answered. 'Will that bother you?'

'Yes,' Aggie might have said. 'I want to go nowhere near those horrible, lustful men who undress me with their eyes.' However, what she did say was, 'No, I will be fine doing that,' and Levingstone was satisfied.

The punters were far from satisfied, though, and the other girls were resentful too.

'Treating her like she is some sort of special case,' Hattie said. 'It isn't fair.'

'Whoever said life was fair anyway?' Brenda asked.

'Yeah, but come on. Nearly all of us have marked Levingstone's card one way or another and then it is over and we're down here and sleeping with whoever. Can you imagine what would happen to us if we said you can look but don't touch?'

'Don't need much imagining, does it?' Hattie remarked. 'We'd be out on our ear, and sharpish too, I think.'

'So what's all this with Lady Muck?'

'I dunno,' said Patsy. 'I mean, I am as mad as you, but it won't be her doing, will it? It will be Levingstone's decision and she'll have to do what she's told, same as the rest of us. He's the boss, after all.'

'He ain't, though,' Rita said. 'That weasel-faced Rogers is boss of the whole shebang. Levingstone

189

is just the manager. Wonder what Rogers will make of this if he ever gets wind of it.'

'They'll be fireworks, I'm thinking.'

Aggie was aware of the slight animosity some of the girls directed her way and was sorry about it, but when she mentioned it to Levingstone he told her not to worry about it.

'It's none of their business,' he said, drawing her into his arms.

'Yes, but—'

'But nothing.' Levingstone kissed her lightly on the lips. 'The only one you need to please is me. Remember that.'

'Well,' said Aggie, 'have you got any complaints in that department?'

Levingstone laughed. 'Not so far. Let's keep it that way.'

'Right, sir,' said Aggie, and gave Levingstone a mock salute. He patted her lightly on the bottom and laughed at her little squeal.

Levingstone didn't know what he did before Aggie had come into his life a mere eight weeks or so before. He had been world-weary, careworn and feeling every one of his forty-three years. Aggie made him feel young and far more alive.

He was worried about her, though, because he didn't know how long he would be able to go on denying Aggie to the punters when some of them were nearly panting with desire for her. He knew Aggie would hate it and he didn't want to share her with anyone either. The thought of some of those men pawing at her made him feel physically sick but he knew he would have to get over that.

When Rogers sent for him a fortnight later, it was almost expected. It was a Friday afternoon and Levingstone faced the man across the desk in the dingy office. His small eyes – blue and as cold as ice in a face the colour of putty – raked over Levingstone, before barking out, 'What's this I hear about the Irish girl you have set on?'

'I don't know,' Levingstone said mildly. 'Tell me what you heard and I will tell you if it is true or not.'

'Don't play games with me, Levingstone,' Rogers said sharply. 'I have been told that you have allowed no one to bed her yet.'

'She was employed as a dancer.'

'Don't give me that,' Rogers snapped. 'Does she dance all night and every night?'

'No, but—'

'There isn't any but in this,' Rogers said. 'They say you want her for yourself. No one has exclusive rights on any girl, you know that. If you want to continue to manage the club then she joins the others tonight.'

'She dances tonight.'

'So?'

'She'll be too tired.'

'For God's sake!' Rogers exploded. 'She is only some tramp. Who cares if she is tired or not?'

'The punters might.'

'That is between you and them,' Rogers said.

'But I'm warning you, if I have any more complaints about you and that Irish girl I will sling the two of you out. Anyway, there is another matter I want to discuss with you and this concerns Tony Finch.'

'Finch!' Levingstone spat out. 'What about him? He's a bastard.'

Tony Finch was the son of a rich industrialist and thought money could buy everything and everyone. It often did, and he had no respect for anything, especially authority. Most decent people gave him a wide berth because he could be brutal if he was crossed.

'He's tried for membership of the club twice already and been refused,' Levingstone went on. 'Seems he can't take a hint. We don't need vicious sods like him.'

'I'm glad you think so highly of him,' Rogers commented wryly. 'He will ask again shortly and this time you will not refuse.'

'Oh, yes I will,' Levingstone said. 'I am not having men like him in the club. He was sent down from Cambridge last year, wasn't he, and for what? He won't say but people who were there with him admit it was because of his aggression. God, he's just twenty-one years of age and already so violent it is scary. He beat up a prostitute so badly she nearly died, apparently. Had she been a normal girl from a good home, he would be behind bars now. But as she was just a prostitute the police didn't want to know, especially with Daddy Finch being so rich and influential. The whole matter was pushed under the carpet and all that happened to Finch was that he was expelled from university. Why should I want a man like him in the club? I have to protect my girls.'

'I repeat, if Finch wants to join, then you allow him to do so.'

'Have you listened to one word that I have said?' Levingstone retorted angrily. 'There is no point in me being manager of a place and you making all the decisions. I should be able to refuse undesirables. You have always given me a free hand before.' He looked at his employer and suddenly knew what this was all about. 'Finch has got something on you, hasn't he?'

It was pointless for Rogers to deny it. He nodded slowly. 'I have certain habits that I would rather not have exposed and Finch has threatened to do just that.'

So, Levingstone thought, it is true. He had heard a rumour that Rogers was into men rather than women – 'boys' his informant had said, 'and the younger the better.' At the time he had thought the matter nothing to do with him, but now his lips curled with distaste.

Seeing this Rogers burst out, 'Don't look at me like that. You are no bloody saint either, and let me warn you,' he waggled his finger, 'I will not go down on my own. If I fall, then so will you.'

'I know that,' Levingstone said. 'You don't have to spell it out.'

'Yeah, well, the only thing to do is keep Finch sweet,' Rogers said. 'He wants membership of the club because he has been denied it and that has made it more attractive than ever. Anyway, the reputation of your little Irish colleen has gone before her and Finch is lusting after her.'

The thought of Aggie in the arms of a man he had such contempt for was so repugnant to Levingstone he felt the bile rise in his throat.

Rogers gave a grim laugh. 'Whatever you imagine you feel for that little scrubber, get over it. She is there to provide a service and that is all, so get a grip on yourself, man. This is the business we are in.'

Levingstone knew that as well as anyone, and he also knew that if Finch was thwarted and did what he had threatened, then all their futures were in jeopardy. He returned to the club a worried man.

That night the club was busier than ever, for all the members wanted to see Aggie dance. They knew they would get nothing else, but for all that, she pulled the crowds in. Levingstone knew from Monday he would have to tell her that she was to be available with the rest of the girls, and that there was nothing he could do to prevent it any longer. But he said nothing to her that night. Time enough to tell her when he had to.

Aggie was changing for her first performance when Levingstone saw Tony Finch enter the club.

He had given orders to the doorman that he was to let Finch in the next time he appeared.

Levingstone, though, was surprised to see Finch that night. He thought he would have a couple of days' grace at least. Rogers must have contacted him as soon as he'd left the office. He saw the girls nudging one another and whispering together as they caught sight of Finch, and he could sense their nervousness. He felt sorry for them and, with the man's reputation, could fully understand their apprehension.

Finch was making his way over to Levingstone to gloat over the fact that he had got entry to the place at last when the tantalising music began and Aggie danced on to the stage. Finch looked up and was mesmerised by the girl who seemed almost part of the music that she danced to in such an evocative way. He wasn't able to take his eyes off her.

'I bet he'll ask for her tonight,' Maggie said, and gave a shiver.

'Levingstone won't allow it, though, will he?' Patsy asked.

'Not for ordinary punters, no, but that Finch is used to getting his own way,' Rita told her.

'What's he doing here anyroad?' Patsy said. 'The doorman told me recently that Levingstone left orders that he is not to be let in.'

'Like I said, Finch is used to getting his own way.'

'Christ! If he asks for Aggie she's welcome to him, 'cos he looks a cruel bugger,' Maggie said.

'Yeah,' Rita agreed. 'Poor cow if he says he wants her.'

'Yeah, well, don't spend too much time feeling sorry for her,' Hattie said. 'When she is around most of the men barely notice us, and Levingstone don't pay us to drape ourselves around the bars alone and drink ourselves stupid.'

'Nowt else to do while she is performing,' Brenda replied. 'Come on, let's have another. She can't dance all bloody night and I reckon it will just whet their appetites for a bit of the other. We might all be really busy later on.'

Aggie finished her first stint and left the stage for her break just as Tony Finch was saying to Levingstone, 'I want that little girl afterwards.'

Levingstone looked at the man that he detested and thought of his harsh, brutish hands groping Aggie's body. 'Not Aggie,' he said. 'She's just a dancer tonight.'

'What're you talking about? When they are down here they are anyone's, you know that.'

'Not Aggie,' Levingstone said firmly. 'Not tonight. Now, any one of the other girls—'

'I don't want one of the other girls,' the man said forcibly. 'I want that little dancer and I mean to have her before I go home tonight.'

'Aggie is different from the other girls.'

'Course she isn't,' Finch said. 'She is a whore like all the rest, or she wouldn't be here.'

'I am sorry,' Levingstone said. 'The answer is still no.' He was watching Aggie making her way

196

towards him, being stopped by this one and that who wanted to congratulate her. A glass of something was pressed into her hand.

Finch said, 'You don't seem to appreciate your position, Levingstone. A word in the right ear could have this place closed down and you out on the street, if not in prison. Where would your little princess be then? Destitute? Living on the streets? Course, I might take pity on her and take her for myself.'

Levingstone looked at the man and knew he meant every word. Aggie reached his side then, flushed with heady success. She smiled at him and his heart turned over. He couldn't smile back, however, because he knew that somehow that night he had to break the news to her that the promises he made that she wouldn't be expected to sleep with any of the punters yet, and certainly not on the nights she danced, were like so much dust beneath her feet. That night, as soon as the dancing was over, she would be given to Tony Finch for his pleasure, whatever it was.

Levingstone followed Aggie to the room at the back where she was going to change her shoes. It was almost the end of the break and she was still filled with exhilaration and slightly light-headed from the drinks she had had bought for her. Everyone, it seemed, had wanted to buy 'the little dancer' a drink. In the end Levingstone had put a stop to it before she was rendered incapable of dancing any more, but even so, he noticed her smile was a little lopsided.

'Are you all right?' he asked.

'Never better.'

'You'll be fine to dance?'

'Of course.'

Levingstone wasn't totally convinced, but there wasn't time to go into it now. He had to break the news to her before the second part of her performance that there was further 'entertaining' she had to do. He also had to impress upon her that, however she felt, she had to please the man, because Tony Finch was a bad enemy to make.

When Levingstone told her, she just stared at him for a few minutes and he had to steel himself to keep looking into her eyes, which were clouded with reproach.

'You said . . .' she began at last. 'You promised . . . it wasn't to be this way.'

'It wasn't,' Levingstone said. 'It wasn't how I had it planned, either.'

'Then why?'

'The man is too powerful and influential for me to refuse.'

'Who is it?'

'Tony Finch, the man I was talking to at the bar when you came off stage.'

Aggie's lips curled. 'Ah God, not him,' she cried. 'I didn't care for him at all. His eyes stick out and they are too close together as well. They were on me all the time, even when he spoke to others, or others spoke to him. I felt almost as if I was standing naked before him.'

'In his mind's eye you probably were,' Levingstone said. 'Anyway, however you feel about him, he wants you, and no one else will do.'

'Alan, please don't make me do this.'

Levingstone shook his head. 'I have no choice. He has threatened to expose this place unless I let him have you tonight, and then we are all in one bloody awful mess. I could be imprisoned and so could many of the girls here, if they didn't manage to escape first, and there is nowhere to run to anyway except the streets. As for you, well, Tony thinks he might take you for himself and there isn't a thing I can do about it.'

'So I haven't any choice in this, have I?'

'In all honesty, Aggie, no, you haven't. To save yourself as well as the rest of us, you must go with this man tonight and endeavour to please him. I am putting you in room ten. It is the one reserved for special customers and all will be ready for you.' And then, as Aggie continued to look at him without speaking, he cried out desperately, 'Come on, Aggie, there is no other option.'

'I know that,' she said brokenly. 'I'm not a fool, but don't expect me to be leaping about with joy about it.' She looked at him with her eyes brimming with tears as she continued, 'My skin crawls at the thought of what I am expected to do with this man, but I will do my level best.'

Levingstone felt as if he had been kicked in the

stomach at the look in Aggie's eyes. He said, 'I'm so sorry, Aggie. If there was anything I could do to make this easier for you, then I would do it.'

'You can,' Aggie said, before panic overwhelmed her completely. 'Pour me a large glass of gin.'

'Do you think that wise?'

'None of this is wise,' Aggie said. 'My heart is jumping about all over the place at the thought of it, and the roof of my mouth is so dry that it hurts to swallow. Getting drunk is the only way to deal with it.'

At last Aggie was finished. The last strains of music drained away, as she curtsied to the audience. The applause was thunderous. Her eyes sought Levingstone. She saw he was at the bar and was forcing himself to stay there, but his whole face looked bleak and sad.

Then she saw Finch making his way towards her through the people clustered around the bar, holding aloft a full bottle of gin and two glasses. When he reached her he used the stage as a table, poured them a glass each and said, 'Shall we go up? I am not in the mood to wait much longer.'

Aggie began to tremble. She took a hefty gulp from her glass before allowing herself to be propelled upstairs to the room assigned to her. Levingstone watched her go and felt a sudden pang of loss. He knew that though she had so far remained virtually unsullied from the trade she was caught up in, that situation was going to change, and rapidly. By allowing Finch to take Aggie, he was setting a precedent. From that moment, she would be common property in the club.

ELEVEN

If Aggie hadn't been so frightened of what lay before her, she would have been surprised by the opulence of the room that had been prepared for her. Her feet sank into the thick carpet; the bed was a four-poster, with the drapes tied back to show the dark red velvet coverlet and the crimson sheets. But all Aggie could remember was Lily's advice to drink enough that she didn't care what was done to her.

Aggie doubted that there was sufficient alcohol in the world to make her not care that she was in this bedroom with a man she didn't know or care for and that she would have to submit to anything he wanted. The idea made her feel sick. She drank deeply of the gin and poured herself another, hoping it would at least stop her teeth from chattering, because she was certain that if Finch noticed he would be vexed.

Finch, however, was too consumed with lust for Aggie to notice.

'Come on,' he said. 'What are we waiting for?'

Aggie barely had time to down her drink in one long swallow before Finch lifted her roughly in his arms, dumped her onto the bed and began tearing the clothes from her. Aggie helped him, frightened he would rip the costume in his haste, but Finch misinterpreted this. He smiled nastily as he said, 'You little whore. You can't get enough, can you?'

Aggie didn't bother answering. She told herself it didn't matter what he thought or what he said. In a little while he would be finished and it would all be over. But when she felt him grabbing handfuls of her flesh roughly with his hard and vicious hands, she couldn't help giving little yelps of pain.

'Shut up, you sodding little trollop,' Finch demanded.

'You're hurting me.'

Finch smiled. 'I haven't started yet,' he said, and transferred his attention to her breasts, pummelling them mercilessly. She bit her lips to prevent her groans of pain, knowing they might annoy him further. She couldn't help crying out, though, when he began to bite her bruised breasts, especially when he attacked her nipples. She tried to push him away from her then, but though her efforts were futile, they annoyed him none the less.

'You are supposed to please me in all ways,' he sneered at the weeping girl as he began to strip. 'Didn't Levingstone tell you that? He wouldn't like it, I'm sure, if I had to complain about your lack of enthusiasm.'

He wouldn't either, Aggie knew. Hadn't he told her as much? She let her hands fall to her sides and Finch, now naked, launched himself on top of her. She had been sleeping with Levingstone for some time and it was always a pleasurable experience, but Finch had hurt and frightened her so she was tense, and when he thrust himself inside her, she thought she would die with the pain of it. She let out a shout, but the next moment Finch clamped one hand over her mouth as he began to bite and suck at her neck causing her excruciating pain.

Aggie thought it would go on for ever – Finch jabbing inside her, his teeth clamping on her neck and the pulsating pain burning like a furnace inside her. Tears trickled relentlessly down her cheeks. She was hurting so much and feeling so wretched and distressed that there was no room left for shame.

That came later, when Finch eventually gave one last almighty shove and let out a cry, so releasing his hold on Aggie's sore neck, much to her relief. For a moment he lay still on top of her as if spent and then began to roll away, and she wriggled from underneath him, sat up and then very gingerly got to her feet.

'That was good in the end and I will tell Levingstone so,' Finch said. 'You were as tight as any virgin I have had the pleasure of bedding.'

Aggie said nothing. She ached or throbbed almost everywhere. She was having trouble staying on her feet and she longed to sink back on the bed, but there was no way she was going any nearer to Finch. Then he swung his legs from the bed and began to dress.

'Shouldn't you put some clothes on?' Finch said. 'Or do you want another dose before I leave you?'

Aggie couldn't prevent the shudder that shook her whole body and Finch saw it too and it amused him. 'Till tomorrow then,' he said. 'Though I might have to wait in a long line when I tell the other punters what a little goer you are.'

Aggie stared at him, horrified. It was bad enough that he had had sex with her and abused her so badly, without it being broadcast throughout the club. She mentally shrank from suffering the same the following night and was terrified that then there might be a succession of men who would want to do the same thing to her.

Her cheeks flamed with embarrassment and Finch saw this as he leaned towards her. 'Don't look like some vestal virgin who has just had her maidenhead taken from her,' he sneered. 'You are a whore and knew well enough what it was all about.'

Aggie continued to stare as Finch got to his feet. He made to kiss her, but she recoiled. 'Naughty, naughty,' he said grimly. 'I may make you pay for that little act of defiance tomorrow evening.'

Prickles of alarm ran all through Aggie, mixed with the self-disgust and degradation that she felt steeped in. Before the door had fully closed behind

Finch, she was vomiting into the bowl of the lavatory in the little room that led off the bedroom. Then she staggered back into the bedroom, stopping only to pick up the bottle of gin as she sank on the bed.

She was bone-weary and needed sleep. Her whole body craved it, but there was little chance of it unless she could blot out the images crowding into her brain. She knew only one way to do that, and she lifted the bottle to her lips.

Everyone knew that Finch had taken Aggie up to the room that night. There were few who hadn't a measure of sympathy for her, for they had heard from some of the street girls what he was capable of even, they said, before he had gone to the university. So when Rita spotted Finch leaving the club, she went back to the dormitories the girls shared, tidied herself up and made herself respectable before going to see if Aggie was all right.

Aggie had fallen into a drunken stupor naked across the bed and Rita could see her whole body was bruised and battered. There were teeth marks all over it, and scratches where Finch's nails had caught her. She was at a loss to know what to do and in the end she went for her friend Patsy to ask her advice.

When Patsy saw Aggie she was as appalled as Rita had been.

'Poor cow!' Patsy burst out. 'God, that bloody man should be locked up.'

'I agree,' Rita said. 'Don't blame her, getting

drunk either, but she has to be wakened and we'll do what we can to try and get her semi-respectable before Levingstone comes looking for her in the morning.'

After the girls had finished with the punters they usually retired to the dormitories they shared with the others. However, Levingstone wanted Aggie to continue to share his bed and so he would expect to find her in bed beside him when he woke the next morning.

When she wasn't, he assumed that she had already risen and he went in search of her, but when it was apparent she was nowhere in his own private apartments, and neither Bessie nor Mary had seen her either, he went down to the club to look for her.

By then Rita and Patsy had done their best, but they couldn't work miracles and knew Aggie was in no fit state to be up. In fact she couldn't stand and had been sick many times in the bowl they had prudently placed within her reach.

Aggie had seemed unaware of their ministrations as they'd bathed her injuries and put salve on, and then clothed her in one of Rita's own nightdresses that buttoned to the neck. So when Levingstone entered the room the next morning, this was what he saw, with Rita and Patsy still in attendance.

He took in Aggie's white, pallid face, the black smudges beneath her eyes and the fact that she was still in bed, and said, 'What is it? What's the matter?'

The eyes Aggie turned on him were vacant, glazed and slightly bloodshot. Her mouth was slack and her inane smile crooked, and he knew that she was extremely drunk. She made no attempt to answer him. In fact, she was so far gone he wasn't sure whether she had heard or understood what he had said. He drew Patsy and Rita away from the bed and looked to them for some explanation.

'She took a drop too much,' Rita said. 'I come in after Finch left late last night to see if she was all right, like, and found her in a bit of a state. She'd been sick and that, and so I fetched Patsy to give me a hand to clean her up and that's all I know.'

'I've never seen her this drunk before.'

'She'll get over it, though,' Patsy told him. 'Look, it were her first time, weren't it? Well, from what I hear, Finch ain't your kind and considerate gentle-manly sort.'

'No,' Levingstone admitted, 'he is anything but a gentleman. I didn't want it, not for Aggie. I said she wasn't ready. Maybe I should find Finch and have a word with him.'

That was the last thing that Rita and Patsy wanted before they had been able to talk to Aggie. Rita said hurriedly, 'You don't know what happened, though, do you?'

'Yeah,' Patsy put in. 'He could have done nothing wrong at all, and Aggie just felt she couldn't cope with it and so blotted it all out in the only way she knew.'

'And it would never do to offend Finch,' Rita said warningly. 'Why not wait until Aggie is more herself and you can ask her what happened?'

'You really think that's best?'

Rita and Patsy both nodded. 'Let her sleep it off, I would,' Patsy said.

Levingstone shrugged. 'All right. I will be guided by you two.'

And Patsy and Rita sighed inwardly in relief.

Early that evening, before they went down to the club, Rita and Patsy bathed Aggie's injuries again, applied more salve and then looked at her in frustration.

''Tisn't good enough, is it?' Patsy said. 'If Levingstone sees the state of Aggie, there is no way on earth we or anyone else will be able to stop him going for Finch.'

'And he will see it, won't he?' Rita said morosely. 'For all we have done, a blind man on a galloping horse would see those marks on her neck.'

'If he goes for him, we are all done for,' Aggie said. 'Alan told me that. It wasn't his choice to have him in the club at all and he told me I had to try to please him or he will have this place closed down.'

'He couldn't know that Finch was going to attack you the way he did, though?'

'Of course not,' Aggie said. 'And he must never know. In the long run how will it help me, any of us, to be tipped out on the streets?'

'I hear what you say, Aggie, and even agree with it,' Patsy said. 'But how the hell are we going to keep it from him? Your neck is all inflamed and the teeth marks are obvious. Here,' she handed Aggie a hand mirror, 'see for yourself.'

Aggie surveyed herself critically, turning her head this way and that. 'They throb too, and I don't want to go near the club. Finch said he will have me again tonight.'

'Ah, Jesus,' Patsy said, 'he is one vicious sod all right.'

'I . . . I really don't think I could stand it,' Aggie said.

'I don't blame you, bab,' Rita said. 'Your body is a mass of bruises and bite marks. Anyroad, if you go down there Levingstone will want you to dance, won't he?'

Aggie shuddered. 'I couldn't dance. I can barely walk.'

'So what is to be done?' Rita said.

'Couldn't you just say you weren't feeling well?'

'He'll hardly believe that,' Aggie said. 'I have spent the day in bed, and anyway that won't help because if I am not to go to the club, then he will expect me to share his bed, and then he will see everything anyway.'

'She's right,' Patsy said to Rita.

Rita thought for a minute or two, then: 'As I see it there is only one answer, and that is to get you in the same state as you was in last night.'

'Oh God,' Aggie said fervently, 'I haven't really

210

recovered from that yet. Anyway, won't Alan be really cross with me?'

'He might be cross,' Patsy said, 'but he'll get over it. One thing in his favour is he never bears a grudge. And at all costs, we mustn't let him see what Finch had done to you. As you said, it is for the good of everyone.'

Aggie gave a sigh. 'You know what? They seem to be able to act in any way they want and just get away with it.'

'Oh, no doubt about it, it's a man's world all right,' Patsy agreed. 'And if I was ever given another crack at it, I would want to come back as a man.'

'Me too,' Aggie said.

'Yeah, well, meanwhile we have to cope with being women and protecting ourselves as much as possible,' Rita commented wryly, handing a brimming glass of gin to Aggie.

Aggie looked at it almost fearfully. 'I still feel a bit sick and I have a thumping headache.'

'More of the same is the only way to deal with that,' Rita declared encouragingly. 'Hair of the dog, see – well-known cure – and anyway, I have mixed some opium in it. That will put paid to any headache.'

Aggie still hesitated and Rita said, 'Come on, Aggie. It really is the only solution. This way you won't have to go down to the club and Levingstone can say that you are indisposed.'

'Yeah.' Patsy gave a wry smile. 'And we'll make

quite sure he will be telling the truth. Be quick, for God's sake, before he comes storming in here and stops you before you are completely incapable.'

Aggie knew the two women were right. She lifted the glass to her lips, swallowed the liquid down and held the glass out to be refilled.

Levingstone had missed Aggie's presence around his own quarters and was very glad he had a meeting to go to that afternoon, because he felt the day to be a long one. When he returned, he was surprised not to see Aggie waiting for him and the maid said she hadn't been in all day.

His lips tightened in annoyance and he went in search of her, certain that she must have slept off all the effects of the booze she had consumed. However, just minutes later he was looking down on Aggie, who was so drunk she was incapable of speaking or doing anything other than lie in bed in a semiconscious stupor.

He was so angry, he wanted to take hold of Aggie and shake her. Instead, he sent for Rita and Patsy to see if they could shed any light on the matter, but they both pleaded ignorance. Levingstone eyed the empty gin bottle and the half-empty one beside it.

'Where did she get the booze?' he asked.

Patsy shrugged. 'Can't say. Maybe she had it hidden away in the room all the time.'

'I can't understand what she was thinking of to get in this state,' Levingstone said, puzzled. 'She knows what she is to do, why I spent so much money on her, and this is how she repays me. They will all be waiting for her downstairs tonight.'

'They'll have to wait then, I'd say,' Patsy said.

Rita added, 'We all have our own ways of dealing with prostitution at the start, and she ain't the first to use booze.'

'Not to this extent.'

'Don't you believe it,' Rita said. 'I remember getting legless a time or two in the beginning. We have all got feelings. I mean, we ain't machines, for all the men seem to think we are.'

'And remember, Aggie is small and slight,' Patsy said. 'A bit of booze usually goes a long way with a person like that.'

Levingstone eyed the bottles. 'I don't call that a bit of booze.'

'All right,' Patsy said, 'maybe she went over the top, but there is nothing to be gained by trying to talk to her now. Try her tomorrow when she is sober.'

'And so what do I tell the punters?'

'That she is indisposed. What else?'

Levingstone knew what the two girls advised made sense. 'Don't know what they will say,' he told them as he took his leave.

They said plenty.

'God,' one of the men fumed, 'Finch told me she was a right one. Gagging for it, she was. I fancied giving her a go myself tonight.'

'You'll have to join the queue then,' another put

in. 'Every man here wants to sample the delights of little Agnes Sullivan.'

'The rule still stands that on the night she dances, she does nothing else,' Levingstone reminded them.

'She did last night with Finch.'

'Well, that was Finch,' said another. 'That man is a law unto himself.'

'Yes. He wouldn't take an excuse like she's indisposed.'

'Aye, he'd indispose her all right.'

The men laughed together. Levingstone was very glad too that Finch hadn't put in an appearance that night, because the men were right. He didn't operate under the same rules as other people. In fact, he seemed to have few rules to his life at all.

'Well, you tell her to get better, and quick,' the first man said. 'We haven't unlimited patience and I'm not the only one who can't wait to give her a try-out.'

Levingstone knew the man spoke the truth and he wasn't happy about it. He didn't know what was the matter with him. This is how he had worked for years: taking girls and bedding them for a while, then once he was tired of them, tossing them to the punters at the club without a qualm. Aggie, however, had almost bewitched him and he was far from tired of her. He didn't particularly want other men pawing and groping her, never mind going much, much further than that. Obviously Aggie didn't like it either. But that was the business they were both in, and she had to accept that and so had he.

Aggie was wakened in the early hours by severe cramps in her stomach. She curled in a ball and pulled her knees up close to her body to try to alleviate the pain, but it didn't ease, and she groaned aloud and rocked in agony on the bed.

Then she felt the saliva gather in her mouth, the familiar nausea in her throat and she knew she was going to be sick. She struggled to sit up and lifted the bowl, but after that first bout of vomiting she didn't really lie down again, for the waves of sickness would assail her if she tried. So she sat on the edge of the bed and vomited over and over.

She was still retching when Rita and Patsy came to see how she was the next morning. By then she had emptied her stomach and all that she was bringing up was yellow bile. The two women couldn't help feeling sorry for her. Aggie wanted to weep from weariness and because she felt so dreadfully ill.

She certainly looked ill. Her face was as white as lint – even her lips looked bloodless – while her eyes were shot with red lines and encircled with black.

Her voice was husky because her throat felt so raw as she said, 'I ache everywhere.'

'You poor sod!' Rita said, examining the marks on her neck. 'I hope we don't have to do that very often, but at least Finch's handiwork isn't quite so noticeable.'

'That's grand,' Aggie said. 'He gets away with it, while I am near dying here.' She gave a sudden moan and wrapped her arms around her stomach, and the girls looked at her with sympathy. Then she thought of something that would make her feel better; it always did if she could keep it down, that was.

She looked across to Patsy. 'Can you fetch me a tincture? Mary, Alan's maid, will make it up for you. Tell her it's for me and she will do it just the way I like it.'

'Oh, bab,' Rita said, 'do you think that's wise? Isn't there gin in that?'

'Aye, but didn't you say yesterday it was the best thing to take?' Aggie said. 'Hair of the dog, you called it.'

'Yes, but—'

'Anyway, she laces it well with opium and that always makes me feel better.'

However, Patsy never came back with the tincture. Levingstone caught her with it and asked who it was for. When she told him, he took it from her. 'I'll take it,' he said. 'I intend to have words with that young lady anyway.'

Patsy gave it to him and when he entered the room, Rita took one look at the anger smouldering behind his eyes and slunk out to join Patsy.

Aggie shrank in the bed. Levingstone looked down on the pathetic and obviously frightened figure, and he felt the anger seeping from him. Her bruised eyes looked enormous in her white face and they were filled with fear as she said in that strange husky voice, 'Are you very cross with me?'

'Not cross, more disappointed,' Levingstone said, sitting on the edge of the bed. 'Come on,' he chivvied. 'Sit up and drink this while it is warm. You look and sound as if you have need of it.'

Aggie took it gratefully and felt the warm sweet liquid soothe her throat and settle her still-churning stomach.

'Never be afraid of me, Aggie,' Levingstone said, stroking her unbound hair gently. 'I hated the look in your eyes just now. I would never hurt you. I thought you knew that.'

'I do know that deep down,' Aggie said. 'But I hurt you. You said I disappointed you.'

'You did, and yet I know the whole thing was alien to you,' Levingstone said. 'I do understand a little of how you felt afterwards.'

'Yes,' Aggie said. 'I did tell you I might not be so good at it.'

'Good enough to satisfy Finch, at least. He's been singing your praises, apparently.'

'Oh God, has he?'

'According to the other men he said you were mad for it, a little wanton,' Levingstone told her. 'Made me a little jealous, to tell you the truth.'

Aggie put one hand on Levingstone's arm and looked into his eyes. 'It was an act, Alan, put on to please him and ultimately to please you.'

'And then you tried to block it out?'

Aggie nodded, and Levingstone continued, 'The trouble with alcohol is that you have to sober up eventually.'

'I know,' Aggie replied. 'And I know how much you have done for me, and I will try to be better.'

'Good girl. The men will be queuing up downstairs when I tell them that.' He gave a sigh. 'I'm afraid for both of us, the honeymoon is over.'

'So, let's get this straight,' Lily said, drawing Aggie into the sitting room. 'You dance for the punters on Friday, Saturday and sometimes on Sundays as well, and on those days you haven't got to have sex with anyone.'

'No,' Aggie said, and added with a sigh, 'Unless it is Finch, of course.'

Lily's lip curled with distaste. 'I didn't realise he was a member.'

'Do you know him, then?'

'God blimey, Aggie, every prostitute knows him,' Lily said. 'Keeps away from him and all, as far as possible, for he is as cruel a bugger as ever walked the earth. Tell you, they nearly had a party when they thought he was off to university. Thought they would be free of him for three or four years, only he seemed to be back more often than he was away. They say he hates women 'cos his mama walked out on him when he was a baby, so the rest of the female population have to pay for that. Mind you,' she went on, 'have to have a tad of sympathy for his mother. Fancy giving birth to that.'

Aggie smiled because Finch seemed indeed to be a good way down the queue when good looks were dished out, for he had a large nose, a weak indeterminate chin and a florid face. It was his eyes though that anyone noticed first, for they were so prominent, they seemed to stand out in his head, and so close together they were unnerving.

'Sadistic sod nearly did for Elsie Phillips last week 'cos she said summat that annoyed him,' Susie put in. 'Strangled her till she passed out, he did. She told me straight that if some blokes hadn't come along when they did, she wouldn't be here now.'

'I can well believe that,' Aggie said grimly.

'And you have had dealings with him, you say?' Lily asked her.

'Aye, yes, I have.'

'A hatpin is a very comfortable thing to have to hand when you are near someone like Finch,' Susie told her.

Aggie shook her head. 'I couldn't do that or anything like it,' she said. 'It is different for you. On the streets, you make up your own rules. We work for Alan and, however we feel, we can't risk upsetting the punters in any way, particularly someone like Finch. Sometimes I am so bruised after a session with him that I have trouble hiding it from Alan, though Finch has never been half as bad as he was the first time. Now he bruises me in places that can't be seen.'

'Why bother protecting him?' Susie said. 'Let Levingstone take the man apart.'

'He can't,' Aggie said. 'Finch has too much influence. A word in the right ear and he could have the whole club closed down. He has threatened to do just that. Alan doesn't know the half of what goes on there. I mean, some of the things we all have been asked to do once the bedroom door is shut . . . well, let's say it would make you sick to think about it.'

'I thought he didn't allow any funny stuff.'

'Officially he doesn't,' Aggie said. 'But a lot of the men only come for the kinky sex they can't get from their wives. If one or two of us refused them, they would stop asking for those girls and that would be that.'

'And how do you cope with all this?' Lily said. 'I know it wouldn't have come easy for you at first.'

Aggie smiled ruefully. 'It didn't and, to be honest, it's not much better now. That's why Alan allowed me to visit you today when I asked him. It's like a reward for me because he knows that I am really doing my best to please the men, and he also knows how difficult I find it. I was terrible at first – so disgusted with myself that I used to get too drunk and drugged to function properly. Alan said I would make myself ill and I must admit I felt ill most of the time.'

'And now?'

Aggie shrugged. 'I don't drink quite as much as I used to, though he knows I have to be well oiled at the start or I wouldn't be able to do anything at all.'

'So he is still good to you, then?' Lily said with a measure of satisfaction.

'Oh, yes,' Aggie said lightly. 'I have few complaints, but I much prefer the nights I just dance for them all. I never mind that.'

'So you are all right and I can stop worrying about you?'

'I didn't realise that you did worry about me,' Aggie said. 'But you can stop now because I'm as right as I ever will be.'

TWELVE

Tom thought that life on the farm was virtually the same day after day, and in a way that suited him. As the years passed, and he and Joe moved from boyhood to manhood, apart from Mass on Sundays, the only time they ever left the farm was some Saturdays when the brothers would go to Buncrana with Biddy.

Joe loved going to Buncrana and he could barely wait until the stuff was unloaded and laid out on one of the trestle tables in the market hall before he would be off with all the other young fellows. Tom never went with him, though, because his mother always had things she wanted him to do. He would find himself at Biddy's beck and call the whole time, and then would return home feeling resentful and annoyed for not standing up for himself more.

Joe couldn't or wouldn't see where the problem lay. He would shake his head at his brother in exasperation. 'Just help her set up the market and then take off like I do.'

'I can't.'

'Why can't you?'

'I don't know really,' Tom would say miserably. 'It's just that Mammy expects that I—'

'Then let her expect, Tom,' Joe would cry. 'Jesus, she will suck you dry if you're not careful. You are a young man and, apart from Mass, this is our one chance in the week to meet up with neighbours and have a bit of a chat. Is that so wrong?'

'Of course not,' Tom would declare. 'It's just that Mammy thinks it is.'

In a way, though, if Tom were honest, he knew it wasn't totally his mother's fault. He didn't feel like a young man. He hadn't felt young from the day he realised he had killed a man. Philomena had done as she said she would. She had sold up the grocery store and moved out of the town only six months after the funeral, which some people thought far too soon.

She told no one where she was going, saying to any who asked where she was bound only that she hadn't decided, that she was just trying to get away from painful memories. Tom didn't think there was anywhere in the world he could go where he wouldn't remember the heinous crime he had committed. He felt almost unworthy to meet and chat with ordinary people who hadn't done such a terrible thing, or come anywhere near it, in the whole of their lives. Better to chain himself to his mother's side. At least that was a penance of sorts.

It was worse when Joe began going to the socials run by the Church every other Saturday evening.

Biddy had tried kicking up about that, tried forbidding him to go, when he told his family that first Saturday night as they sat eating around the table, but he stood his ground. 'I am over twenty-one and you have no right to forbid me anything.'

'No right,' Biddy shrieked. 'I am your mother, I have every right.'

'No, you haven't,' Joe said in a low, but firm voice. 'This is my leisure time, which I have earned. As long as I do all the work that Daddy wants, then how I spend my leisure time should be my own decision.'

'The boy's right,' Thomas John said. 'All work is no good to anyone. I used to like a dance at the same age, as you did yourself, Biddy.'

'Aye, but in a neighbour's house, just.'

'Times have changed, Biddy. Give the boys their head,' Thomas John said. Glancing across the table to Tom, he asked, 'I suppose you will be going along with him?'

'No,' Tom said. 'Tell you the truth, I have no fancy for it.'

'I should like to go,' Nuala said.

'Huh, you,' Finn said disparagingly. 'It's not the place for weans.'

Tom smiled at his pretty wee sister, who was getting more like Aggie with every passing year. 'Time enough, pet,' he said. 'When you are a wee bit older.'

'But, Tom, it takes so long to grow up.'

'Aye, and there is not a blessed thing you can do to hurry it up,' Thomas John said.

'And, anyway, I don't want my wee girl grown into a woman too soon,' Biddy added.

'There are great advantages for you in being a child, anyway,' Finn said. 'You are expected to do nothing and get away with blue murder.'

'I do not. That's not true.'

'Oh yes it is.'

'That will do, Finn,' Thomas John said.

'I was only saying.'

'Well, don't say. We don't want to hear it.'

'Aye,' Biddy put in. 'Don't be teasing and upsetting the child.'

'I wouldn't be upset by anything he says, Mammy,' Nuala said. She tossed her head and gave Finn a withering look. 'He probably can't help being horrid.'

Tom and Joe burst out laughing and Joe gave his younger brother a cuff as he got to his feet. 'Follow that, boyo,' he said as he made his way to the bedroom to change.

'You should come with me,' he suggested to Tom, who had followed him in.

'Sure, I am no good at the dancing,' Tom said, 'nor talking with women. I never know what to say. They would think me a dull old stick.'

'Aye, they'd think that, all right,' Joe said ruefully. 'A complete dullard and one set to inherit this farm one day. I tell you, Tom, that alone will guarantee your popularity from all the mamas there. They would be pushing their unattached daughters your way all night long.'

'That's not something I am up for either,' Tom said with a shiver.

'What is the matter with you?' Joe asked.

'Nothing. I am just different from you, that's all.'

'But you go nowhere and see no one.'

'Well, what of it? I don't go running to you complaining.'

'But it's not a natural way to be going on at all.'

'It's my way and I am happy with it.'

'All right,' Joe said. 'If you want to die a sad and lonely old man then it is your lookout.'

'Right,' said Tom. 'I'm glad that we have established that at least.'

He knew that marriage was not for him. How could he convince any doting mama that he was an honest and reliable man, well able to take care of her daughter, when he had another man's blood on his hands? And if he was to overcome that and marry one of the buxom beauties he had glimpsed a time or two at Mass, he would have to confess to the dreadful thing he had done. There could never be such a big secret to hang between a wife and her husband. Joe knew nothing of that, of course, nor did he have to know. It was a burden for Tom to carry alone.

'Anyway,' he said, 'can you just see Mammy welcoming another woman in here?'

'I can't believe I am hearing this,' Joe said. 'Are

226

you going to let Mammy dictate to you all the days of your life?'

Tom shrugged. 'Yeah,' he said, 'I probably am.'

'God Almighty!' Joe said. 'No wonder Aggie ran away.'

Tom turned instinctively to the door that opened on to the kitchen as he cautioned, 'Ssh, Mammy will cut your tongue out if she hears you speak Aggie's name.'

'Well, she isn't likely to through the door, is she?'

'I don't know so much,' Tom said with a grin. 'She has ears on her like a donkey.'

'Well, anyway, the whole thing is stupid,' Joe said. 'I remember the hullabaloo when she went missing and it is a mystery where she disappeared to and all, but never to be allowed to talk about it since is madness. You mind Finn cried for her for days because she had the rearing of him nearly as much as Mammy, and now all that will have faded from his mind.'

'Aye, and Nuala won't know that she ever had a sister.'

'No, she won't,' Joe agreed. 'Tell you the truth, I have trouble remembering what she looked like.'

'Nuala is her double,' Tom said. 'Course, Aggie didn't have the fine clothes that Mammy buys for Nuala, or as much time and attention spent on her hair, and Aggie was often grey with exhaustion for Mammy allowed her little leisure time, but essentially they are very alike. Nuala has something else

227

too, the confidence that she is loved by each and every one of us.'

'Doted on, more like, don't you mean?' Joe said. 'Don't know why we bother either, because Mammy and Daddy between them could do a decent enough job on their own. Finn wasn't so far wrong tonight.'

'Finn is as bad as the rest of us, for all his teasing,' Tom said. 'It is very hard to refuse Nuala anything with her cheeky face and those eyes that dance in her head.'

'Aye, and the smile that looks as if someone has turned a light on inside her.'

'Do you mind when she was wee and we did cartwheels and somersaults to get her to smile at us like that?' Tom said.

'I mind it very well,' Joe said. 'And I will tell you something else too: we haven't changed that much.'

Tom laughed. 'No, you are right there, Joe.' He added, 'But I wish Mammy wouldn't praise her so much outside of the house.'

'Aye,' Joe agreed. 'I mean, to hear Mammy talk, Nuala is the most beautiful, clever and talented child in the whole of Ireland. There is none to match her.'

'I know. And she keeps on saying it. She doesn't seem to see that going on like that is bound to upset some of the townsfolk, particularly if they have daughters of their own.'

'Well, you'll never change her,' Joe said. 'Mammy is a law unto herself.'

228

'Aye,' Tom said glumly. 'Don't I know that well enough?'

After Nuala turned twelve and left school, she began making the weekly trip to Buncrana as well. If she was there to help her mother, Tom would often elect to stop behind on the farm. There was always plenty to do, though Finn couldn't understand him.

'Don't you ever want to get away from this place?' he asked as he and Tom stood in the yard and watched the old horse pull the cart up the lane.

'What place?'

'The farm. Where else?'

'No, not really.'

'God, Tom, you're an odd man altogether.'

'Maybe it's because I know the farm will be mine one day.'

Finn shook his head. 'No,' he said. 'I know that even if I was handed the farm on a plate, I would still want to leave it sometimes. As it is . . .'

'What?'

'Well, there will be little for me here,' Finn said. 'And I don't intend to spend my life grubbing about in this place for little or no reward.'

'You would always have a home here,' Tom replied.

'Thanks,' Finn said, 'and I know you'd never throw me out, but a man wants more from life than just a roof over his head. Don't worry about it, I realised some time ago that the farming life is not for me.'

'Joe says much the same.'

'Good job you like it then.'

Tom shook his head. 'Don't know whether there was much like or dislike about it,' he said. 'I just knew as I grew up that this farm would be mine one day and I think I just sort of got on with it, whereas you and Joe . . .'

'Are different, and no worse for that,' Finn said. 'We didn't start off talking about me and Joe, though, did we, but about you?'

Tom grinned. 'Not a lot to say about me. And what there is can be dealt with in a couple of sentences.'

'Oh, Tom!' Finn cried, exasperated. 'Where is your fire and enthusiasm for life?'

Tom was a wee while answering, and then he said, 'You know I don't recall having much of that type of thing myself, not even when I was your age.'

'Don't you ever wonder what is out there, beyond Buncrana?'

'I might have wondered a time or two but never had any desire to go and find out.'

'All right,' Finn said. 'Let's stay in Buncrana, that great metropolis. Why don't you go to the socials with Joe a time or two, or ask some of the girls mooning after you at Mass if they would like to walk out with you that afternoon?'

'Don't be daft, Finn,' Tom said. 'No one moons after me.'

'They do then.'

'They don't,' Tom said firmly. 'You're making it up.'

'I'm not,' Finn maintained. 'I don't even know why you are acting so surprised. You are a fine and handsome man. Look at the fine head of hair you have and those big brown eyes. Your only bad feature is that you don't smile enough. When you do you are really handsome, far better-looking than Joe, and added to that you are decent and respectable.'

Tom, however, knew that he was far from being decent and respectable, and he never thought of himself as good-looking in any way. But he was intrigued enough to ask, 'Go on, then. Who are these hordes of females who think I am so wonderful?'

'Oh, no,' Finn said, 'you will get no names from me. If you were less pious and more worldly you would have discovered them for yourself. Have a peep around next time. And some of them are, well, you know,' he said, letting his hands trace a woman's figure in the air, then gave a knowing wink.

'Finn!'

'Don't tell me you don't think of it in your bed at night, for I'll not believe it,' Finn said. 'Anyway, I am not going to wait for the girls to fall at my feet at Mass. I am going looking for them.'

'Now, what do you mean?'

'I mean that I am going to go to the socials with Joe.'

'But you are only—'

'Sixteen, I know,' Finn said. 'Other fellows my age go, because they have told me.'

'You're mad,' Tom declared. 'Mammy will never stand it.'

'She will have to stand it,' Finn said, 'for I am determined upon it, and whether she likes it or not I will be away tonight with Joe.'

And Tom knew he would. He would risk his father's displeasure and even his mother's terrifying rage. He would stand firm and in the end get what he wanted. Joe did that too. It was only Tom that couldn't seem able to cope with that.

Maybe, he reflected, something had been left out of his make-up, or maybe it was the result of his upbringing or the dreadful events of that Sunday afternoon. Whatever it was, he knew that while his brothers would probably go out and conquer the world, he would plod along on the farm and stay with his parents all the days of his life. As for the girls Finn said had an eye for him, well, they would have to cast it elsewhere.

'Come on, then,' he said to his young brother with a smile. 'Let's get all the jobs finished before they get back, for if everything isn't done to my satisfaction, I might be the one stopping you going to the social.'

Finn went willingly enough. Tom was all right, as big brothers went, he thought, though he never would understand him in a million years.

*   *   *

Later, Tom always thought that it was from that morning that he sensed a change in Finn. He had always been restless, as if he had a spring coiled inside him that was going to unravel at any time and surge out of him. This personality wasn't particularly good on a farm that dealt with animals. In fact, Thomas John didn't particularly like him at the milking because he said he could get only half a pail of milk from any cow, whereas he and Tom could get a full pail, and even Joe usually managed three-quarters of one.

Now Finn's restlessness turned almost to belligerence. He seemed to be constantly at odds with his parents, demanding things that Tom and Joe had never even given a mind to – like a wage, for instance.

Biddy bought all the clothes she thought they needed. Once, most of Finn's had been handed down from his brothers, but the strip of wind he had been at sixteen had developed into a well-muscled young man only slightly shorter than his two brothers as he neared eighteen, and that was no longer an option. Finn said he should have some say in the work clothes he wore nearly every day of his life, not to mention his suit and shirts for Mass. This suit he also wore to the socials he went to with Joe, for he had fought and won that battle. He also wanted money in his pocket to spend as he wished.

Biddy couldn't understand him at all. Hadn't he food in his belly, clothes on his back and a

233

good fireside to sit beside, she asked, and didn't she give him money when he went out with Joe?

'Aye, and what a paltry meagre amount it is,' Finn said scathingly. 'Doled out like I was a wean.'

'You're little more,' Thomas John growled. 'And not too big for a good hiding, my boy, and don't you forget.'

Finn looked at him pityingly, for Thomas John had never laid a hand on any of them, leaving that job to Biddy. Finn had asked him about it once, and he had said he was too big a man to go around hitting weans. Many times, as Finn was growing up, he had wished his father had got over this aversion, for he had the feeling he would not have hit them with the full force of his hand. Their mother, on the other hand, would hit them with all the strength she had. Any sort of measured response had no place in her life at all.

But it did mean that Finn was not afraid of his father, and for all his truculence he valued Thomas John's opinion. Not that he was afraid of his mother; the time was dead and gone when she could terrorise him. So now he said to his father, 'I don't see why I am threatened for asking for a wage for the job of work I do. It isn't a strange thing to ask for. The least job a man does in Buncrana he gets a wage for.'

'You're not a man, not yet.'

'Then don't expect me to work like one,' Finn retorted.

'Your brothers have never made demands like

this,' Biddy said, her lips a slash of ill humour on her face. 'They have more respect.'

Finn's eyes strayed to the window where his brothers were walking down from the fields for their dinner, laughing about something, and suddenly Finn felt on the outside of his family – not a part of it, but as if he were a stranger looking in. He turned to face his parents.

'I am not like my brothers, though, am I? No one person is like another. Everyone is an individual and you can't seem to see that.'

Later, with nothing resolved and the meal eaten, Thomas John told Finn to go to the woodshed where there were piles of wood to saw and chop. Usually after dinner they sat before the fire with cups of tea, while Thomas John and his two elder sons would have a smoke of their pipes.

For a few moments Finn, after staring at his father, did not move, until Tom wondered if he intended to defy him. In fact Finn did consider it. It was as if everyone was holding their breath. Then Finn got to his feet slowly, scraping his chair on the flagstone floor. Tom was able to breathe easily again as he watched his brother pull his jacket from behind the door and leave the cottage in a flurry of discontent.

Nuala gave a sigh. She knew that Tom and Joe wouldn't have any idea why Finn was acting the way he was, but she had been in the room during Finn's earlier altercation with their parents, though she had said nothing, knowing that it wouldn't be

235

helpful. She knew her mother wouldn't let her help with washing the dishes, because she always said it would make her hands red and rough. Biddy would let Nuala do so little that she often felt bored, and so as soon as she could, she slipped out of the door.

She found Finn sitting on the chopping block in the woodshed with the wood that he had obviously made no start on scattered about his feet, and his face the picture of misery.

'Why are you so cross?' she asked.

'You'd hardly understand,' Finn said. 'Don't you get everything you want and your own way in everything?'

Nuala was too truthful a girl to try to deny this and she said instead, 'Doesn't mean that I can't listen.'

Finn sighed. 'All right then. This isn't what I want, for a start.'

'What isn't?'

'This,' Finn cried, throwing his arm out expansively. 'The farm, this life, everything. I feel a bit like a cuckoo in a strange nest, for all I have been born and bred to this. I want to travel and see different things and meet different people. I want to live a bit before I get tied down. Can you understand that?'

Nuala nodded. 'For all you say I have everything, and I know that you're right, some days I am so bored that I could scream. I can't help feeling that any man who takes me on will have made a

236

bad bargain because I won't have the least idea of how to cook or clean a house, and when the babies come, dear Lord, I won't know the least thing about babies.'

'I thought that sort of thing came naturally.'

Nuala shrugged. 'I don't know, but in my case I hope it does.'

'That's another thing,' Finn said. 'How will I ever find a girl and settle down?'

'Do you want to settle down now?' Nuala asked.

'No, not particularly.'

'Well, then . . .'

'I suppose I will one day, though. And how will I ever be able to court a girl without ever having a penny piece on me, regardless of how much work I do on the farm?'

'Put like that, it doesn't sound very fair,' Nuala said. 'And Mammy and Daddy can't see your point of view?'

'No, not at all,' Finn spat out. 'And, after all, I am eighteen in June.'

Nuala shivered, for the February day was bleak and cold, and the skies gunmetal grey, dark and forbidding, and June seemed a long way off.

'And what of you, Nuala?' Finn asked suddenly.

'Me? What about me?'

'Well, what plans have you for your life? You are turned fourteen now and have been left school two years.'

'I have never even thought about it,' Nuala said truthfully. 'I mean, I haven't actually got plans.'

'Maybe you should have,' Finn suggested. 'The thing is, do you want to stay here on the farm all day and every day until some burly farmer carts you off to his place for more of the same?'

Put like that it didn't sound a very attractive prospect, yet Nuala replied, 'Isn't that what most girls do?'

'Is it what you want to do?'

'It's probably what Mammy and Daddy want me to do.'

'That isn't what I asked.'

'It amounts to the same thing.'

Finn suddenly took Nuala by the shoulders and said firmly, 'Now you listen to me. We only get one crack at this future business and it belongs to you and only you, and if you want to do something other than what Mammy and Daddy have planned out for you, then you take hold of it with two hands and don't let go. Remember they cannot live your life for you, and if you let an opportunity go you may resent it all the days of your life.'

'I couldn't go against them, Finn,' Nuala said.

'You could if it mattered enough to you.'

'No, no, I couldn't,' Nuala insisted. 'I am not like you.'

'Then I am sorry for you,' Finn told his sister. He released her shoulders and said, 'Go in now, Nuala. It is too cold to be out. I could feel you shivering beneath my hands.'

'What about you?'

'Oh, I'll be all right when I get started on this

wood,' Finn said. 'And I best do that if I don't want the head bitten off me. Anyway, it will work my temper off.' He grinned and added, 'You'll see the difference. When I have this pile cleared I will be like an angel of goodness and light, so I will.'

'Oh, that will be the day,' Nuala remarked, but she was laughing as she left her brother.

THIRTEEN

Just after Easter, Nuala was in Buncrana with her mother in the post office when she caught the eye of Lady Carrington. The Carringtons were Protestants, the most prestigious family in the area, and lived in a large house set in its own grounds on the edge of the town towards Derry.

Biddy had little to do with them. In fact, they were seldom seen in the town for most things they needed were delivered, and fresh produce collected by their maid. But that day the maid had become ill and the lady of the house had decided that, as the day was dry and warm, she should take the carriage and go into the town herself.

She had popped into the post office to post letters to her family, many of whom lived in the Midlands in England and she came face to face with 'a vision of loveliness', which was the way she described Nuala to her husband, Gerald, later.

She barely noticed Biddy, for her attention was

taken by Nuala, who looked delightful that day. She had on the clothes her mother had had made up for her to wear for Easter Sunday: a blue and white checked dress that gathered beneath the bust and went to just above her soft leather shoes, she also had a soft blue shawl to put around her shoulders, and a straw hat on her head trimmed with the same blue as the dress.

Nuala, feeling the woman's eyes on her, turned and smiled. Lady Carrington actually gasped. She lingered in the shop until Nuala and her mother left, then she said to the postmistress, young Nellie McEvoy, 'Who was that gorgeous child?'

'That's Nuala Sullivan,' the postmistress told her. 'Pretty as a picture, isn't she? And a pleasant little thing, despite the mother, who is a right braggart about her. Mind you, there is not so much of the child about her now. She must be fourteen or so.'

'Really, are you sure? She barely looks it.'

'I'm pretty certain that she has been left school close on two years now.'

'Is she looking for a job?' Lady Carrington asked.

The postmistress laughed. 'I doubt it. Her mother barely lets the wind blow on her. What sort of job?'

'I need a nursemaid. My present one is leaving to get married, and I always like to have someone young with plenty of energy to play with the children. Even children like prettiness around them, don't you feel?'

Nellie muttered something noncommittal. She thought whatever the woman wanted, she hadn't a hope in Hell of getting Nuala to work for her, or anyone else.

Lady Carrington, though, was used to getting her own way. As she made her way home, she decided she would talk it over with her husband, though in domestic matters she had the final say, for he seldom concerned himself with such issues. It was only as the coachman helped her alight from the cab that she realised she hadn't bought the purchases that had taken her into Buncrana in the first place.

Biddy was extremely flustered when a carriage rolled down the lane to stop before the cottage a few days later. She hurriedly dried her hands on her apron and went to the door to welcome her visitor, Lady Carrington, though she hadn't any idea what she was doing there.

'Come in, my lady,' she said, opening the door wide. 'This is an unexpected honour.'

The room Lady Carrington stepped into was quite dark after the sunshine, for the light came through only one small window. But for all that, she saw that the place was clean and tidy, and the child Nuala was there. She smiled when she saw who the visitor was and bobbed a curtsy, which pleased Lady Carrington enormously.

Her husband had been right when he advised her to visit the house and see the type of people the girl came from. 'I'm sure you will have whoever you choose, Julia, my dear, and I will not go against you, as you well know, but if she is to care for our children then we must know that she is from good and respectable stock.'

'You are right, Gerald, of course. I wonder I hadn't thought of it myself.'

And now here she was, and saw that Nuala and her mother were decently clad, the house was a more than adequate one, and the girl had been taught manners and her place in life. She knew she would fit into her household with ease and be such a help to Nanny Pritchard, who was getting on a bit. She had been with the Carrington family years, taken on originally to be nanny to her husband and his brothers and sisters, but she was getting too old now to run after young children.

Lady Carrington accepted the cup of tea and slice of barmbrack from Biddy as she went on to say how impressed she had been by Nuala when she had met her in the post office the other day. Biddy accepted that as due praise, for few met Nuala who were not struck by her charm and beauty.

However, she knew that it wasn't likely that Lady Carrington had come all the way out to their cottage to say so, and when she told her the real reason for her visit, Biddy was both astounded and annoyed.

'A job, my lady?' she repeated a little tight-lipped.

'Nursemaid to three children?' She shook her head. 'We hadn't thought of Nuala getting any form of employment. There is no need and, anyway, she is such a help to me in the house, d'you see?'

Nuala knew that was a lie, for she was let do very little and was bored often, as she had told Finn. Besides, she liked babies and children, for all she had had little to do with them, and would love the chance of caring for them. Then too she would see people other than members of her family, day in and day out, for all she loved them dearly.

Nuala wasn't aware how expressive her face was. Lady Carrington had been watching her and when Biddy had finished speaking she said, 'I do understand about Nuala being such a help to you, but maybe she should be given this chance. I can see by her face that she wants to.'

Biddy looked at her daughter. Her whole face was lit up, almost glowing. Biddy said, 'Surely you don't want to do this?'

Nuala nodded vigorously. 'I do, Mammy,' she said, 'Really I do.'

Biddy looked at the child that she loved more than life itself. She had refused her little all her life so far, but Nuala, like Tom, had been a compliant, eager-to-please child. Biddy was confident that her daughter would see how ridiculous the whole plan was and would bow to Biddy's will as she had always done before.

This time, however, Nuala remembered what Finn had said to her a couple of months before in the woodshed that the future was hers and hers alone, and she had to grasp opportunities with two hands and not let them go. She had said at the time that she couldn't stand against her parents and Finn had told her that she could if it mattered enough. Now she understood what he had meant.

So when Biddy said disparagingly to Lady Carrington, 'You see, Nuala is just a child yet and doesn't see how unsuitable this is,' the girl felt her hackles rising.

She faced her mother and in a tone that she had never used before said, 'I am not a child, Mammy. I am turned fourteen. Many girls in the town have already been working for two years.'

'You are not some girl from the town,' Biddy ground out.

'Yes, but—'

'Enough, Nuala!' Biddy snapped. 'Goodness, where are your manners? My mind is made up. I'm sorry, Lady Carrington, that you have had a wasted journey.'

Biddy was affronted when, even as she was getting to her feet, Lady Carrington glanced at Nuala and said, 'Is that your answer too?'

Nuala knew that she only had to nod her head and the woman would walk away, and she knew too that if she allowed her to do that she would regret it always. Her mother's face was like thunder, but Nuala gathered all her reserves of courage, swallowed the lump in her throat and said, 'No it isn't. I am sorry, Mammy, but I really want to do this and I would like it if you would allow me to.'

'I have told you—'

'Yes, but, Mammy, that is what you want me to do,' said Nuala. 'But this is what I want to do. Shouldn't it at least be considered?'

'I have never heard such insolence in all my life.'

'Mammy,' Nuala said in a conciliatory way, 'I have no wish to be rude, but shouldn't we at least ask Daddy before the matter is resolved?'

Biddy had known from the first that Thomas John's opinion should be sought, and she had hesitated only because she knew that her husband would lift the moon from the sky if Nuala had so desired it. She had never known him refuse her anything. Yet, on the other hand, if he wasn't at least informed, he could be very vexed indeed, especially if Nuala complained about it, which she was likely to.

'We'll ask your father's advice when he comes in to his dinner,' she said grudgingly.

'And I will come to your house this afternoon and give you our decision, my lady,' Nuala said to Lady Carrington.

The woman shook hands with both Nuala and Biddy, and Nuala followed her into the yard where her carriage and footman waited. Just before Lady

Carrington got in, she turned and put her hand on Nuala's shoulders.

'I do hope the news you bring is favourable, my dear,' she said. 'I would very much like you in my employ, and, incidentally, I admire your pluck.'

Those words helped Nuala when she entered the cottage and her mother went for her in a way she never had before. Nuala bore it without complaining because, in a way, she had almost expected it.

Thomas John had been in the lower fields with his sons and so was unaware of the visit of Lady Carrington and the purpose of it. At first he too was affronted that the woman should assume that he was unable to afford to keep his daughter at home and that she should have to seek employment elsewhere like many of the poor families around them. That was before he caught the light of excitement dancing in Nuala's eyes, however.

He said almost incredulously, 'Do you want to do this?'

'Yes, Daddy, very much.'

'Why?'

'Lots of reasons,' Nuala said. 'I am often bored at home – Mammy has her own way of doing things – and I miss the friends I used to have at school. With the best will in the world, Daddy, there is little companionship to be had from you or the boys when you are all out in the fields all day.'

'She's right, Daddy,' Finn said. He had been as amazed at the turn of events as his father when he was first told. Then he caught his sister's eye and was determined to support her, and so were Tom and Joe, though they knew nothing of the talk in the woodshed.

'Let her do it if she wants to, Daddy,' Tom said.

'Aye,' said Joe in agreement. 'Sure, she can come to no harm. She will only be a step up the road, when all is said and done.'

Biddy saw the way the conversation was going and snapped out, 'Not one of you has given one thought to me and what I am to do without Nuala to give me a hand.'

Finn laughed. 'Oh, come on, Mammy,' he said. 'Nuala doesn't give you a hand and you know it, because you won't let her. You will barely let her put her hands in the washing-up bowl.'

'Aye, because I don't want her worked to death, and now she is proposing to do that for someone else.'

'Hardly that, Mammy,' Nuala said. 'I will be looking after the children. There are only the three of them and they already have a nanny. I like babies and children, yet I have no experience. I can learn such a lot if I set my mind to it and I will be better fitted to look after my own when the time comes.'

'I shouldn't let on to the Carringtons that you are

using their children to practise on,' Joe commented drily.

'Aye. You would be out on your ear sharpish,' Finn said with a wide grin.

'You are talking, all of you, as if it is a foregone conclusion,' Biddy said, 'but neither your father nor I have given permission, and I have voiced my objections.'

'Which were not based on accuracy, Mammy,' Finn said. 'You would not miss the help that you allow Nuala to give.'

'That is not for you to say.'

'All right, then, but Nuala has a right to say it.'

'Finn is right, Mammy,' Nuala said. 'And you know he is.'

Thomas John knew it too. He had seen Nuala mooning about the farmhouse many a time and had even said to Biddy that the child often looked lonely. He had no real wish to see her anywhere other than within his own four walls, and yet he didn't want to be the one to dim the light dancing in his daughter's eyes. Maybe she did want more in her life than they were able to give her.

'It will do no harm to give it a try-out, at least,' he said at last. 'She hasn't to stay if it doesn't work out. Let's say she gives it three months or so.'

'So my wishes are of no account in this house,' Biddy said sharply, 'is that the way of it?'

'Now now, my dear,' Thomas John said. 'Your wishes weren't the only ones to consider in this case and I had to be fair to Nuala too. I think that a three-month trial is the way forward and at the end of that time the situation can be reviewed.'

'Oh, thank you, thank you, Daddy,' Nuala cried. She leaped up and threw her arms around Thomas John's neck, and planted a kiss on his cheek. 'You are the best daddy in the world.'

'Aye, well, this daddy wants to eat his dinner in peace now,' Thomas John admonished, but with a twinkle in his eyes. 'So let us do justice to the meal your mother has prepared and after it you go and tell Lady Carrington and say that you will take the job she offered for an initial period of three months.'

Nuala had never been anywhere near the Carringtons' house before – there had been no need – and that afternoon she stood inside the wrought-iron gates and stared for a few minutes at the magnificent structure built of honey-coloured bricks, trying to gather the courage to walk up the gravel path towards it.

'Now, remember,' her father had said, before she set off, 'the likes of us don't go up to the front door of these places. Go around the back and you will likely find the kitchens. They will put you right.'

Nuala found it just as he had said. The cook seemed to be expecting her. She smiled at her as she opened the door and then told the kitchen maid to take the young lady to the morning room and then inform the mistress that she had arrived.

Aggie surveyed the room while she waited for Lady Carrington, awed by the splendour of it. Patterned rugs covered the floor, and two cream brocade sofas were either side of the fireplace. The mantelshelf was full of delicate ornaments and the fireplace itself covered by an embroidered black velvet fire screen, the hearth enclosed by a gleaming brass fender. On the opposite side of the room was a large clock in a glass case, the heavy pendulum swinging relentlessly, and a writing bureau was set against the window.

Lady Carrington came in. 'I am so pleased to see you again, my dear,' she said. 'I do hope the news you bring me is good.'

Nuala had already decided to say nothing of the trial period of three months and just said her father was agreeable to her taking the job, but she wouldn't be living in. She would be brought in every day by her father or one of her brothers and taken home again each evening. Lady Carrington said that was quite in order and she took Nuala to the nursery to introduce her to Nanny Pritchard, the nursemaid who would be leaving at the end of the week, and the children: four-year-old Billy, two-year-old Isabella and the gorgeous roly-poly baby, Reginald, who was six months. Nuala knew instinctively that she would be happy in that house. She was astounded, though, by the array of toys those three children had and told her family about it as they sat around the table that evening.

'Most aren't new,' she said. 'Nanny Pritchard told me that. But think of any toy imaginable and those children have it. There is a magnificent doll's house, with all the tiny furniture in each room and a little family of people. There are lots of dolls of all shapes and sizes with clothes for them all, a large pram to wheel them about in and a crib as well. There is also a Noah's ark, and the oldest boy, Billy, lined all the animals up two by two to show me. There is a fort as well and two armies of soldiers. Nanny Pritchard said there is a really large railway in the massive toy cupboard, which the master will set up when the boys are older. Then there are games and jigsaws and shelves full of books, and a wonderful rocking horse that even I could ride.'

'Lucky children,' Biddy said, her lips tightened in disapproval.

Nuala took no notice of her mother's ill humour. 'I'll say they are,' she said, with a smile. 'And lucky me too, for I am going to get as much fun playing with them as the children.'

Nuala would often entertain her family in the evenings by telling them of the gossip from the Big House, which she got from Amelia, the kitchen maid, with whom she had become friendly. She also spoke of Nanny Pritchard, with whom she got on so well and respected so much, and the cute

252

things the children did or said. The weeks slipped by.

'Madam is never away from the nursery,' Nuala said one night when she had been at the Big House almost three months. 'Nanny Pritchard says that is unusual and that she has worked in houses where the children saw their parents once a day for about half an hour. Madam is always popping in and thinks nothing of feeding the baby, or getting down on the floor to play with Billy and his toy soldiers, or help Isabella dress her dolls. Even the Master comes up each night as soon as he arrives home.'

'You like them?' Thomas John asked. 'They are good to you?'

'Oh, yes,' Nuala said. 'It's a happy house. I like Nanny Pritchard and Amelia, I get on well with all the other staff too, and I love the children.'

'You intend stopping then?'

'Yes, please.'

'Biddy?'

'Oh, my opinion is asked, is it?'

'Come on, Biddy,' Thomas John said. 'Your opinion was asked and taken into account, but I said to let our Nuala try it out and the three months is almost up. It obviously suits Nuala because she has a smile on her face every evening when I drive the cart up to the back of the house to fetch her home.'

Biddy grudgingly had to agree her daughter did look happier these days, but she wasn't going to share that. Instead she growled out, 'Well, she best stop there then, seeing as it seems to suit everyone else so well.'

So, she had won, Finn thought, quite enviously. And what was he to do with his life? All that fine talk he had given Nuala, which she had so obviously taken so much to heart, about grasping opportunities, and he was doing nothing to help himself, though he had now turned eighteen.

Just a few weeks later, Finn had the chance to change the course of his life. He had been unaware of the rumblings in an unsettled Europe until Britain declared war on Germany on 4 August 1914, after Germany had invaded Belgium and France. That had been on a Tuesday, and by Saturday the news has filtered through to Buncrana and the whole town was buzzing with it. Tom went out, bought a paper and read all about it.

'England has declared war on Germany because they invaded two other countries,' Tom told the others as they sat eating their midday meal. 'That is about the strength of it, and no one can see the irony of that.'

'What do you mean?' Joe asked.

'Well, isn't that what England has done to us?' Tom said. 'Who rules Ireland now? Not the Irish, that's for sure.'

'Aye,' Thomas John said. 'And that means anything that involves England automatically involves us too.'

'You mean the war will?' Finn asked.

'Of course I mean the war, boy. What else?'

Finn coloured both in anger and embarrassment. He hated being called 'boy', especially in front of his brothers. Now he was eighteen he was a boy no longer.

'So you think there will be call-up here?' Joe asked.

'Don't see how we will get away without it,' Thomas John said.

'Maybe they are hoping for volunteers,' Tom said. 'After all, the young English boys have volunteered in droves. The recruiting offices have been hard-pressed to cope with the number who want to take a pop at the Germans. So the paper says, anyway.'

'And why would Irish boys volunteer to fight for a country that has kept them down for years and years?' Thomas John demanded.

'The carrot that they are holding out might have something to do with that,' Tom said.

'What's that?' Joe asked. 'Have to be some bloody carrot, for I would not volunteer to lift one finger to help England.'

'The paper claims that the government will grant Ireland independence if they get Irish support in this war.'

'Let me see that,' Thomas John said, and Tom passed the paper to his father. He scanned it quickly, then said, 'That's what it says, all right, and I don't believe a word of it. To my knowledge, England has never kept any promise it has made to Ireland. For my money they can sink or swim on their own. We will keep our heads down and get on with our lives. It does no good to go out seeking trouble. In my experience it will come knocking on the door soon enough.'

There were murmurs of agreement from Tom and Joe. Only Finn was not of the same mind as the others. To him, war was new and exciting, and there was nothing comforting for him that their dull and ordinary lives would go on unaffected by the battles being fought just across a small stretch of water.

If he was to join in the fight he would be on a level playing field with all the other recruits. There would be no one there to look down on him because of his youth – rather in wartime it would be praised and valued – and no one to call him 'boy' in the disparaging way his father had. He didn't share these thoughts, instinctively knowing that not only would they be unpopular, but that it would be more reason for them all to pour derision over his head.

Only Nuala saw the look of defiance and determination on her brother's face when she was told the news after she came in from work that evening. Watching Finn's face she knew much of what he was thinking and sincerely hoped that he wasn't going to do anything stupid. She shivered inside for her impetuous brother.

However, two weeks passed and she thought

she had been worrying unnecessarily. War dominated the news, of course, and after the first week there were pictures of the first troops to go overseas. Many were looking out of train carriages, all happy and smiling. They would soon kick the Hun into touch, they said, and be home by Christmas with the job done. Finn looked at the pictures and ached to be there amongst them.

The following Saturday the Sullivans set out as usual for Buncrana. Now that Nuala was working, Tom was once again there to help his mother sell the produce. Joe had been left behind to see to things with Thomas John. As they pulled into the town, Biddy pulled out her purse and, dropping some coins into Finn's hand, told him to go to the harbour and buy some fish for their dinner.

Finn nodded, jumped from the cart and then wished he hadn't, for it started his head spinning and his ear throbbing painfully from the cuff his father had given him that morning for spilling a pail of milk in the byre. Thomas John had never raised his hand to any of them before, but rage at the waste of the milk and the mess they had to clean up caused him to lash out at his son and knock him to the floor. Then he called him the stupidest bugger he had ever known and claimed a five-year-old would be more use than he was.

No one helped Finn to his feet. In a way he was glad because he would have hated his brothers to see the tears he brushed away surreptitiously.

He burned with anger and resentment against his father, so that his face was as red as his afflicted ear.

That was still his mood as he reached Buncrana. He was pleased to be away from his father for a while, but not so pleased that he was directed to the harbour with the coppers his mother had doled out to him as if he were still a child.

Finn, however, never got to the harbour. As he turned down Main Street he heard a military band and saw the line of soldiers at the bottom of the hill. In front of this company was a tall officer of some sort, in full regalia, and so smart that even the buttons on his uniform sparkled in the summer sunshine. He held a stick in his left hand.

Suddenly, the brass band behind him began to play and the officer led the soldiers up the hill to the marching music, the beat emphasised by the young drummer boy at the front. The officer's boots rang out on the cobbled street, answered by the tattoo of the soldiers' tramping feet following on, all completely in time.

Shoppers and shopkeepers alike had come to the doorways to watch the soldiers' progress. As they drew nearer, though, Finn was unable to see the officer's eyes, hidden as they were under the shiny peak of his cap, but his brown, curly moustache fairly bristled above the firm mouth in the slightly red and resolute face.

Finn felt the excitement that had begun in his

feet swell within him so that it filled his whole being. Tom, brought out of the market hall like all the rest, saw the zeal filling his brother's face and he was deeply afraid for him, but the press of people made it impossible for him to reach Finn.

And then the company stopped, and while the soldiers stood to attention, the officer spoke words that were like balm to Finn's bruised and battered soul. The officer talked of the pride and integrity and honour of serving in the British Army, whose aim was to rid the world of a nation of brutal aggressors. Their armies would crush the enemy who marched uninvited into other countries, taking away their freedom and liberty, and harassing and persecuting the people. Many, he said, had already answered the call to halt this aggression against innocent men, women and children, and now he wished to see if young Irish boys had what it took to join the British in this righteous fight. To see if they felt strongly enough for the poor peoples of Belgium and France, their fellow human beings, and he urged any who wanted to join the fight to step forward bravely.

At the time, freedom and liberty were what many Irish people longed for too, and so those words burned brightly inside Finn. If he was to join this company, like he saw more than a few were doing, then Ireland would gain her freedom too, for wasn't that the promise given?

His feet stepped forward almost of their own volition.

'Finn, what in God's name are you doing?' Tom cried. He had broken through the crowd and had his hand on his brother's shoulder as he spoke.

Finn shook him off roughly. 'What's it look like?'

'You can't do this.'

'Oh yes I can. You heard what the man said. They need our help and if enough Irish men do this, then Ireland will be free too.'

'This is madness, Finn . . .'

'Now then,' said the sergeant beside them. 'What's this?'

'I want to enlist,' Finn said firmly. 'My brother is trying to prevent me, but I am eighteen years old and the decision is my own.'

'Well said,' the soldier told Finn admiringly, and he turned to Tom. 'As for you, fine sir, you should be ashamed at trying to turn your brother from what he sees as his duty. If he is, as he said, eighteen, he can decide these things for himself. It would look better if you were to join him rather than try to dissuade him.'

Finn shot Tom a look of triumph. How very seldom had he been able to decide things for himself. He said rather disparagingly to the man, 'Tom can't join just now, for he has an urgent errand to run for our mother.' And then with a cheeky smile he dropped the coins his mother had given him into Tom's hand and said, 'I'm going to be busy for a while, so you must get the fish for Mammy.'

He turned away before Tom could find the words to answer him and followed behind the sergeant to find out how he could qualify to join the carnage already being enacted on foreign fields not that far away. All Tom could do was watch him go with his heart as heavy as lead.

If Finn was honest with himself, he joined more for himself than for anyone else. He was fed up being pushed around, barked at to do this or that because, as the youngest boy, he was at the beck and call of everyone. Yet he couldn't seem to do anything to anyone's satisfaction and he never got a word of thanks.

Even if he expressed an opinion it was often derided and mocked. And then for his father to knock him from his feet that morning for spilling a bit of milk . . . it was not to be borne.

According to the army, he was a man and could make a man's decision concerning his future. This way led to excitement and adventure. He might easily get his wish to travel and see other places, and he could hardly wait.

By tacit consent, neither Finn nor Tom mentioned to Biddy what Finn had done. Finn broke the news that he had enlisted as they sat eating their dinner.

'I am to report in the morning,' he said. 'I'm in the Royal Enniskillens.'

Biddy and Joe had sat open-mouthed with shock at the news, and Thomas John had gone puce with anger.

'Are you, begod,' he snapped, thumping his fist on the table. 'Well, you are not. You will not do this. You are just a boy yet and I will accompany you tomorrow and get the matter overturned.'

'This is the army, Daddy, not school,' Finn said. 'And I am not a boy any more, not in the army's eyes, that is. I signed my name on the dotted line of my own free will and that is that. There is not a thing that anyone can do about it.'

Thomas John sat back in his seat defeated, for he knew that Finn spoke the truth.

'But why, Finn?' Biddy cried out.

'I am surprised that you can ask that, Mammy,' Finn said. 'For nothing I do pleases you either. As for Daddy, it's Finn do this or that, and when I have done it, he yells at me for not doing the job properly, for all I have done my level best. And why am I working my fingers to the bone anyway for a farm that one day will be Tom's? I shall have nothing, not even a penny piece to bless myself with, because it seems to be against your religion to actually pay us anything like a wage.'

'You watch your mouth, boy,' Thomas John thundered.

Finn faced his father unafraid. 'Or what?' he asked. 'You hit me this morning for the first and last time. I will not stand and take it a second time, and you remember that. And I am no longer a boy, and you remember that too.'

'Finn,' Biddy rapped out, 'how dare you speak to your father like that?'

Thomas John, however, said nothing. He knew he no longer had any jurisdiction over this son he loved more than the others yet he seemed unable to show it. The boy had stepped into a man's world, only he had chosen a dangerous route and his father would worry about him constantly.

His brothers had a measure of sympathy for Finn, although Tom was concerned for him and said so.

'Why worry?' Finn said. 'They say they fight in trenches and sure, a French trench mustn't be that different to an Irish one, and those I am well familiar with. And if I pop off a few Germans along the way, so much the better.'

'You don't know the least thing about fighting.'

'Neither do any of us,' Finn said. 'We'll be trained, won't we? And after that, I expect I'll be as ready as the next man to have a go at the Hun. And there is something else, Tom. They say the French girls are hot stuff. Know what I mean?'

'Finn!' Tom said, slightly shocked. 'And how do you know, anyway? Just how many French girls do you know?'

'God, Tom, it's a well-known fact,' Finn said airily. 'And don't get on your high horse either. A fighting man has to have some distraction.' And then Finn laughed at the expression on Tom's face.

Much as he could reassure his brothers, though, he dreaded breaking the news to Nuala when she came home. He had missed her when she began work, more than he had expected and more than he would admit to. She had always listened to and often championed him. She did the same that day, for all she said she would worry about him, and urged him to be careful and come back to them safe and sound. Finn told her he would do his best, glad to have someone even partially on his side as he prepared to dip his toe into alien waters.

FOURTEEN

Levingstone was becoming worried about Aggie. She told him she had arrived in England in February in 1901 when she was fifteen, although she had turned sixteen just after coming to the club, and now in 1914 she was twenty-nine years old, and in June of the following year, she would be thirty. Very few girls were kept on after that age. And how long, Levingstone thought, would she be able to dance with the same verve and energy? Not that he had seen her slow down at all yet, but he accepted that she couldn't go on for ever. Yet if at all possible he wanted to keep her off the streets. He didn't understand himself because he had never felt this way about any of the other girls.

In the end, he confided in Lily, telling her of his concerns for Aggie. When he had finished, Lily could see only one solution.

'Why don't you marry the girl, Alan?'

Levingstone looked at Lily as if he couldn't believe his ears. 'I am too old for Aggie,' he said.

'Besides, Rogers would never stand for it. He told me when I started as manager that I could take all the delights the girls had to offer me, but I wasn't to start marrying any of them. Apparently it upsets the punters. I told him then that there was little fear of that because, to tell you the truth, I did think I wasn't the marrying sort. I mean, what I have seen of marriage has never convinced me that it is a particularly good thing. My parents' marriage wasn't happy and most of the men we see down the club, bedding a new girl every day of the week, are married.'

'That's as may be,' Lily said dismissively, 'but there are good and happy marriages too. Anyroad, I can't see any other way of protecting Aggie other than marrying her.'

'I can't ask her to tie herself down to an old man,' Alan cried. 'For Christ's sake, Lily, I'm nearly double her age.'

'Didn't stop you bedding her, your age,' Lily snapped. 'Didn't think of it then.'

'I know,' Levingstone admitted. 'To my shame I used to try most of them out; thought of it as a sort of perk of the job.'

'Till Aggie?'

'Yeah, till Aggie. She's really got under my skin. I have never had another girl in my bed since the day I took Aggie in, nor have I wanted to.'

'I think you love her, Alan.'

'Christ, Lily, what's love anyway?' Levingstone said. 'I haven't had any experience of love. All I can say is that I feel more for her than I have ever felt for anyone in the whole of my life.'

'And what does she feel for you?'

'What could she feel but gratitude? She is so very beautiful. Born into another life, she could have married anyone. They would have been queuing up.'

'I know that,' Lily said sharply. 'Probably so does she, 'cos she ain't daft. But she weren't born into a different life, was she? This is the only one she has, and if you marry her you will be her saviour, because if that girl goes on to the streets she will be destroyed.'

'I know, and that's eating me up inside,' Levingstone admitted. 'Even at the club, the loathing for what she has to do is in every line of her body. She hides it well and only someone like me, who knows almost every beat of her heart, can see her shame and deep sadness. She seems to lose a small part of herself every time, and afterwards she drinks far too much and has too much opium as well – to help her forget, she says.'

'It's the only way she can cope, I suppose,' Lily said. 'She might not have such a great need for it if you were to marry her, though. Put it to her. She'll know what the alternative is. She isn't a bloody imbecile.'

'Rogers won't like it,' Levingstone said.

'Bugger Rogers!' Lily cried. 'Anyroad, I would say you had taken that man at his word nearly all the years of your adult life and didn't think a thing

267

of it. But this is different and you've said as much. I mean, it isn't as if you were getting married every other day of the week, is it?'

'No, but—'

Lily put her hand on his arm and, looking him straight in the eyes, she said, 'Alan, you have a right to a life of your own, and so does Aggie. It isn't a lot to ask.'

'You're right,' Levingstone said decisively. 'I will square it with Rogers first and then talk to Aggie.'

That evening, Aggie was in the bedroom dressing before going down to the club when Levingstone came into the room. When she turned and smiled at him, he felt his heart turn over. He wanted Aggie by his side legitimately and always, because he loved her dearly. Now there was not the slightest doubt in his mind.

He put his arms around her, kissed her gently and then, taking her hand, led her into the sitting room and pulled her down onto the sofa beside him.

'I need to talk to you, Aggie.'

Aggie was filled with apprehension. She had been watching the calendar herself, and knew that approaching thirty was the thing that most of the girls looked on with dread. She was as sought after as ever, though, and she still danced as well as she ever did. Surely that counted for something?

But Alan was looking at her in such an odd way. She was totally stunned when he suddenly kissed her fingers lingeringly before asking, 'What do you really think about me, Aggie?'

'You, Alan?' Aggie cried. 'Why, I am surprised that you have to ask. I love you dearly. But you must already know that.'

'No, I don't. I mean, I wasn't sure,' Levingstone said.

Aggie saw how nervous he was. She had never seen him in any way vulnerable before and she felt for him, so she leaned forward and kissed him gently on the lips.

Levingstone grasped her and held her tight. 'Do you truly love me?' he demanded. 'With all your heart and soul?'

When Aggie had said she loved Levingstone she had meant it, but despite the fact that she slept with him, she thought of him as her protector, almost a father figure. However, she knew instinctively that that wasn't what he wanted to hear and she also knew that her future would be decided by the way she answered him. So she said, 'Yes, Alan, I love you with all my heart and soul. I cannot imagine life without you.'

'I love you too,' Alan said. 'But I am twice your age.'

'You will never be old to me, Alan,' Aggie assured him. 'I said once that you were timeless and I stand by that.'

'I am asking you to marry me, my dear.'

Aggie gasped. Never, ever in a million years had she expected that. Levingstone had told her many times that he would never marry one of the girls, that his bosses wouldn't allow it. Anyway, he had said he had never felt like making the brief flings he had had with most of the girls into something more permanent.

'My God, Alan, you have taken me totally by surprise,' Aggie admitted. She threw her arms around his neck and hugged him tight, feeling suddenly so light-hearted and happy. Marriage to Alan would mean the end of prostitution for her. Oh God, what a blessed relief that would be.

But she had to be sure. She would hate to have this redemption, this stab at happiness dangled in front of her, and then see it snatched away again, so her answer was slightly tentative. 'The answer is yes, of course, a million times yes, but will you be let marry me?'

Levingstone, for a moment, recalled the blistering row he had had with Rogers after he had spoken with Lily. 'Rogers wasn't happy about it, but he came round when he saw how determined I was.'

Aggie sighed. 'You have made me the happiest woman in the world. Really, you have. I can't find the words to tell you just how much your proposal means to me.'

Levingstone held the slight girl in his arms, their lips met, and he knew with certainty that he would love Aggie till the breath left his body. She was still insecure, however, and asked, 'What about Rogers?'

'Don't fret,' Levingstone said. 'It really is all right. All I was asked to do was to keep it quiet for now.'

Aggie pulled away from him. 'Ah God, and I wanted to shout it from the rooftops,' she said, disappointed. 'Why have we got to keep it quiet, as if it is something to be ashamed of, instead of something that we should be celebrating?'

'Because Rogers demands it,' Levingstone said. He put his arms around Aggie again and drew her close because he knew what he had to say wouldn't please her, but it was the compromise that he had had to make for Rogers to agree at all. 'Sweetheart,' he said gently, 'you know how popular you are with the punters, and Rogers knows too of course, and not just because I have mentioned it. Your reputation goes before you, my dear, and so naturally he doesn't want to lose you just yet.'

'What are you saying, Alan?'

'I am saying that we can get engaged now, but secretly.'

'Secretly?' Aggie repeated. 'What is the point of that?'

'Only for a time.'

'How much time?'

'A year.'

'A year? Oh, Alan, come on,' Aggie cried, scarcely able to believe it. 'Waiting a whole year before we can tell anyone is just a joke.'

'Believe me, Agnes, it is no joke,' Levingstone said. 'And I have no alternative but to agree if I want to stay on as manager of the club. And to be quite candid, darling, I know nothing else.'

'Yes, but—'

'Listen, pet,' Levingstone said, giving Aggie's shoulder a squeeze, 'whenever we announce our engagement the news might not be popular because from that moment onwards you will be off limits to all the punters.'

'You have no idea how good that sounds.'

'I know how you feel about that – how you have always felt about it,' Levingstone said. He remembered trying to explain that to his furious boss when Rogers had said to him, 'If you are determined to be wed, though for the life of me I can't understand why, then why marry one of the strumpets that work for you? You are a well-set-up man and could have someone respectable.'

Levingstone smiled inwardly and imagined the reaction a respectable girl and her family would have at the realisation that her future home would be above the club, not to mention the line of work he was in. But, no matter, he didn't want a respectable girl, or any girl at all but Aggie. 'Agnes isn't like the others,' he'd told Rogers.

'Oh? So she doesn't sleep with men, then?' Rogers asked sarcastically.

'Yes, of course,' Levingstone said. 'But—'

'Then she is a whore, a harlot like all the rest.'

'No, she's different. She was forced into it,' Levingstone went on. 'She was raped and—'

'Surely you haven't fallen for that old line?'

Rogers said contemptuously. 'I bet she asked for everything she got. Still, if you are so adamant that you must marry her, then you say nothing about it until Christmas 1915, if you want to keep your job. You can get engaged then, and marry the following year. I tell you now, if she had been much younger I wouldn't even have considered this. But, as you say, she will be thirty next summer and so her usefulness at the club is coming to an end anyway.'

'She'll not be happy about waiting so long.'

'Do you think I give a damn about what these women are happy or unhappy about?'

'You should,' Levingstone said. 'They do have feelings, you know. After all, you have made plenty of money from them.'

'And why not cash in on the girls who can't wait to have sex with any Tom, Dick or Harry?' Rogers said. 'They are not real women and don't deserve any normal understanding. You tell your woman that's the way it is.'

So Levingstone told Aggie. Then he went on to say, 'Aggie, you know it will break my heart too, seeing you, who are promised to me, go off with other men. Next year will be a hard one for both of us, but it will pass eventually and then in the spring of 1916 we will become man and wife.'

Aggie saw Levingstone's concern for her furrowing his brow. She felt sorry for him because she knew he was being forced into this just as much as she was. However much she protested, there was no alternative, so she kissed his lips gently and said, 'Roll on 1916.'

The war had little impact on most of those in Buncrana, but the Sullivan family took more of an interest in it because of Finn's involvement. He wasn't the only one, by any means, though, as more and more Irish boys answered the call. The Sullivan men would buy the English as well as Irish papers in Buncrana on Saturday and scrutinise them carefully.

This was a war the like of which had never been seen before. The family read with horror of the machine guns that could rip a platoon of soldiers to bits in seconds, and the new naval weapon, the submarine, that sailed below the water. It also soon became apparent, as 1914 drew to a close, that this was no short skirmish that would be over by Christmas and that soon, with his training over, Finn would be in the thick of it.

His family always looked forward to his letters. He wrote just as he spoke so it was like having him in the room for a short time, and while he was training he wrote regularly. He mentioned marching till he had blisters on top of blisters, rifle practice and attacking a straw dummy with a bayonet attached to a rifle, and he could see a purpose to those sorts of exercises. Some of it, though, seemed so pointless, like the proper hospital corners they had to have on the beds and the shoes that had to be polished so that their sergeant could see his face in them.

Tom didn't care how boring or pointless the training was because he knew while Finn was there he was safe. And then in early December, with his training completed, he mentioned he had a spot of leave coming up. It was only three days, so he said he would not make it home. Though everyone said that it was embarkation leave, no one knew for sure. He added that if they were heading for France he hoped that the French girls lived up to expectations.

The tone of Finn's letter amused Tom, Joe and Nuala, but it annoyed Thomas John, who said the boy wasn't taking the war seriously enough.

'God, Daddy, won't he have to get a grip on himself soon enough?' Tom said. 'From what I hear, war is no picnic and it will affect Finn as much as any of the others.'

Biddy pursed her lips. 'War or no war,' she said, 'Finn has been brought up to be a decent Catholic boy and I can't believe he talks of women the way he does. Of course you get all types in these barracks. I just hope he doesn't forget himself and the standards he was brought up with.'

Joe sighed. 'Do you know what I wish? Just that Finn keeps his bloody head down. That's all I want for him.'

'Don't speak in that disrespectful way to your mother,' Thomas John admonished.

'I'm sorry, Mammy,' Joe said. 'But, really, isn't Finn's survival the most important thing?'

'Anyway,' Tom put in, 'it's likely the way he copes. He's probably a bit scared, or at least apprehensive.'

'Doesn't say so,' Thomas John said, scrutinising the letter again. 'According to this, he can't wait.'

'Wasn't he always like that?' Joe said. 'Claiming he was scared of nothing, even as a wee boy?'

'Aye,' agreed Tom.

Nuala said suddenly, 'Why are we bothering about the words he writes in a letter? I agree with Joe. All I care about is that Finn will come home hale and hearty when this is over.'

'That's all any of us cares about, cutie dear,' Thomas John said gently. 'We just have different ways of expressing things. Didn't know myself how much I would miss the boy until he wasn't here. He would irritate the life out of me at times and yet I would give my eyeteeth now for him to swing into the yard this minute, back where he belongs.'

Finn's regiment was apparently sent to the Western Front, and he was now in France. His letters home were more spasmodic and he could tell them little. All the soldiers had been warned by their commanding officers against worrying the people back home.

The papers, though, were full of battles at places the family had never heard of – Gallipoli, the Dardanelles and Ypres – resulting in such terrible casualty figures. It was estimated that as many as 250,000 men had died by the summer of that year, and the constant worry about Finn was like a nagging tooth.

About 125,000 Irish men and boys had volunteered for war, and by the late summer of 1915 some of those injured began to arrive back home. People were shocked to see the young, fit men who had marched off return with missing limbs, or wheezing like old men as their lungs were eaten away by mustard gas. Others were blind or shell-shocked. Many more were killed, their bodies left behind in foreign fields.

'And for what?' Thomas John asked. 'We were promised Home Rule by the end of last year and now here we are, halfway through 1915, and it seems as far away as ever. Put on hold, they said, because of the war. Forgotten about, more like.'

'That is only what you expected,' Joe pointed out.

'Aye, I know,' Thomas John said, 'but it gives me no pleasure to be right and think that my youngest son is risking his life for nothing.'

'We are only going to control twenty-six counties anyway,' Tom put in.

'Well, what do we control now?' Thomas John demanded. 'Bugger all! That's what! Small wonder that some of the lads are joining that Citizens' Army,' he added. 'I hear they have guns and ammunition and all, down in Dublin.'

'Aye, and it's known as the Irish Volunteer Force now, Daddy,' Joe said. 'And haven't the Ulster Volunteer Force their own stash of weapons and had them this long while?'

'Aye, and under the eye of the British Government too,' Thomas John said. 'It will end in civil war yet, mark my words.'

It had been one of the hardest years of Aggie's life and she loathed the thought of another man's hand mauling her when she felt that now she belonged totally to Levingstone. He had taken her out and bought her a large diamond ring, which for the moment she was not allowed to wear. He promised that he would announce their engagement on Christmas Eve, and ever after that she could wear the ring.

He said she could tell Lily, knowing that she was longing to, and he took her over to her friend one day. Aggie found the world to be a strange place outside the club, which had cocooned her from the war and its effects. She saw women driving omnibuses, cars and even lorries, and she asked Lily about it.

'That ain't all, girl, either,' Lily said. 'There's girls working in Dunlops in Rocky Lane – them that makes all the rubber – and they're in all the munitions factories around as well.'

'Munitions?'

'You know, weapons, bullets and that.'

'Oh . . .'

'Well, someone's got to do it with all the men called up,' Lily pointed out. 'Well paid, they say it is, as well. Plenty of jobs for women today. Need it and all, many of them, for a soldier's pay and the separation allowance a wife is paid is little more than a pittance. Mind, there ain't much in the shops to buy and even less when the nobs buy it in loads to stockpile in their houses. They don't go themselves, of course, and mix with us riffraff. They have their carriages parked down a side street and they sent their coachmen in. Course, that's if the grocer is as bad as they are. Some of them are rationing stuff now, however much money you have, which is fairer, of course. I don't expect this affects you at all.'

Aggie shook her head. 'I don't know how Bessie manages it, but she is a first-rate cook and produces some lovely meals. I suppose I should feel guilty that the war hasn't changed my life at all.'

'Why feel guilty?' Lily said. 'It ain't your fault. Anyroad, haven't you had any young officers down in the club for you to "entertain"?'

'A few.'

'Well, that's doing your bit – flying the flag, as it were.'

'Some of them are a lot nicer than your average punter,' Aggie said. 'And caught unawares their eyes often look so sad, almost bleak. I had an officer in just a couple of weeks ago, a young man – early twenties, no more – and he had to tell the soldiers in his command that if they are side by side with a brother as they go over the top and one is killed, then the other must step over him and go on. The officer did as he was told and he was haunted by it. He said good, decent men, often with loving families back home, men he had had a laugh and joke with just minutes before, he had to order over the top and see them mown down or blown to pieces. Not in ones or twos, he said, though that would have been bad enough, but wave upon wave of them. And yet he had to swallow the bile that would rise in his throat and signal for another batch to be butchered, on and on till the trenches were empty and the ground was littered with bodies, or parts of bodies and the organs inside them. Body pieces, he called them.'

'God . . .' breathed Lily in horror.

'He didn't want sex,' Aggie said, and added after a moment or two, 'And you know it is one of the times I wouldn't have minded, if it could have brought him some ease.'

'What did he want?' Lily asked.

'To cry,' Aggie replied. 'Weep about the terrible things that he had been forced to do that he had no control over, and he wanted a woman's arms around him, giving him comfort while he did it. He was so full of guilt and shame, and I held him tight and I think that sort of told him that it was all right for him to cry his heart out, that it didn't make him a coward or a cissy or less of a man because his stiff upper lip had wobbled a bit.'

'Bloody awful, ain't it?' Lily said. 'I mean, I know it is a man's world all right, and I seldom feel sorry for the buggers, but they can't have a damned good old cry like we can.'

Aggie shook her head sadly. 'No, they can't.'

'Finch still around?'

'Oh, yes.'

'He'll get called up if he ain't careful.'

'They haven't got call-up yet, though, have they?' Aggie said. 'And when they do, his daddy will probably get him off it. He thinks anything can be bought for a price, but I wish to God he was in the army because it would solve all my problems. I mean, he doesn't come every night or anything, but he only has to enter the club and I start trembling inside.'

'And it's still you he wants?'

'Oh, yes, and he is as brutal as ever.' Aggie shuddered. 'But seldom where it shows. I keep the lights low in the bedroom, and if Alan does see anything I always pass it off as nothing, say I walked into something. I'm not at all sure how much he is aware of, though he is not stupid. Alan says, when we are officially engaged that side of things will come to an immediate stop.' She looked at Lily, her eyes nearly standing out in her head. 'Tell you something for nothing, the announcement of the engagement can't come soon enough for me.'

When it was announced, however, at the club's Christmas Eve Ball, to a great fanfare of trumpets and roll of drums, the look in Finch's eyes frightened Aggie. There were cheers and roars of approval from the majority, though. Levingstone's hand was pumped up and down, and Aggie was hugged and kissed. But through it all, she couldn't get the look in Finch's eyes out of her mind, especially as the man had said not one word either congratulatory or otherwise. She told herself not to be silly, he could look all he liked, he would never get near her again. She was under Levingstone's protection now.

Sometime during the evening, she lost sight of Levingstone. Finch also proved elusive and she presumed and hoped, that he had gone on somewhere else. She always liked to know where he was at the club because then she could keep well away for as long as possible.

She gave a sudden shiver and realised she hadn't brought down the wrap she usually had with her so she popped back upstairs to collect it. She realised as she got to the top of the stairs that Alan and Finch were inside Alan's apartment and arguing, their voices raised and angry.

'And I have told you once already,' she heard Alan say, 'only you seem hard of hearing, so I will say it again. You are not bedding Aggie any more and I don't care what you are offering to pay.'

'We'll see what Rogers has to say about that.'

'I checked it out with Rogers,' Levingstone said. 'He knows all about it.'

'He couldn't,' Finch said. 'I was with him tonight and he never said a word.'

'Oh,' Levingstone said sarcastically, 'I wasn't aware that Rogers discussed all our business and personal arrangements with you.'

282

Finch shrugged. 'He knows that I have an interest in the club in general, and Agnes in particular.'

'Well, you must allow that interest in Agnes to wane,' Levingstone said. 'Agnes has agreed to be my wife and we are to be married in the spring. As for you, the club downstairs is awash with girls.'

'And none of them suits.'

'Then you are a hard man to please,' Levingstone snapped, tight-lipped. Then, suddenly losing patience, he said irritably, 'Look, I am not going to discuss this any more, Finch. I have told you how it is and if we talk from now until doomsday, the situation will not change. Either accept the rules, or take your custom elsewhere.'

'You will be sorry for that, Levingstone.'

Levingstone gave a sigh. 'Possibly,' he said. 'But for now I would like you to leave.'

Aggie hid until she saw that Finch had gone. Then she went into the sitting room. Alan had sunk on to the sofa and he had his head in his hands. She was across the room in seconds and put her arms around his shaking shoulders.

'Alan,' she said in surprise, 'you are trembling as much as me.'

Alan looked up at her and she saw his eyes were still afire and his cheeks were crimson. 'Perhaps, my dear,' he said, 'but my shaking comes from trying to control my anger, not my fear.'

He pulled Aggie down beside him and, with his arm around her, he said, 'But you need fear him no longer, my dear. Cross him out of your life.'

Levingstone hadn't seen the look Finch had cast Aggie's way earlier that evening and a cold shiver ran down her as she realised why it had totally unnerved her. It was a sort of promise – unfinished business – and she knew she would never be really safe while Finch lived.

FIFTEEN

Levingstone had expressly forbidden Aggie to go to Lily's on her own, saying the streets around there were far too dangerous, peopled as they were by footpads and pickpockets, not to mention the more violent element that would murder a person for the watch on their wrist.

Aggie thought he was being unduly cautious. Lily and her friends worked on the same streets night after night and they never said anything about it.

She knew, though, that Alan's warning was just another measure of his concern for her, and it was a lovely feeling to be cosseted so. In just a few days that would be the pattern of her life. She would have Alan by her side and the bad times behind her, as if they had never happened.

She hadn't truly loved Alan as a woman should love a man she has agreed to marry when she had accepted his proposal, but that had all changed now. His love for her was so all-consuming, and he demonstrated how he felt about her so often, she couldn't be other than affected by it. Now she could say, hand on heart, that she truly loved Alan Levingstone.

The age difference had never been an issue with her and wasn't now. The only regret was that they probably wouldn't have as many years together as they would if Levingstone were younger. When Aggie had said that, just the previous night, he had told her not to worry about the future, let it take care of itself. What they had to do was take joy in each day.

When Alan had left on business that morning, Aggie hadn't a thought in her head of going to Lily's, but after lunch she saw a long afternoon stretching out before her, because Alan had said he didn't expect to be back until it was almost time to open the club.

She really wanted to see Lily and the other girls to discuss the wedding. They had been so pleased when they heard of her engagement. Levingstone had taken her over to tell them and show them the ring in January and they had been delighted for her. The sun was shining from a sky of cornflower blue. What harm could happen to her on such a day? So she set out after lunch without a word to anyone.

She reached Lily's with no problem at all, and when she told her what Alan had said, Lily took her hand and said with tears in her eyes, 'It's all plain sailing for you now, bab. He will look after you right and treat you well, and I know many would change places with you this minute for that fact alone.'

Aggie smiled happily. 'I know. I know too how lucky I am. And it's not that alone either. I truly love him. I tremble whenever he is near me and I long for his touch, or his lips on mine.' She laughed at the expression on Lily's face. 'Yes, Lily, I am a totally hopeless case.'

'No you ain't,' Lily said emphatically. 'You are just bloody lucky, and thank God for it, because it is about time summat went right for you. What about that snake in the grass, Finch?'

'Oh, that is even better,' Aggie said, 'because he's gone. Well, at least he hasn't been near since the argument that he had with Alan on Christmas Eve that I told you about.'

'So, where is he now then?'

Aggie shrugged. 'Taken his custom elsewhere, I suppose, like Alan advised him to do if he didn't like the rules. I don't care really. Each night after that, I was always looking over my shoulder, certain he would be in, causing trouble. But now, well, it's weeks, isn't it? He will be off to pastures new, inflicting his special brand of vicious love-making on some other poor cow. I pity her, whoever she is.'

The other girls came back then and they were delighted to see Aggie and hear her news. Their congratulations were warm and sincere, and the time slipped by as they chatted together. It was only when the girls said they had to change to go to work that Aggie realised how much time had elapsed. The afternoon had been replaced by evening and she was concerned that Alan would be home before her and then she would be in trouble.

'I must go,' she said to Lily.

'You best get on the tram,' Lily said. 'It goes right up the Pershore Road.'

'I'm all right,' Aggie said. 'The walk will do me good.' She was never given money of her own and though she knew she could have borrowed the tram fare from Lily, she had never ridden on one before and was scared stiff of them.

Although Aggie had left on a lovely afternoon, fog had descended as she had sat in Lily's sitting room, and visibility was bad. But Aggie was not afraid of the dusky evening. In Ireland there had been no lights after sunset, only the moon and the stars. All she was concerned about was getting home as quickly as possible.

Finch had been visiting a lady friend, who was extremely free with her favours. She lived on the other side of Cannon Hill Park, which wasn't far from the club, and as he walked across the park he toyed with the idea of going back to the club that evening. He had avoided it for months because of his fixation with Aggie. However, now he had this woman in Edgbaston who was a real little goer and didn't even mind the rough stuff – seemed to like it, rather – he wanted to know if Aggie would have the same effect on him.

Suddenly, as if his thoughts had conjured Aggie up, he thought he saw her approaching, though he wasn't totally sure with the swirling fog. If it was Aggie, he'd be surprised to see her out alone. People said Levingstone kept a firm hold on her, hardly letting her out of his sight.

As she drew nearer, he saw it was Aggie. To reach home, he knew she would have to pass close by a small terrace of shops. The shops were all shut for the night, but in the middle of them was a central alley and he crossed the road, slipped into this and waited.

When he felt himself harden at even the thought of her drawing closer, he knew he wanted her more than ever. He recalled telling Levingstone that he would be sorry for the way he had spoken to him. What sweet revenge it would be to take his woman almost on the eve of their wedding.

As she drew level, he stepped from the shelter of the entry and said, 'Good evening, Agnes.'

Aggie stood stock-still, her mouth suddenly as dry as dust. Even in the half-light, she could see Finch's eyes shining demonically, and the curl of his thin, cruel lips. Dread seemed to be gripping her innards and she began to tremble.

'What do you want with me, Tony?' she asked.

Finch heard the tremor in her voice and could almost taste her fear. He smiled. He was determined that she would have reason to fear him before he was finished with her and he snarled at her harshly, 'Why ask the road you know?'

He grabbed hold of her shoulders, digging his nails into her skin as he dragged her into the dark of the entry. 'I have been missing you all this time,' he hissed in her ear.

She tried to pull away, but he just held her tighter and she said as firmly as she could, 'Let me go. You have no right to touch me. I am engaged to Alan Levingstone now, as well you know.'

'Oh, yes, I know that all right,' Finch said breathlessly, desire to take this woman almost consuming him. But by admitting this, even to himself, he was exposing a weakness. All women were bitches, he reminded himself. 'Wants you for himself, the dirty old sod,' he snarled at Aggie.

'It's none of your business,' Aggie yelled. 'Just leave me alone.' She was angry, despite her intense fear, that Finch should think he could get away with this. She gave a terrific lunge forward that Finch wasn't prepared for and felt her skin tear beneath his fingers as she cried, 'Leave me be. If you touch me I shall scream the place down. Someone passing will hear me. You shan't get away with this.'

The punch took her unawares and she thought for a moment that she had been blinded. She felt the blood dripping from her nose and mouth, but the second punch knocked her against the entry wall. At the third, she fell to her knees and the fourth knocked her on her back on the ground, dazed and whimpering in pain and fear.

'Scream, will you?' Finch gloated, landing on

top of her. 'By the time I am finished with you, you will be in no fit state to even cry for your mother.'

He took hold of her coat and ripped it open. Aggie vaguely heard the buttons popping off, but her senses were reeling and she was drifting in and out of consciousness. Her dress and petticoats he ripped down to the waist so she lay bare, her breasts exposed, and these he pummelled mercilessly before yanking off her boots and ripping off her bloomers and her silk stockings so that she lay naked before him.

His hard, groping hands became more brutal than ever and Aggie was roused by the agony he was inflicting. She couldn't prevent the groan when he entered her, however, because it hurt her so badly. It seemed to last for ever and each thrust caused her to moan aloud, because the pain was excruciating. In the end, Finch put his hand over her bruised and bleeding mouth lest she be heard by someone in the street.

But at last it was over, and for a minute he lay on top of her, spent. Then he hissed in her ear, 'Tell Levingstone that this is the sort of thing that happens when a man annoys me. You hear me?'

Her eyes were closed and he smacked her on each cheek until she opened them and tried to focus. Finch grabbed her under the chin. 'I said, do you hear me?'

'Yes,' Aggie mumbled, indistinctly because of her damaged mouth. Finch was satisfied, though, and he got to his feet, fastened himself and melted away.

Tears seeped from Aggie's eyes and trickled down her cheeks, causing the grazes to sting afresh. She knew she had to get out of this place, but she was in too much pain to move. She lay back and her eyes closed almost by themselves as a great lethargy stole over her.

Eventually the cold roused her and she opened her eyes in a panic. She had no idea how long she had lain there, but she knew she had to get home and as quickly as possible. She was shivering, and tried to pull her coat around her to cover her nakedness. There were no buttons left to fasten it, so she left it hanging open as she tried lurching to her feet, only to keel over almost immediately. She tried again and again with the same result. In the end, she crawled down the entry on her hands and knees, the rough ground scoring into her bare feet, legs and the palms of her hands.

When she reached the street she once more tried to get to her feet, holding on to a wall for grim death. Every bit of Aggie ached and throbbed as she gingerly moved her feet. One step, then another and another. She was gasping with pain as she tried to push herself forward. Sometimes she stopped, for the street refused to stay still and she had to stay hugging the wall until it righted itself and she could go on again, for she knew she was very close to the club now. It was just a little further.

She was just yards from home when her head began to swim alarmingly. Desperate to reach safety, she took another step forward and staggered. Sudden blackness surrounded her and there was a roaring in her ears as the ground rose up to meet her.

Levingstone wasn't concerned at first, when he arrived home to find Aggie was not there, convinced that the maid, Jane, would know where she was. The two of them were great friends. When Mary had left to get married, Aggie had asked Levingstone to allow her to choose the next maid and so Jane Potter came into their lives. She was a trim girl with a mop of brown curls. She had a pleasant and open face with brown dancing eyes and a mouth shaped like a rosebud, which turned up slightly as if she were constantly amused about something. She and Aggie had hit it off straight away and Levingstone would often hear them laughing together over something. This would please him, for he knew Aggie sometimes felt a bit lonely.

But Jane couldn't help him that day. 'She was here until dinner time, that I do know, sir,' she said. 'But it was my afternoon off. I am not long in myself. Do you want me to check whether her coat and boots are missing?'

'No, I'll do that,' Levingstone said. A few moments later he had to face the fact that Aggie had disregarded his words and gone out unprotected, and had not returned.

'She must have gone to Lily's place, for she know no one else,' he told the maid. 'I'll go and fetch her home. Tell the coachman to get the carriage ready.'

The maid knew that for the master to go into that area at night, and in a carriage too, was madness. But her mother was always telling her not to try to understand the minds of those she worked for, just to do as she was told, so she said, 'Yes, sir, I'll go directly.'

The coachman wasn't that keen either, but as he told Jane, 'Orders is orders, but I'll tell you summat for nowt: if anything has happened to that lass, then our lives won't be worth living.'

Jane sighed. 'Don't I know it?' she said. 'Let's hope you find her safe and sound.'

Lily's house was in darkness. Levingstone wasn't really surprised, for most of the prostitutes would be working at that time, but then where the hell was Aggie? He knew where many of the women's pitches were, and so he set off to find Lily. He saw the girls standing in provocative poses in door-ways and on street corners, and while some watched him pass silently, others called out, their wares on offer. He barely heard them, though his eyes scanned each face. He was dismayed that Lily was nowhere to be seen in the roads she usually worked.

He didn't know what to do and he told the coachman to just drive around and he hoped he would come upon her. He didn't, but he did spy Susie a couple of streets away. He saw her eyes light up speculatively at the sight of a man in a carriage beckoning her over, until she realised who it was.

'Is anything up, Mr Levingstone?'

'Yes, I'm looking for Lily.'

'Oh, she's gone off with some geezer,' Susie said. 'I was just coming to work myself and saw her.'

'Right,' Levingstone said. 'Well, I really want to know if she saw Agnes today.'

'We all did. She came round.'

'Thank God!' Levingstone said. 'So where is she now?'

'No idea,' Susie said. 'After a bit I went up to get changed to come out, like, and when I come back down she was gone. Lily said she told her to take the tram home, but she said she'd walk – that it would do her good.'

'About how long ago was this?'

Susie shrugged. ''Bout two hours ago.'

'At the outside, it would take her forty minutes or so to walk home,' Levingstone said, 'and yet there is no sign of her.'

'Christ,' Susie breathed.

'I just don't know what possessed her to come round like that,' Levingstone said. 'I've told her I don't want her walking the streets on her own.'

'She was excited about her wedding and that,' Susie said. 'Who wouldn't be in her position? Like a dog with two tails, she was, and wanted someone to talk it over with, that was all. It's worrying, though, that she ain't come home.'

'Anything could have happened her,' Levingstone said.

'Have you thought of informing the rozzers?' Susie asked.

Levingstone avoided the police as much as possible, as did the prostitutes. 'No, not yet,' he said.

'You are going to, though, ain't you?' Susie insisted. 'You'll have to.'

'I know,' Levingstone sighed. 'I tell you, Susie, if anything terrible has happened to Aggie, I will no longer want to live.'

Susie caught sight in the lamplight of the devastated look on Levingstone's ashen face and thought wistfully: if just once in my whole life a man had loved me so wholeheartedly, I'd have thought I had died and gone to Heaven. What she said was, 'Come on, Mr Levingstone. Don't go thinking the worst straight off. I'd advise you to go home. She might be there by now and if she ain't, well, that's time enough to worry about it and get the coppers in.'

Levingstone knew that Susie spoke sense, and he couldn't think of anything else he could do anyway, so with the cries of the prostitutes ringing in his ears, the coachman thankfully turned the cab for home.

Bob Tyler, the club doorman, stepping outside for a walk and a smoke before the doors were opened officially, saw the crumpled shape on the ground as soon as he turned the corner. He threw his cigarette to the ground and hurried closer to see who it was. When he realised the person was Aggie, the shock was so great it was a wonder he was not rendered senseless on the ground alongside her.

She was naked with just a coat covering her shoulders, and he pulled it around her for modesty while he put his fingers on her neck to check for a pulse. He was mightily relieved when he found one, for he had never seen a person so badly battered.

For a moment Bob wasn't clear what to do. Should he fetch a woman from the house? But he would hesitate to leave Aggie in this state. Anyway, he reasoned, a woman would hardly be able to lift her. Surely it was better to get her indoors as soon as possible. When he put a hand on her, though, Aggie shrank from him, though her eyes remained closed.

'Don't you fret, Aggie,' he said softly. 'You're home now, and safe. We will have you nice and comfortable as soon as we can.' And he lifted her as gently as he could.

Bob wondered what Levingstone would do when he saw what some vicious thug or thugs had done to his Aggie. He knew he would not rest until he found out who her attacker was, and he wouldn't blame him if he tore the heart from the man, for every bit of poor Aggie was bruised or bleeding.

Anyone who could beat a defenceless woman so badly didn't deserve to live. He felt a wave of compassion flow over him at what Aggie must have suffered and how frightened she must have been.

'Mother of God, what has happened?' Jane asked as she opened the door to Bob's frantic knocking.

'We can go into what happened to her later,' Bob said. 'Run up and turn the bed down, there's a good girl.'

But when Bob laid her on the bed and said to Jane, 'Will I help you get her coat off?' Jane shook her head.

'You can't do that,' she said. 'You're a man.'

'I've just carried her in.'

'Even so,' Jane said firmly, 'it wouldn't be seemly. I'll get Cook to help me; you would be better employed fetching the doctor.'

'You don't think we should wait for Levingstone to get back?'

'No,' Jane said, 'I think that he would want us to use our common sense and do the best we can for Aggie. That girl needs a doctor, and quickly, I would say.'

Bob couldn't disagree with that, but Jane hadn't finished. 'And when you have done that, then wait outside for the master and try and prepare him in some way, if there is any way in the world to prepare anyone for such a sight.'

And Aggie was a sight. The fronts of her legs were lacerated, and her hands, and the rest of her was a mass of swelling bruises. The skin from her shoulders had been ripped off. Her bloated face, though, almost defied description. Both lips were split open and the blooded nose was a very odd shape. Around her eyes, blackened with bruising, was so swollen the eyes themselves were mere slits.

'God, the master will go off his head when he sees her like this,' Bessie said brokenly, weeping as she helped Jane bathe Aggie tenderly with warm water. 'He thinks the bloody world of her.'

'I know,' Jane said, dabbing at her eyes. 'It's lovely to see them together.'

'And now some bloody bastard tries to do her in.'

'Poor, poor Aggie.'

'Aye, and poor Mr Levingstone,' the cook said. 'He'll never manage without her.'

The doctor was already in the room and examining Aggie when Levingstone burst through the door, having been told what had happened by Bob. He approached the bed almost cautiously, and then the doctor had to steady him as he looked at his beloved Aggie's face. The doctor wasn't surprised, for he had been similarly stunned by the injuries. And then he saw the deep sorrow in Levingstone's eyes replaced by the white heat of anger, and knew he intended to find and kill the man who had done this.

The doctor bandaged Aggie's face so that only the slits of eyes were left uncovered. She didn't regain consciousness, nor did she move when the doctor bandaged the lacerations on her hands and legs.

'Believe me, I understand how deeply upset and shocked you were,' the doctor said to Levingstone as he closed up his bag. 'In all my professional life I have never seen a person beaten so badly. Any ideas who it was did this?'

'No,' Levingstone said through gritted teeth, 'but I intend to find out.'

'Are you informing the police?'

Levingstone shook his head. 'No police.'

'Alan, you might be the one in trouble if you deal with this yourself.'

'That is not your concern,' Levingstone snapped. 'You just look after Agnes.'

The doctor shrugged. Maybe he would feel the same if one of his own loved ones was attacked in such a vicious manner. And there was no doubt that Levingstone truly loved his Agnes. His love seemed to seep from the very pores of his skin.

Levingstone was actually in acute pain, affecting all of his body as if his nerve endings were exposed, and his suffering was apparent to everyone in the room.

Even the doctor knew it was no good telling Levingstone to pull himself together, as he had done to other worried men, for he was past hearing that. His haunted, saddened eyes worried him, and he would have been happier if Levingstone had agreed to accept some powders to calm him a little and enable him to sleep, but he would have none of it.

'Have you given some of that stuff to Agnes?' he asked.

'No,' the doctor said. 'She was found in that unconscious state. But don't worry about that, not just yet anyway. That's the mind closing down so that the body can heal. Probably the pain was too much to bear. She will come round in her own good time, I'm sure, and for the moment she needs full-time care.'

Levingstone gave a brief nod. 'I'll see to it.'

'He will never survive this if she doesn't make it,' the doctor remarked to Jane as she showed him out.

Jane was shocked. The thought that Aggie wouldn't pull through had not occurred to her. 'D'you think she might not?'

'Who knows? Maybe she hasn't the stamina or will to fight such an attack. She is a very sick young woman at the moment, I know that. I have done all I can and now the next twenty-four hours are crucial. Send for me, if you are worried – about either of them, mind. Levingstone won't have anything yet, but he might be glad of it before he is much older.'

'Yes, Doctor,' Jane said, and returned to the room of sadness and sorrow.

Levingstone couldn't seem to sit still. One minute he was ranting and raving, promising that he would find who did this to Aggie and tear them to shreds, beat them to pulp. The next minute he was kneeling by Aggie's bed and promising her the earth if she would just recover from this, pleading and beseeching her. The sight was so moving that both Jane and Bessie felt tears sting their eyes.

The knock at the door took them all by surprise and Jane went to answer it. She knew straight away who the woman was. She was a street woman, and Jane wrinkled her nose in disgust. She knew that Levingstone ran houses for the street women – everyone knew – but never in all the time she had worked in the house had one of those women come to the door, so she could sort of forget about that side of things.

She'd never associated with the girls in the club either, except Aggie, though she considered what they did a tad more respectable than trawling the streets looking for men.

Lily saw the lift of Jane's chin, but she was too worried about Aggie to take Jane to task.

'I've come about Aggie,' she said. 'My mate Susie told me she was missing, like, and I come straight up. Has she got home yet?'

'Yes,' said Jane. 'She's back, but . . .'

'What is it?' Lily asked urgently, seeing the look on Jane's face. 'Is she all right?'

'No,' Jane said. 'She's far from well. She has been beaten up.'

'Beaten up! Dear Christ! Do they know who by, what for, or anything?'

'No,' Jane said. 'Maybe you'd better speak to Mr Levingstone.'

'Oh, is he here?'

'Yes,' said Jane. 'What name shall I say?'

'Lily.'

Jane had never expected to see Mr Levingstone so pleased to hear that one of his street women was in his own private quarters. As soon as she mentioned the name, he was up from the chair, while she took his place by the bed.

'Oh, Lily,' he cried, almost in relief.

Lily knew she was looking at a man in torment, his face grey and drawn.

'Your maid that let me in said Aggie was beaten up,' she said.

'That's right.'

'It must have been as she was making her way from our place.'

'I suppose. I know so little.'

'I blame myself,' Lily said. 'I should have insisted she used the tram.'

'Can't everyone be wise after the event?' Levingstone said. 'You're not to blame for this, Lily.'

'Can I see her?'

'Of course. But she is unconscious and she is also heavily bandaged.'

Afterwards, Lily was glad that Levingstone had warned her about this and so she was able to hide her shock. Levingstone had dismissed Jane so there were just the two of them in the room. Lily said, 'God, that must have been some beating she took.'

'It was,' Levingstone said. 'The doctor said he had never seen anything like it. His voice says she'll recover, but his eyes say different.'

'Nonsense!' Lily declared emphatically. 'He doesn't know the girl like I do. She might look like a strip of wind, but she has got guts. She is a fighter. I didn't drag her from the jaws of death fifteen years ago just to let her succumb to this now.'

And then Alan remembered the little girl who had shared Lily's room for weeks after she had found her half dead and pregnant in the street. The little strip of a thing who had danced for him and taken away a piece of his heart. Now she had it all and he wouldn't, couldn't lose her. Life would have no meaning if he didn't have Agnes by his side to share it with him.

'Would you do it again?' he asked. 'Nurse Agnes, I mean. I will see that you don't lose by it. Agnes cannot be left. Jane can't do it all and I don't want to engage someone that Agnes won't know and might feel nervous of.'

Lily thought about it and knew she would like to do that. She thought a great deal of Aggie, and so she said to Levingstone, 'I will do it on one condition.'

'And what is that?'

'That you talk to that young girl who opened the door to me,' Lily said. 'Tell her I'm not some slug to be ground beneath her feet. I plainly saw the look of disgust in her eyes and the way her lip curled and the nose that she had lifted into the air. I wish to be treated civil and spoke to civil and then I dare say we shall get along well enough.'

Levingstone gave a grim little smile that didn't reach his eyes. 'Same old Lily. Don't believe in pulling your punches. I will see to it that no one, absolutely no one, looks down on you in this house and I will start putting that right straight away.'

'So be it,' Lily said. 'And between us we will get Aggie right. Just see if we don't.'

SIXTEEN

On the Tuesday after Easter, the postman told Biddy of the insurrection that had begun in the GPO in Dublin the previous day.

'Surely not,' Thomas John said, when Biddy told him after he and Tom and Joe came in for breakfast. 'They would not be so stupid as to take on the might of the British Army.'

'I don't know so much,' Joe said. 'There are plenty of stupid fellows in that Irish Republican Brotherhood, or whatever they call themselves these days. That's what people say, anyway. Some fellows were talking about it only last Saturday. They seem to think that England has her hands full fighting Germany.'

'Oh, aye,' Thomas John commented drily. 'So they expect them to wave good-naturedly when this motley bunch takes charge, do they? Jesus, Connolly and Pearse are leading them to be slaughtered, and what will they gain? Bugger all, that's what.'

'Who really cares about what is happening in Dublin anyway?' Joe said.

Thomas John rounded on him immediately. 'Well, you should, for a start,' he snapped. 'All of us should care what is happening in our own country. Someone of us must go to Buncrana and buy a paper.'

In the end, Tom went in on the old horse. When he got home, regardless of the jobs awaiting attention on the farm, Thomas John spread the paper on the table.

'Just a thousand of them,' he said in disgust. 'What on earth can they hope to achieve?'

'They have both sides of the Liffey covered, though,' Joe put in, impressed despite himself. 'And taken over the GPO in Sackville Street like the postman was after telling Mammy.'

'Hoisted up the tricolour flag too,' Tom said.

'And the other one,' Joe said, pointing to the picture. 'Paper says it has a green banner and has a golden harp and "Irish Republic" written on it.'

'It might be ill-timed, stupid or whatever you want to call it, Daddy,' Tom said, 'but isn't it a fine sight to see the tricolour flying in Ireland again?'

'Aye, it is, son,' Thomas John said rather sadly. 'And take joy in it, because it won't flutter there for long. It wouldn't hurt to get a paper each day and keep abreast of things.'

Britain's response was immediate. Thousands of troops arrived in Dublin. Field guns were installed and by Wednesday a gunship had sailed up the Liffey and begun shelling the place to bits. Dublin was burning. Few supplies were getting through as the rebels had control of the railway stations, and those shops not shelled or burned to the ground were closed up. The Dublin people were starving, and looting became commonplace, despite the army shooting anything that moved.

'What did they expect?' Thomas John said. 'It's their own people that these bloody rebels are hurting. And in the end it will be for nothing. You'll see.'

He was right. By Saturday it was all over and the rebels marched off to Kilmainham Gaol – apart from de Valera, who had an American passport and was taken to Richmond Barracks.

The speed of the execution of the leaders of the insurrection shocked the nation. De Valera's passport saved his life, but the others were given very brief court martials, the outcome a foregone conclusion. With no process of appeal, the first leaders, Pearse, Clark and MacDonagh, were shot in the stone breaker's yard in Kilmainham Gaol on 3 May, and the others in the following days. The flame of the mini rebellion, which had burned brightly for six days, had been successfully snuffed out.

In the middle of all this, Tom received an impassioned letter from Finn. He mentioned not one word about the uprising, which Tom had written and told him about. He was interested in matters much nearer his heart and said that the whole company was on the move. No one knew where and he was heartbroken at leaving behind his beloved Gabriella, the French girl he had met and he fancied himself in love with.

Tom wrote back in conciliatory tone, though he wasn't too worried about his brother's predicament. He was sure Finn would soon get over the loss of Gabriella. Someone else would no doubt take her place because it was likely that he would fall in love many times before wanting to settle down.

No one in the Levingstone household was the least bit interested in the insurrection in Ireland either, and even the events of the war just skimmed the surface. All their energies and their thoughts centred on Aggie's recovery. Thirty-six hours after the doctor had first examined her, he called again and said that as she had hung on so long, she probably would make it.

This was good news, there was no denying it, and yet Aggie still lay like a stone. The doctor couldn't say whether or not she would ever recover totally. Seeing Aggie comatose and unresponsive every day, Lily too had her doubts, so when Aggie opened her eyes the evening of the day she should have been married, Lily, sitting with her at the time, was terribly pleased, even though she shut them again almost immediately and there was no further movement.

'It is the very first sign of any improvement at all,' she told Levingstone later. 'I think we have to expect it to be a long time till Aggie recovers totally from this. Mind you, we will need to get some food into her soon. She was thin as a lath before this, and if she goes much longer without sustenance, she will be just skin and bone and not fit to fight anything.'

The doctor said much the same two days later when he called to take the bandages off and see how the skin was healing underneath. Lily was helping him when Aggie's eyes opened again, though there was no recognition and they were vacant as they watched the doctor almost fearfully.

'I have left her mouth exposed now,' he told Lily and Jane later. 'It is still a bit swollen and tender, but the loose teeth have bedded down nicely. Maybe in a day or so you can encourage her to try drinking through a straw.'

Lily and Jane agreed with that, but Aggie still slept most of the time, and it was two days before Lily was able to encourage her to take a little milk. That time when Aggie opened her eyes, the swelling was slightly reduced, and Lily saw immediately that the blank look had gone and that Aggie knew who she was.

'Hello, bab,' she said. 'Christ, you gave us a bleeding scare, you did.'

Aggie didn't answer. She wasn't sure she could, for though she had tried moving her tongue about her mouth, it hurt her too much to do more than that. Anyway, she didn't want to talk, didn't want to do anything, because it was too much effort and she was so tired.

Lily saw her eyes glazing over and closing. She said quickly, 'Will you take a wee drop of milk to please me?'

Aggie looked at Lily as if she hadn't heard right. 'I mean through a straw,' Lily explained. 'I'll help you.' And then, as there was no response, she urged, 'just a wee drop, half a cup.'

Aggie wasn't keen on taking anything, her mouth felt too sore, but to please Lily she allowed her to lift her head and place the straw between her swollen lips. The liquid made her mouth throb, and her head, lifted from the pillow, began to pound, but she saw that Lily was ridiculously pleased with the relatively small amount that she had taken.

Aggie wished that she could go to sleep and never wake up again. She was more afraid than she had ever been in her life, and when she was awake she relived every moment of that attack and knew she would never have the courage to go out alone again. How easy it would have been just to slip away in her sleep and never have a worry or care in the world any more.

But then Alan would be sitting by her bed, holding her bandaged hand in his own as if he were willing strength into her limbs, the love light shining in his deep brown eyes. His soft voice would soothe her soul and he urged her to get better soon, telling her over and over how much he loved her. Then she thought she couldn't leave this wonderful man, who loved her with an abiding love that she knew would last a lifetime.

And because of that love, he could never learn the name of her attacker, because that would be too dangerous for him. When she began to talk again, she knew she must bury Finch's name and never let it surface.

Later, Lily was to see that day as a break-through with Aggie, although that wasn't apparent at first. The next day, Aggie took her milk without protest and the day after that she mumbled, 'Thank you,' as Lily lowered her onto the pillow. It was husky and indistinct, but it was a start. Aggie even felt the muscles in her face move at the delighted look in Lily's face and knew she was trying to smile, a thing that she thought she would never do again.

'Oh God, Aggie, that is the best sound I have heard in bloody years,' Lily cried. 'I would like to hug you to bits. I know I can't, but you have made me one happy woman and you just wait till his nibs hears the news. He'll be like a pig in muck.'

Aggie knew that he would be, and not least because he wanted to know what she remembered of the attack and preferably who it was that had beaten her so badly. Not that he had said one word about it, but she had seen the speculative light in his eyes sometimes and knew what it meant.

He waited another week before asking Aggie anything. By then she was able to sit up in bed for her meals and the menu had become more varied as she was able to tolerate the spoon in her mouth, especially as she could hold the spoon herself, although the food still had to be puréed. She had also practised her speech and, though still not great at long conversations, her voice sounded more natural.

Aggie knew that Levingstone would ask her something that night. She had felt the unease in him even as he came into the room, as he did every night as soon as he came home. Then if someone was sitting with her they would leave, Levingstone would sit on the chair, take up one of her hands and kiss it gently.

Tonight, though, she read the trepidation in his eyes and she said gently, 'What is it?'

'What do you mean?'

'Something on your mind?' Aggie said.

'It's just . . . well, I don't want to upset you.'

Aggie took pity on him, but said, 'I can't help you.'

'You saw nothing?'

'I was jumped from behind, dragged into the entry. It was dark.'

She saw Levinstone's face redden with rage and his hands ball into fists as he said, 'I am so angry at what you have suffered at the hands of some bloody pervert. If I had the man before me this minute, then I would kill him with my bare hands.'

Aggie knew he meant every word. She put her hand on his arm and pleaded, 'Let's put this behind us.'

There was nothing else they could do, but Levingstone was frustrated that he was not able to avenge the damage, hurt and degradation inflicted on the woman he loved more than life itself.

As for Aggie, she was content to watch the early summer unfold in the dusty Birmingham streets from her bedroom window, where she felt safe. May gave way to June and she began to get up each day, but at first she tired easily, and Lily insisted that she rested every afternoon. She looked forward to her wedding, which had been rescheduled for late June, when she imagined she would be fully recovered.

Pleased though Lily was at Aggie's progress, she wished that they knew the identity of Aggie's assailant. She was more persistent in questioning Aggie about it than Levingstone because she had a concern for the women on the streets.

One evening in mid-June, she said to Aggie, 'Maybe you should have had the police in at the beginning. I know that Alan don't like them – well, who in their right mind does? – but it might have helped, like.'

'How d'you work that out?'

'They could maybe have found out who did it.'

'Even they need something to go on,' Aggie said.

'Yeah, but the coppers know the right questions to ask, don't they?' Lily said. 'And they know the people into this kind of thing.'

'It wouldn't matter what questions they asked, or what people they know,' Aggie protested. 'I couldn't identify anyone.'

'Yeah, but, Aggie, you can't have maniacs running the streets, attacking any they don't like the look of,' Lily cried. 'All the street women are jumpy now it's come out what happened to you. I saw a couple of them when I was out shopping yesterday and they told me some are afraid to go out. It's their living, Aggie. As they said, no woman is safe.'

Aggie thought of all the women in the house that Lily shared with. She imagined how fearful they would be. She also remembered Levingstone saying that Lily could keep her own counsel if she was asked to and she made a decision she would regret for the rest of her life. She took Lily's hands between her own and said, 'Stop this, Lily. I know for a fact that the man who attacked me will not go on to do it to anyone else.'

'How can you be so sure?'

'Lily, I want your solemn promise that you will not repeat one word of what I am going to tell you to a living soul,' Aggie said, 'though you can tell the girls that their areas are as safe as they ever were, that the attack was personal to me and me alone.'

'Oh God,' Lily said, and the blood drained from her face. 'It were Finch, weren't it?'

'Ssh,' Aggie cautioned. 'I don't want Jane to hear.'

Jane didn't hear, but someone else did. Levingstone had arrived home unexpectedly early. The hall was empty and he crossed to the bedroom quietly, intending to burst in and surprise both women. Instead, he was the one surprised. He stood with his hand on the doorknob and, as he listened he felt his body fill with fury.

'Are you off out again, sir, and you just in?' Jane said, coming into the hall as Levingstone was lifting his coat down from the hook.

'Yes, I have to go out,' Levingstone said. 'There is someone I have to see.'

Levingstone had thought that it might be Finch when he first looked on Aggie's bruised and battered body, but he had had no proof and, anyway, Aggie's survival was the first priority. And then, when he was able to ask her, she said she didn't know who it was. If it was Finch he knew she would be fully aware of it because she had had so many dealings with him over the years and she had always said there was a special smell emanating from him, a smell of evil and sheer wickedness.

He didn't blame Aggie for keeping the name from him because he knew she was afraid he would get either hurt or in trouble or both. He didn't care, nor did he care that Finch was twenty years his junior. Now he knew the name of the man who had raped and nearly killed the woman he loved above all others, he couldn't let him go unpunished.

He had no idea where Finch spent his time now and so he went first to Rogers. Rogers looked at the man before him dispassionately. He had never seen him in such a state before; he could almost see the barely controlled rage surging through him.

'Why do you think that I would know where Finch might be?' he asked mildly.

'Because the pair of you are as thick as thieves,' Levingstone said through gritted teeth. 'And I warn you, Rogers, I am in no mood to play games.'

Rogers shrugged. 'So who is playing games? What do you want him for, anyway?'

'That's my business.'

'Not if you want information it isn't.'

Levingstone had the urge to lift the smug Rogers from behind the desk and throttle the life out of him. 'All right then,' he yelled. 'I have just found out he is the man who raped and attacked my Agnes and left her for dead. He is not getting away with that.'

Rogers' sharp intake of breath was inaudible. He had asked Finch at the time and he had sworn he had nothing to do with it. Rogers wasn't totally surprised, though, for he knew Finch had a fixation for that little whore, so much so that he had asked Rogers to stop Levingstone marrying her.

Rogers had said he could push Levingstone only so far and that he didn't own the man body and soul. Finch hadn't liked it, but, God Almighty, what he had done to that girl was horrendous. He remembered how distraught Levingstone had been and the injuries he had described.

Maybe it was time that Finch was taught a lesson.

'Try the 501 Club,' he said.

Levingstone knew the 501 Club was on the edge of the Jewellery Quarter of the city, where there were lots of alleyways and courtyards, a hive of industry in the day but deserted at night. It would suit Levingstone's purpose very well. He wanted no witnesses to what he intended to do to Finch.

'If he isn't there, try Flamingos off Broad Street,' Rogers said. 'But try 501 first, and if I were you I would take someone with me.'

'I need no one else,' Levingstone said. 'It would be wrong to involve anyone, anyway. This business is between Finch and me.'

Rogers shrugged. 'Don't say I didn't warn you,' he said, and extended his hand. 'Good luck, and I hope you find him.'

Knowing the clubs would not be open yet, Levingstone made his way to the city centre and into a pub for a bite to eat and a few pints of beer to while away a few hours. Not too many beers, though; just enough to fuel his anger.

*　*　*

Aggie was concerned that Alan was so late coming home. Then Jane came to see her. She hadn't known that Levingstone had not seen Aggie when he was in earlier and so presumed that she knew all about the person he had to see that evening.

'As the master is going to be late, do you want to wait to eat with him, or have your meal earlier, Cook wants to know?' she asked.

'How do you know that the master is going to be late?' Aggie asked.

'Well, he said he had to see someone when he left.'

'When was this?'

'Just a while ago.'

Aggie stared at her incredulously. 'Jane, the master hasn't been in this evening yet.'

'Pardon me, ma'am, but he has,' Jane insisted.

'But he couldn't have,' Aggie cried. 'He would have come into the bedroom if he had come home. He always does.'

Jane looked troubled. 'Don't know about that, ma'am, and I didn't see him come in, because I was in the kitchen helping Cook, but when I come in again, it was to see the master lifting his coat off the hook. I assumed that he had already been to see you. Anyway, I made a comment about him leaving when he was just in, like, and he said he had to go out unexpectedly to see some-body.'

'But it's so odd.'

'It is, ma'am,' Jane agreed. 'Tell you something

else too, if you won't feel that I'm speaking out of turn, like.'

'Is it relevant?'

'Don't know, ma'am,' Jane said. 'It is just with his behaviour being out of character, like . . .'

'All right then. Go on.'

'It was just this, ma'am.' Jane said. 'The master's face was all red and he looked murderous. Yes, murderous is the only word for it. I mentioned it to Cook. Said I wouldn't like to be the person he was going to see, like.'

Jane didn't go on to say that in any normal household, they might assume the master and Aggie had had a few words – they didn't seem to have words like other couples – but none could deny that the master's behaviour was decidedly peculiar that evening.

Finch had been expecting a visit from Levingstone, but long before this, feeling sure that as soon as Aggie had recovered herself enough, she would tell him the name of the one who had made such a mess of her and raped her into the bargain. He had got himself a couple of heavies to go round with, so sure was he that Levingstone would show up. But as time had gone on, he had begun to think that maybe Aggie was going to say nothing and he had let down his guard a little and almost told the heavies they were no longer needed. How glad he was he hadn't done that when he saw Levingstone approaching him that night just as they neared the 501 Club.

Levingstone couldn't believe his luck at actually meeting Finch on the road. He thought he might spend all night trying to find him, but there he was before him, delivered into his hands as if it was meant. He didn't notice the heavies detach themselves from Finch's side and melt into the night, knowing instinctively that Levingstone would be unlikely to start on Finch in open view of any that might pass. His eyes were boring into Finch's and he strode up to him and said, 'I think you and I have got some unfinished business.'

Finch regarded him with a supercilious smile. 'Really? I don't think so.'

'I know so, but not here,' Levingstone said. 'There are too many people about. When I knock you to kingdom come I want as few witnesses as possible. I want to knock that smile off your face, for one thing.'

'Oh, do you?' Finch said, and added goadingly, 'and how is dear Agnes these days?'

Levingstone could no more have stopped the punch that he levelled at Finch after that remark than he could have stopped the sun from shining. There was such power and anger behind it that Finch was nearly rendered senseless. Levingstone took full advantage of his stunned state to take him by the scruff of the neck and drag him into one of the alleyways where he threw Finch to the ground, saying as he did so, 'You are not even worthy to speak her name.'

'What, speak the name of a common prostitute?'

Finch said. 'Or are your wits so addled with her that you forget the profession she is in?'

'I forget nothing,' Levingstone ground out, 'and that includes the state you left her in just a few weeks ago. I am going to teach you a lesson you will not forget in a hurry.'

Finch knew he could do it too because he was angry enough, despite the fact that Finch was a much younger man. When Levingstone had flown at him he had knocked him to the ground. Levingstone was unaware of the stealthy footfall behind him and the arm raised until it was too late. He turned and the karate chop caught him at the side of the neck. With a grunt, he fell forward unconscious.

The second heavy helped Finch to his feet and he looked at the unconscious heap on the floor. He adjusted his clothes, which had become disarranged in the tussle, and said, 'You know what to do. Deal with him.'

In the end, Aggie had her dinner with Lily at about nine o'clock in the apartment dining room, but she was too worried to feel hungry and just pushed the food around her plate.

'Try something, Aggie,' Lily urged.

'I can't,' Aggie said. 'What can have happened to him?'

'Nine o'clock isn't late,' Lily pointed out.

'It is for Alan,' Aggie said. 'The club has been open for an hour already, and no one knows about this strange meeting he had because Bob Tyler came up to see if everything was all right when Alan hadn't put in an appearance.'

'Surely they can run the place without him for the one night?'

'Of course they can, but you are missing the point,' Aggie said. 'Why isn't he here?'

No one could answer that question, however. The minutes ticked into hours and still there was no sign of Levingstone. Twice more Bob Tyler came up, and eventually he realised that the club would have to do without Levingstone that night.

Aggie became so agitated in the end that Lily was all for fetching the doctor, but she said she would refuse to see him, that it was Alan she wanted to see. Eventually, she was so weary that she lay on the bed in all her clothes except for her shoes, as she had refused point-blank to get undressed, and fell into a doze. Lily didn't undress either, but resumed her old place on the chair by Aggie's bed and closed her eyes.

The pounding on the door roused her. As Bob and Jane had gone to bed it was Lily who answered the door, glancing at the clock in the hall as she did so.

'Four o'clock,' she said to herself. 'Almighty God, what now?'

When she saw the policeman outside she wasn't unduly surprised. Normal mortals didn't nearly knock doors down at four in the morning, but still she asked, 'Can I help you?'

'I have news about a Mr Alan Levingstone.'

'Bad news?' Lily asked, and when he nodded her stomach gave a lurch. 'You had best come upstairs and speak to his fiancée.' Then once inside the apartment she said, 'If you wait in the sitting room for a moment, I will see if she is awake.'

Aggie was more than awake. She was up and putting on her shoes. 'It's a policeman,' Lily said. 'He wants to speak to you.'

Aggie nodded as if she wasn't surprised, though her mouth was so dry she could hardly swallow. When she entered the room she flew at the policeman crying, 'It's Alan, isn't it? Something has happened to Alan.'

The young policeman recognised Aggie from the photograph found in Levingstone's jacket pocket. He said, 'Yes, miss, I am afraid it has. Mr Levingstone was found in an alleyway in the Jewellery Quarter.'

'Is he badly hurt?'

'I'm sorry, miss,' the policeman said. 'I should have said Mr Levingstone's body. I am afraid that he is dead.'

The primeval scream that came from deep within Aggie woke Jane and Bessie, and sent them scurrying from their beds to see Aggie on the floor in a dead faint. Lily was tending her, although tears ran down her own face, while she instructed the young and very nervous-looking policeman to fetch the doctor for Aggie, and quickly.

'What's happened?' breathed Jane in an awed whisper.

324

Lily was so distressed, she could barely get the words out, and then Jane and Bessie wept too. And that is how the doctor found them: one unconscious on the floor and the other three sodden with weeping.

SEVENTEEN

The doctor sedated Aggie because, although she had come round after the faint, she was so over-wrought he was afraid that she was going to lose her mind.

'This is all connected, isn't it?' he said to Lily, later. 'Levingstone should have gone for the police about Aggie in the first place and let them deal with it.'

'I wanted him to,' Lily said, 'but Aggie claimed then that she didn't know who did beat her up, that it was too dark and that. You know she did because she told you the same. Anyroad, Levingstone weren't keen on getting the police in either, because they snoop around and ask questions. When a person is in this line of business, it is better to involve the police as little as possible.'

'Aggie was lying, though, wasn't she?' the doctor said. 'She did know who her assailant was.'

Lily nodded. 'She told me who it was and the reason she said nothing to Levingstone was to prevent him doing just what he did: go after him, and his death is the result. Point is, whether we wanted to involve the police or not, this time it has been taken out of our hands. But,' she went on, 'doesn't matter who investigates this, the man concerned will get away with it because he won't have done the dirty on Levingstone himself. He will be high and dry with a cast-iron alibi, I bet.'

'Couldn't Aggie go to the police now?' the doctor asked. 'Tell them what the man did to her?'

'D'you think she is up to coping with that?'

The doctor remembered the frail woman he had sedated for her own good. He knew how close she was to breaking point and he shook his head. 'No,' he said, 'you are right, she would never cope with that.'

'And if she could,' Lily went on, 'd'you think the police would take the word of a prostitute, for that's what she was, especially as the man responsible for her attack is influential and powerful? Aggie could easily find that she was the one banged up. But just say by some miraculous chance they did believe her, she'd know as well as I do that if she tried to point the finger, her life wouldn't be worth tuppence. She hasn't even got the partial protection of Levingstone any more. In fact I really don't know what in God's name she is going to do after all this.'

'What are *you* going to do?' the doctor asked.

Lily sighed. 'Go back on the streets, I suppose,' she said. 'It is all I know. But as I get older it gets harder to get the punters. I did hope that that part of my life was over. Levingstone almost said as much, and I think he intended keeping me on here, but both Aggie and me are completely scuppered by this.'

'You could always work in one of the munitions factories,' the doctor said. 'In fact you both could. The money is good, and they are so desperate for any help they can get, they don't ask that many awkward questions or even need references at some places.'

Lily thought about the alternative: going out night after night, regardless of the weather. She realised that she had gone soft, living in Levingstone's place, and she was beginning to feel her age. The more time went on, the less she wanted to go back to her old life.

'It's dangerous work,' the doctor went on, 'I'll not deny it, and normally I wouldn't be recommending it at all, but . . .'

'It's a sight less dangerous than here, believe me, Doc,' Lily said. 'The lesser of two evils, I'd say. Jane told me that her sister had gone into it and she said she was earning two pounds and ten shillings a week. I could save a good bit on that sort of money; salt it away, like, for when the war is over. Have a bit of a nest egg for the first time in my bleeding life.'

'So you will think about it?'

Lily nodded. 'I will, and it will be a solution of sorts for Aggie, and all. I'll talk her into it. Not yet, 'cos she ain't ready, but as soon as I can.'

*   *   *

Rogers, who felt guilty that he hadn't done anything to stop Levingstone going for Finch that night, called to see them to offer his condolences, but Aggie was so heavily sedated that only Lily was in a fit state to see him. When he offered to organise and pay for the funeral, Lily was surprised. Rogers wasn't known for his acts of charity, but she accepted gratefully.

'Terrible business,' he said. 'Kicked to death was the way I heard it.'

Lily blinked back tears. 'He was, and left in a pool of blood. Christ, he dain't deserve to die, but to die like that . . . It were just plain wicked, that's what it was. The coppers asked me to go and identify the body. I mean, Aggie couldn't go. The doctor has her heavily sedated 'cos he says her mind can't cope with it yet. By Christ, was I glad she was spared that, because the state of him . . . well, it was enough to turn anyone's brain. I mean, I had to identify him by the clothes he had on and the gold wristwatch he always wore.'

She looked at Rogers and continued, 'I have known Levingstone all my bleeding life. We grew up in the same street and I am going to miss him a great deal, but I suppose you will want us out of here as soon as possible?'

'Yeah. Well, I'm not going to throw you out or anything, but as soon as the funeral is over I am going to put this place on the market,' Rogers said.

Lily's eyes opened wide in surprise and Rogers smiled grimly. 'Been thinking about it for a few weeks now, and this business has knocked me for six.'

'So what will happen to all the girls?'

'Well, I hope to sell it as a going concern,' Rogers said, 'so the girls will probably be all right, but Aggie – well, she was in a special position, wasn't she?'

'Yeah,' Lily said. 'In just under a week she would have been Levingstone's wife.'

'I know,' Rogers said in a conciliatory tone. 'Terrible business.'

'Don't concern yourself about us,' Lily said. 'I have some irons of my own in the fire. I will see to Aggie and the pair of us will be out of here as soon as possible. I am very grateful for you organising and paying for the funeral, and I know that Aggie will be when she is more herself.'

'Not at all,' Rogers said. 'It is the very least I can do.' It also went some way to salving his conscience because he knew in his heart of hearts that he could probably have prevented Alan Levingstone's death. No need, though, to share that knowledge with anyone else.

The next day, Lily tried to tell Aggie about the funeral arrangements. She had got out of bed, but was moving around like a zombie. Since the policeman's visit she had eaten nothing, but when Lily offered to make her a tincture she had shaken her head.

Since the announcement of her engagement, Aggie had seriously cut down on the amount of

gin and opium she had been taking. She knew that
Levingstone had been pleased about this because
she was well aware how much he hated seeing her
getting so drunk and drugged every night of the
week. When he praised her cutting back so much
and so thoroughly, she had kissed him and assured
him that she didn't need to blot anything out since
she was off limits to all the punters. Lily was almost
as pleased as Levingstone, because she had been
worried at the amount that Aggie had been taking,
and guilty too because she had not only started
her on the opium and gin, but encouraged her to
keep taking it.

Lily had reviewed her own situation, cut down
her intake too, and had stopped altogether when
she had moved into Levingstone's place to nurse
Aggie. It was no good getting drugged up or drunk
and expecting to nurse someone effectively, especially when that person was as sick as Aggie was.
Lily had had a few uncomfortable days, when she
would have the shakes and sweat profusely, and
in the early days she often felt sick and was unable
to sleep, but all that had gone now.

'I don't want to start taking drugs and booze
any more,' Aggie told Lily now. 'A lot of the time
when I did that before, I wasn't aware of much
some days and yet I had the abiding love of a
good, kind man. I don't think the aching loss will
ever go away completely. His funeral is the last
service I will be able to do for him and I want to
be in full control of myself. I will not besmirch

Alan's memory by doing the very thing he disapproved of.'

'I am that proud of you, Aggie,' Lily said, putting her arms around Aggie's shoulders. She expected tears but there were none, and Lily realised with a start that Aggie hadn't cried at all, not once. It was as if she were frozen inside.

The following day, the vegetables were delivered to the kitchen. Jane used the sheets of newspaper that lined the box to make up the fire in the sitting room. It was as she left the room to get wood that Aggie crossed to the hearth. She would be glad of the fire because she felt cold inside, yet she knew it wasn't the sort of cold that any fire would reach. She had always liked to see a cheering fire in the grate, but she doubted anything would cheer her at the moment, for she felt full of misery and despair.

It was as she gazed at the screwed-up newspaper that she caught sight of Alan's name. She withdrew the sheet of paper from the grate and smoothed it out. She had not seen a paper – she imagined that they had not let her see one – but this paper was a few days old and the headline screamed: 'Club Manager Kicked to Death in Alleyway'.

Aggie took the paper into the bedroom and there she read of the gruesome end of the man she had loved. She knew the fear and desperation he would have felt, and the agony he would have suffered at the merciless attack until he died in a pool of blood. She felt as if a heavy weight was pushing down on her and a tight band of pain was encircling her waist so that she cried out like an animal in deep distress, and great gulping sobs racked her body as the tears spurted from her eyes.

Lily came running, and though she enfolded Aggie in her arms, and rocked her gently, she thanked God that Aggie had shed those much-needed tears, while Aggie felt as if she were breaking up inside, as though her heart was shattering into a million pieces.

Much, much later, when the tears were spent at last and Aggie was limp and lifeless, Lily tucked her into bed and she slept long and deeply.

'She'll do all right now,' Lily remarked to Jane and Bessie.

'What d'you mean?' asked Jane.

'She did what she had to do, and that was mourn and grieve for her man,' Lily said. 'She will always miss him and a piece of her heart will be with him for ever, but she will survive this and eventually will be able to look forward again.'

After Aggie had cried for the first time, she seemed unable to stop. It was as if she had opened the floodgates. By the day of the funeral her eyes were red-rimmed and encircled with black. She was glad her hat had a veil attached that would hide her white, ravaged face.

As Aggie and Lily were leaving the apartment

to get into the funeral carriage Rogers had ordered for them, Aggie said fiercely, 'Finch should be the one being laid in a hole in the earth. I would dance on his grave.'

'And you wouldn't be on your own,' Lily said.

'There will never be another like Alan,' Aggie said. 'I feel sort of lost. He has been so much part of my life for fifteen years.'

'I know that too, and after the funeral is over, you and I must have a talk about where we will go from here.'

'Lily, I don't think I want to go on.'

'What sort of talk is that?' Lily said sharply. 'You are a young woman.'

'Don't say I have my life before me or I will laugh, 'Aggie said. 'Because my life from now on will be spent on the streets and I would rather die than have that prospect dangled before me.'

'It won't necessarily be that sort of life, though,' Lily said. 'I have got some ideas up my sleeve.'

'What d'you mean?'

'Not now,' Lily said. 'There's not time.'

It was as they were in the carriage, with Witton Parish Church in view, that Aggie suddenly grabbed Lily's arm and said, 'If Finch is there I will go for him. I will not be able to help myself.'

'He won't be,' Lily said confidently. 'He can't risk being linked in any way.'

Lily was right, Finch was not there, but so many others were, the church was packed solid. Aggie felt proud that she had been associated with such a wonderful man to whom so many wanted to pay their last respects, and most looked with sympathy at her as she entered the church.

That sympathy sustained her during the service, and kept her upright and on her feet when she really wanted to sink to the floor and let the world go on without her. The worst was at the grave-side, thronged with people to hear the last prayers said, and she had to step forward in front of them and throw the first clods of earth onto the mahogany coffin.

Afterwards, at the reception, her hand was shaken many times by people who told her what a great man Alan was. She didn't need telling really, though it soothed her a little, but did nothing to lift the huge weight of sadness that seemed lodged inside her.

Lily was at her side, as she had been most of the time, and three hours later Aggie was so weary she sighed and said, 'Oh, Lily, I know that this is very fine and all, and it was kind of Mr Rogers and everything, but I wish it was all over now.'

'And me,' Lily said. 'But it won't be long, you'll see. Now the food is nearly eaten, some have already dwindled off. I'm sure that is what some people attend funerals for, to get a good feed, because they certainly pay more attention to that than to anything or anyone else.'

Lily was right, and soon the party broke up and people went their separate ways. Lily and Aggie were able to leave.

'I wonder,' Aggie said as she went into the flat that day, 'how long I will be able to consider this place home.'

'Not long,' Lily said. 'Rogers is selling the club, and then it might be all change for a lot of people.'

'And where will that leave us?' Aggie asked. 'As if I don't know.'

'That is what I wanted to talk to you about,' Lily said, 'but are you ready for it today, after the funeral and all?'

'Lily,' Aggie said earnestly, 'if you have a plan to keep me from selling my body on the streets of Birmingham, then I am always willing to listen.'

'All right,' Lily began. 'Why don't the two of us go into the munitions?'

Aggie stared at her. 'Lily, I know nothing about making guns and things like that.'

'I should imagine most of the people in the factories was the same once,' Lily said. 'And what they can learn we could learn just as easily. The doctor says they are crying out for people.'

'The doctor?' Aggie repeated in surprise. 'Don't say he was all for it as well? I've heard they can be dangerous places to work.'

Lily nodded. 'He agreed they was. But he said it was our chance to get out of this. I think he would like to see us respectable.'

'I dearly wish I was,' Aggie said.

'So do I, bab, in my heart of hearts,' Lily admitted. 'And, anyroad, I am too old now for the streets, so how about it?'

'What about references?'

'The doctor doesn't think they are too fussy,' Lily said. 'You can say you are newly arrived from Ireland after your parents died or summat, and come to stay with me, your auntie, and that we both want to register for war work. Anyroad, if there is a problem, Jane said her sister will vouch for us.'

'Does Jane's sister work in one of these places then?'

'Yeah, she works in a place called Kynoch's and gets two pounds ten shillings, or even three pounds sometimes, if she puts in a bit of overtime.'

'It's good money.'

'Not half,' Lily agreed. 'And that ain't all, bab.'

'Oh, come on. What else have you thought up to frighten the life out of me?'

'I ain't trying to frighten the life out of you, I am trying to protect you,' Lily protested. 'Think on this: however dangerous munitions work is, does it measure up to you meeting up with Finch one dark night? Think what the bloody hell he could do to you the next time.'

Aggie shuddered. 'Don't.'

'You need to be kept off the streets and preferably out of this area,' Lily said. 'The place where Jane's sister works is in an area called Witton, the same place we was at today, and we could get lodgings and live near at hand. Every second person there is offering rooms to let, apparently. That way, while the war lasts, you would be totally safe from Finch.'

'You don't know how happy that makes me feel,' Aggie said. 'Can we take a dander up to see the place tomorrow?'

'I don't mind,' Lily said, 'but we'll have to go on the tram. Thought you was scared stiff of them?'

'I am nervous,' Aggie admitted. 'But I can conquer that. What I have no control over is my fear of Finch. In fact I am bloody terrified of meeting up with him again. How does a short tram ride compare to that?'

'Huh, well, I know which I'd rather,' Lily said. 'All right, you're on, bab. The pair of us will go up tomorrow.'

They found the Kynoch works on Witton Road, not far from the cemetery, just as Jane had described it to them. Built of brick, it was a low building with huge metal gates at the front.

'Shall we go for it, girl?' Lily asked. 'Go right up this minute and ask if they have any jobs?'

'What have we got to lose?' Aggie said.

'Nothing at all,' Lily replied determinedly, and she approached the gates with a purposeful air. Immediately a man came out of the little hut at the side of the gate and asked them to state their business.

'We're both after jobs,' Lily said. 'Any going, is there?'

'I should think so,' the man sad. 'Usually is.

You'll have to speak to a Mr Witchell. Decent enough fellow.' He unlocked the gate with a large set of keys as he spoke, swung it open for them to enter and locked and bolted it carefully once they were inside. Then he led the way down the alley alongside the factory to a building at the back, and ushered them inside to a small waiting area with wooden chairs around the bare brown walls. 'Wait here,' the man said. 'I'll see if Mr Witchell is free.'

Witchell was not only free, but he seemed pleased to see them, and when he looked at the forms they both filled in he was surprised that they were both single, especially the younger and very beautiful one.

It was to Aggie that he spoke when he said, 'We employ a lot of young women here and we often have them no sooner trained than they get married and leave us. I know that you are wearing no ring, Miss Sullivan, but is there some young man in the offing?'

'No,' Aggie said, proud that her voice held not a tremor of emotion. 'I was engaged and my fiancé was killed. It was then I decided to do something for the war effort.'

From this Mr Witchell thought that Aggie's fiancé had been killed in the trenches and Aggie did not put him right. 'Dear, dear!' he said. 'This terrible war, such heartache and tragedy at every turn. My greatest sympathy to you, Miss Sullivan, and how commendable, my dear, that you should offer your services for war work in this way.'

Aggie wondered how Mr Witchell would behave if she were to blurt out the truth. Very differently, she knew, and she felt guilty at taking his condolence at her loss.

Lily, knowing Aggie and how her mind worked a sight better than their prospective boss, saw her flushed face and put in quickly, before he could ask her anything else, 'As for me, I thought it was about time I did my bit too. After all, we have to support our boys. Can't fight nobody without bullets and guns, can they?'

Mr Witchell smiled at Lily, but she had achieved her aim and got his attention from Aggie so she had a minute to compose herself. Afterwards, walking towards the tram stop, she said to Lily, 'When I said that about Alan, he presumed—'

'Yeah, he presumed,' Aggie said. 'That was his problem. You never said a word of a lie, and what's it matter to him how Alan died? We will work as hard as the rest. You do want this job, don't you?'

'Of course I do.'

'Well, then, keep your lip buttoned,' Lily said sharply. 'It's a bloody jungle out there. Survival of the fittest and all that. Still, no harm done in the end, and we start on Monday morning prompt at half-past seven. Did you see Mr Witchell's face when we said we could be ready for Monday morning? He couldn't believe it.'

'We hadn't sorted out lodgings then either,' Aggie said.

'No,' Lily said. 'Nice of Mr Witchell to recommend Mrs Palmer's in Albert Road to us.'

They had gone straight down after leaving Kynoch's. The house was neat and well kept. Both Aggie and Lily had been drawn to the woman who opened the door to them, for she had an open, friendly face. She also had a mop of natural brown curls that they were to find she was always complaining about, deep brown eyes, with gorgeously long black lashes, and her cheeks were just dusted with pink. Her smile lit up her face when they explained why they were there. She introduced herself as Polly Palmer, bade them come in, and they stepped into the room.

Two children were playing on the rug by the door. They got up when they saw they had visitors and approached their mother, but while the boy appraised both women openly, his younger sister hid behind her mother's skirts and put a finger in her mouth. Aggie saw immediately that they had taken their looks from their mother. For the first fifteen years of her life she had been surrounded by siblings and she was drawn to these beautiful children of Polly's, and so she smiled and said, 'Hello.'

The boy gave a cheeky grin in return and then, because his mother had told him that they were having lodgers, and he had never seen these two women before, he said, 'You coming to live in our house?'

'Charlie, don't be rude,' Polly said sharply.

'I ain't being rude,' the boy said indignantly. 'I'm just asking.'

'They haven't even seen their rooms yet, so how can they say?'

'Would you mind if we did live here?' Aggie asked, and the boy shook his head. 'No,' he said. 'I get to sleep in the attic and it's smashing. It has got a window in the ceiling. I'd hate it if I had to sleep with our mom like Clara.'

Aggie bent down and said to the little girl trying to bury herself further into her mother's skirts, 'Will you mind us coming to live in your house, Clara?'

She was a lovely child, Aggie thought. Her untamed curls framed her pretty face and her eyes looked enormous. She didn't take her finger out of her mouth, but she shook her head and gave a shy little smile.

'I'll show you to your rooms,' Polly said, and led the way upstairs with the children bringing up the rear. Aggie and Lily had a room each. The sheets were crisp and clean, and there were plenty of blankets and bright bedspreads. Oilcloth covered the floor but there was a rag rug beside each bed, and they each had a chest of drawers and a wardrobe too.

They were much better lodgings than they had anticipated and both women were delighted with them.

'We'll take them and gladly,' Lily said. 'I think I can speak for Aggie as well, for I see by her face that she is as pleased as me.'

'Oh, I am,' Aggie said. 'These are wonderful rooms.'

'Yours used to be my room,' Charlie told Aggie. 'Only Mom cleaned it up for you, like.'

'Cleaned it up!' Polly repeated. 'I'll say I cleaned it up. It was like a tidal wave had gone through it.'

Aggie laughed. 'Well you did a good job of it, anyway. What rent are you asking?'

'Does five shillings each sound all right to you?' Polly asked. 'You would have breakfast and an evening meal for that too.'

'I think that is very generous,' Lily said.

'Are you sure that that is enough?' Aggie asked.

'Quite sure. And now if that is settled maybe we should go downstairs to have a cup of tea to seal the bargain.'

It was as Aggie was following Polly and Lily down the stairs that she felt her hand grasped gently and, turning round, she saw Clara's little hand in hers and a tentative smile playing around her mouth. Aggie felt her heart turn over. She held Clara's hand a little tighter as she remembered her earlier life with her brothers and sister, which had been ripped from her.

Polly said she didn't mind if they wanted to push the two beds into the one room and make the other room into a sitting room that they could use in the evenings. She also told them about her husband away at the Front, and how she worried about him and missed him because they had never been apart before.

Both Aggie and Lily heard the loneliness in her voice so Aggie was pleased when Lily said, 'If it's all the same to you we'll leave things as they are. I think I would rather stay down here in the evening, that is if you don't mind, of course.'

They saw the relief in Polly's face and weren't surprised when she said, 'Oh, I don't mind. Not in the slightest. Tell you the truth, I would be glad of the company.'

'Oh, I think we've fallen on our feet right and proper this time,' Aggie said as the tram rattled along the rails. 'They're so lovely, both Polly and her children.'

'Yeah,' Lily agreed. 'About time summat went right for us, I think. And I watched you with them kids, Aggie. It's a bleeding shame you ain't got a man of your own and a houseful of nippers 'cos you're a natural.'

'I don't think I could ever have children, Lily,' Aggie told her. 'Look how many men I have slept with over the years, and there has never been a sign. Most of the girls had to get themselves seen to – and more than once, some of them – but I never did. I always thought that when I miscarried that time I damaged something. I didn't bother about it then. It was better that I couldn't get pregnant. It was when I thought I would be marrying Alan that I thought of it again.'

'You might be right about damaging yourself,' Lily said. 'But I doubt Alan Levingstone would have wanted kids at his age, anyroad.'

'Maybe not,' Aggie said. 'But I bet he would have given me children if I had wanted them badly enough, because Alan loved me with every shred of his being.'

'You're right there, girl, anyroad,' Lily said. 'Some silly bugger once said it was better to have loved and lost than never to have loved at all. Not so sure of that myself. No time to ponder it now, though, 'cos this is our stop and we have packing-up to do.'

'Don't worry,' said Aggie with a grimace. 'I can pack up the last fifteen years of my life in no time at all.'

They were ready to go by Sunday morning, but weren't due at the Palmers' until the afternoon. Lily suggested they buy a paper and see what was going on in this war that they soon would be making detonators for. Working and living in the club, Aggie had been shielded from much of it. She had no idea of the extreme poverty of many people and how the sight of the telegraph boy struck terror into many a heart. Lily, living where she had been, knew a little more, but neither woman had the least idea of the battles raging and the condition of the average soldier's life in the trenches.

However, on Saturday, 1 July, the Battle of the

Somme began in France. Newsreel cameramen and photographers were allowed on the battlefield for the first time, thereby bringing the horror of it into people's homes in a way that had never been done before.

Aggie and Lily spread the papers out before them and even with the grainy newsprint pictures the brutal bloodbath was easy to see. They saw the limbs of half-submerged and very dead soldiers, peeping through the slurry and mud of the trenches, men lying on the blood-slimed battlefield with their legs shot from under them, or impaled on wire, and soldiers continuing to run towards their enemies' guns over the bodies and bits of bodies of those who hadn't made it.

'God, it's awful,' Aggie said. 'The younger officers who came to the club were all damaged in some way. One had a tremor that he couldn't control and he felt so embarrassed about it, as if it betrayed some weakness in him. And there were some with red-rimmed, bloodshot eyes that they were afraid to shut, for they said if they did they relived the terrible carnage all over again. Most of them were unable to share the memories with anyone, partly because they had been told not to worry the people back home and partly because what was happening was so shocking. Yet their pain and the horror of it all were written over many of the faces. Most drank too much, of course.'

'And who can blame them?' Lily said, shaking

the paper angrily. 'It says here twenty-one thousand allied soldiers were killed at the Battle of the Somme in the first hour.'

'Dear God, such numbers don't bear thinking about,' Aggie said aghast. 'How can you even visualise such numbers?'

'All we can be grateful for is that none of our loved ones are caught up in all this,' Lily comforted her.

'You can say that again.' Aggie sighed with relief, little knowing that her youngest and headstrong brother, Finn, had been one of the Somme's first casualties and his body left in a foreign field.

EIGHTEEN

It was Sunday, 9th July 1916, and the three Sullivan men were just finishing the milking when Tom, glancing up through the open door of the byre, saw a boy in a uniform of sorts clatter across the cobblestones on a bicycle. He saw him throw this down before the cottage and take a telegram from the bag around his shoulders.

None of the Sullivans had ever received a telegram, but Tom remembered Joe had said that was how the army informed the relatives if a man was missing or dead. His mouth suddenly felt very dry.

He looked back into the byre, where his father and brother were tipping milk into the churns, and called out, 'There's a boy here with—'

He got no further, for they all heard Biddy give a sharp cry of distress. Tom, bursting on to the yard, saw the boy standing apprehensively before the open cottage door. He looked thankful to see Tom, and he said, 'She sort of fell over when I gave her the telegram.'

'It's all right,' Tom assured him. 'I will see to her now.'

As the relieved boy mounted his bike, Tom turned to his mother. She was kneeling on the floor, keening in deep distress, the tears pouring from her eyes and a crumpled buff telegram clutched to her breast. His father and Joe were at his heels.

'What is it?' Thomas John cried, but in his heart of hearts he knew.

Tom didn't answer his father, but instead lifted his mother to her feet and, putting his arms around her, led her to one of the easy chairs pulled up before the fire, saying, 'Come on, Mammy, don't take on like this.'

He was moved by the bleak expression in his mother's dark eyes. 'Oh, Tom,' she said, and handed him the telegram.

He scanned it quickly. 'It's Finn,' he said to his father and Joe, standing staring at him.

'Well, of course it's Finn,' Thomas John snapped. 'I haven't a rake of sons in the British Army. Is he dead?'

Tom nodded and Thomas John felt a deep and intense pain inside him at the loss of his youngest son. 'Ah God,' he cried. 'What a tragic waste of a young life.'

Biddy began crying afresh and Tom busied himself making tea so that none would see his own wet cheeks. As the eldest he remembered Finn from the day that he was born. He recalled the cheeky grin he had and how funny he had been as a wee boy. He would trail after him all the time, and plague him to death with questions. What he wouldn't give to hear those same questions now, he thought as he handed out tea, noting that Thomas John's eyes were glittery with unshed tears and even Joe's were brighter than normal.

No one went to Mass that Sunday, but they sat on and talked of Finn, their memories punctuated with Biddy's sobs. 'I will have nothing of his,' Biddy said suddenly, 'not even a grave to tend.'

'Well, that's the way of it in wartime,' Thomas John said brusquely. 'And you won't be alone either. There will be many families, both sides of the Irish Sea, mourning the loss of a loved one this day, I'm thinking.'

'Maybe, but that doesn't help me.'

'Nothing will help,' Thomas John said. 'Nothing but time.'

In the end, because Biddy was incapable, Tom and Joe made a stab at making some breakfast for them all, though his mother could eat none of it and even Tom had little appetite.

Eventually, he could stand the atmosphere no longer. When Joe saw him cross the floor and lift his jacket from the hook behind the door, he said, 'Where you off to?'

Tom shrugged. 'Nowhere in particular. I just want to try and walk some of the sadness out of me.'

'Do you want company?'

'Aye, come along with me if you want to.'

For a while the two brothers walked in silence, and then Joe said, 'It's unbelievable really, isn't it? Finn seemed so alive, had more about him than either you or me.' He gave a sad little smile. 'D'you know what the little fool said to me when I told him to be careful?' And without waiting for a reply he continued, 'He said not to worry about him. That he would catch the bullets in his teeth and spit them back.'

'Aye,' commented Tom wryly. 'Maybe he found that more difficult to do than he anticipated.'

'Obviously.'

'I mean, when a person joins the army, especially if the country is at war at the time, you take on board the risks, or you think you do. It was the first thing that crossed my mind that day in Buncrana when he stepped forward to answer the recruiting officer's call. Inside, though, you hope and pray that your loved ones will come home safe and sound.'

'Aye,' Joe said. 'And now we know that that is not going to happen I think Nuala should be told. Course, in the normal way of things she would have been at home on Sundays with the rest of us, if her employers hadn't asked her to go in as a favour.'

'She'll know something is amiss with none of us at Mass today,' Tom said.

'She is sure to,' Joe agreed. 'And I want to tell her about Finn before the news leaks out and someone else tells her.'

'You're right,' Tom said. 'Shall we go up to the house now, d'you think?'

'Aye,' Joe said. 'Daddy won't want to go today and leave Mammy on her own. She is powerful upset, all right.'

'Come on then, what are we waiting for?'

'Nothing, I suppose,' said Joe. 'I just dread doing this. Nuala will be heartbroken, for the two were very close.'

Nuala was in the window of the nursery, rocking the fractious baby and wondering why none of her family was at Mass that morning. She should have gone up after Mass and seen that everything was all right, but she had promised Nanny Pritchard that she would be straight back. The point was, the master and mistress were out for the day and it meant that Nanny Pritchard had charge of all the children on her own, and there were four of them now. This was more than enough for anyone, especially with the new baby, wee Sophie, teething and letting everyone know about it.

Suddenly, she saw her two brothers turn into the gravel drive from the road. They had never called at the house before, and at the look on their faces and the determined strides of them, she felt her spine suddenly tingling with alarm.

'My brothers are here, Nanny,' she said, turning from the window. 'Will you have the baby? I must see what they want.'

'Aye, give the child to me and get yourself away,'

Nanny Pritchard said. 'I know you have been fretting that something was wrong at home.'

She watched Nuala leave the room, biting her bottom lip in consternation, and hoped that she wasn't going to hear bad news.

Nuala flew through the house and arrived in the kitchen where the preparations for dinner were in progress and the various aromas of it wafted in the air. Nuala wasn't a usual visitor in the kitchen and the cook had just turned from the stove to ask her if she wanted something when there was a knock at the door. That too was unusual, and grumbling slightly, she went to open it.

Tom had just asked if he could have a word with Nuala and she was there before him, her eyes full of foreboding as she asked in a voice that trembled slightly, 'What is it? What's wrong?'

Tom's heart felt like lead and he said gently, 'It's Finn, Nuala. We had the telegram this morning.'

'Dead?' Nuala's voice was little more than a whisper. 'Are you telling me he is dead?'

'Aye.'

She looked at Tom and Joe with eyes so full of pain that Tom had to glance away.

'Finn assured me that he would be all right,' she said in a small voice, brittle with anguish. 'That any bullets would bounce off him.' She suddenly covered her face with her hands. 'Oh God, I can't bear the thought that he is dead,' she cried. 'I really can't bear it.'

She staggered then and would have fallen but the cook steadied her and then, feeling so sorry for the girl, she put her plump and motherly arms around her while she wept.

'Take her home,' she said to Tom, when Nuala was calmer at last. She turned Nuala to face her and said gently, 'You need to be with your own at a time like this, and be some level of support to your poor mother.'

'But Nanny Pritchard—'

'Amelia here will go up and give a hand,' the cook said. 'And we will cope. You go on home, for the loss of that poor boy will be a grievous one for you all.'

Nuala knew the cook was right and she stopped only to fetch her coat from the nursery and tell Nanny Pritchard the news.

'You poor child,' Nanny Pritchard said, laying the baby back in the crib and putting her arms around Nuala.

'Don't,' Nuala warned. 'You will have me wailing again and my brothers are waiting. Cook says I am to go home.'

'You must,' Nanny Pritchard said. 'Your poor, poor mother . . .'

Nuala walked home, a brother either side of her, numbed by the tragedy of it all and no one could think of a word to say. Nuala had never experienced directly the death of anyone before, and she didn't know how to cope with the loss of her very dear brother. She remembered the time when they had been playmates when they were children, the only one of her brothers her mother had allowed her to play with, and they stayed close as they grew up. Nuala had known Finn better than any of them and she knew she would always miss him sorely.

Biddy found it hard that there was no funeral and no grave, and that evening she went with Thomas John to arrange a commemorative Mass for Finn the following Sunday. The priest was so very sad to hear of his death. He had known Finn well, for he had been an altar boy for years. The sincere sympathy he expressed at their loss was nearly Biddy's undoing and she was barely able to hold on to her tears until she and Thomas John reached home again.

The news of Finn's death began to spread. Many neighbours called at the cottage to offer their sympathy and their help if they needed anything. Others had a Mass said for the repose of Finn's soul and Biddy displayed the Mass cards on the mantelpiece.

But life had to go on. Nuala returned to the Big House two days after she left it, though the mistress said she could take all the time she wanted to get over the tragedy.

'I am better at work,' Nuala said. 'When I heard first I really thought I couldn't bear the thought of never seeing Finn again. I even said as much, but you have to bear it because you can do nothing to change the situation. Finn was my very dear brother, who I will never forget, but I must get on with my life, as he would expect me to.'

'You are very brave, my dear,' Lady Carrington said. 'And you have been missed. The children have asked constantly when you were going to come back. They will be delighted to see you.'

They were, and Nuala tried to be as natural with them as possible, but there was an air of melancholy that she carried around with her that had not been there before. She never cried in front of them, though. Any tears that she still shed for Finn were wept when she was in her bed at night.

For Joe and Tom, in one way nothing had changed, and yet in another everything had. Finn's absence had been temporary before. Thomas John often said things like, 'When this war is over and Finn back where he belongs, I might get a few more cows.' Or, 'When the lad's back home, I've a mind to till that top field that's lying fallow just now.'

Now that wouldn't happen, and while it was hard for Tom and Joe, it was devastating for Thomas John. He seemed to age twenty years.

'There is a pain in my heart every time I think of Finn,' Thomas John said to Biddy, as they sat together one evening. 'It's like I've strained it in some way.'

It was so odd for Thomas John to speak of his feelings this way that Biddy just stared at him. 'I loved him, you see, better than the other two, and I was so afraid of showing that favouritism that I was even harder on him. Dear Christ, if I'm honest, I barely threw him a kind word all the years he was growing up.' He passed a gnarled hand over his wet face and said, 'I think of every bad thing I have said to him – and over the years there has been a fine collection of them – and now they come back to haunt me. Mind the time I clouted him across the head for spilling a drop of milk? For God's sake! As if it bloody mattered.'

'Don't do this, Thomas John,' Biddy said. 'You are a grand father, none better. You have barely laid a hand on any of the children. You were vexed with Finn that day, that's all. And he was a happy child growing up. Didn't he always go around the place with a smile on his face?'

'He did that,' Thomas John said, a sad little smile playing around his mouth at the memory. 'And his laughter used to echo across the yard. He was forever after Tom, d'you mind that? He had more patience with him than either Joe or me, for the child wanted to know the whys and where-fores of every damn thing. Tom never seemed to mind and he answered his questions every one, or he would toss him up on his shoulders, or have him on his back and gallop him around the yard.'

'Tom,' snapped Biddy, 'is as soft as clarts. Always was and always will be.'

'A man can be worse things than that,' Thomas John said. 'Don't you think you're a mite hard on Tom at times, Biddy?'

'Well, he's not a proper man,' Biddy said. 'He never sticks up for himself like Joe does, or Finn did. He is afraid of me. I can see it in his eyes and I find it hard to respect a man like that.'

'Tom is a grand worker,' Thomas John declared stoutly. 'He is my true right-hand man, with more of a feel for the land and the animals than Joe. He is also honest and reliable. Can you not respect him for those qualities?'

'If you say so,' Biddy said impatiently. She wouldn't change her opinion of her eldest son. He had almost been born to be bullied, but she would keep that to herself. 'But we didn't start this conversation talking of Tom,' she went on, 'but of Finn, and I hope I have made you feel better about that and remember he died doing something he had chosen to do.'

Thomas John sighed. 'Aye, I have to accept that now, though I doubt any of the boys really knew what they were going into. According to the papers, in Britain anyway, conscription is now extended to married men if the unmarried recruits fall below fifty thousand a month. Think on that. Fifty thousand a month to be sent overseas, to be mutilated, maimed and murdered. At the end of it all, if more Germans die than British, it's counted as a victory. It is almost obscene!'

Aggie and Lily presented themselves to Miss Morris at Kynoch's factory in Witton at a quarter-past seven on Monday morning.

She was waiting for them in the office with straightforward forms for them to fill in and then, when the first rush of girls had gone, she took them over to the time clock. 'Every morning when you arrive and every evening when you leave, you have to take your card from this rack here,' Miss Morris said, handing Aggie and Lily the cards she had made out for them. 'Then put them in the slot in the side of the clock and pull the handle and it records the time for you.'

She watched while Lily and Aggie followed her instructions, then nodded in approval. 'It will become second nature for you after a while,' she said. 'And the next thing we must do is sort out overalls for you.'

They were voluminous, dark green and quite hideous. The only consolation was that everyone else had to wear them too, Aggie thought as she struggled into hers. All jewellery had to be removed, including rings and watches, and even kirby grips had to taken out of the hair – anything metal that might cause a spark that could possibly lead to an explosion. Then every vestige of hair had to be tucked under the oversize hats.

Seeing them struggle with these, Miss Morris said, with a slight smile, 'I know that it isn't the height of fashion, ladies, and the hats are the worst, I think, but you will be glad of those hats when I take you into the factory, for the dust gets everywhere.'

Aggie knew exactly what Miss Morris meant

when she had been in the factory just seconds, for the swirling dust that danced in front of her made her eyes itchy and sore, while the stink hit the back of her throat and she started to cough and splutter. Lily was in no better shape.

'Most people are like that to start with,' Miss Morris told the two women. 'I was myself, but you soon get used to it.'

Aggie hoped she would, because whatever happened she had to stay there as long as she could. Through her bleary eyes she saw that the long room was dimly lit generally, though above the tables round which the girls were grouped, a naked bulb sent a pool of light over everything. Miss Morris put Aggie with a woman she called Miss Potter, while Lily was taken further down the factory.

As soon as Miss Morris was out of earshot, Miss Potter leaned towards Aggie and said, 'I can't be doing with this Miss Potter lark. My name is Chris – Christine, if you want to be posh – but never Miss Potter.'

'I feel the same—' Aggie began, but the other woman interrupted her. 'I know who you are. You are Aggie Sullivan.'

'How on earth do you know that?'

'Can't you guess?' Chris said with a laugh. 'I am Jane's sister.'

'Jane Potter, of course,' Aggie said. 'I always called her Jane, see; barely knew her last name.' She scrutinised Chris and said, 'Now that you have told me who you are I can see the resemblance to Jane.'

'Yeah, we have got the same ordinary brown hair,' Chris said.

'Ah, yes,' Aggie said, 'but it's naturally curly. You should be grateful – mine's as straight as a die – and you have both got lovely dark brown eyes and about the longest eyelashes I have ever seen.'

'I know we are alike,' Chris said with a grin. 'People used to think we were twins, when we were younger. Course, there is only a year between us.' And then, with a glance at her companions to see they were absorbed in their work, she whispered to Aggie, 'Our Jane thinks a lot about you. She has told me all about you and you needn't think it will get any further 'cos it won't. I think you have had enough bad things happen in your life and this lot don't need to know anything about it.'

'Oh, thank you,' Aggie said in relief. 'It will be lovely to start with a clean slate with everyone.'

'No reason why you shouldn't either,' Chris said. 'Oh God! Old Morris is on her way back up. I'd better start teaching you what I am supposed to be, or she will have me by the short and curlies.

'These here detonators come to us semifinished,' she explained, 'and we have to fit three things on them in a special order. They are in the numbered trays in front of you and I will show you how to fit them on. Then you clip them into the metal canisters in the basket to your right and put the finished article into the crates on your left. That's all there is to it. I think you will pick it up in no time.'

Aggie did, though she was all fingers and thumbs to start with.

Jane told her to go slower. 'Speed is essential, but that comes with practice. Accuracy is even more important. No good sending detonators out at a rate of knots if, when they get where they're going to, they don't flipping work, is it?'

'I suppose not.'

'I know not,' Chris said. 'So you concentrate on getting it right for the moment. The more you do, the quicker you will get at it.'

Aggie saw the sense of that and got on well with Chris, for all she was a good few years younger than Aggie herself, and she began to relax and not worry so much.

One thing intrigued Aggie, though, and that was how yellow the girls' faces were. When they removed the regulation hats at home time she noticed most of them had a coppery tinge to their hair. She didn't want to ask them, fearing they might be offended, so she asked Lily if she knew anything about it on their way home.

'It's the sulphur, bab,' Lily said. 'It's what makes the dust and all, and the bloody stink.'

'That dust gets everywhere,' Aggie said. 'It speckles all our clothes and I have seen it on girls' eyelashes. And with older women with lined faces, it settles into the creases by the end of the day.'

'Yeah, well, the sulphur works its way into the skin and the hair,' Lily said. 'People call them that work in munitions canary girls. Does that bother you?'

Aggie thought for a minute. 'Not in the slightest. I've been called far worse things.'

As summer slipped into autumn, each day got a little easier for Aggie and Lily. Despite the depressing war news and the growing casualty lists, Aggie was enjoying her new life better than she ever thought she would. Though she didn't particularly like the job, she knew it was a million times better than the alternative. It was nice also to feel you were doing your bit. The girls were a friendly bunch and they could have a good laugh together.

Each evening when Aggie and Lily arrived home, the Palmer children gave them a riotous welcome. Polly said it was doing them good to have other people in the house. Aggie had no problem playing with them and could even inveigle Lily to join in sometimes. Aggie liked nothing better than tucking them up in bed. She would tell them the stories from Ireland that she used to enthral her brothers with, or read the books Polly had got them from the library, and thought there was nothing like the feel of a little one's arms about her neck, or their lips on her cheek as she bid them good night.

Polly was glad of Aggie's willing help with the

children, and was more than glad that, with the children in bed, she wasn't alone night after night. In no time the three women had become good friends, but Aggie and Lily knew there were certain things they could never tell Polly.

One day, she had said with a sigh, 'I am so glad that you two came to live here. When Georgie suggested we get lodgers in to help out a bit, I wasn't impressed. Please don't be offended, but trying to raise two children decently is hard enough, especially on my own, and I know some who work in munitions are often heavy drinkers and rough types, immoral even. I am so glad I got two respectable ladies like yourselves.'

And, Aggie thought, anyone seeing them now would think them just like anyone else. Neither frequented pubs any more, nor bought gin or anything else from the carry-out, and wouldn't know where to get their hands on opium if they wanted it. Being totally sober was safer in the work they did, for as Lily said, 'Got to have your wits about you in that place, I'd say.'

'And steady hands,' Aggie said.

'I'll say,' Lily agreed. 'Remember that woman was telling me that early on in the war, a girl was working with detonators just like we do and she just suddenly dropped one. She was killed outright and the girl on her right had her arm blown off and the one to her left was blinded. Don't pay to take chances.'

They didn't tell this tale to Polly; she worried

enough about them working in such a dangerous place as it was. Polly was one of life's worriers. As Lily said, if she had nothing to worry over, then that would worry her as well.

Aggie, though, could understand Polly's concern for her husband, for she was often frantic if his letters were delayed.

'You must think me very feeble, worrying about him so much,' she said one evening. 'But he has been gone since 1914 really, apart from one short leave, and I miss him dreadfully.'

'I thought they didn't take married men at first?' Aggie asked.

'No,' Polly confirmed, 'they didn't, but Georgie volunteered. See, he was out of work, had been for more than two years and not a snifter of anything going. Then we heard of the Germans doing terrible things to Belgian women and children and that they might do the same to us if we didn't stop them. Well, my Georgie said, he mightn't be able to provide for us, but he could damn well fight for us and then at least he would be doing something useful. He thought I would have more money. He honestly thought the government would look after us properly if he volunteered for the army.'

'And I bet you get a bleeding pittance,' Lily said.

'Too right I do,' Polly said bitterly. 'When Georgie joined up, he got a shilling a day – King's shilling, see – and I got the grand sum of one shilling and one penny a day that they call Separation Allowance.

Then Georgie has to give me another sixpence, plus a penny for each of the children, and the government add another twopence each. If you add that up it comes to eight shillings and seven pence, and the rent was three shillings a week.'

'God Almighty!' Lily exclaimed.

'Don't mind telling you I was on my beam ends and terrified of being turfed out of the house because I couldn't bear to hear the kids cry with hunger. So I sometimes had to hide from the rent man. Georgie sent me what he could but he hadn't much either. Anyway, in 1915 they doubled his pay and he sends that increase direct to me. Not all husbands are so good. You must have seen the scrawny kids about, and not all of their mothers are wearing the widow's bonnet.'

'I have seen them,' Aggie said, 'and been shocked, to tell you the truth. They look so thin and cold and hungry, and some of them are barefoot. I mean, we wore no shoes in Ireland during the summer, but the nights are drawing in now and chilly with it.'

'Yeah, and many that have boots have *Evening Mail* stamped on them because they give them to the poor,' Polly said. 'They supply the lot sometimes; the kids couldn't go to school else. They give out jerseys, gymslips, trousers and stockings all stamped so they can't be pawned, see.'

Aggie didn't see. She had never heard the word 'pawned' before, but she understood poverty all right. 'We have a religious organisation do a similar thing in Ireland,' she said. 'It's called St Vincent de Paul. They get clothes for the poor and even give vouchers for people to trade for groceries in the shops.'

'That would be a good idea here,' Polly said.

'Yes, but the wife and children of a man fighting for his country shouldn't be reliant on handouts and charity.'

Polly sighed. 'They are, though. It's the way of the world. Mind you, no one expected this war to last long. Kick the Hun into touch and be back by Christmas, that's what everyone thought.' She stopped and then said, 'I worry sometimes that the children will forget who their father is. I mean, he came home early last summer. He had been in some place called Gallipoli and so many men died there that Churchill resigned over it. So Georgie was one of the lucky ones. Anyroad, Clara was only three then, and she wouldn't have anything to do with him, and even Charlie was a bit off, though he was five. I show them the photograph I have of Georgie often and tell them it's their dad, but what's it all mean to a nipper?'

'Not a lot,' Lily agreed. Many children were without fathers now that the call-up had begun, and married men were included, and they all knew some of those men would never come back.

'I don't think you feeble,' Aggie declared to Polly. 'I think you are jolly brave, if you want to know.'

Despite all the dangers of the job, Aggie was happier than she had ever been. 'This is the sort of life I thought I would be having in Birmingham when I first arrived all those years, once that Gwen Halliday had helped me get rid of the baby,' she told Lily.

'There are lots of things to do and see in a city like this,' Lily said. 'I mean, we have plenty of picture houses on our doorstep. Maybe we should make use of living in such a place and go out a time or two after work.'

Much as Aggie longed to go to a picture house, she was reluctant at first, for she thought in some way it would be disloyal to Alan. Lily, however, wore her down in the end and Aggie began to enjoy herself so much that if it wasn't for the rising casualty figures, she could wish the war would go on for ever.

NINETEEN

One evening in early November, Aggie and Lily were hurrying through the dark, damp streets when someone called out to them. Aggie spun round, then cried, 'Jane! How lovely to see you again. Are you waiting for your sister?'

'Well, I will wait now that I am here,' Jane said. 'But I really came to see Mr Witchell. I am joining you lot on Monday. Finch has bought the bloody club.'

'Finch?' Aggie repeated aghast. 'Oh, thank God we got out when we did, Lily.'

'Not half.'

'He went mad when he realised you'd gone,' Jane said. 'He couldn't believe that we didn't know where you were. I played dumb. It is easy enough for me to do, but Bessie said she had heard tell you had gone back to Ireland.'

'Oh, good for her.'

'She's leaving as well,' Jane told them. 'She says anything she cooked for Finch she would lace liberally with arsenic and he isn't worth hanging for.'

'He isn't,' Aggie said fervently. 'And yet I have fantasised about doing the selfsame thing. But where is Bessie going to go?'

'To her sister's down south somewhere,' Jane said. 'Her sister's husband died three years ago and she has been urging Bessie to go and live with her since. Mr Levingstone knew all about it; promised to set her up with a pension. Course, all that has gone by the board now, but she says she has saved a good bit over the years. Anyroad, her mind is made up. So Finch hasn't a clue where you are and no way of finding out either.'

'That's the way I like it,' Aggie said.

As they walked home that evening, Lily said, 'I like that young Jane, though I thought she was a stuck-up miss when I went first to the club, after you had been attacked.'

'Jane, stuck up?' Aggie repeated. 'I find that hard to believe and yet I have never heard you tell a lie.'

'Believe it,' Lily said. 'She looked at me as if I had crawled from under a stone. When Alan asked me to help her to nurse you, I said that I would only do it if she gave me proper respect. Well, I don't know what he said to her – we never discussed it after – but she came to find me before she went to bed that night and apologised. I always think it takes guts to apologise and so I shook her hand and said there was no harm done. We got on like a house on fire from then on.'

'Well, I saw that as I recovered,' Aggie said. 'I wouldn't have said there was ever bad feeling between you.'

'There wasn't,' Lily said. 'I didn't let it develop into bad feeling. I nipped it in the bud straight away. Point is, will it be awkward for you at the factory with Jane working there too?'

'I don't think so. Why should it be?'

'You know, you being the mistress and her the maid in a previous life?'

'Oh, I never felt that way with Jane,' Aggie said. 'We were friendly from the start. I didn't see why someone had to wait on me at the table and clear up after me. She had to do these things, of course – Alan employed her for that – but she was well aware of what I thought. Anyway, she has proved to be honest and reliable. I like her sister and I am looking forward to working with Jane as well.'

'Me too, bab,' said Lily. 'Yeah, me too.'

Thomas John found it hard to shake off the despondency that had surrounded him since the news of Finn's death. The fact that he was one of many fathers grieving depressed him still further and he hoped that 1917 would be a better year for them all. It didn't start at all well, though. There seemed to be unrest everywhere, and then a revolution in Russia, of all places, and bad enough to make the Tsar abdicate.

But spring was a busy time on any farm, and Thomas John and his two sons were out every day.

Thomas John welcomed the work that ensured he slept each night, and he didn't mention the vague pains he had in his chest now and again, which sometimes made him feel breathless. He knew what it was: heartache over losing Finn, because that was when they began and there were no pills or potions made that would ease that type of pain.

No one was surprised when America declared war on Germany in April 1917, for the Germans seemed intent on clearing the seas of any ships but their own. They sank two hospital ships, one of them called *Donegal*. When Thomas John read this he declared that any nation that could justify sinking hospital ships must be peopled by barbarians. Most people thought that of the Germans anyhow, but Tom was depressed over America's involvement. Whichever way you looked at it, it was an escalation of a war that had already claimed so many young lives.

By June 1917 the rebels from the 1916 insurrection who had not been executed had all been released from prison, including Eamon de Valera.

'The whisper is that the Irish Republican Brotherhood is regrouping,' Joe said one Saturday after returning from Buncrana. 'They say that lads are climbing over each other to join and they are calling themselves the Irish Republican Army.'

'Bloody fools,' Thomas John burst out. 'Have they learned nothing?'

'People don't, Daddy,' Tom said. 'If they did there would be no wars ever again.'

*　　*　　*

Aggie was delighted to find that Jane would be working alongside her and Chris, and then in the spring Lily was moved to join them. The four women got on really well. Aggie could be open with them because they knew all about her and she found she could relax in their company. Chatting together also helped the day pass quicker and as long as they talked quietly and still got the same amount of work done, no one took much notice.

Aggie couldn't help noticing and envying the close bond between Chris and Jane. 'It's even better now I am living back home again,' Jane told Aggie one day in the canteen. 'Me and Chris share the same bed again, like we did before I left to go into service with you and Mr Levingstone. It's like old times. Mom and Dad prefer it too. They were never happy about me sleeping out, not that they were jumping about with joy that I was joining our Chris in munitions either.

'I never told them about the goings-on in the club, you know. God, if they had known the half of it, they wouldn't have let me within a mile of the place, and it would have been no good me telling them that I never met any of the girls and was not expected to set one foot inside the club itself. Still,' Jane gave a shrug, 'that's parents for you, and I suppose at least it shows they care.'

Aggie couldn't speak for a moment, she was so choked with emotion. She wished fervently the last fifteen years had not happened. She would still have the love of her parents, the companionship of her siblings, and likely be married by now and have children of her own to love and cherish. She felt her eyes sting with tears she could not let fall. God, sometimes she found life very hard.

She could have blessed Lily and Chris who joined them at that point, their chatter slicing through the silence that had started to settle between Jane and Aggie.

The friendship between Polly, Aggie and Lily also grew deeper. Then one evening in March, Lily said she wasn't up to gallivanting out to the pictures as she and Aggie had planned to do that evening. Aggie was disappointed but her concern was all for Lily.

'Why not?' she asked. 'Are you feeling ill?'

'Nothing a quiet night by my own fireside won't cure.'

'Are you sure?' Aggie said. 'I could get the doctor in.'

Lily laughed. 'I want no doctor, girl. Don't fuss. I am getting no younger, have been on my feet all day and I am too jiggered to go out tonight, that's all I'm saying.'

'If you're sure?'

'Absolutely certain,' Lily said. 'There's no reason for you to stay in, though. Maybe Polly would like to go with you. I would be here to see to the nippers.'

Aggie didn't need the surreptitious wink that Lily cast her way to know what she was about.

She had heard it in the tone of her voice. Only the other day she had said that she thought it a shame that Polly didn't seem to have much of a life and that she never crossed the threshold of her house unless it was to go shopping.

'Oh, I couldn't,' Polly said.

'Why couldn't you?'

'Well, I'm a married woman.'

'I had noticed that,' Lily said with a wry smile. 'Does that mean that you are chained to the house twenty-four hours a day, seven days a week?'

'It's just that it wouldn't seem right, me going out to enjoy myself, especially when Georgie is maybe in the thick of it.'

'Well, you staying in will not help him whether he is or not,' Aggie said. 'Look, what is wrong with going a few yards to the picture house and then afterwards going to a coffee house for a cup of coffee before we come home?'

'Put like that, not a lot, I suppose.'

'Well, that is all me and Lily do,' Aggie said. 'And if I can't persuade you to come, then I must stay in as well because I can't go on my own.'

Polly knew how much Aggie looked forward to a night out, and she hated to disappointment her. If she was truly honest she really wanted to go herself. 'I've never been to a picture house,' she admitted, 'nor have I sat in a coffee house. As for the music hall . . . I can only imagine it, but I should think it would be magical. We hadn't money for such things before, you see.'

'Well, now you have,' Aggie said. 'Are you going to go out with me or not?'

'I am,' said Polly with an emphatic nod of her head. 'And thank you, Lily, for making it possible.'

'Huh, I did very little,' Lily said. 'And the only payment I want is a smile on your face when you come back in tonight.'

Aggie found that Polly was a different person when she was away from the house for a few hours. She had a very good sense of humour and was a lot of fun to be with. The two women had a wonderful evening.

'We must do it again,' Aggie suggested as they returned to the house. 'It does you good to get out. It sort of refreshes you.'

'You're right,' Polly said. 'I can't remember laughing like that in ages. With the war and all, there hasn't been much occasion to laugh.'

'No,' agreed Aggie. 'I know you worry about your Georgie every day, and with reason, but pushing it to the back of your mind for a couple of hours or so isn't being disloyal.'

'No,' Polly said. 'When I write to Georgie and tell him about this he will be pleased. He was worried about me coping on my own before you came. I have told him all about you and the fine woman that you are. Now I shall write and tell him that you are the very best lodgers anyone could have.'

Despite the success of Polly's first foray out to the pictures the war news did dominate most of the conversation around the table in the evenings. Aggie and Lily sometimes gleaned information from the girls at the factory and they always bought a paper on their way home from work.

When America entered the war, they didn't know whether it was a good thing or not.

'Couldn't do owt else, though, could they?' Lily said. 'After all, no country can stand by, watch its ships blown clean out of the water and do nothing.'

'You're right,' Polly said, 'but what bothers me more than that is those towns that them dratted Germans bombed on the south coast, and I know there was some bombs in London before. I mean, what's it all about? Soldiers kill each other, not ordinary people.'

'Yeah,' agreed Lily. 'And I think there has been enough killing in this war to satisfy anyone's blood lust.'

'Exactly,' Polly went on. 'So why bomb ordinary people? I mean, what if I'm sitting here with the babbies, minding my own business, like, and a bloody great bomb lands on top of us?'

It was monstrous, Aggie thought. War surely shouldn't be waged on women and children. 'Don't,' she said to Polly. 'It doesn't bear thinking about. Birmingham is probably as safe as anywhere, though, for we are so far inland.'

'Oh, yeah, there is that,' Polly said with a sigh.

Aggie was glad she had allayed her fears a little and she just hoped what she said was true. What the hell did she know about bombs or the planes that carried them?

'It's the kids I worry about most,' Polly said. 'Keeping them safe, you know?'

Aggie knew full well. It would be what any mother wanted. Polly loved Aggie's company if she took the children out to the park on a Sunday afternoon. Lily would use this time to put her feet up, and Aggie didn't blame her, but she loved those outings with Charlie and Clara.

Georgie had managed to procure a football for Charlie before he enlisted. It wasn't a new one, but a ball was still a ball.

'Don't ask where he got it,' Polly said, the first time she produced it from the cupboard, 'because I haven't a clue. He arrived home with it one day and when I asked him how he had come by it, he said them that ask no questions will be told no lies. So now you are as wise as me.'

However Georgie had got the ball, Aggie, Polly and Charlie spent many hours pounding after it in the park. Even little Clara joined in the chase, though she could barely keep up and seldom got near enough to actually kick it.

Eventually, though, other boys would sidle up and ask to play, and in the end, Aggie and Polly would sneak away and let the boys play their own version of football. Clara would usually find some little girls to play with and Aggie and Polly would talk together for hours.

'It's a shame that you haven't children of your

own,' Polly said one afternoon. 'You are so good with them and they love you too.'

'Children without a husband?' Aggie said with a smile. 'Shame on you. Anyway, I don't think I can have children. I think there is something wrong inside me.'

'Oh, that is sad,' Polly said. 'Is that why you are not married?'

Aggie paused before saying, 'Oh, there are many reasons why I am unmarried.'

She didn't say what they were, though, and after a few minutes of awkward silence she jumped to her feet asking, 'Shall I start rounding the children up? It's about time we were heading back.'

Polly never broached that subject again, sensing that Aggie didn't want to answer personal questions about her past. The children had no such restraint.

Sometimes, though, Aggie brought this on herself. Polly remembered Charlie's open-mouthed astonishment when Aggie told him the milk he was pouring on to his porridge came from a cow.

Charlie had never seen a cow, but the thought that milk came from any animal at all fascinated him, especially when Aggie explained how it was extracted.

'We get our milk from a woman what comes round,' Charlie said.

'Yeah, Mommy says before the war a man did it,' Clara put in. 'But it's this woman now and we have to take a jug out and she fills it up.'

'Well, it starts off in a cow,' Aggie said. 'And you make butter from milk too.'

Charlie looked a little sceptical. 'How do you do that?'

Aggie went on described the churn the milk was poured into and the paddle that had to be pounded until the milk separated and began to solidify.

'By then,' she said, 'you feel as if your arms are going to fall off, but you have to scoop the butter out, mix it with salt, pat it into shape and wrap it in muslin.'

The children were hanging on her every word. 'Tell us some more?' Charlie urged.

Aggie shook her head. 'I would be late for work if I did,' she said. 'I'll tell you more another day.'

They didn't forget and in time they knew all that Aggie was prepared to share. She told them of the little whitewashed cottage she had grown up in, and the thatch on the roof that was made from the flax that was grown in the fields. 'Lots of things are grown in the fields,' she said. 'Things you eat like cabbages, swedes, turnips and potatoes.' She explained how they were planted in the spring and then harvested in the autumn. She described, when they pressed her, about the woolly sheep on the hillside, the velvet-flanked cows with their deep brown eyes, and the very smelly pig and squealing piglets.

One day, when Polly had managed to get her hands on a few eggs, Aggie told the children of the rooster that had woken them every morning with his cock-a-doodle-doo, and of the hens strutting about the yard.

'Did you have lots of chickens?' Clara asked.

'A fair few,' Aggie said, 'and I could collect a whole basket of eggs every morning.'

'Did you eat them all?'

Aggie laughed. 'No, there were too many,' she said. 'The others we would sell at the market in the town on Saturday and the excess butter would go there too.'

'Are they bothering you?' Polly asked anxiously.

'No,' Aggie said. 'They learn by asking questions. To tell you the truth, they remind me very much of my little brother, Finn, when he was small.'

It was the first time that Aggie had mentioned any of her family and she knew that she had made a grave mistake.

'What age would he be now then, your brother?' Polly asked.

Immediately, it was as if a shutter had come down, with Aggie on one side of it, and Polly the other.

'Oh, all grown up,' Aggie said vaguely. 'I haven't heard of him in years.'

Polly's eyes narrowed and she wondered what had happened in Aggie's past. She obviously once had had a family and yet all the months she had been there she had never had a letter. Lily had – from her brother in America, she said – and Polly had always assumed that Aggie was alone in the world. She was bursting with curiosity, but not

381

prepared to badger her with questions she'd not want to answer. After all, everyone was entitled to privacy.

It was obvious by 1918 that the war was starting to bite financially. Meat rationing was introduced, which didn't really affect the poor in Birmingham, who already seldom saw meat any day of the week. But fuel was rationed too, and so theatres, cinemas and restaurants were forced to close early and the age for conscription was raised to fifty.

'Bloody Hell,' Lily remarked when she heard this, 'We are fighting a highly trained and disciplined German army with a load of granddads.' Seemed she was right as well, when the Allies suffered a massive defeat in Ypres and 400,000 were killed in three weeks.

'Seems like the end of the war is as far away as ever,' Lily said. 'And that means they need as many detonators as we can make.'

'I know,' Aggie agreed. 'I would like to feel sorry about it. I mean, I am sorry about the loss of life; you would have to be a real heartless soul not to feel sad about that and wish it wasn't happening. But this is the first time in my life I have made money, legitimate money that I feel entitled to spend in any way I choose. I know that is a really selfish way to look at things, but . . .'

'It ain't selfish a bit, duck,' Lily assured her. 'The dice were stacked against you long enough. We can't do aught to shorten or lengthen the war and there ain't no sin in enjoying the money you are earning, honestly. And we are earning it at the moment,' she added. 'Because now the summer has arrived, I feel some days that I am going to melt under them bloody overalls, and all that will be left of me by the end of the day will be a puddle of sweat.'

Aggie knew exactly how Lily felt. The weather was unseasonably warm for a British summer, and the heat in the factory could get very uncomfortable indeed.

One Friday in early July, Lily, Aggie and Jane were glad to be among a party of six to be sent into the yard to help unload the deliveries that had arrived that morning. There was no breeze, and the day was heavy with heat, but to be out in it was more pleasant than had being indoors.

They had just remarked on this fact when there was a gigantic explosion that flung the women and the two van drivers to the ground. Aggie felt as if all the breath had been knocked from her body and all her bones had been loosened. She sat up gingerly and felt everywhere, and she knew she was not seriously injured, though she might have a mass of bruises develop later on.

'You all right, Lil?' she asked.

Lily pulled herself into a sitting position with a groan and said, 'I'll live, and that's probably more than can be said for them poor sods over there.'

'Oh God!' Aggie breathed. Their section of the factory was no longer there. It had crumpled inwards, and was now just a mass of tumbled bricks, blackened and fractured roof beams, shards of glass and broken slates. The acrid stink of brick dust, smoke, sulphur and cordite filled the air. 'Chris is in there,' Aggie whispered, horrified.

'And plenty of other poor sods,' Lily said, heaving herself to her feet. 'Come on, let's give them a hand before the whole bleeding thing disappears altogether.'

Jane was already there, pulling desperately at the debris while tears ran down her face and sobs shook her body. Aggie wanted to say something to the distraught girl, but couldn't think of anything that might help. Instead she worked alongside her, moving the rubble piece by piece, for the whole structure looked unstable.

Others came to help – the other three girls, the van drivers and people from parts of the factory not affected – and the crushed body of Miss Morris was uncovered before the emergency services arrived.

Jane looked at the mangled face of her supervisor and let out a howl of fear. 'I won't be able to bear it if anything has happened to Chris.'

Aggie put her arms around Jane's heaving shoulders, feeling the distress running all through her. She was hardly aware that tears were streaming from her own eyes and she said nothing for she couldn't assure her that Chris would be fine, or urge her not to worry or upset herself. All she could do was hold her tight. Lily's eyes were full of compassion for them both.

Now that the rescue services were in charge, they had just to watch, for it was deemed too dangerous for untrained people to help. They stood in the heat-filled yard, the air still so fetid and sour it was hard to breathe in, and the shock and sorrow all around was so palpable that it could almost be touched. Some keened and cried, but most stood in silence. As each body was brought out, a sigh rippled around those watching. Jane shuddered as each was carried past her to be laid in the yard and covered with a blanket.

When the dust-covered body of Mr Witchell was carried out, all hope that there might be survivors seemed to seep out of Jane, and when her sister was the next body to be pulled out she had almost been expecting it. That didn't prevent her cry as she saw how badly she had been crushed, apparent from her disfigured face to the strange angle of her body.

Many were crying along with Jane, Lily and Aggie amongst them. They hadn't known Chris that long, but they had become friends almost straight away. Aggie knew that Jane would always mourn the loss of the sister she had loved so much, and the family would be rent asunder by the tragedy.

Through bleary eyes she saw a middle-aged couple approach Jane, who spotted them at the same time.

'Oh, Mom!' she cried in anguish, and her mother enfolded Jane in her arms, though Aggie saw the tears glinting in her own eyes.

Her father patted her gently on the shoulder and said, 'Let's away home, lass. There is nothing to be gained by staying here.'

'But Chris . . .'

'Doesn't need our ministrations,' Jane's father said. 'And I will do the necessary. But you, my dear, have done enough and I want to get you home where you will have your mother to tend you and maybe you will be a measure of comfort to each other.'

Aggie and Lily watched the sad little group walk out of the yard.

Lily said, 'Do you want to do the same?'

'Go home, do you mean?' Aggie said. 'Oh, yes. I am too burdened down with sadness to stay any longer.'

The yard was filling with people as the news of the explosion was spreading, but no one stopped Aggie or Lily as they walked out of the gates and made their way home.

TWENTY

The day of the explosion Polly had been shopping. For a change she had gone into the Bull Ring in the city centre and she was unaware of anything untoward happening at Kynoch's factory. When she arrived home, she found Lily and Aggie already there. They'd had to come home in their overalls, as the cloakroom, with their coats and bags in it, was one of the areas in the factory that was crushed. But by the time Polly had got home they'd washed and changed.

Polly was appalled at the news. 'My God!' she cried. 'You could have been killed.'

'We know that,' Lily said. 'If some of the other girls had been chosen to help with the unloading, then we would have been inside the building that got the full force of the blast. It's finished me with munitions, for the next time we might not be so lucky.'

Eighteen people, mainly women, had died in the explosion. Others were injured and needed treatment in hospital. These were sad and sorrowful days.

Mr Witchell was the father of six children and it upset Aggie greatly to see them all in church, dressed in black, their sorrowful eyes standing out in their white strained faces, and their mother coping with tremendous dignity in the face of such a terrible tragedy. The saddened elderly parents of Miss Morris seemed bemused by the whole thing, as if they couldn't quite believe it, and Aggie's heart went out to them too.

There was so much unhappiness and anguish, so many funerals. The worst for Aggie and Lily was that of Chris Potter, where they saw her parents and Jane bowed down with grief, and Jane's two younger brothers manfully trying not to cry. They were invited back to the house and welcomed as friends of Chris, but they didn't stay so very long.

Jane caught up with them at the door before they left. 'Going so soon?'

Lily nodded. 'The strain is beginning to tell on your parents,' she said. 'They don't need strangers at a time like this.'

'I know,' Jane said. 'It's awful, isn't it? I can barely believe she's gone, that I'll never see her again.'

'What are you going to do now?' Aggie asked gently.

'My aunt Peggy is taking me back to her place in Cheshire for a bit,' Jane said. 'She asked Mom too, but she won't leave Dad and the lads; said they're all going through it too. I know they are, but I really need to get away. What will you do?'

'Get another job,' Lily said. 'What else can we do?'

'Nothing, I suppose. In munitions again?'

'Huh, not likely,' Lily said. 'I think me and Aggie have had our fill of places like that.'

'The point is,' Lily said to Polly later, 'we don't really know where to look for work.'

'Well, what line of work were you in before?' Polly asked.

It was a reasonable question to ask, and though it had never come up before, the two women had their stories ready.

'We were in service together,' Lily said. 'And we hardly want to go back to that.'

'I don't blame you,' Polly said. 'I couldn't bear being at someone's beck and call like that.'

'And the wages were awful,' Lily said. 'It was the money tempted us to try for the munitions. Jane was working with us, and her sister, Chris, had a job at the Kynoch's works and told us of the big money we could be earning.'

'And wasn't it Chris's funeral you were at today?'

'Yes, that right.'

'What a shame!' Polly said. 'Thank God you are coming out of it. But, I suppose there might be other war-related work that isn't as dangerous.'

'Ah, we have talked about this,' Lily said. 'We think it would be better for us to get jobs we can

389

still do when the war is over. Otherwise, we might be competing for work with the demobbed soldiers.'

Polly nodded. 'I can quite see that. I should try Aston Cross. There are all sorts of factories there and it's only a short tram ride away.'

Lily grinned at Aggie and said, 'Have to get over your aversion to trams then, bab, if we get set on at Aston Cross. You was a dithering wreck when we went up to Kynoch's that time to find out about jobs in the munitions place. I ain't putting up with that performance every bloody morning.'

'I know,' Aggie retorted, 'and you won't have to. I know I will just have to get used to it, that's all, like everyone else does.' And she knew she would. God, she would walk over hot coals if it meant at the end of it she had respectable employment. What was a short journey on a tram in comparison to that? Nothing, that's what, and she was determined to conquer her fear.

The women were in a better position than they had ever been before to get respectable employment, for not only did they have references, they also had a genuine reason for leaving Kynoch's. They were delighted to be taken on at HP Sauce, which was at Aston Cross, within days. Though the money would be just under half what they were used to, it was perfectly adequate for their needs.

'We'll need other lodgings too,' Aggie said on

the way home to tell Polly the good news that they were employed again. 'Polly will not want us there when her husband comes home.'

Polly, however, wouldn't dream of them leaving. 'Wait till the war is officially over, at least,' she pleaded. 'I have got used to having you around.'

'And we don't want you to go either,' Charlie added, overhearing what Aggie had said. 'Do we, Clara?'

'No, we don't,' Clara said, and to make absolutely sure they understood that, she wrapped her little arms around Aggie. 'We want you to stay for ever.'

'For ever is a long time,' Aggie said, 'but we will stay until the war is over and then we will be moving out because your daddy will be coming home.'

Charlie and Clara were too young to remember a time when the country hadn't been at war – it was just there all the time – and so they were satisfied by Aggie's reply.

With the children in bed, Polly confided in the two women, 'It might be a bit awkward at first when Georgie comes home. I'm a bit nervous, to tell the truth. I mean, Georgie won't be the same man as the one I married, will he? Stands to reason. He'll have seen things and done things that's bound to have changed him. He was different when he came home last time – shorter-tempered, like.'

'And you will have changed too, don't forget,' Aggie said. 'It'll take time to get back to living together again, that's all. And that is time on your own. It will be even more awkward if we are here too. But for now we'll stay put.'

HP Sauce workers had to wear overalls too, and again their hair had be hidden under caps, but the working apparel was a lot smarter than that worn at Kynoch's. Here there was no swirling yellow dust and the only smell that of vinegar. The women worked on a conveyer belt, packing bottle after bottle of tomato sauce into crates, for the troops, the other girls said.

'So,' said Lily, as they went home that first night, 'we are still doing our bit, for how would the men manage to kill Germans without a bit of sauce? And this way we don't risk being blown up for our war effort.'

On 11 November, the church bells started to peal out joyfully. The factories sounded their hooters and people spilled onto the streets, aware that the war, that dreadful war that had lasted for four terrifying and bloody years, was finally over.

Children were released from school and many factories closed down for the day, HP Sauce included. People seemed to have a need to be together. The streets were so filled with happy, celebrating people that many drivers, unable to get through the grid-locked roads, abandoned their vehicles and joined the mêlée. Aggie felt so sorry for those in the widows' bonnets. For them peace had come too late.

That night she said to Charlie and Clara, 'The

war's over and your daddy will be home soon. Won't that be nice?'

However, for Charlie and Clara, their father was a shadowy figure that they could barely remember, while Aggie and Lily were real flesh-and-blood people that they loved dearly. Charlie remembered Aggie saying she would leave when the war was over, so he gave the question serious consideration and then said, 'Dunno, really. Don't know what a daddy does. I really think that I would prefer it if you and Lily stayed.'

'And I would,' Clara echoed.

Aggie was saddened by the children's response and recounted it the next day at work.

'At least that Polly has got her man and he is coming home,' Aggie's workmate said. 'As for the rest of us, I can't see as there will be that many men left to go round.'

'Yeah, the best of them are littering some foreign field,' put in another.

'Like my bloody fiancé, killed in 1914,' said the first woman. 'God, he had only been in the army weeks. No, I reckon this will be a generation of spinsters and widows.'

'She could well be right,' Lily said when Aggie told her this on their way home.

'Good job I am not in the market for a husband then,' Aggie said. 'And for God's sake don't look at me like that. I want no man. Don't you think that I have had enough to do with men already to last me a lifetime?'

'Your life could be different now, though,' Lily protested. 'Respectable.'

Aggie shook her head. 'I want no man in my life,' she said. 'None of that malarkey ever again.'

Lily and Aggie knew it was time for them to move on and they began to look for new lodgings. They tried in the roads around Aston Cross first, to save on tram fares and travelling time. Most places were only too willing to let out rooms to two respectable-looking women in full-time employment.

In the end they rented two rooms in Vicarage Road, just a step away from HP Sauce. One room was a bedroom with two beds side by side, a wardrobe, chest of drawers and a dressing table. The other room was a living room with a small kitchenette leading off from it. This had a sink and slopstone, running water from a tap, a couple of gas rings, a few battered saucepans, a kettle and a shelf with assorted crockery on it. To the two women it was like a palace, especially when they learned that there was a bathroom of sorts on the floor below, with a boiler to boil the water for a bath if they wanted one.

'Our own place,' Lily said. 'And we'll soon have it brightened up.'

'Yes,' Aggie said. 'Only one thing worries me and that is it's on the third floor and you were puffing like a steam engine when you reached here today. Will you be able to do that every day?'

'Course,' Lily said confidently. 'And twenty

times a day if I have to. I am not as young as I used to be, that's all, and there's not a thing you or I can do to change that so don't start fretting until there is something worth fretting over. This is another chapter in our lives, Aggie.'

When the children realised that Lily and Aggie were leaving, they were inconsolable. It tore at Aggie's heartstrings that they cried themselves to sleep that night.

'I'm as sad as the children,' Polly confessed that night, when it was eventually quiet upstairs, 'and I knew it was coming. Can't you stay a little longer? Till we have word that Georgie is demobbed, perhaps?'

Aggie shook her head. 'No, we really must go. I am sad too because I will miss you all so much. But from what the children said to me the other day, they can't remember their father. In fact, Charlie said he didn't know what a daddy did. You must use the time before Georgie comes home to tell them about their daddy. Dredge up all the nice times you remember and tell them so that they will look forward to their father coming home. And, believe me, it will be much easier to do that without us around muddying up the water.'

'She's right, lass,' Lily said. 'And you're luckier than many, for your man will soon be by your side to help raise the children. Charlie in particular needs a father, and yet many boys his age will be without one.'

'I do know how lucky I am really,' Polly said. 'It's just that we have got on so well. I have never had such good friends.'

'We'll only be in Aston Cross,' Aggie reminded her. 'We can still see each other.'

'It won't be the same.'

'Course it won't,' Lily said. 'Nothing will be the same, and for you it will be better.'

'You must come for Christmas,' Polly urged. 'It will make the day for the children and there is precious little in the shops to buy them anything in the way of toys.'

Aggie and Lily knew how true that was so they agreed to spend Christmas Day at the Palmers' house.

The men began to dribble home from the war just before Christmas, but many of them were unaware that they were incubating a terrible disease that they inadvertently passed on to their families and friends. It was called Asian flu, and was said to be spread by the fleas that fed off the rats that shared the trenches with the soldiers. Soon it ran rampant through the population, killing thousands.

The speed the disease took hold overwhelmed the doctors and hospitals, for there was no cure. It all depended on whether a person had the resilience to fight the infection or not. Many in that city were too thin and undernourished to fight anything so virulent and lethal, and the flu claimed many lives, initially amongst the very old, very young, the frail and the weak.

Christmas was low-key that year, for people were generally disheartened. As a nation they were still reeling from fighting a war of unparalleled magnitude that had killed and maimed so many. For those same people then to be attacked by a killer virus seemed monstrously unfair and totally terrifying.

But for the children Christmas was still Christmas, and Aggie and Lily were determined to find something for Charlie and Clara's stockings. By searching diligently Aggie was able to find a skipping rope for Clara and a bag of marbles for Charlie, and Lily bought Clara a book of fairytales and Charlie tales about Ali Baba and the Forty Thieves. They delivered these to Polly on Christmas Eve. So on Christmas morning the children had full stockings for Polly had already packed each of them with an orange and an apple, a small bar of chocolate and a silver thrupenny bit. For Charlie and Clara, then, Christmas was wonderful and made more especially so when Lily and Aggie arrived.

The day had been a special one for all of them. By next year Georgie would surely be back in the bosom of his family and then things would undoubtedly change. With promises to visit again soon, Aggie and Lily took their leave after tea. As they walked through the dark and near-empty streets, for there were no trams running, it began to snow.

'Seems right, doesn't it?' Aggie said. 'Snow on Christmas Day?'

'Yeah,' Lily agreed. 'I think problem times are over for us at long last, so let's look forward to 1919. All we've got to do is dodge this bloody flu.'

But the flu was a serous threat. As the year turned and more and more men were demobbed, the scale of the infection rose. People previously thought to be strong and healthy became ill, and a fair number of these did not recover. The government was in a panic. Theatres and cinemas closed and people were told to avoid crowded places. Though everyone was scared, as Lily said, people had jobs of work they had to go to and to reach those jobs many had to travel on crowded trams and omnibuses.

Ireland had its share of the flu too, of course, but as the number of Irish men and boys enlisting had been much less than in England, with even fewer returning, their problems were not as catastrophic as Britain's. Anyway, Ireland had its own concerns. It was a very unstable country to be in at that time.

Nuala's mistress was very jumpy about the regrouped IRA roaming the countryside, armed with guns. They began by attacking RIC barracks and shooting soldiers and others in positions of authority. When the British response was to take reprisals, killing men from surrounding towns and villages, the violence escalated as the IRA began forcing Unionists to leave their homes before setting light to them.

Lady Carrington spent a lot of time in the nursery and was scared to let the children out of her sight. Eventually, by the spring of 1919, her husband decided to take the family to their other house in England. This was on the outskirts of an area called Sutton Coldfield, which was a small market town just to the north of Birmingham.

Nanny Pritchard elected not to go. It was past her time to retire. Her employers agreed with her, but wanted to take Nuala with them as head nursery maid. Nuala was more than agreeable but didn't think her parents would countenance the idea.

At first they didn't, though Lord and Lady Carrington even went to the farm together one morning and in front of Biddy's implacable face pleaded their case. They said how well Nuala was thought of and how the children loved her.

'They are distressed enough to be leaving here,' Lady Carrington said. 'Ireland is all they have ever known and they are distraught that Nanny Pritchard is not coming with us. I don't know how they would cope if they were to lose Nuala too. Nuala herself is agreeable to come with us and it will be a step up for her, for she will have a size-able increase in wages and will be in charge of two junior nurserymaids working with her. Please think about it?'

'There is nothing to think about,' Biddy said. 'I could not bear for my daughter to be so far away from me. The light would go out of our lives if Nuala was to leave here.'

'We would care for her like one of our own,' Lady Carrington said. 'We are more than fond of the girl.'

Biddy shook her head. 'No. I am sorry.'

The men had all been working in the lower field that day and hadn't been aware of the visitors at all. When they came in for their dinner Biddy told them what the Carringtons wanted and her reaction to it. Thomas John was in full agreement with his wife, and Tom too was glad that his sister was to stay at home a wee while longer.

Joe expressed no opinion at first. Then he said, 'Maybe you could reconsider.'

'And just why would we do that?'

'For Nuala's own safety, maybe.'

'What nonsense is this?'

'Listen, Mammy,' Joe said earnestly. 'These are dangerous times and some of the fellers in the IRA are like madmen and would sacrifice their own mothers to further "The Cause". I met up with a couple of them last Saturday in Buncrana. They had actually singled me out to give me a warning.'

'A warning?'

'Aye, for Nuala,' Joe said. 'They started by saying that all that were not for Home Rule were against it, and which side of the fence was this family on? I said that we wanted a united Ireland and the autonomy to rule our own country as much as the next man. They asked me, was I sure? One of them said we were Proddy sympathisers and reminded me that Finn had lost his life fighting for the English. "And now," he said, "that sister of yours is working in a Proddy house, kowtowing to the people who have taken her homeland from her." I started protesting then that it was only a job and all, and the other one, this chap with hard, hooded eyes, said, "I would tell her to mind her back, if I was you."

'Course, I had the man by the throat at that, but the other threw me against the wall, nearly knocked the breath out of me and said not to try any of that. He said that I wouldn't be much of a farmer with two busted kneecaps. They said they had come to give me a warning and it was up to me what I did about it.'

'Why did you not say anything sooner?'

Joe shook his head. 'I didn't know what to do. To tell you the honest truth, I don't want to be part of an Ireland that is won by terrorising and threatening young girls because they don't approve of their place of work. In my rational moments I think that the whole thing is crazy, but then some of these men *are* crazy.'

'So what do you think we should do?' Thomas John asked, a frown creasing his brow.

'Nuala has been given a lifeline,' Joe said. 'Let her take it and get her away from here until Ireland is a more stable place.'

Alarmed for the safety of their younger daughter, Biddy and Thomas John went up to the Big House that afternoon. Biddy was awed by the splendour of the room that they were shown into to wait and she thought it would be a tragedy altogether if the place was set light to, though she knew in the present climate that could easily happen. Joe was right: Nuala was better out of the way altogether.

Lady Carrington saw them on her own, her husband having returned to work, and though she was pleased with their decision, she was horrified with what had been said to Joe in Buncrana.

'Maybe it would be better not to tell her this,' Thomas John said. 'It would only frighten her and would serve no purpose.'

'I understand that perfectly,' Lady Carrington said. 'My husband is making arrangements to travel as soon as possible.'

Thomas John felt a failure as a father and knew his life would have little meaning when Nuala moved out of it. As for Biddy, she felt an actual pain at the thought of Nuala living apart from them. She had adored and cosseted the child from the moment she was born. And that was why she had to let her go. It was better living anywhere than ending up dead in some ditch.

Although Nuala wanted to go to England, she shed bitter tears the day she left, knowing she would miss her family greatly and might not see any of them again for years. As Thomas John held his beloved child close, he felt again the pain in his heart that he had known often since Finn's death. This was sharper than usual and he gasped.

Nuala was immediately concerned. 'What is it, Daddy?'

'Nothing, child, but the realisation that you are leaving us,' Thomas John said.

Though Nuala was satisfied with that and kissed her father's weathered cheek, Tom wasn't convinced that that was all it was. He had heard his father give that sudden gasp before and each time the blood had drained from his face, as it had that time. He had tried asking him about it but got nowhere. Now wasn't the time to go into it though, because the moment belonged to Nuala.

He lifted his sister onto the seat of the cart and sat up beside her to take her to the station at Derry where she would meet up with the family as there wasn't room in the carriage for them all.

'You'll write, sure you will?' Biddy asked as the cart began to roll across the cobbles.

'I will, Mammy,' Nuala said, 'often, for I will miss you all so much.'

They waved till the cart reached the head of the lane, when they could see it no more, then Thomas John put an arm awkwardly around his wife and led her into the cottage.

Nuala wrote regularly as she promised, and she painted pictures for them of the place she lived in: the large house with many servants that was in the small market town of Sutton Coldfield, which was no bigger than Buncrana; and Holy Trinity Catholic Church, which the master had found for her and where she went every Sunday morning. The family were also close to a place called Sutton Park, which was, she said, beautiful.

It is so big there are roads running all through it. There is such variety, woodland, pastureland and rippling streams feeding into the five large lakes, and it's very popular with courting couples.

'If you ask me that girl thinks about boys too much,' Biddy said darkly.

Joe hooted with laughter. 'Well,' he said, 'if she wasn't thinking of boys then there would be something wrong with her. I know if you had your way you would have her tied to your apron strings all the days of her life.'

'I will not have you speak to me in that way,' Biddy said. 'Thomas John, have you nothing to say to your son for the way he has just spoken to me?'

Thomas John thought Joe had a point. Although he loved Nuala with all his heart and soul, and his life was poorer without her in it, he had accepted that that was how it must be. He knew that one day she would surely marry and then another man would be the most important one in her life. Biddy, though, would like Nuala by her side all the time. That wasn't going to happen and she had to come to that understanding. Besides, Thomas John had no wish to quarrel with another of his sons. He was often haunted by the thought that, had he not argued so much with Finn, the boy might not have enlisted.

He chose his words with care. 'I don't think

that he was being at all offensive, my dear,' he said. 'He was just making a point. As for the tone of Nuala's letter, I don't think she said anything untoward either. Both of us have to realise that Nuala is not a little girl any more.'

Biddy, though, was worried by the thought that Nuala might meet an English boy and marry him. If the child was to marry at all, she wanted it to be to a boy in Buncrana and for her to live down the road, where she could see her every day and have a big hand in raising any children she might have.

As far as Thomas John was concerned, Nuala was happy and that pleased him because he certainly didn't want her to come back home yet. Ireland was in a worst shape than it had been when she had left it. The violence had escalated still further and so had the reprisal attacks. Nuala was much better off being left where she was for now.

Another letter told them of her first trip to a place called the Bull Ring in Birmingham city centre. She went on the tram for the first time and, knowing that none of her family would have seen anything like it, she wrote:

Honest to God, they would frighten the life out of you. They're big and clanking, and they run on rails like a train, only on the road with all the other traffic. They rattle along at a fair old pace, too fast, in my

405

opinion, and they sway from side to side and
you feel any minute the thing will tip over
and you will be flung out. The other girls
laughed when I said this and said I will soon
get used to them, but I am not so sure.

The Bull Ring, she said, was a big bustling place
with a market hall ten times larger than the one in
Buncrana, selling all manner of goods, and barrows
grouped outside piled high too. She imagined anything
a person wanted could be bought there.

She went on:

Some of the other girls told me that on
Saturday night the market is open till late and
all lit up with gas flares – like fairy land they
said it is; and there is great entertainment
to be had there then. Mind you, there is
entertainment aplenty in the city centre if a
person has the money and the inclination, for
there are pubs and picture houses galore, and
theatres, dance halls and something called
music hall, where, the others told me, there
are all manner of acts on and it is a great
night out.

'Seems to like it well enough,' Biddy said after
scanning the letter.

'Isn't that what we want?' Thomas John said.
'Wouldn't we worry about her if she was unhappy?'

'Yes, but . . .'

'Mammy is unhappy because she doesn't say she misses us on every line,' Joe said teasingly. 'Isn't that right?'

'Not every line,' Biddy protested. 'But she never mentioned it, not once.'

'Mammy, what would have been the point?' Tom said. 'Can't we take it as read that she misses us? Everything is different for her and she is making the best of it, that's all. I'm with Daddy here. I'm glad that she is so happy.'

'You can see the appeal to a young girl,' Thomas John ventured, noticing Biddy purse her lips slightly at the tone of the letter. 'She is doing nothing wrong and if she wants a bit of fun, where is the harm? Nuala is a good girl and knows right from wrong.'

'Aye,' Joe said. 'Don't spoil it for her, Mammy, writing censorious letters. Everyone needs a bit of fun in their lives now and again.'

So Nuala had her fun and it sprang from the pages of every letter she wrote, as she sampled all the delights the city centre had to offer in her evenings off, and wrote and told them all about it, including the dance halls where she said the girls wore shorter skirts than she was used to, and the music too was strange to her ears, but pleasant enough for all that. And she wrote that the other girls were teaching her to do the new dances from America, like the charleston and the shimmy, and that she was having the time of her life.

*   *   *

In the late autumn of 1920, Thomas John suddenly keeled over when he was working in the fields alongside his sons. They carried him to the house and Tom was dispatched to fetch the doctor. He told them that Thomas John had suffered a heart attack, quite a big one, and it hadn't been his first.

'He admitted that he has been having pains for some years,' the doctor said.

Tom knew the attacks had been getting more common of late, but Thomas John had shaken off the concern that he and Joe expressed and forbade them to tell their mother.

So though Thomas John's collapse and the doctor's diagnosis weren't a total surprise to his sons, Biddy was stunned, especially when the doctor went on to say that Thomas John was on borrowed time.

'He will recover from this,' he said, 'but he will never be the man he was once. He is not fit for any but the lightest duties on the farm and he must be untroubled in all other ways. I will be brutally honest with you: a sudden shock could kill him.'

'Then,' said Biddy, 'I will see that he shall have no shocks and my sons can take on the duties on the farm.'

Later, when the doctor had gone, Tom said, 'Shall we write and tell Nuala?'

Biddy thought about it. If they did so, Nuala would come home. To have her in Ireland at that time would be a further worry for Thomas John, and the doctor had said he wasn't to be troubled in any way. If anything should happen to Nuala he would never forgive himself, and it could so easily happen, for violence was everywhere. Anyway, the doctor said he would recover from this and then, provided he took life easy and had nothing to upset him, he could live for years. So Biddy said, 'I don't think Nuala should be told anything just yet. It will worry her and for no purpose.'

Tom thought she ought to be told, prepared almost, but he never defied his mother, so Nuala never knew how seriously ill her father was.

TWENTY-ONE

In the summer of 1921, Nuala wrote and told her parents about meeting a man she liked called Ted Maguire, who, she said, was an Irishman originally from Fermanagh though he now lived in Birmingham. She also said he was decent, honest and respectable. He had asked her employers' permission to walk out with her, and she would like her parents' blessing as well.

Biddy was incensed. Wasn't this what she had feared from the first? That her daughter would fall for some smooth-talking Englishman, and an Irishman living in England was just as bad. If she married this man, she would be living apart from them for ever.

'Write and tell her to come home immediately,' she told Thomas John.

'I can't do that,' Thomas John said. 'For one thing, Ireland is no safer now than it was when she left – worse, if anything.'

'And there is the small matter that the girl is over twenty-one,' Joe put in.

Biddy ignored Joe and went on, 'And what gives them Carringtons the right to give their permission for this man that we have never clapped eyes on to walk out with our daughter?'

Joe was astounded. 'Listen, Mammy,' he said. 'Nuala is twenty-one years old and therefore an adult. Any decisions she makes are hers to make, surely. In asking permission to walk out with her, this Ted Maguire was showing Nuala's employers respect. They have obviously met the man and approve of him so why shouldn't they give their permission for them to see each other? What do you say, Daddy?'

'I say that you are right, son,' Thomas John said. 'And I will go one step further. We will not alienate our daughter by being awkward about this. We will give this liaison our blessing and ask her to come home for a few days with this Ted Maguire so that we may meet him too.'

It wasn't what Biddy wanted to hear, but Thomas John was the one man that she respected and so she said nothing further and wrote the letter as he had directed her to.

Nuala's answer was swift and in it she said how pleased she was that they had raised no objections to her relationship with Ted Maguire. She said she loved him a great deal and he was a fine man who had a grand job too in a country where many

411

hadn't. However, she also said that neither of them could come to Ireland just then because the family were going away to the seaside for a month and she was going too, but she would be over as soon as she could manage it.

Just over a month later she wrote that Ted had asked her to marry him and she had accepted. Thomas John read that bit of the letter out to them as they were all around the table having breakfast after the milking, and he felt a momentary pang that his Nuala would soon belong to another. The girl that left Ireland's shores was no more and he longed to see the woman she had become and the man she had chosen to spend her life with.

But, the letter went on:

I know that you will probably find this hard to understand, but Ted isn't a Catholic. He was brought up a Protestant, but he says he will have no problem with me following my own religion.

The words blurred on the page as the tears sprang to Thomas John's eyes. Nuala couldn't do this disgraceful thing: shame them all by marrying a Protestant. Before his eyes was the image of the Black and Tans, now roaming the country, shooting innocent men in reprisal attacks, or razing whole villages to the ground and laughing while they did so. And his Nuala wanted to marry one who would approve of such things. It wasn't to be borne and he didn't care how old she was. There was a sudden tight band around his chest and a worse pain than he had ever had before. He opened his mouth to cry out against it, but he made no sound. He toppled forward from the chair and was dead before he hit the stone floor with the crumpled letter still in his hand.

Biddy, with a shriek at the sight of her beloved husband now lying so still on the floor was beside him in seconds. 'Do something,' she cried to Tom and Joe. 'Fetch the doctor.'

Joe put his hand on his father's neck to feel for a pulse, and when he found none he gave a small shake of his head to Tom. Tom had known his father was dead – he had seen the death mask on his face before he reached the floor – and he turned to his mother and lifted her up.

'He's gone, Mammy,' he said, gently. 'We must go for the priest as well as the doctor.'

Biddy's pain-filled eyes met his. 'He can't be dead,' she said. 'He was alive and well just a moment ago. The doctor said some shock . . .' She sprang forward suddenly and snatched up the letter. When she read it she knew what had killed her husband. 'Nuala killed your daddy,' she told the two men before her. 'That fine man that she has become engaged to is a Proddy. There, what do you think of your fine sister now?'

Tom was shocked, there was no denying it, for it was the very worst thing a Catholic could do, especially with the state Ireland was in at that time.

He took the letter from his mother and scanned it quickly.

Poor Nuala, Tom thought. She would be devastated by the news of their father's death, and if she thought her letter had hastened it in some way she would always feel guilty.

'I am going for the priest,' Joe said, making for the door, 'and then I will go on to Buncrana for the doctor and to send a telegram to Nuala.'

'Saying what, pray?' Biddy asked, her voice so cold that the words fell from her mouth like shards of ice. 'Are you going to tell her that she has killed your father stone dead?'

'Mammy, she didn't know about Daddy's bad heart,' Tom put in.

'No matter,' Biddy snapped. 'News such as that would be enough to stop the heart of the healthiest person.' She shook her head almost in disbelief. 'And for it to be Nuala to do this. Almighty Christ, your daddy thought the sun shone out of her backside. No wonder the shock killed him. Well, now Nuala will be told nothing, not now, not ever. From this day forward, she ceases to be part of this family, to be my daughter and your sister.'

'Mammy, you can't do this.'

'Oh yes I can,' Biddy almost screamed. 'I have given birth to two daughters. One ran away and one is marrying a Proddy, so by their actions they have cut themselves off from their family and that is that.'

Tom knew his mother was building up for a fine rage, the sort that had terrified him from when he was small.

Joe knew it too and also knew there was no reasoning with her in that sort of mood and so, feeling sure she would come round in the end, he shrugged and said, 'I'll just go for the priest and doctor then, shall I?'

The doctor, who came after the priest, was surprised that Biddy wasn't almost prostrate with grief. Her eyes were ravaged with raw pain, but they were dry. There were no tear trails on her face and her eyes were not glittering with unshed tears, which worried him.

He had come in his trap. He asked Tom to guide the horse up to the head of the lane for him and Tom knew the doctor wanted a quiet word. Barely had they started up the lane when the doctor said, 'Tom, has your mother cried at all?'

'No,' Tom said. 'None of us has and that is strange, for I thought a great deal of my father and I know Joe did too. It's as if dying the way he has left us all in a state of shock. I know you warned us about his heart and all – not that he took a blind bit of notice of you telling him to take things easy – and I know too that sudden death is the nature of a heart attack, but I don't think I have really got to grips with the fact he has gone yet.'

'Do you think that your mother feels the same way?'

Tom smiled ruefully. 'I gave up trying to work out how my mother's mind works a long time ago. But I think this time she is so eaten up with resentment against Nuala, who she blames totally for Daddy's death, that there is no room in her head for anything else.'

'Yes, she told me that,' the doctor said. 'Showed me the letter too. The point is, though, your father's death might not have had anything to do with that letter and I told your mother this. Your father's heart was in such bad shape, it was like living with a ticking time bomb. I told your mother this when your father had that collapse and I reminded her just now, but she is adamant that it is all Nuala's fault.'

'Mammy wouldn't let us tell Nuala how bad Daddy's heart was,' Tom said, 'and now she won't let us tell her that he is dead.'

'Said in the heat of the moment,' the doctor assured him. 'She will come round when she is thinking more clearly.'

They had reached the head of the lane and Tom bid goodbye to the doctor and turned towards the house. He didn't bother contradicting the man but he knew his mother a sight better than the doctor did, and he knew that she would never change her mind over this.

Tom was right. Biddy did not change her mind. In fact, as each day passed, she became more and more entrenched in her resentment against Nuala.

She railed against her almost constantly in the house until Tom and Joe were sick hearing about it, and she was the same at the funeral a few days later.

Nearly the entire town turned out for the funeral of Thomas John Sullivan, for the man was well known and very well liked. Many said this as they passed their condolences to the family. Tom was glad of the turnout – he felt it gave his father proper respect – but he was bitterly ashamed that his mother had forbidden him to contact Nuala, especially when another letter had come from her the day before. He didn't know what was in it – no one did – for Biddy had thrust it into the fire.

Biddy lost no time in telling everyone what Nuala had done to hasten her own father's death. Even when the people blatantly didn't want to listen, or were embarrassed, she went on and on about it anyway. No one who was at Thomas John's funeral could be in any doubt that he was laid in the ground because of his daughter Nuala.

The days slid into weeks, and Tom and Joe were still trying to come to terms with the loss of a man they were beginning to realise had been the unassuming helmsman for them both. Tom missed him more with each passing day and there was an almost constant ache in his heart.

He thought he could possibly have coped with it better if he didn't have to listen to his mother's carping voice and vitriolic tongue constantly berating the person she had once held up as perfect. He was often relieved to escape to the byre and Joe felt the same.

'Phew, dear Mama is on her high horse right and proper tonight,' Joe said one night as he and Tom began the milking.

'Not half,' Tom said with a heart-felt sigh. 'And I wouldn't be surprised if the shrieks and screeches of her were heard in Buncrana. God, she gets worse instead of better. I mean, it's over two months since the funeral.'

'I think Daddy used to curb Mammy's excesses,' Joe said. 'She has probably always been this way and Daddy stopped her going too far. You know how she always listened to him?'

Tom nodded. 'Aye she did. I think you are right. Now there is no steadying influence, and Nuala has slipped off her pedestal, and so is fair game for her bones to be picked clean.'

'That is about it,' Joe said. 'And Nuala won't know any of this, or why she gets no replies to the letters she writes every few days.'

'How d'you know she writes every few days?' Tom asked. 'We are always in the byre when the postman comes.'

'Aye, but I met the man himself in Buncrana last Saturday,' Joe said. 'He said my wee sister was a fine one for writing the letters and seemingly she had something to say every few days because he had the lane to the farmhouse worn down he had to deliver so many.'

'Ah, d'you know I can't help but feel sorry for her.'

'I feel very sorry for her,' Joe said. 'Why don't we defy Mammy and write and tell her about Daddy anyway? She has a right to know.'

'Can you imagine Mammy's reaction if we did that?' Tom said.

Joe laughed. 'Honest to God, Tom, you shouldn't let yourself be so scared of Mammy.'

'I know I shouldn't,' Tom said. 'But she has me that way since I was a boy. Anyway, this isn't just about me, but about Nuala. I couldn't guarantee her safety if she was to come here, and that is the first thing she would do if we wrote.'

'You think that Mammy would actually hurt her?'

'I am certain sure she would,' Tom said, 'and then there's Mammy's mental state.'

'What about it?'

'I think it is precarious.'

Joe grinned. 'What a nice way of putting it, Tom. The woman is clean bloody barmy.'

'All right then, however you want to put it. But can we risk making her worse?'

'All right, yes, I can see all you say,' Joe agreed. 'But all this might happen anyway. I mean, Nuala might take it upon herself to come over to see what's what. After all, she's a free agent.'

Tom shrugged. 'If she does, she does,' he said. 'And we will have to deal with it the best way we can. But we won't have instigated it.'

Joe sighed. 'So I suppose Nuala will be another one whose name we are not allowed to mention?'

Tom nodded. 'Aye, Mammy said that this evening before I left the house.'

'Like Aggie, who people say ran away with the gypsies,' Joe said. 'Rum do, that, altogether. I mean, running away with bloody gypsies.'

Tom looked at his brother and said quietly, 'Aggie ran away with no gypsies. What happened to Aggie was unbelievably tragic.'

'And what do you know about it?'

'Everything before she left here, and after that nothing at all, but I know where she was making for and it wasn't the gypsy encampment. This isn't up for general release, Joe. I don't know why I am telling you all this now, except that with Nuala estranged from the family I think you need to know what happened to Aggie. After all, there are only the two of us left.'

'I won't tell a soul, Tom,' Joe said. 'You have my word.'

And so Joe listened to the fantastic tale of the dreadful things that had happened to his sister when she had been just fifteen years old.

'And you have no idea what happened to her since?'

'No,' Tom said. 'How could I know? I was even more worried about her when Philomena – you may not remember her, but she was McAllister's wife – when she tried to contact his sister in Birmingham after he died, and the letter was returned. They said she was not known at that address. I am pretty certain that that was where McAllister was sending Aggie, but if the woman wasn't there, what happened to Aggie? What did she do? What could she do?'

'God, yes, because she knew no one else,' Joe said. 'Jesus, it's dreadful though, isn't it?'

'Terrible,' Tom said. 'I have often thought it myself. For years I have worried about her.'

Joe sighed, then burst out angrily, 'God, it is a good job that McAllister is dead, for if he wasn't then I would strangle him with my bare hands.'

The truth about what really happened to McAllister trembled on Tom's lips but he decided to keep silent. Joe was already coping with the estrangement of their younger sister from the family for marrying a Protestant and reeling from the revelations about Aggie. Tom didn't think he also needed to hear that his brother was a murderer.

That was his burden to carry to the grave.

The harvest was a good one that year. It was all gathered in before the weather broke and the autumn chill beginning to steal into the days when Joe spoke to his brother as they milked the cows one evening, which was virtually the only chance they had to say anything even remotely private.

'Tom, I know this puts you in a bit of a fix, but I want to leave here and try my hand in America.'

Tom gaped at him. 'America? But why?'

Joe shrugged. 'Many reasons. I mean, with first Finn, then Daddy gone, and Nuala disappeared from our lives, the place is not the same at all.'

'I know.'

'Then there's Mammy and the way she goes on,' Joe said. 'Tom, you are a bloody saint to put up with her, especially when she talks like you are a piece of scum. I could never cope with her the same as you do.'

'That's because I am a coward, as you have pointed out before,' Tom said. 'If I let her go her own way and say what she likes and not oppose her, my life is easier.'

'You might need to oppose her one day,' Joe said, 'stand up for yourself.'

'If I opposed Mammy at every turn where would it leave me?' Tom said. 'In the long run, my life would be worse. I am a boring man, Joe, and I realised that a long time ago. I am, essentially, a man of peace.'

'You'll never have peace with Mammy.'

'I'll have my kind of peace. If I do what Mammy wants, when she wants, then she leaves me alone.'

Joe shook his head. 'I couldn't stand it.'

'I know,' Tom said. 'You argue with her at every turn and yet she has more feeling for you than she has me. I see it in her eyes.'

Joe felt immensely sorry for his brother. He knew he spoke the truth and to leave him to cope with everything was dealing him a hammer blow, but he couldn't stay. He felt in that small place in that small country the life was being squeezed out of him, and he would lie in bed some nights, unable to sleep because of the restlessness inside him.

'Tom, you are the best in the world,' Joe said. 'And the finest brother a man can have, but all this will be yours one day. If you should take a wife—'

Tom shook his head. 'I will never marry, Joe.'

'Have you put that idea out of your head because of Mammy?'

'Not entirely.'

Joe looked at his brother sceptically and said, 'I'm not sure I believe you, but no matter. I will probably take a wife one day. If I stay here, what future could I offer anyone and maybe provide for offspring?'

'I'd never have you leave here empty-handed,' Tom said.

'Tom, I know you mean well and you would like to treat me decently, but you are master in name only. Mammy controls the purse as she controls every other damned thing on the farm.'

'Aye,' said Tom, 'but she doesn't know it all.'

'God, she's slipping,' Joe said with a grin. 'Go on, what doesn't she know?'

'She doesn't know about the top field with the sheep in that Andy Murray has been after this long while. You know he holds the field adjoining it already?' Joe nodded and Tom went on, 'Andy was at Daddy about that field before he died, but

423

Daddy always refused him, but I was thinking of letting it go. I would have to anyway when you leave, for I would have my work cut out with the cows and the ploughing and the planting and all. So what do you say that I let him have the field and then you will have your money for America?'

Joe felt the worry slide from between his shoulder blades. It was all right to have grand notions about starting in that brave new world the other side of the Atlantic Ocean, but it would be hard to do it without a penny piece in one's pocket. He had thought he would have to take employment in the town somewhere for a few months through the winter and save his wages, but here was Tom, offering him the solution on a plate. Joe slapped his brother on the shoulder. 'Christ Almighty, Tom, but you are a brother in a million,' he said, his voice thick with emotion.

Tom smiled. 'I take it you approve of that notion,' he said sardonically. 'I will set the wheels in motion immediately. Now, not a word to Mammy till the deed is done and the money is in the bank.'

'I am not an idiot altogether,' Joe said.

'No?' Tom asked sarcastically, and Joe laughed and punched him on the arm.

While negotiations for the field and livestock were going on, Joe helped Tom get the farm ready for the winter. They made numerous trips to the bog, cut the peat, cleaned out the well and coated it with lime, and replaced any thatch that looked as if it needed replacing. Tom, though grateful for his brother's help, was morosely aware that it was the last time they would do such things together. He knew he would miss his brother a great deal and he dreaded telling his mother.

Biddy's rage when Joe broke the news to her reached mammoth heights. She shrieked and screamed, while abuse spewed from her mouth. Tom had the urge to rush to the barn and put his hands over his ears as he had sometimes done as a boy. He marvelled that Joe should face her so unafraid. Biddy forbade Joe to go to America or any other such place, and he even managed a wry smile as he said, 'You can't forbid me anything. I am a grown man and you have no jurisdiction over me.'

'You are my son.'

'Aye, just that,' Joe said. 'Not joined at the hip.'

'Your place is here.'

'I don't think so.'

'Well, where is the money to come from?' Biddy demanded. 'For I'll tell you here and now, you will never get a penny piece from me.'

'Isn't that Tom's decision to make?' Joe asked. 'Isn't he the master here now that Daddy has gone?'

Biddie's eyes slid over to the son she regarded as spineless and she said contemptuously, 'Tom will do as he is told.'

And he would, Joe thought. That was the bugger of it. He didn't even bother protesting at what

Biddy had said, probably because he was well used to it. 'The time I ask you for money will be the time that you can have a say in how I spend it,' Joe said. 'And let me tell you that day will be a long time coming, though I could take a goodly portion from the profit of this farm for the years I have grafted unwaged.'

'You could not.'

'Yes I could,' Joe said, 'and any court in the land would uphold that claim. There was a piece in the paper only recently about that selfsame issue, but I want nothing from you. I have money of my own.'

'But where did you get it?'

'That, Mammy dear, is my business.'

His remark enraged Biddy so much that she lifted the poker. Joe spun around in front of her, so angry that his nostrils were dilating and his eyes wild. He spoke through gritted teeth: 'If you so much as touch me with that it will be the last thing you ever do, so now I am telling you.'

Biddy was startled enough at the look in Joe's eyes to replace the poker. She turned to Tom, the one she could always intimidate, and said, 'Where did he get the money?'

Aware that she would have to know anyway, though his knees were knocking together, Tom said, 'I sold the top field and the sheep in it to Andy Murray.'

'You did what?' The shrieking voice nearly lifted the thatch from the roof. Joe, seeing his brother quailing before this fresh onslaught, said mildly, 'I don't think you really need to ask that question. I think you heard what Tom said perfectly clearly.'

Biddy ignored Joe and said to Tom, 'You sold one of our fields without a word to me?'

Tom gathered all his courage. 'Aye, Mammy, aye, I did. You didn't need to be consulted. It was my decision and I took it.'

'You are too stupid to make these sorts of decisions for yourself,' Biddy said disparagingly. 'The man would have you fleeced. How much did he offer you for it?'

'Luckily Andy Murray didn't think me too stupid to deal with,' Tom said, 'and he offered me the same price he offered Daddy before he died.'

'But your father didn't sell, numbskull.'

'Yes, but not because he thought Andy was offering too low a price. He told me that the man had been very fair, but then with three of us we could cope with the sheep. With two it is difficult, and by myself it would be impossible.'

'So how much did you get for it?'

'That really is our business,' Tom said. 'I gave Joe the money and, as he said, it was only what he was due if everyone has their own.'

'I make that decision,' Biddy snapped.

Tom contradicted quietly, 'No, Mammy, I do.'

Biddy saw her sons ranged against her, Tom taking courage from his brother's presence. She would let Joe go his own way, as he would in any case. He hadn't the same feel for the land as Tom

– Thomas John had always said so. As long as she had Tom she would be all right. He would never leave her, she knew, the man hadn't that much gumption. And she would soon bring him back in line when he hadn't his brother at his back.

With the veil of secrecy lifted, the word quickly flew around that small community that Joe Sullivan was leaving for America and nothing would do the townspeople but they hold a party for him to wish him well. No one suggested having it at the house and Tom was glad, knowing his mother would never have allowed such a thing anyway. In the end, Grant's Bar offered their back room for the venue and donated a couple of barrels of beer to help the party go with a swing.

Because of Joe's habit of going around the town talking to people when he went into Buncrana on a Saturday, he was well known and well liked, and they wanted to give him a party he would re-member. Tom took them both in on the cart, for he had the impression that his brother would be in a less than sober state when the party drew to a close.

He was right, and the more Joe drank, the more nostalgic he became about these people that he might never see again. He would be back, he promised, when he had made his fortune. He would be home with his pockets filled with gold pieces. Tom was embarrassed but Joe's friends just laughed at him and said it was the beer talking.

Later, some of these people helped load the comatose Joe into the back of the cart and the consensus seemed to be that he was a grand fellow and would be sorely missed. Tom had to unload the grand fellow at the other end, and suffer a tirade from his mother as he virtually carried him to the room Nuala once had. Then he laid him on the bed, semi-undressed him, left him to sleep it off and went out to deal with the horse and cart. When he sought his bed that night he was bone weary and aware that in a few hours' time he would have to be up again to do the milking.

The next morning, Tom didn't even try to wake his brother as he sneaked across the bedroom. He did the milking alone and told himself to get used to it: that was how it was going to be from then on, for Joe was leaving the following day. When he returned to the cottage, it was to see Joe outside the door tipping a pail of water over his bent head. He looked at Tom shamefaced.

'Sorry.'

'It's all right.'

'Jesus, have I got one thick head,' Joe said. 'It was a good night, what I remember of it. I didn't disgrace myself or anything, sure I didn't?'

'Not really,' Tom said. 'I suppose you could

have been worse. You talked a lot of blethering nonsense about coming back when you make your fortune in America with your pockets full of gold.'

'Did I upset anyone?'

'Not really,' Tom said. 'God! Half of them were nearly in the same state as yourself and will barely remember much of the night themselves, if any thing at all. They all still think you a grand man altogether and they will be not the only ones that will miss you when you go off tomorrow.'

'Tom . . .'

'The time for talking is past,' Tom said. 'Let's go in. I am that hungry I could eat a horse.'

Early the next morning, the cart clattered up the main street of Moville, which was on the other side of the Inishowen Peninsula, on the banks of Lough Foyle. The liners to America were anchored in the deep waters of the Lough and the passengers first got into tenders from the pier in Moville and were rowed out to board the ships.

Tom drew the cart to a halt at the Square, tethered the horse to one of the posts and lifted Joe's bag out of the back of the cart. With Joe carrying the case, the two brothers started down the Main Street towards the pier with their boots ringing on the cobbles. There was the usual cluster of people at the pier, some like Joe, chancing their arm in America, and others like Tom, waiting to see them off.

Joe had butterflies in his stomach and wasn't

at all sure that he was doing the right thing. What worried him most was Tom.

'You must try and stand up to Mammy,' he said earnestly.

'Haven't we travelled this road more than enough?'

'Aye,' Joe said. 'But you did all right when we told her I was leaving and she went on about the field and all.'

'Aye, but that is not my normal way of going on.'

'I know,' Joe said meaningfully. 'I have seen your normal way of going on. The woman treats you like a rubbing rag.'

'I'm all right,' Tom said. 'Don't worry about me.'

'I can't help it. It's a habit that I have got into,' Joe said as the tender drew alongside the pier and the little crowd surged forward. 'And don't give up on having a woman in your life. You have a lot to offer.'

Tom laughed. 'The point is, a woman might gladden my heart and warm my bed but she'll have to have miraculous qualities too: the ability to sweeten my mother.'

'Oh Lord, I don't think they make any women like that.'

'Then I will stay as I am,' said Tom. 'And now will you get into that tender before it goes without you?'

The brothers embraced and then Joe stepped forward. The tender pulled away from the shore and Joe turned to wave. Tom felt suddenly bereft and very lonely. He knew that now it would be him and his mother in that small cottage together till at least the end of his mother's life, and he looked forward to the future with no enthusiasm whatsoever.

TWENTY-TWO

By the late summer of 1925, the euphoria that the Great War was over was long gone, Birmingham was in dire financial straits and many of the residents of that beleaguered city were only too aware of it. Aggie and Lily had been with HP Sauce for nearly seven years by then, and they knew how lucky they were to be in regular employment when so many others weren't. Each evening, they would leave the factory on Tower Road and have to walk down past the tall, green, four-faced clock tower at Aston Cross, standing on its own little green island, to reach their lodgings.

As often as not, the island was filled with men, their grey pinched faces barely visible beneath the caps pulled well down.

'That's to hide the desperation in their eyes,' one girl at work said.

Aggie could well believe it, and yet these were just some of the city's many, many unemployed. They were all dressed in a similar way: grey caps, thin, raggy and totally inadequate clothing, and well-cobbled boots. Some wore army-issue greatcoats to show they had done their bit.

'Bloody disgrace,' Lily said one evening as they passed many of these despondent men. 'Land fit for heroes, my eye. Land for unemployment and despair, more like.'

She had a point. Even the families of those who had paid the ultimate price had been betrayed, and it pained Aggie to see the barefoot starving children. A sizeable group of them clustered around the factory gates at night, begging for anything the workers might have left from their lunches. Aggie and Lily weren't the only workers to have the odd sandwich left to give to the starving children.

'The government should be ashamed,' another said fiercely.

'The government! When has the government ever been interested in the likes of us?'

'When they wanted our men to fight their wars and the women to run the country and make the arms for the men, that's when,' the first woman replied.

Aggie knew all they said was true and yet, unbidden, for she seldom thought of that shadowy time in her life any more, she remembered the damaged young officers, with their haunted eyes and shaking hands, who had visited the club. But she said nothing and pushed the memory away.

'Good job Polly's Georgie got work in the end,' Lily remarked as they made their way home one night. 'I'd have hated to see her children out here begging.'

Georgie had been out of work for two years after he had been demobbed. Aggie and Lily would have liked to help the Palmers, but Georgie wouldn't allow it.

'I do know how he feels,' Polly had said. 'It is bad to be beholden to people, but we all have to eat. Charlie and Clara would be barefoot if it wasn't for the *Evening Mail* Fund, and, as it is, I am never away from the pawn shop.'

Neither woman liked to see Polly as distressed as she was about money and she could hardly discuss any of this with Georgie as he already felt such a failure. They were as delighted as she was when an old mate from the army spoke up for him and got him set on at Fort Dunlop just off the Tyburn Road.

All Polly had to worry about then was the black carbon dust that clung to Georgie's clothes and became ingrained in his skin.

'I tell you,' she told the two women, 'he comes home from work as black as any miner. And the stink of it seems to seep through the pores of his skin.'

And yet when Charlie had left school the previous year, when he turned fourteen, Polly had no objection to him following his father. Jobs were still few and far between and, as she said, beggars couldn't afford to be choosers.

Aggie and Lily knew they were well off. They

were well paid and they had good working conditions too. In fact, Aggie and Lily had full and happy lives as the years passed.

The only regret that Lily had was that Aggie stayed single. Despite there being not that many men around, more than a few had shown an interest in Aggie, who still was a very attractive woman. She was always pleasant and polite to them, but she never went any further than that, and she told Lily she wanted nothing to do with men ever again.

Lily, though, would have liked her settled. She was past sixty-five and she knew she wouldn't live for ever. In fact there had been a few worrying times recently when she'd had trouble breathing that she had to hide from Aggie. She worried what would happen to her when she was no longer there.

Aggie would be all right financially, at least in the short term, because for years Lily had been salting away money from her work on the streets and it was safely stored in the Post Office. Originally she had saved to visit her brother in America. Even when it became apparent that he didn't want her there, she continued to save, because it had become a habit by then. Levingstone too had been extremely generous, and then there had been the work at the munitions.

Lily wanted Aggie to have it all when she was gone. The lady at the post office told Lily that she would have to change the name on the book otherwise it would go to her next of kin, the brother in America, and she didn't want that.

So one night, she broached the subject with Aggie. At first Aggie didn't want to hear anything about a time when Lily might not be around, and when Lily mentioned the money she threw up her hands in horror.

'Lily, I don't want your money. I don't even want to talk about this.'

Lily caught Aggie's hands between her own and looked into her eyes. 'Listen to me, bonny lass,' she said. 'One thing no one can do is deny the grim reaper indefinitely. If you don't take this money then it will go to my brother when I am gone. He didn't want me in any part of the nice clean life he had carved for himself in America, though it was my whoring put him there, and so I don't want him to get his paws on my money. Now you and I have been through thick and thin together, and I love you like the daughter I was never allowed to have.'

Aggie sighed. 'Oh, Lily, I really don't know what I am going to do without you.'

Lily felt tears stinging the back of her own eyes, and in an effort to prevent them falling she said quite brusquely, but with the ghost of a smile, 'Don't take on, you silly sod. I ain't intending to pop me clogs just yet, but I would rest easier if you would do this to please me.'

Aggie wiped her eyes and tried to take a grip on herself. 'All right,' she conceded. 'Maybe sometime, but we haven't got to think about this now, have we?'

'No time like the present,' Lily said. 'I want us to go up the post office and get it sorted this Saturday morning, and then we need never have this conversation again.'

Eventually Aggie said, 'I will do this, because you so obviously want me to, but I hope it is years yet before I benefit from it.'

It was after this that Lily started to fail, almost as though now that she had put her house in order, she could give in to the illness that she knew was sweeping through her body. Aggie begged her to stay at home, to take it easy, see a doctor, but she took no notice.

When she almost collapsed one late September afternoon, the firm wanted to call the doctor, but all Lily wanted was to go home. Aggie had to bear most of her weight in the street, and was surprised how light she was, for she had once been such a buxom woman. Had she been any heavier, Aggie might have had trouble getting her up the stairs, but she managed it, and once they had reached their rooms she helped Lily undress and put on her nightclothes. And then, with her tucked up in bed, she went for the doctor, despite Lily's protest that she would be as right as rain in a day or two.

The doctor didn't think so. After examining Lily he went to find Aggie. 'She has a tumour,' he said. 'It's on her lungs.'

'Is that serious?' Aggie asked anxiously. 'Will she recover?'

'It's very serious and I'm afraid it is just a matter of time.'

Aggie's hand flew to her mouth and blood drained from her face so effectively that the doctor was alarmed. 'Is there anyone we can contact to be with you?'

Aggie shook her head. 'There is no one,' she said, and realised bleakly how true that was. When Lily was no more she would be totally alone and that thought chilled her to the bone. But, she chided herself, this wasn't the time to think of herself.

'Have you any idea how long Lily has?' she asked the doctor. 'She has a brother in America. Should he be sent for?'

The doctor looked at Aggie and wondered how he could tell her that her dear friend might be taken from her at any moment, when she seemed to have no one around to support her at all.

However, Aggie was no fool, and when the doctor said gravely, 'I think that her brother should be contacted immediately,' she knew the words he was hesitant to say.

'I have written a prescription for something to help with the pain,' the doctor said.

'Is she in a lot of pain?' Aggie asked in surprise.

'Considerable, I should say,' the doctor replied. 'And for some time too.'

'She's never said a word about that.'

'She isn't saying it now either. Not the complaining sort, I would have said. Anyway, this medicine

439

might ease things for her, and if you soak a flannel with warmed camphorated oil and lay it across her chest it might ease the congestion there. Any chemist will sell it.'

The nights were drawing in and the streets dusky when Aggie set off a little later for the chemist's shop at Aston Cross. With her head down as protection against the mizzling rain she cannoned into someone who hadn't seen her approach because she had her umbrella raised in front of her. They both apologised together, and then, in the pool of light spilling out from a gaslamp, they stared at one another.

The other woman recovered her wits before Aggie and exclaimed, 'Aggie! By Christ, you're a sight for sore eyes, all right. Everyone thought that you had gone and dropped off the bleeding planet.'

'Hello, Susie,' Aggie said. In a way she wasn't that pleased to see her, for she was a link to that part of her life that she would rather forget. But then she felt a little ashamed of herself. She smiled and said, 'Not quite, as you can see.'

'Is Lily with you?' Susie asked.

'She is, but she is ill in bed now. I've just had the doctor and I've come out to get the prescription made up,' Aggie said. 'What about you? What are you doing around these parts?'

'Been to visit my mother in Upper Thomas Street.'

'Oh, it's a wonder I haven't caught sight of you before.'

'Not really,' Susie said. 'I seldom come near the place. Black sheep of the family, I am. Mom lives with my sister, Carol; has done for years. Anyroad, the old woman took bad and Carol sent for me. Don't know if I done any good or even if the old codger was the slightest bit pleased to see me. I wouldn't half like to see Lily again, though.'

'Well, come with me to the chemist,' Aggie said, 'and then I'll take you up to where we live now.'

'You're on,' said Susie, and fell into step with Aggie, holding the umbrella aloft over the two of them.

When Susie saw Lily propped up in the bed, she knew she was looking at a dying woman. There was no sign of this, though, as she said to Lily in a jocular manner, 'What did you mean, you old bugger, running out on us without a word like you did?'

Lily let her eyes slide around the room and saw the door was closed and that Aggie was nowhere in earshot, before saying in a husky voice that rasped in her dry throat, 'I had to do it that way. It was safer for Aggie.' She closed her eyes as if the effort of speaking had exhausted her, and her chest rattled.

Susie felt immensely sorry for her, but to mention it would do no good and so she said, 'Do you want to tell me why? I don't want to tire you.'

Lily smiled grimly. 'I'll tell you,' she gasped. 'And don't worry about tiring me. I will soon have

441

all the time in the world to sleep.' And then she went on, 'That time that Aggie was beaten up, remember?'

'Yeah, I remember.'

'Well, it were Finch very nearly killed her, and later did for Alan Levingstone as well, but you probably worked that out.'

'Sort of,' Susie said. 'I mean, we all know what the vicious sod is capable of. Don't blame you getting Aggie away either. He nearly tore the place apart looking for her and dain't believe we dain't have as much as a hint of where you might be.'

'That's why she had to be kept off the streets,' Lily said. 'He'd have found her easy – not that she was mad keen doing that, anyroad.'

She stopped, too breathless to go on. Susie's eyes were sympathetic as she watched her friend of many years fighting for breath. Eventually her chest stopped heaving quite as much and Susie poured her a glass of water from the jug by the bed and helped her drink it. At last Lily was able to go on.

'Any job you needed references for,' she said, ''cept for the munitions, that is. They couldn't get enough people to do that sort of work and we were at Kynoch's in Witton until an explosion almost destroyed the place in the summer of 1918. After that we got them precious references, found jobs at HP Sauce and we moved here.'

'God,' Susie breathed, 'so Aggie was almost

under Finch's nose all the time. That bloody man is evil. And I'll never give a hint of where you are, so don't fret.'

Lily knew that Susie would never betray her, but she was suddenly incredibly tired and Susie saw the difficulty she was having keeping her eyes open. 'Lie down and rest yourself, Lil,' she said.

Lily didn't protest and Susie helped her. She settled on the pillows with a sigh of contentment and her eyes were closing as Susie stole from the room.

'Will you let me know if anything happens?' Susie said to Aggie, and Aggie knew what she was saying. Yet she said, 'How? I never go anywhere near that area.'

'I wouldn't expect you to,' Susie said. 'If you tell our Carol, she'll get word to me. Lots of the girls will want to pay Lily respect.'

'Ah God, Susie, I don't know what I'm to do without her.'

'And it won't be long. You do know that?'

'Course I know,' Aggie said. 'I am not blind, and the doctor said as much anyway. I'm going in to work tomorrow and trying to arrange time off. I think I have holidays owing. If I have to have it without pay, then I will. Lily was always good to me and I won't leave her now.'

Susie nodded approvingly. 'You do right,' she said. 'She thought the world of you.'

Aggie was too choked to speak. She managed to take down the address, then shut the door on

Susie, leaned against it for a minute and let the tears trickle down her cheeks.

Aggie shared one tragic week with Lily, tending her gently and watching her deteriorate rapidly. She had sent a telegram to her brother, telling him how ill she was. He replied that he was making arrangements to come home to see her. She only hoped he made it before Lily lost her tenuous grip on life.

Lily never saw her brother, however, for she slipped into a coma and died two days later. When finally Aggie's tears were spent, she sent for the doctor and, remembering her promise to Susie, went to see her sister, Carol, who promised to relay the message. Then Aggie went to tell Polly, and she cried too at the loss of that kind and feisty woman. She went back with Aggie that night and helped lay Lily out. Aggie hesitated to do more, certain that Lily's brother would like to make arrangements for the funeral. However, the day after Lily died, Aggie received a letter from her brother, expressing regret that he would be unable to return to England after all.

Aggie felt such anger as she remembered all the years when he never once came near the sister who had reared him, or invited her over for a short visit to meet his wife and children. She knew it would have meant the world to Lily and now he couldn't even come to the funeral. Well, Aggie decided her dear friend would be tossed into no pauper's grave. She would be buried with dignity.

Lily's funeral was held in Aston Parish Church and was attended by a great many people, colleagues from HP Sauce and the prostitutes from Lily's earlier life. Aggie was glad to see, however, that the latter were all respectably and decently dressed, and no one could possibly have guessed what their profession was.

She was particularly pleased about this because she would have hated Polly and George to find out about her earlier life when they thought she had been in service. Charlie and Clara, now fifteen and thirteen years old, had also insisted on coming, and Aggie was gratified to see how much they had thought of Lily.

She had written to Jane, who had never returned to Birmingham from Cheshire, but married a local man there. Jane had sent a telegram back saying she would be there to say goodbye. Aggie remembered how well they had got on and was glad she had asked her. She knew she would like to see Jane again too, but wished they could have met under happier circumstances.

There was also someone else watching the cortège going into the church, then come out again, and the hearse and the mourners make their way to Witton Cemetery where Lily was to be buried, and that someone was Finch. The rent on the houses had been due that day, and although Finch employed a rent man, he knew the women were scared of him so he sometimes used to collect the rents himself. His menacing presence never failed to give them the jitters and he enjoyed that. Kept them on their toes, he thought, for he didn't stand any messing about by any whore.

So that morning when he called at two houses and got no reply he was annoyed because the girls were to go nowhere until the rent was paid. However, the door of the third house he knocked on was opened by a prostitute that had been working the streets for just two years and was one of the few in that area not attending Lily Henderson's funeral. Knowing this, all the other women had given her their rent books and money to pay Finch when he came.

She knew nothing about the fixation Finch had about Aggie because it had happened long before her time. So when Finch asked where the women had gone to she saw no harm in telling him they had all gone to a funeral at Aston Parish Church.

'The woman used to live around here,' she went on. 'Name of Lily something. Lily Henderson, or something like that.'

Finch couldn't believe his luck. So the old trout had kicked the bucket, and about bloody time too. He had always known that Aggie and Lily were together somewhere and he knew Aggie would be at the old crone's funeral. Maybe it was time to renew their acquaintance, he thought as he climbed into his car and turned it towards Aston.

By the time another week had passed, Finch knew all there was to know about Aggie: where she lived and worked, what time she left home in the morning, what time she finished work, and that she walked home alone. He wondered what he should do with that knowledge. He could just leave her alone, let her continue the way she was. Why should he concern himself with the little scrubber? He didn't know the answer to that himself except that Aggie had got under his skin like no girl ever had before, and he hated that.

Anyway, why should she go around as if she was as respectable as the next girl when he knew where she came from? She had no right to mix with decent people and to try to pass herself off as one of them. As far as he was concerned, once a whore always a whore, and he knew exactly how to teach Aggie a lesson. Now that October was halfway through, it would be pitch-black by the time that Aggie left work each night, and that suited his purpose very well.

Lily had been such an integral part of Aggie's life for so long, her dying had left a gaping hole that no one else could fill. She thanked God that she had her job to occupy her waking hours, and the company of her colleagues, who were sympathetic because they had seen how close the two women had been.

Most of the workers looked forward to it being Friday but Aggie didn't. As she bade farewell to her workmates and started for home that evening, she knew she had two days of loneliness stretching out before her. Polly had urged her to visit them, but Aggie hesitated to do that at the weekend with Georgie home. The weekend was a family time and, with Lily gone, the worst days in the week for her.

She gave a sigh. She knew she would have to take a grip on herself. She wasn't yet forty years old and she was fit and healthy. She had to stop feeling sorry for herself. In this reflective mood she was crossing over Upper Thomas Street when she felt her arms suddenly grasped from behind, and her hands twisted up her back while a smelly sack was thrown over her head.

Her screams were muffled by the sack and she began thrashing her head from side to side and fighting against the restraining arms until a blow to the head rendered her unconscious.

When Aggie came to, she was in a bedroom that she had never seen before. A strange man was sitting on a chair not far from the bed, and when he saw her eyes flicker open, he got up and approached her. Aggie flinched, expecting another blow, but the man neither touched her nor spoke to her. Then he turned and left the room, and Aggie heard the key turn in the lock.

She was still scared, but she wouldn't let herself

just lie there like a frightened rabbit. She heaved herself out of bed, but immediately her head began to thump, the room swam before her eyes and she felt a little sick. She held on to the bedpost till everything stood still again and the nausea had passed.

Knowing the door to be locked, she was making her shambling way to the window to try to establish her whereabouts, at least, though it was as black as pitch, when suddenly the door opened. She wasn't even surprised to see Finch – he would be the only person on earth who wished her harm – but still she felt her blood turn to ice.

Finch had a smirk of satisfaction on his face and he curled his lip as he said, 'Well, well, well. Look what the cat has dragged in. How do you do, Agnes Sullivan?'

Despite her fear, Aggie was suddenly very angry. 'I'll tell you how I do, you slimy toad,' she said. 'Much worse for seeing you. What right have you to have me captured in the street and brought to this place? Let me go this instant!'

'Can't do that, my dear. You belong to me now.'

'I do not,' Aggie retorted.

'Oh, but you see you do,' Finch said. 'When I bought the club I bought everything in it, and that included you, but when I took up residence there, I found that the bird had flown.'

'Don't be stupid!' Aggie cried. 'You can't go around buying people like that.'

'But I have, you see,' Finch said. 'Now you will

work for me.' And then he added, 'On the streets, in the gutter, where you belong.'

'No,' Aggie cried. 'That part of my life is over now and you can do what you like to me, but I would never work for you if you were the last man on earth. I despise you.'

Aggie expected the blow and, though she tried to dodge it, Finch caught her full in the face. A second was delivered to her stomach and doubled her over, and when Finch hit her again in the face he knocked her to the floor. Aggie's body was one mass of pain and she was terrified, but she willed herself not to show fear.

Sheer willpower kept the tears at bay as she spat out through her swollen bleeding lips, 'I will not work for you and it doesn't matter what you do. I would rather die than stoop to that.'

Finch recognised a quality in Aggie that had not been there before, a confidence and assurance, and he knew that if he beat her senseless, she wouldn't change her mind. If he turned his back for one moment she would run away, no matter what the consequences would be.

He had lost some of the power he had over Aggie and he had to regain it somehow but he knew just how he was going to do that.

'You will do as you are told in the end, my dear, never fear,' he said in a voice that made Aggie's skin crawl. 'Just remember there are more ways of killing a cat than drowning it.'

* * *

450

When Finch had gone, Aggie crawled back into bed to try to ease her aching body. She probably looked a sight because she could feel the dried blood coating her face, but there was no mirror in the room and no way of cleaning herself up either. She wondered what other delights Finch had in store for her, and though her mind recoiled from further pain, she was determined that she would not work on the streets for him or anyone else, and would get away from him at the first opportunity.

She woke and thought it was probably morning, though it was still dark outside. She got out of bed and padded to the window. She could see nothing, for shutters had been fitted to it from the outside. Her heart sank: there was no possibility of escape that way.

When her eyes had adjusted to the semidarkness she saw that something had been left by the door – a slice of dry bread on a plate and a large glass, which was full of gin.

She was both hungry and thirsty. When she was lifted the night before she had been looking forward to a good meal and now her stomach growled in protest. She tore at the bread and had eaten it in minutes but it took only the edge off her hunger. She didn't want to drink the gin. She hadn't touched gin or opium since 1916 and she didn't want to go down that road again. She held out as long as she could, but in the end she took little sips of it. These served only to dampen her mouth, so in the end she had to gulp it, and knew from the taste that opium had been added to it.

When she had drained the glass, the room began to spin, and she barely made it back to bed before passing out. Twice more that day, she was given a bare slice of bread and a glass of gin, and the second time a bucket was placed in the corner of the room.

Her mind recoiled from that. It was obviously there for her to relieve herself, and she realised Finch was going to keep her locked in the room till she gave in. Well, he could rot in Hell for she had no intention of doing that. But as time passed it was hard to remain focused because there was nothing in the room but the bed, nothing to do to pass the time, and she welcomed the oblivion drinking the opium-laced gin induced in her.

The food was brought by a large man who never spoke a word, or even looked at her, not even when she asked him what she was doing there and where Finch was.

On the third day, she was left a bottle of gin with the bread, and though she tried to ration it, she was unable to. She felt filthy for she was still in the clothes she had worn when they had brought her in, the bucket stank to high heaven and she had seldom felt more miserable. She was rousing herself to drink only enough to send her back into a stupor, and by the end of the next week there was little resemblance to the working girl she had once been.

* * *

After three weeks of giving Aggie such a lot of gin heavily laced with opium, Finch gave orders that it was to stop and so was the bread. Aggie at first could not believe that there was nothing waiting for her when she opened her bleary eyes. She lay back and closed them again, but she was unable to sleep, for her whole body had started to tremble and she knew that she needed a drink badly.

After a little while, she could stand it no more, and she hammered on the door. She heard the key being turned and the man who always brought her food was looking at her questioningly.

'I need a drink,' Aggie said.

'Mr Finch says no more for you.'

'You don't understand. I need it.'

The man shrugged and Aggie clutched at him. 'Please?'

He shook her off and she sank to the floor sobbing. The man left her and closed the door.

When Finch entered the room later he saw Aggie curled in a ball on the bed and groaning, for the shooting pains in her stomach were so severe they were making her feel sick.

'You look like something you would see lying in the gutter,' Finch said. 'Get up.'

'I can't.'

'You had better or the toe of my boot will help you.'

The thought of Finch kicking her in the stomach caused Aggie to stumble to her feet. She was unable to stand upright, though, and was leaning forward like an old woman on trembling legs that threatened to give way at any moment, the pain causing globules of sweat to gather on her brow.

'Look at you,' Finch taunted. 'Your clothes are a mess and filthy dirty, and you stink to high heaven. Your hair's in tatters and your mucky face is all caked with dried blood.' He shook his head as if he was unable to understand her foolishness. 'And to think the solution to stop all this is in your hands.'

There was only one thing on Aggie's mind, and she fell to her knees before Finch and implored, 'Please, Tony, let me have a drink.'

'Of course, my dear, when you earn it.'

'Tony, I really can't go out on the streets,' Aggie said. 'Please don't make me do this.'

'I am not making you do anything, my dear,' Finch said with an evil smile. 'You just don't eat or drink until you do. And get away from me. You disgust me.' He gave her a push and so she lay spread-eagled on the floor.

Aggie could scarcely believe that he had left her like that. She hammered on the door till exhaustion overcame her and she sank to the floor and slept.

By the evening of the second day she knew she couldn't take any more. She would do anything to have the drink and opium her whole innards were craving for, but no one came, though she hammered the door and shouted.

When Finch came in the following day she was almost hysterical. She flung herself at him.

'I'll do it,' she said, 'anything, but please let me have a drink first?'

Finch detached Aggie's arms from his clothes and brushed himself down fastidiously. 'I am glad you have seen sense at last, Aggie, but at the moment, no one with any sense would go within a hundred yards of you. I will have water sent up and clothes for you to change into after your wash.'

'And a drink?'

'Not until you have earned it, my dear,' he said with a leer.

Aggie was taken in Finch's car to one of the roughest areas of Birmingham, where there were three pubs close together.

'Plenty of trade,' Finch said, almost rubbing his hands with glee. 'You will open your legs a good few times tonight, I think.'

Aggie felt as sick as a pig when the first drunk nearly stumbled over her on his way home. In the lamplight she saw his eyes gleam when he caught sight of her, knowing immediately what service she was offering.

When he leaned towards her the stink of beer nearly knocked her on her back, and the sight and smell of the brown rotting teeth when he opened his mouth caused the nausea to rise in Aggie's throat. She wanted to push the man away from her, but of course she couldn't do that.

'How much?' the drunk growled out.

'Half a crown.'

'Half a crown? Better be good for that. I like to get me money's worth. Come around the back so we're not disturbed, like.'

Aggie thought she would die with shame when she allowed that vile, smelly man to pull down her drawers. Then he expected her to take his throbbing member in her hand and rub it a bit to get him in the mood. Suddenly he spread her legs wide with his hands and she lifted her skirts. When he entered her she bit her lip to prevent a cry escaping because she thought that she had been ripped in two.

Finch was right. When the news filtered through the pubs that there was a whore outside ready and willing, she had a steady stream of customers. By the end of the night, Aggie's degradation was complete. She knew her life was effectively over now, for she could no longer do without the gin and the opium, and would do anything it took to get hold of it.

Finch pocketed her earnings as they went back in the car. As he passed her the gin bottle he said, 'Not bad for an evening's work. Now you listen to me, Aggie. You do this every night and if you earn enough then you will get fed and have as much gin and opium as you want, but if you don't earn enough, you will get nothing. Do we understand each other?'

Aggie understood, all right. She understood that Finch owned her, body and soul. He had been right at the outset: she now belonged to him.

TWENTY-THREE

Tom too thought his life had ended. Every day was just one long line of chores with no let-up at all, and he could see the same life going on year after year. This was against the background noise of his mother's incessant whining and complaining voice. Nothing he did seemed to please her, and in the end he accepted that that was the way it was going to be. If he retaliated then his mother would be even worse. He knew many of the townsfolk thought him weak and spineless and he could hardly blame them.

He lived for his brother's letters, glad, as the years passed, that one of them at least was doing well. On reaching New York, Joe had almost immediately got a job at an engineering works owned by a man called Brian Brannigan, a former Irish immigrant himself, who had made good.

'Good God!' Tom said when he read Joe's account of this. He was sure if Joe had fallen in a dung heap he would have come up smelling of roses. His good fortune did not just end there, either. Over the years he had risen through the firm in a most spectacular way, and ended up marrying the boss's daughter, Gloria.

However, in 1929 came the Wall Street Crash and Joe's father-in-law, bankrupt, killed himself because of it. Joe was left almost penniless and destitute, with both a distraught wife and mother-in-law dependent on him.

He tried to get a job, but it wasn't easy, for America was sunk in a deep depression. Tom urged him to come home, but he said that his mother-in-law would not leave the land where her husband lay buried and so they were stuck in America for the time being.

Then in the autumn of 1934, Gloria gave birth to a son they called Benjamin Joseph, and Joe's joy was muted by the responsibility of another mouth to feed.

Biddy was almost gleeful that his household seemed closer to starvation. Tom felt quite help-less. He would willingly have sent Joe his last halfpenny, but he was never given money of his own. All he could do was write encouraging letters to Joe and Gloria, and hope and pray that their lives would improve before too long.

The day was a fine one and just one of many that spring, Tom thought with satisfaction as he sat and ate his dinner. It was 24 April, and already the crops were ripening in the fields and the two new calves and the litter of pigs growing up fit and healthy. Suddenly, through the window his eyes caught a movement in the lane and he turned to his mother, who was at the other side of the table. 'There's a garda coming here.'

'Here?'

'Aye. Shall I see what he wants?'

'No,' Biddy said, getting to her feet. 'I will.'

Tom shrugged and returned to his dinner, and Biddy opened the door to the young and nervous garda and stepped into the yard to find out what he wanted. The voices were muted and Tom could not distinguish what was said, but he thought he would know all soon enough.

The garda however was quite appalled by Biddy's reaction to the news he had just given her. When he got back to the station he said to the garda behind the desk, 'My mammy always said that Biddy Sullivan isn't right in the head and, honest to God, it makes you wonder. I mean, I have just given the worst news ever to a mother and she looked . . . well, she almost looked pleased.'

'Maybe she was in shock?' the other policeman suggested. 'That can affect a body in all sorts of strange ways.'

The young garda shook his head. 'She didn't look in shock to me,' he said. 'She had a smile on her face as if was good news I had given her.'

And Biddy considered it to be good news. When she turned to face Tom, the expression on her face unnerved him, for she was smiling. Tom hadn't seen that very often and he watched the light dancing in her cold eyes as if she was truly delighted about something.

'What did the garda want?' he asked tentatively.

'He came to tell me what I have wished for many a year. Your sister Nuala and her husband have been killed in a car crash in Birmingham.'

Tom was stunned. He felt a pang of loss for he had loved his sister dearly and missed her dreadfully when she had first gone to England.

And now she was gone, her young life snuffed out along with that of her husband, and his mammy was saying it was what she had wished for. He met her gaze and said steadily, 'Mammy, that's a dreadful thing to say.'

'She killed your daddy,' Biddy spat out, and she remembered the overpowering grief she had felt the day that Thomas John died. From that moment she had prayed for something bad to happen to Nuala.

'You can't be certain of that,' Tom answered, 'and even if you are right and the news in the letter did hasten Daddy's death, she didn't know. It wasn't her fault.'

'Well, I think differently,' Biddy snapped. 'And I am glad that she has got her just deserts at last. Now if you have eaten your fill, shouldn't you be about your duties and not arguing the toss with me?'

Tom was only halfway through his dinner, but both the news and his mother's response to it had

461

taken away any appetite he might have had. Without another word, he returned to the fields. But as he toiled that afternoon, memories of his beautiful sister kept invading his mind.

Everyone had been Nuala's willing slave and Tom always admired the dainty loveliness of her as she grew up. Little did he know when he had seen her off on the train in Derry so many years ago that he would never see her again. Tears ran down his face, not just for the death of her, but for the wasted years when he could have made contact with her and yet he had taken the coward's way out rather than risk upsetting his mother.

Then he saw his mother come out of the cottage and scurry up the lane. Tom stood up, easing his aching back and shading his eyes from the sun, watched her heading off towards Buncrana. Now what is she up to? She never went to Buncrana on a week day. Whatever it was he knew he would only find out about it when she was willing to tell him.

He had always known she had funny notions, different from other people's. However, from her reaction that morning he had to acknowledge that she was a very wicked woman. He truly hoped, though, that with Nuala dead and gone, Biddy would at last get rid of the resentment she had carried around with her for so long.

That same evening, as they sat before the fire, Biddy told Tom that she was going to Birmingham the following day for Nuala's funeral, and that she had sent a telegram to those in Birmingham telling them this. Tom's mouth had dropped open in shock for he could hardly believe his ears. He hadn't thought either of them would actually attend the funeral service, knowing how his mother had felt about Nuala. He would have been surprised if she had sent flowers or had a Mass said for her, but this . . .

'Why go now, when she is dead?' he asked in genuine amazement.

He was further staggered by Biddy's reply. She said she was going to see the set-up of the place.

'There are children, more than likely, and they are going to no Protestant to rear. They will come to me to be raised in the one true faith. I know my duty.'

Tom knew that his mother didn't like children. It was clear now that her resentment against Nuala was as deep as ever, and any children Nuala might have had would receive little love or understanding. He couldn't help hoping the marriage had been a childless one.

However, Nuala had two children and, once in Birmingham, Biddy wrote to tell Tom all about them. Molly was thirteen, and even more bold and disobedient than her mother. Her brother Kevin, at five, was just as defiant as his sister, as well as being totally spoiled. But she would put manners on the pair of them before they were much older.

Tom had shivered in apprehension for the offspring of Nuala.

The townspeople of Buncrana mourned the passing of Nuala and her man, and felt sorry for the poor wee orphaned children. The Mass Tom had said for them was attended by half the town. Tom told the townsfolk that his mother was bringing the children back with her and he saw that many were surprised. As they said later, out of Tom's hearing, they didn't know that Biddy had a charitable bone in her body.

However, the whole business took longer than Biddy had imagined it would, and Tom thought he had never known such peace as he did in those few weeks when his mother was away. He could cook enough to keep body and soul together, and he washed things as he needed them, so he got by all right without help, though many offered it.

In the meantime, letters and telegrams were flying backwards and forwards. Soon the townspeople were aware that the wee boy had been ill and it had been decided to leave him in Birmingham with his grandfather. However, Biddy was bringing Nuala's daughter, Molly, back to the town where her mother was born and bred.

When Tom saw Molly alight from the train at the station in Derry, he felt his stomach tighten as he gave a small gasp, for it was like his poor, dead sister had been returned to him, her daughter was so like her. Tom's gentle heart turned over in sympathy, for the suffering of his poor niece was so very evident and he saw too that his mother disliked the girl intently.

Tom was soon aware that his mother intended to make no allowances for Molly, and yet as well as coping with the loss of her parents he knew everything would be strange to her. A farm on the edge of a market town was a long cry, he would imagine, from Molly's home in a bustling city. And she had left all that behind, and the friends and neighbours she had had, not to mention her grandfather and little brother.

What had she come to instead? A malicious old woman, who seemed determined to punish Molly for the sins she imagined Nuala had committed, and an uncle afraid of his own shadow.

Biddy continued to heap humiliation and condemnation on Molly's head, for whatever she did wasn't right. This was apparent to the townsfolk, who had seen plainly how harsh she was with the girl that first Sunday at Mass. In the end Molly began to look forward to the quiet peaceful times in the byre with her Uncle Tom, finding it soothing to lean her head against the velvet-flanked cow and see the bucket placed between her knees fill with the white foamy milk.

It was in the byre with her uncle that Molly heard what had happened to the family over the years. Finn had died before Nuala had left Ireland, but she hadn't known that Joe had emigrated to America, and Tom told Molly all that had happened to him there. He also told her just how his own father had died and about his bad heart. He said her mother was not to blame, and saw that Molly was relieved by his assurance.

Tom and Molly got on very well and yet Tom knew his company was not nearly enough. The point was, as his mother well knew, Molly should have been at school every day. Biddy, however, had decided she had more than enough book learning, and instead the woman kept her at it from morning till night. In fact, from the moment Molly stepped over the threshold of the cottage, his mother had seemed to lose the use of her limbs, for it was Molly who did everything, while she presided over her and found fault with every damned thing she did.

There was the matter of the letters from Molly's grandfather and the next-door neighbour that Biddy destroyed. She not only forbade Molly to write to them any more, she wrote to the people concerned in Birmingham and said that there was to be no communication between them and Molly.

The way Molly stood up to Biddy over that shamed Tom for she was just a slight, wee thing and so many tragic things had happened to her. Yet she had stood stoically before the woman who had always frightened the life out of him. Molly eventually lost that fight when Biddy would not back down.

Tom felt that he had let her down, and it didn't

make him feel good about himself. He was determined to make amends and he spoke to the postmistress in Buncrana, Nellie McEvoy. She of course knew all about the letters that had arrived and she had even tried remonstrating with Biddy about the letters she sent to Birmingham, forbidding Molly's grandfather and the neighbour, Hilda, writing to her.

'I told her I thought it hard,' Nellie said, 'and got my head bitten off for my trouble. But I do think it is a dreadful thing to do, Tom, to cut the poor girl off from all she holds dear, even her wee brother.'

'So do I,' Tom said grimly. 'And this has decided me anyway. I know that you have asked Molly up to tea tomorrow afternoon and I am determined that she will go, but I know too that I may have to stand against my mother to do that.'

'And will you be able for that?'

'I won't like it one bit,' Tom admitted. 'But I will do it for Molly's sake. God, Nellie, the child is desperate for company and your youngest, Cathy, and she are the exact same age, aren't they? All things being equal, they would have met at school and it is my mother's doing that they don't.'

'But we won't waste any more words on her,' Nellie said. 'We'll see Molly tomorrow then.'

That was the beginning of a deep friendship that Molly developed with the whole McEvoy family. She and Cathy were soon close friends.

Nellie became like a pseudo mother to her, and Cathy's big, burly father, Jack, acted as the father Molly also missed so much.

Tom insisted on coming over every Sunday evening to walk home with Molly from the McEvoys', and he took to sinking a few pints with Jack in Grant's Bar in the town, which he had never done before.

Tom had just never got into the habit of socialising, but now he decided a man could be too much on his own and he enjoyed the pints and the company of the men in the town on Sunday night.

He had also taken to having a pint or two on Saturday while he was collecting the fish from the harbour, like most men did. One Saturday the Guinness Tom consumed gave him the nerve to demand a wage for his work, and for the first time he had money in his pocket to spend as he wished. Biddy approved of none of it, of course, but then, Tom asked himself, when did his mother approve of anything?

In fact one of the things he enjoyed most about those walks home on Sunday night was the opportunity to get to know Molly better, when the friendship begun in the byre could be expanded on. She told him lots about her father, who had had a fine job in that depressed city. 'It was because of the Great War,' she told Tom. 'Dad was a hero. Mom used to say that any who fought in that war was a hero like her brother Finn, but Dad was a real hero. He got a medal because he crawled into the battlefield to rescue an injured officer, a man called Paul Simmons.'

'And did he survive it?' Tom asked.

'Oh yeah,' Molly said. 'Good job and all, 'cos he didn't behave like some toffs did afterwards and forget Dad. He had taken over his father's factory. As he had one leg shorter than the other, he found driving difficult so Dad would drive him places and then do anything else he wanted him to do. Mom said that if Dad hadn't had a good, well-paid job her employers wouldn't have allowed them to court, never mind marry. Just think, Uncle Tom,' she went on with an impish grin, 'I might not even have existed, and that I'm sure would have pleased your sainted mother.'

Tom laughed, realising how much he loved and admired his young niece. She had wormed her way into his heart, all right, and he welcomed the opportunity to get to know her better.

Molly was sixteen in February 1938 and began counting the days till she could leave the farm. Tom didn't blame her one bit, though he knew he would miss her sorely.

Then Joe wrote to say that his mother-in-law had died and the way was open now for his family to leave America. They would not be returning to Ireland though, Gloria would never settle there, having been born and bred in a city. They would, he said, make for London.

* * *

Eventually Joe settled in a place called Tottenham and got work on the docks with no problem at all. He set about providing properly for his family again, but in his letters home he spoke often of the possibility of war with Germany in the near future.

He said he wasn't fooled by Neville Chamberlain going to see Hitler in Munich in the autumn of that year. He came back on 29 September, waving a piece of paper in his hand and declaring, 'There will be peace for our time.' It was the headline in every newspaper, both in Ireland and Great Britain at the time, but Joe wasn't the only one who was sceptical.

Christmas came and went, the year turned, and as the spring unfolded Tom began to feel that they were balanced on a knife edge. Joe saw war as almost unstoppable and wrote advising Tom to get a wireless in.

'These are dangerous times and even in Ireland, it is as well to keep abreast of things.'

Tom knew his brother was absolutely right, and he wasn't averse to getting a wireless anyway. When he mentioned it to Molly later that day as they ate around the table, she hugged herself with delight.

'Ooh, it will be terrific to have a wireless in the house,' she said. 'The McEvoys have one and it is great entertainment. There are plays and comedy shows and music and programmes for children, all sorts of things.'

Tom smiled at her. 'I have it mainly for the news, Molly.'

'I know that,' she said, 'but no one can listen to the news twenty-four hours a day.'

'You won't listen to it at all, miss,' Biddy snapped. 'I'll see to it that you won't have time to sit and listen to any wireless.'

'You don't have to sit and listen to it,' Molly said. 'That is the beauty of it. I can listen and still do my work. In fact, working away to music helps to lighten the load.'

It was not Biddy's intention to have the load lightened for Molly, the exact opposite, in fact, but she concentrated her energies on Tom. 'Boy, money must burn a hole in your pocket.'

Tom had had a drink and that gave him the courage to snap back, 'I am no boy, and when I ask you to give me something towards anything I buy, then you may express an opinion. What I do with my own money is my business.'

The Spanish Civil War had finally ground to a halt in March of 1939 with the dictator Franco as the victor. In the same month the Czechoslovakian people, dissatisfied with their government's decision to give away part of their country to appease Hitler, began to protest. The government, afraid of revolt, asked Hitler for help in restoring order. His answer was to invade and take over the country. Tom wrote to urge Joe to come back to Ireland with his family before it was too late and war broke out.

Joe's answer was swift. He said that people

couldn't just run away when the going got tough and that he wanted to stay and fight if necessary to prevent that madman Hitler from overrunning Great Britain too.

In May, he wrote of the Territorial Army being recalled and in the same month conscription began of men of twenty and twenty-one years of age.

Molly was glad that the McEvoys had worked out a subterfuge years before so that she could receive her letters, addressed to Cathy, at the post office.

The loving concern of her granddad and their next-door neighbour, Hilda, had sparked from the pages over the years, while Kevin's had sometimes made her laugh, though with each one she was aware of him growing up without her, and she yearned to see him again.

All in all, though, the letters had sustained her through many of the bleak times, and now they were able to tell her how Birmingham was preparing for war. In July, Molly's granddad told of the trenches being dug in the parks and brick-built reinforced shelters being erected. The children, Kevin included, were recruited to fill sandbags to line the outside.

'*He is more excited than worried about the possibility of war,*' Granddad wrote. '*He sees it as one big game.*'

But the adults knew it was no game. In August, Britain signed an alliance with Poland, which promised Britain would go to Poland's aid if she were attacked.

'Hitler's armies are nearly on the borders now,' Molly said. 'Jack showed us in the map he had inside the paper last Sunday.'

'Aye, I know,' Tom said.

'Granddad is going to get an Anderson shelter,' Molly told him. 'He said it's made of corrugated iron. You have to dig a pit to sink it in your garden and pile earth on top. I would rather they be there than in the brick-built surface shelter. I don't really see how they can be much safer than a house.'

'I agree,' Tom said. 'God knows what Joe will do, for they live in a flat with no garden at all. Anyway, Joe said once war is official he is going to offer his services as a volunteer fireman. They are advertising, apparently. Foolhardy, perhaps, but then someone has to do these things. Tell you, Molly, I'm glad we got the wireless in. Even if Ireland is neutral we have loved ones that will be in the thick of it. We need to know what is happening.'

There was to be an announcement from the British Prime Minister, Chamberlain, just after eleven o'clock in the morning of Sunday, 3 September. What he was going to say was almost a foregone conclusion for the German Army had invaded Poland two days before. Yet Tom and Molly needed to hear the dreaded words actually said.

'*I am speaking to you from the cabinet room*

*of 10 Downing Street. This morning the
Ambassador in Berlin . . . no such undertaking has
been received and that consequently this country
is at war with Germany.'*

Tom sighed.

'So, now we know for definite.'

'You knew before,' Biddy snapped. 'That is,
unless you are a complete and utter numbskull.
But it won't affect our lives in the slightest.'

'Maybe not you, Mammy, but both Molly and
I have people in Britain that we will worry about.'

'Joe has a perfectly good home here where they
all would be safe,' Biddy snapped. 'If he has chosen
not to avail himself of it, then it is his own lookout, and Molly has no reason to concern herself
with people who were part of her past life.'

'You know one person shouldn't tell another
how to think or feel,' Molly said to Biddy. 'And
for your information, I love those people in
Birmingham just as much as I did the day I left.'

'Nonsense, 'Biddy retorted. 'How can you say
that? You hardly know them any more.'

Molly hid her secret smile and after, in the
cowshed, she said to Tom, 'She really thinks that
I have had no correspondence with my family for
four years, because she knows nothing about the
letters. I will never tell her, though, however much
I long to throw it in her face, because it will
impinge on the McEvoys and they will have to live
here after I leave.'

'Are you leaving?'

'Not yet,' Molly said. 'Nellie advised me to wait until I am eighteen because she says that then your mother will have no jurisdiction over me and will not be able to force me to return. But that isn't that long. I will be eighteen in February next year. I can go any time after that.'

'I will miss you.'

'And I will miss you,' Molly said sincerely. 'Isn't it odd, really? I mean, I didn't know you at all for the first thirteen years of my life and yet I have grown to love you so much in the time that I have been here.'

Tom suddenly cleared his throat and turned away so that Molly wouldn't see the tears gathering behind his eyes. He knew that when Molly left, it would be like someone turning off the light in his life.

The war drew a little closer to the Sullivan farm, for the Royal Navy had commandeered Derry as a naval base, called HMS *Ferret*. Lough Foyle, which separated the British North from the Free State, was filled with military craft for convoy duty protecting merchant ships, and a company of soldiers was positioned at Buncrana to guard Ireland's neutrality. Tom wondered what chance the few soldiers would have against a highly disciplined and so far invincible German army bent on invasion. He kept these thoughts to himself, though; it would help no one to give voice to them.

Molly's eighteenth birthday came and went. In May Germany invaded the Netherlands and Belgium, and Hitler launched his promised blitzkrieg on Rotterdam, leaving nine hundred dead in one night. Knowing that what Hitler could do in Rotterdam could easily be done in Birmingham, London or any other damned place the madman wanted it to, Tom and Molly sent letters off to London and Birmingham, pleading with their loved ones to take care.

A few days later the papers were full of the hundreds of Allied soldiers trapped on the beaches of Dunkirk and France and the frantic efforts to rescue them after the surrender of Belgium. France fell towards the end of June and everyone was well aware that only a small stretch of water separated Hitler and his armies from Britain. The Luftwaffe began blitzing coastal towns and invasion was on everybody's lips. Molly's granddad urged Molly to stay where she was for the time being.

Molly chafed at the delay.

'You can't blame your grandfather for wanting to protect you,' Tom said. 'He hasn't seen you for going on for five years. Although in his head, he knows you are eighteen, probably in his mind is the picture of you still the child that you were when you left Birmingham, afraid and sad and just thirteen years old. Probably the greatest thing he can do, in memory of your parents, is keep the two of you as safe as possible, and with you here he just has Kevin to worry about.'

'I hear all you say and even understand it, but no one is thinking of me in this.'

476

'Believe me, Molly, everyone who loves you has your welfare at heart,' Tom said. 'Everyone is waiting for and dreading invasion. Bide here a little longer until we see what transpires.'

TWENTY-FOUR

The first bomb fell in Birmingham on 9 August, according to the wireless and the paper, though Birmingham was always referred to as 'a Midlands town'. After that, there were more sporadic attacks throughout the month. Molly worried about the people back home, but her granddad wrote that he and Kevin were just fine and that she was not to think of returning just yet.

The first attack in London was in September and centred around the docks area. Tom was concerned for the safety of Joe and his family. However, there was nothing either he or Molly could do to help, and meanwhile life had to go on.

The raids increased in ferocity in October and then suddenly the letters from Birmingham ceased. By the time October gave way to November, Molly's letters to Birmingham had a distraught edge to them. Intense fear dogged her every waking moment until she felt she couldn't bear it any more. She knew that she had to return to Birmingham, and without delay, to find out what had happened.

Tom didn't want Molly anywhere near to Birmingham, though he knew the level of her concern. Each time she mentioned leaving, it brought to Tom's mind Aggie's desperate flight and the nagging worry of what had happened to her that had never truly left him.

Molly did her best to assure him that she would be all right, but as he couldn't share Aggie's story, her words couldn't help him. The point was, his two sisters had been making for the same city. From the moment Aggie climbed into McAllister's cart, and many years later, Nuala – in very different circumstances and with the grudging approval of her parents – had mounted the train at the station in Derry, he had never seen either of them again.

He was terrified of allowing his slight, wee niece that he had come to love dearly to travel alone to that same city, especially with the danger of bombs toppling from the sky. But how could he prevent it? She was old enough to make decisions herself and her fears for her loved ones were no longer unfounded. She needed to know. Even if the news was bad she needed to know, but he knew he would worry about her every second that she was away.

He was both relieved and pleased when Molly was able to tell him of her money from Paul Simmons, the man that her father had rescued way back in the First World War. Apparently he had been sending her money since she was fourteen years old, which she had saved in the post office. When she told him how much it was, he knew that, even with the fare taken out of it, she would have plenty to find lodgings somewhere while she sorted everything out.

The fiercest air raid on Coventry, on Thursday, 14 November, only strengthened Molly's resolve. The following Saturday she went into Buncrana to book her passage to England.

However, she sought out her uncle at the pub by the harbour just a little later and, drawing him to one side, away from the press of people, she thrust an envelope into his hand that had been waiting for her at the post office. Tom noted that the scrawled address was written in pencil before withdrawing the scrap of paper from inside. It had jagged edges as if torn from a pad, but the cryptic message was clear enough.

'Molly, come and get me. It's horrible in this place – luv Kevin.'

Kevin's unhappiness leaped from the page and tore at Tom's heart, but at least it showed the child was alive, or had been when he wrote the letter. That was the best scenario Molly could hope for.

'Where is he, do you think?' Tom asked.

Molly shrugged. 'I have no idea, but as soon as I get to Birmingham, I will search until I find him, and also find out what has happened to Granddad and Hilda, our old neighbour. I won't rest until I do.'

Tom nodded. He knew nothing would stop Molly now. 'I see clearly what you must do and, indeed, what I would want to do myself in your shoes, and I will do all in my power to help you.'

'Thank you, Uncle Tom,' Molly said quietly. 'That means a great deal to me.'

Molly left the following Tuesday, 19 November. Tom had bought her a fine torch and plenty of extra batteries, a money belt to keep her cash safe, and food and drink enough to feed a small army.

He'd intended taking her as far as the station, but as they stood on the slight hill above it and Molly saw the lights of the station twinkling, she would let him go no further. As he watched that stalwart figure walk away from him down the hill, he knew that Molly was taking a piece of his heart with her.

Later, with his head reeling from the tantrum his mother had flown into when she realised Molly had left, he sought out Nellie McEvoy, needing the company of sane and ordinary people.

'How are you feeling?' she asked him, noting his sad and strained face.

'Inadequate,' he admitted.

'Will you stop blaming yourself for all the world's ills?' Nellie said in exasperation, though she smiled at him. 'What in God's name could you have done that was in any way different?'

'It's just—'

'It's just that farms don't run themselves, Tom.'

'I know that,' Tom said miserably, 'but it isn't just the journey and all and travelling to a country at war. What if the news is as bad as it gets?'

'What if it is?' Nellie said. 'I am really not being heartless, Tom, but take heart from the fact that that young boy was alive when he wrote that letter. I am sure that Molly will be using that knowledge as a sort of talisman to hold on to.'

Tom knew, however, that he wouldn't stop worrying about Molly until he received a letter from her saying that she had arrived safely. All other news could wait, but knowing how worried her uncle was, she had promised to write immediately and let him know that she was all right.

It had spread around Buncrana, as these things do, that Molly Maguire had gone back to Birmingham to see that her grandfather and brother were all right. Many townsfolk asked about her and at first Tom said confidently that he was sure they would hear from her any day.

Three weeks after she had left, he was beside himself with worry.

'Maybe she hasn't had the time yet,' Nellie said, though she too was anxious. 'Maybe she is waiting until she has something to say before she writes.'

'No,' Tom said. 'She promised me.'

'Och well, you know what these young ones are,' Nellie said with a dismissive flap of her hand.

'Not Molly,' Cathy put in. 'She is as straight as a die. If she says she will do a thing then she will. I've never ever known her tell a lie.'

'Nor have I,' Tom agreed.

Silence settled around them and each was busy with his or her own thoughts. Anything, just about anything, could have happened to Molly in that city bombed to bits most nights.

'We must just wait and see,' Nellie said at last, for there was nothing else to say. 'Sure, she might write any day. Does your mother express any opinion about it at all?'

Tom sighed. 'Oh, yes,' he said. 'Happiness.'

'Happiness?'

'She says Molly has gone the way of her mother. Dead and gone, and good riddance.'

'Jesus, the woman must be mentally deranged.'

'I think she is,' Tom said. 'Molly always thought it, and Joe. I mean, she was never an easy woman, and without Daddy our upbringing would have been very harsh indeed. Daddy wanted his pound of flesh all right, and we helped on the farm virtually as soon as we could walk, but he was fair. Well, to be completely honest, he was fair with me and Joe. Aggie had a special place in his heart and he fair doted on Nuala, as we all did. Finn seemed to irritate him and he often got the rough edge of Daddy's tongue, yet I saw him sometimes look at Finn, when he thought himself unobserved, with a soft look in his eyes. I think deep down Finn was his favourite, but Daddy would think that was an unfair way to go on and so would be harder on him because of it.

'Mammy cared for none of us but Nuala and

Daddy, and when he died it was as if something snapped in her brain. Just at the moment, I am so worried about Molly, and Mammy's attitude is hard to take.'

'I'll say it is,' agreed Jack. 'I'd want to strangle the old harridan. Let's away to sink a few pints and forget all about her for an hour or two at least.'

'Aye,' Tom said wearily, getting to his feet. 'I'm up for anything that will block out my mother's gloating face.'

Birmingham wasn't the only city to be bombed, of course. London was going through it too. Tom wrote every week to his brother urging him to take care. It was a pointless exercise really because not only did Joe work on the docks, which was a favourite place for some of the bombers to drop their lethal loads, but he was also a volunteer fireman, which was one of the most dangerous jobs of all.

Not, of course, that Joe could tell him anything in his letters, but he didn't need to, for the newscaster on the wireless would often pronounce how many bombers had attacked the capital and in which area the buildings were set ablaze. You didn't need much imagination to understand the danger that Joe would be in, fighting those fires.

Even Joe, though, was concerned that Tom had heard nothing from Molly. He thought that she must be dead. He had seen plenty of dead bodies since the bombing began, and he knew Molly would be counted as just one more casualty of a war that had already killed thousands of innocent men, women and children.

He did feel a pang of regret for the young woman that Tom had described in such glowing terms, and also described the hellish life their mother had put her through. He wasn't surprised, for if Molly had resembled Nuala even half as much as Tom said, then their mother would make the most of it, punishing her because she couldn't get to Nuala. Joe wrote a warm and sympathetic letter to Tom, offering comfort and support while gently suggesting he should not raise his hopes of hearing from Molly.

He wondered for a moment about Molly's brother, Kevin, whom she had gone to find, and the grandfather who had been looking after him. It was likely the grandfather was dead too, but the boy might be alive. He had been over a month ago, when he wrote the note to his sister that Tom had told him about. Pity he had put no address on it, because he wasn't that much older than his own son, Ben, just a boy yet, and now possibly alone in the world. God, he would hate the same thing to happen to his own son, and so in his letter he also asked about Kevin and whether Tom had received any further information, but he had none at all.

Nellie and Cathy kept their hopes alive until Christmas. They had letters, presents and cards to send to Molly as soon as they had an address for her, but as Christmas and the New Year passed with no word at all, Nellie and Cathy too lost heart that they would ever see Molly again.

The townsfolk had stopped asking about her as well, having drawn the same conclusions. Though many were saddened, Nellie and Cathy seemed burdened down with sorrow for the girl they had known so well, and they were often tearful.

Tom was the same. The tears flowed sometimes when he tilled the soil, or milked the cows, and mixed with his sadness was guilt. He blamed himself for allowing Molly to go alone to Birmingham.

He was glad of the heavy springtime workload. He was out from dawn till dusk, which at least ensured that he went to bed exhausted. It wasn't just that there was twice the work without Molly; somehow it all seemed more of a chore. He hadn't realised how much she lightened his days, and sometimes he couldn't see the point in any of it. Breaking his back for what? His mother? And after her day, what then? Work and more work, and for bugger all. It wasn't as if he had a son to pass it on to. If he envied Joe at all it was because he had a son.

Then, in mid-March, he went into the post office one Saturday and saw that Nellie had a big smile on her face.

'You look like the cat that's got the cream,' he said.

'Better than that,' Nellie replied. 'I've had a letter.'

Tom's heart seemed to stop beating. Hardly daring to hope, he said, 'Not from Molly?'

Nellie felt immediately contrite. 'No, I'm sorry, Tom. I should have thought that you would assume that. It's from Hilda, Molly's old neighbour and she— No, I won't tell you.' She lifted the counter. 'Come through to the back and you can read it for yourself in peace.'

Tom read the letter and was totally confused.

'So what do you make of that?' Nellie said, as he folded up the letter and returned it.

'I don't know what to make of it,' Tom said. 'Molly left here on the nineteenth of November, so where was she and what was she doing until three weeks ago, when she called on her old granddad's neighbour?'

'And where is she now?' Nellie said. 'She knows now her granddad is dead and her brother in some sort of orphanage, because the neighbour knew that much.'

'What terrible news for that young girl to shoulder on her own.'

'I know,' Nellie said. 'And think what that wee boy has gone through. Fancy your mother not only refusing to take him in when Social Services asked her to, but also saying there was to be no further communications between the siblings.'

'That is desperate altogether,' Tom said. 'The child must have felt totally abandoned and yet you know I'm glad he didn't come here. He would be one more child for me to try to protect from

Mammy. I would give my eye teeth to know they are all right, though, and I hope to God this Hilda gets to know something.'

'That's what I am hoping for too,' Nellie said fervently. 'That letter came a few days ago, and I wrote straight back and said that we had not received one word from Molly since she left here. I told Hilda that we were delighted to know that Molly was alive and obviously well, and if she had any news of her we would be pleased to hear it.'

'I should go over myself.'

'Talk sense, Tom,' Nellie said. 'You can't leave the farm and, anyway, what chance would you have of finding Molly in a city the size of Birmingham? Maybe now we have Hilda as a contact we will hear something soon.'

'I hope so, certainly,' Tom said, 'because you're right, of course: I cannot leave the farm, much as I might want to.'

'Wait and see,' Nellie advised. 'Really, it is all we can do.'

The summer and then autumn passed and Molly's friends in Ireland were no nearer finding out where Molly and Kevin had disappeared to. Hilda too had drawn a blank.

The war rumbled on. Then, in December 1941 Japan bombed Pearl Harbor, bringing America into the war. As the year drew to a close Tom faced 1942 with little enthusiasm.

* * *

Tom came in stamping his feet, for the day was raw, the fields and hedges, seen now in the half-light of a dull morning at the beginning of February, were rimed with frost, and icicles hung from the thatch.

'It's a cold one, all right,' he said to his mother as he set the bucket of milk on the stool. 'Coldest yet, I'd say.'

Biddy made no reply to this. Instead she said, 'There is a letter there from your brother.'

'Joe?'

'I was under the impression that you had only the one brother,' Biddy remarked. 'That Yankee strumpet he married wrote it. Apparently Joe is injured.'

Tom ignored the derogatory reference to Gloria, for his mind registered only one word. 'Injured!' he cried, catching up the letter from the table.

'Not to be wondered at with the job he was doing,' Biddy went on. 'I mean, for God's sake, what the hell does he know about putting out fires?'

Tom barely heard his mother. He was scanning the letter where Gloria had written that Joe had been injured when a flaming building had collapsed on him, and that he had quite extensive burns, and internal injuries from being crushed. Tom was completely shaken by the news, especially when Gloria added that Joe was a very sick man and she thought the family should be told. Tom felt sick at the thought that he might actually lose his brother. He turned to his mother.

'Don't you think that this is the most upsetting news, Mammy?'

'News I expected as soon as he told me he had volunteered as a fireman,' Biddy stated flatly.

Tom gazed at her and his eyes narrowed in bewilderment. 'Mammy, I have said it before and I shall say it again, you are as hard as nails,' he said. 'Aren't you the tiniest bit upset about Joe and his family?'

Biddy's eyes narrowed maliciously and she almost spat out, 'I am used to loss. It has been the pattern of my life. I had my man and my youngest son taken from me, another son is fighting for his life and my daughters are dead to me too. And what am I left with? A gormless imbecile like you, that's what. That upsets me a great deal.'

'So now we know where we stand, Mammy,' Tom said, tight-lipped. 'But don't kid yourself that you are upsetting me by this type of talk. I have heard it more than enough. You have never made any secret of the scant regard you have for me. Maybe it would please you more if I left you to fend for yourself.'

However, Tom knew he wouldn't, and his mother knew it too, and that was the rub. While his mother lived he was bound to the land, and though he might fret about the brother lying desperately ill in a hospital bed in London, he had as little chance of seeing him as he had of flying to the moon.

That night he sat down and wrote a letter to

the sister-in-law he had never met, expressing his deepest regret at what had happened and assuring Gloria the whole family was in his thoughts and prayers constantly.

'D'you want to put a wee note in yourself before I seal up the envelope?' he asked his mother.

'I doubt your brother is up to receiving mail.'

'I meant a note of support for Gloria.'

'Joe's wife is of no interest to me,' Biddy said. 'It was because of her that he didn't come home here to Buncrana where he belonged when he left America.'

'No it wasn't,' Tom said. 'He told me himself he likes city life. He isn't that keen on farming. You must know that. It isn't everyone's cup of tea, you know.'

'Don't give me that,' Biddy snapped. 'He was born and bred to this life. He would soon have settled down to it again. I know whose fault it was they went to live in London, and it wasn't Joe's. It was all the fault of that American wife of his, and I will never forgive her for it.'

TWENTY-FIVE

By the end of April, Derry was reputed to be full of Yanks. 'Oversexed, overpaid and over here' they were widely dubbed.

'People say those camps have been there all the time,' said Jack, as he and Tom made their way to the pub one Sunday evening. 'Only the soldiers wore British uniforms then. Disguise, I suppose.'

'Aye, but sure they would only have to open their mouths for people to know it was all so much eyewash.'

'Probably didn't allow people that close,' Jack said.

'So how do they know, then?'

'I don't know,' Jack admitted as they reached the doors of the pub. 'How do people get to know anything anyway? They just do, that's all.'

Tom hadn't time to reply because as soon as the regulars saw him they wanted to know how Joe was. Remembering the send-off he'd been given when he went to America, Tom hadn't been surprised at the popularity of his younger brother even now.

The point was, Joe was a fighter. He had survived the series of operations to repair his damaged spleen, kidneys and liver, and to restore his shattered ribs, and had even overcome the subsequent infection and fever that threatened to kill him. Gloria had told Tom this much. She also said that Joe now faced some weeks of painful skin grafting.

Tom had great admiration for Gloria and how well she was coping with everything, for she had written to him often when Joe had been too ill to write himself, and he had got to know her quite well. He asked after the boy, Ben, from the beginning, aware that, as the child was no baby, he had probably been worried to death about his father.

It would do him no harm, he thought, to know he had a caring uncle not that far away. He knew that sweets were rationed in England, for Joe had mentioned the rationing in an earlier letter, and so he made a parcel up for Ben and in it he put sweets and chocolates and a couple of comics. The child had been delighted and wrote such a lovely thank you letter back that Tom did the same thing every week or two.

Gloria was grateful for the things he sent to Ben, and for his interest in them generally, because she often felt very isolated. She had expected Joe's mother to write and thought it odd that she hadn't, especially when Joe had been so sick. Joe had always said she was a difficult woman, but still Gloria thought it wouldn't have hurt her to include a wee note. She mentioned this to Joe when he was on the road to recovery.

Joe had been neither surprised nor upset. He told Gloria that Tom would convey any news to her, and, knowing his mother as he did, added that she was probably disappointed with him for choosing to come to London when she wanted him to go straight back to Buncrana.

'Surely you remember the letter she sent?' he asked Gloria.

'Yeah, sure I do,' Gloria said. 'And she was pretty mad then, I know, but that was in '38, Joe. It was four years ago. People get cross and disappointed all the time and have to get over it. I have had nothing but disappointments since the Crash and Daddy killing himself. But you can't keep harping back, can you? That does no good at all.'

Gloria, however, was talking about how the majority of normal people cope. She had no experience of how Biddy Sullivan's ill humour and displeasure quickly turned to resentment that was never forgotten and could span generations.

Gloria liked Tom, though, who wrote to them every week without fail. She knew Tom was a worrier – that had come across in his letters – so when their block of flats was destroyed in a raid when Joe had been in hospital about six weeks, she gave only a sketchy account of it to Tom. She said she and Ben were fine and were being housed in a church hall, and that many more were in a similar position.

She also asked him not to tell Joe; there was no need for him to know yet. He knew nothing about it and she didn't want him upset. Tom was appalled by what had happened to them. However, he could do damn all about it. He agreed with Gloria that there was nothing to be achieved by letting his brother know anything just yet.

Joe had been in hospital over four months when, in July, the hospital wanted to discharge him.

'He is not really fit for much yet,' the doctor said, 'but we are desperate for the bed and we have done all we can for your husband. He just needs time to rest and recover now.'

Gloria was in a dilemma. She knew of the shortage of beds, and she thought of the church hall, which she shared with many other families. That it wouldn't do for a man as infirm as Joe still was, who needed peace and quiet to recover fully. There was only one place they could go, and though she would hate it with all of her being, she could not be selfish about it. Joe's health was at stake here.

When Tom received the letter from Gloria, explaining the position they were in and asking if they could come over and stay with him until Joe was fully recovered, he couldn't have been happier. He longed to see Joe again, and meet his wife and child that he had got to know so well during Joe's illness. In his mind's eye, he saw them all happily settled at the farmhouse, though he knew Gloria in particular would find it strange at first, and he was determined to do all in his power to make it easier for her.

He decided that he would vacate his bedroom at the end of the cottage for them to use, so that he wouldn't disturb them when he was getting up early to milk the cows, and he would have the one that Molly had used when she lived there, which he could share with Ben.

He was so glad that there would be a child about the farm again, and this time there would be his parents as well as himself to make sure Biddy behaved herself.

When Tom told his mother that Gloria had written asking if the family could bide in Ireland while Joe recovered totally from his injuries, and that he had invited them, she was furious.

'Without so much as a by-your-leave,' she snapped. 'You are getting above yourself. It was my decision to make, not yours.'

'It wasn't a decision to make at all really, Mammy,' Tom said. 'We could do nothing else. Joe is in need and we are in a position to help him. And that, as far as I am concerned, is that.'

'I can't believe that I am hearing this,' Biddy said. 'I will not have that American strumpet under my roof.'

'Gloria is no strumpet, Mammy.'

'And how do you know?'

'Because I trust Joe's judgement, as you should,' Tom snapped. 'God Almighty, just listen to yourself. Let's get this clear,' he said. 'First of all this is my roof, and Joe is coming to share it with me and so are his wife and son. I would offer the same hospitality to a perfect stranger if they had suffered as much as Joe has, especially when the alternative was them all lying on the floor of a church hall shared with all the people of the neighbourhood. When it's your own flesh and blood, there is no issue there at all. And if you can't get on with Gloria and young Ben, then you must deal with it, for the problem, I'm sure, will be yours and yours alone.'

Tom saw his mother's eyes widen. He knew he had surprised her and he was glad. This time he intended laying it on the line for his mother before Joe, Gloria and Ben arrived.

When Tom saw Joe alight from the train at Derry, he was shocked. He had never carried excess weight but Tom saw he was positively gaunt, his face almost cadaver lows and his dark hair now more grey than brown. But the careful way he carried himself was just as worrying, and Tom didn't need to see his eyes glazed with pain to know the discomfort he was in.

He hugged him gently. 'Welcome home, Joe,' he said, and then turned his attention to Gloria by his side. She was a lovely-looking woman, he thought – stunning, in fact, for the hair coiled around her head very becomingly was naturally blonde and her eyes were violet blue. She smiled at Tom and he knew why Joe had been so captivated by her.

'I feel as if I know you already,' she said, as Tom hugged her. 'I am so glad to get to meet you.'

'And I too am glad you are here at last,' Tom said. 'All of you. And this,' he said, bending to the young boy at Gloria's side, 'must be Ben.'

He saw straight away that the child got his looks from his mother, for his eyes and even the shape of his face was the same. His hair was blond too, and worn rather longer than was usual, and because he was younger, the golden colour was even more vibrant so that it glowed like a halo around his head in the sunlight.

He grinned up at the uncle who had been so kind to him and said, 'Hello, Uncle Tom.'

'And hello to you, young Ben,' Tom said, clapping the boy on the shoulder. 'I'm sure you and I will get on like a house on fire. Now let's get you all up in the cart and I'll have us home in no time at all.'

'I hardly think so, with this horse,' Joe commented with a laugh.

'There is nothing at all wrong with this horse,' Tom said, matching his brother's bantering tone.

'I didn't say there was,' Joe said, 'but not even you, Tom, can say he was bred for speed.'

'Dobbin will get us there in his own time and at his own pace, but it will be a damned sight more comfortable than walking, and are you going to stand arguing about it all the day or get into the cart with the others?'

Joe gave the grin that Tom remembered so well and said, 'All right then, but I will ride on the top with you.'

'Are you sure?' Tom asked. 'It's quite high.'

'Don't fuss me, Tom,' Joe said. 'You know that I could never abide it, and I have had enough just lately to last me a lifetime.'

So Tom didn't fuss, although he did extend a hand to help Joe, and saw him wince with pain as he pulled himself up and lowered himself to the seat.

'Bad trip?' Tom asked quietly and Joe nodded.

'A damned uncomfortable one. I will be glad to reach the cottage, I don't mind telling you.'

And then before Tom could ask him anything else, he turned carefully around in the seat and said to Gloria and Ben, 'Well, this is where I grew up. What do you think?'

Ben was enchanted. He had never seen so much green. He looked around in delight. 'It's real fine, Dad.'

Gloria didn't think it fine at all. In fact, the further Gloria got from Derry, the more despondent she became. She was a city girl and she felt that she had left civilisation behind her. She was no lover of the wide open spaces and had a horror of being buried in the country. But she couldn't say this, she realised, and so she said, 'It's certainly beautiful.' That at least was true because the countryside had never looked lovelier. 'And I'm sure I will soon settle down.'

'That's my girl,' Joe said proudly, because he knew his Gloria so he guessed how she really felt, and she hadn't met his mother yet.

'How does Mammy feel about us landing on her like this?' he said to Tom quietly.

'Fine.'

'Tom, you are talking to me, your brother,' Joe said, 'and Mammy is never fine about anything.'

'Why ask the road you know then?' Tom said. 'She did kick up, as might be expected, even though she knew there was no alternative. It isn't you she doesn't want; it's Gloria and the boy.'

'We come as a package, and the sooner Mammy realises that, the better everyone will be,' Joe said grimly. 'Gloria has already put up with so much, and Ben is the light of both our lives. Mammy will treat them properly or answer to me.'

'I don't blame you either,' Tom said. 'But you don't know Mammy like I do, and I can envisage many battles ahead.'

Tom was right, but he was to find that Gloria was no slight, wee girl burdened down by sadness, as Molly had been, but a young woman of spirit. She had already suffered such poverty, indignity and deprivation, it would have felled a lesser woman. What was all that set against one sad and embittered old woman with a terribly twisted mind?

She had refused point-blank to take on the entire burden of the house, but said the work should be shared equally, and of course there was no talk of her helping with the milking, or in the fields as Molly had. Biddy hated Gloria with a passion, but she seemed unable to make a dent in her at all. In fact, when she began one of her rages, Gloria would stop whatever she was doing and say quite calmly, 'I see you are not behaving well at the moment. I will come back when you are in a better temper,' and walk out.

The first time she had done this, Biddy had had the urge to run across the room and prevent her leaving, but she didn't know how Joe would react if she laid a hand on the wife he seemed so fond of. Only the day before when she had smacked the boy for accidentally breaking a dish, Joe had been in such a towering rage that Biddy thought he would strike her. He didn't but he threatened to do so if she was to hit the boy again. 'I am his father and Gloria his mother, and if there is any chastising to be done, then we will do it. Have you got that, Mammy?'

And when Biddy elected not to answer this, he had fair bellowed at her, 'I said, have you got that?' And she was forced to mumble that she had.

'Right,' Joe said. 'Ben broke the dish by accident and apologised immediately, and that should have been the end of it. I do not punish my son for accidents.'

So what would he do if she was to manhandle

his wife? Biddy decided not to put it to the test and so she had just watched her walk up the lane with narrowed and malicious eyes.

In fact, none of this was turning out as she had hoped. Joe would just look at her almost pityingly if she got in a temper about something. 'For goodness' sake, Mammy,' he would say, 'if you could only hear yourself. This is no rational way to go on at all. Now, if you are prepared to talk to me, then I will listen.'

It completely took the wind out of Biddy's sails, and Tom would marvel at the easy way in which Joe controlled his mother.

Ben, he knew, was nervous of her, though any child with a modicum of sense would be wary of her, he thought. However, in everything else Ben had never been happier. He had more space and freedom than he had ever known existed, and there were no sirens, no bombs, no mounds of rubble and air that stank every time you took a breath of it.

And best of all, his father was getting better.

The only fly in the ointment, as far as he was concerned, was the crabbed old woman, his grandmother, who always glared at him so angrily, even when he couldn't think of a thing he could have done that might have upset her.

'Listen, son, everything has got its down side because that's life,' Joe told Ben when he complained of this. 'Personally, I don't think that your grandmother's mind works the same as everyone else's.'

'You mean she's mad?' Ben asked; he could well believe that.

'Not quite mad,' Joe said, 'more a little unbalanced.'

'Right . . .'

'And we have to cope with it as it is,' Joe said. 'OK?'

'I guess so.'

'I know so,' said Joe, punching Ben lightly on the arm.

As the boy's laughter reached Biddy's ears she pursed her lips together tight. God, she thought, she would like to beat that laughter out of him, but she knew her hands were tied.

In September Gloria thought there was something the matter with Biddy and she told Joe that she was eating virtually nothing, her eyes were rheumy and bloodshot and her face a funny colour.

'Are you sure?' Joe said. 'Her voice is as vitriolic as ever. Did you hear how she went for Tom earlier? God, I don't know how the man stands for it.'

'She always goes for Tom,' Gloria said. 'And he stands it because he is that kind of man. As for your mother, I think her carping voice will be the last thing to go because she appears to like the sound of it so much. It wouldn't surprise me if she was still going on when they were nailing the coffin lid down.'

Joe laughed and put his arm around his wife

and said, 'You may be right, but you think she is really ill this time?'

'Well, let's say that it wouldn't hurt to get her to see a doctor,' Gloria said. 'And it has to be you who tells her.'

Joe did his best, but Biddy not only refused to see the doctor, she also refused to see that there was anything wrong with her, and all Joe got for his trouble was an ear-bashing. He knew that Gloria was right to be so concerned because, now she had brought the matter to his attention, it was obvious that there was something drastically wrong with his mother. Tom could see it too. But there was nothing they could do about it, and they watched as she deteriorated over the following weeks so that she was slow and ponderous in anything she did.

Joe had just decided to have another talk to her when she suddenly swayed forward one day as she was stirring stew in a pot over the fire. She would have tipped into the embers if Joe hadn't been close to her. He caught hold of her and lowered her into the chair before the fire.

'Right, that is it, Mammy. We will have no more nonsense. I am going to the doctor's and he is going to come out and see you,' he insisted.

Uncharacteristically, Biddy said nothing. If she was to admit it, the incident over the fire had unnerved her but she saw illness as a weakness and had not had a doctor near her in years. Perhaps, though, this was the time. Eventually, she ground out, 'All right then. If you want to waste your money get the damned man.'

While Joe was away for the doctor, Tom helped Gloria changed the beds around. In order for Biddy to have some privacy it was decided that she would have the room at the end that Tom had given to Joe and Gloria on their arrival. They would share Tom's old room with Ben while Tom would take his mother's bed.

She grumbled about it, of course, and said it was a lot of fuss about nothing, but neither of them took any notice. And when she was in bed and screamed at them both to 'Get out and leave me alone,' they knew whatever had happened to her had not improved her temper at all.

A little later Dr Green faced them across the room and said gravely, 'I'm afraid that Mrs Sullivan is extremely ill. She has a tumour the size of a small football in her stomach. I wanted her to go into hospital for tests, but she wouldn't hear of it.'

Tom hid a wry smile for he could just imagine how Biddy told the doctor that.

Joe asked, 'What is the treatment, Doctor?'

'Something for the pain is all I can offer.'

'You mean . . . ?'

'I mean your mother is dying,' the doctor said. 'I am sorry, but there is nothing further I can do for her.'

Tom and Joe looked stunned, but Gloria wasn't really surprised. 'Does she know, Doctor?' she asked.

'I haven't told her in so many words,' the doctor said, 'but the woman is no fool.'

'And how long has she?'

The doctor shook his head. 'Not long, weeks. Certainly before Christmas.'

At the very end of October, with his mother going downhill fairly rapidly, Tom was surprised and overjoyed on going into the post office to find a letter from Molly. He ripped it open eagerly and scanned it quickly. How disappointed he was then, for the letter was stark and totally uninformative and gave no explanation of why she had not written before, or what she was doing now, but stated only that her grandfather was dead and she had found Kevin in an orphanage. The only good thing to say about it was that it showed that Molly and Kevin were both alive.

Nellie had received a similar letter, and so had Cathy. As she told Tom, it was what Molly didn't say, more than what she did say, that was the most worrying part.

Tom agreed. His first inclination was to go to Birmingham but Molly had put no address on the letter so he still had no idea where in Birmingham she was.

Just over a week later, Joe, now beginning to help around the farm, had taken the churns to the head of the lane to await the truck from the creamery to collect them, while Tom was cleaning out the byre, when the postman put his head around the door.

'Your brother said that I would find you here,' he said, delving in his sack. 'I have a small package for you from England in a hand I don't recognise, and Nellie said to bring it straight to you in case it was important.'

Tom took the package from the postman, who asked, 'Any idea who it's from?'

'Not until I open it,' Tom said. He wanted to be on his own when he did that because he was totally mystified. The postman would have liked to have lingered, but he had other letters to deliver and Tom waited until he was cycling up the lane again before he broke the sealing wax.

The package was from Paul Simmons. Tom had to think for a moment before he remembered that he was the man who had employed Molly's father and later sent money to Molly every month. He launched a blistering attack on Tom in the letter he wrote.

What in God's name were you doing letting Molly, a young and defenceless girl, go alone to Birmingham, a city that has been bombed to blazes? Your irresponsibility in this matter beggars belief. When your mother took on guardianship of Molly, I consoled myself that at least the child would be cared for adequately, and I now find that you have failed in that duty too. You are an absolute disgrace and I would be surprised if you could sleep in your bed at night. And just in

case you think I am overreacting, and
possibly Molly has not kept you up to date, I
am sending you the cuttings of the trial.
There were reports in the *Despatch* and the
Evening Mail, which you can read for yourself while I make arrangements to contact
Molly without delay.

When Tom read the cuttings he could hardly believe
it. He learned how his innocent and naïve niece
was abducted at New Street Station by two
depraved individuals. The city was being pounded
by the worst raid in the war and Molly, who'd
had no experience of raids at all, was understand-
ably terrified. In the guise of helping her, the men
soon had her ensconced in a flat and pumped so
full of drugs she didn't know what she was doing;
or that the men were preening her for the whore-
house.

It was a man called Will Baker that rescued her
and hid her at great risk to himself and his family.
However, later, vicious thugs tracked her down,
attacked her and injured her so badly she nearly
died. It tore at Tom's heartstrings that Molly should
suffer at the hands of such corrupt and perverted
brutes. He didn't underestimate either the bravery
it took for her to face the men who had sought
to hurt her, even kill her, and to say what dreadful
things they had done to her in front of a jury of
perfect strangers.

Tom wasn't offended by what Paul Simmons

wrote to him. He deserved that and more, and he put his head in his hands and wept.

He was still in tears when Joe returned to the byre and he made no attempt to explain his distress. He just passed over the package and let Joe read everything for himself. He read it all in silence and when he eventually finished and looked up, Tom noted his eyes were very bright and his voice a little husky as he said, 'God, Tom, this is terrible. I am shocked to the core.'

'I just feel so bloody inadequate.'

'How could you have done anything different?'

'Oh, I don't know, Joe,' Tom said, 'but something, surely to God. I'd like to go over and see her now this minute and yet Mammy is so sick, I daren't.'

'You don't know her address either, do you?'

'No.'

'This Paul Simmons must have it if he is going to contact her.'

Tom shrugged. 'Maybe he has, but if so, he would hardly give it to me. The cuttings said she worked at the Naafi in Castle Bromwich Airfield and so maybe he will get in touch with her that way.'

'Well, couldn't you do the same?'

'Aye,' Tom said. 'And I will as soon as Mammy . . .'

'We could send for you if she took a turn for the worse.'

'Come on, Joe,' Tom said. 'You know as well as I do that any turn Mammy takes for the worse now will be her death.'

'You owe her nothing, Tom.'

'She is my mother,' Tom said. 'Bad as she is, I can't leave her now.'

Three days later a very welcome letter came from Molly. In it she said that Paul Simmons had been to see her and told her of the letter he had sent to him, and Molly had told him he had been wrong to do that. She went on:

I told him there were no words written that would have stopped me going to Birmingham at that time, especially after I received the note that Kevin wrote. You have probably read all this and more in the cuttings Paul said he sent you, but what happened to me in Birmingham was partly my own fault. I might have fared better if there hadn't been a massive raid, which began just after I had alighted from the train. I must admit, it scared me witless. I hadn't a clue what to do in the event of a raid. The two men who approached me used to trawl the stations on the lookout for runaways and the like, and they took advantage of my fear and confusion. They were so kind and attentive that I was taken in, and very soon I couldn't remember who I was or why I was in Birmingham because they had pumped me full of drugs.

Even after I was rescued and had recovered my wits enough to remember what I was doing in the city, I was too ashamed to write to you, or explain why I hadn't written earlier. I am sorry about it; I know you must have been worried.

I did manage to locate Kevin and he is living with me now. We are both grand and I have met a wonderful man called Mark Baxter, who I would like you to meet, as he has become very special in my life.

Tom treasured that letter. This time Molly had included her address, so Tom wrote a long letter back and told her he would be over as soon as he saw his mother buried.

TWENTY-SIX

Each day Tom, Joe, Gloria and, especially, Ben waited for Biddy to breathe her last.

'It's just awful, isn't it?' Tom said. 'We're sort of willing her to die.'

'Tom, she has no quality of life,' Joe said. 'Gloria is quite worn down with her demands and abuse.'

Tom knew that was true. Gloria looked quite drawn at times, and in early December she had actually told Joe she didn't know how much longer she could continue.

A couple of days later, in the throes of one of her many tantrums, Biddy suddenly went stiff and her eyes rolled in her head.

'A stroke, and a bad one at that,' the doctor pronounced. 'Something I have been expecting for years.'

Biddy had no movement below her neck and was unable to speak. Joe asked Gloria if she wanted his mother to be transferred to the hospital. Gloria, however, said she had managed so far, and in a way it was easier dealing with someone who wasn't constantly shouting at her and slapping out all the time.

'She can't go on much longer like this, I wouldn't have thought,' Tom said, but Biddy lasted seven more weeks, until the end of January 1943, to die a tormented and painful death.

Biddy had few mourners at the funeral, which was held on Friday, 4 February, and they stood shivering in the snow-capped graveyard, listening to the priest intoning prayers for the dear departed, his breath causing whispery trails to spill from his mouth into the icy air.

Then Tom stepped forward to drop the first clod of earth on top of the coffin. He had no sense of grief at his mother's passing, just relief that it was over at last, that he was free. There was no wake, just a few drinks down at Grant's Bar. Though Tom's hand was shaken many times, and he was bought numerous drinks, no one actually said they were sorry that his mother was dead.

Tom and Joe didn't stay late and yet it was pitch-black when they stepped out of the pub, and the air so raw it caught at the back of Tom's throat. It had snowed earlier that day so the tramp of their boots made little sound. Around them the countryside was hushed and the night was a clear one so the full moon, like a golden orb, cast its light on them as they walked, and twinkling stars peppered the sky.

Tom couldn't help comparing his mother's funeral with that of his father, which nearly the whole town attended. He said to Joe, 'Not much of a turn-out.'

'Huh,' Joe said. 'And can you wonder at it?'

'No,' Tom said with a sigh. 'What a wasted life, when all's said and done. Mammy was eaten up with bitterness and died virtually friendless.'

'It was her own doing,' Joe said. 'Look how stupid she was about things, like we weren't even allowed to mention Nuala's name after that letter, remember? Or Aggie before that? I feel so sorry for Aggie having to cut herself off from the family the way she did.'

'It was the only solution at the time,' Tom said. 'There was no way around it. Poor Aggie.'

'Course, she could be dead and gone by now,' Joe commented.

'Well, she could,' Tom replied with spirit, 'but she was only two years older than me, you know, and I don't intend to go heavenwards for a long time yet.'

'Who said you will be going heavenwards anyway?' Joe said. 'I reckon it will be the downward spiral for you.'

'I'll meet plenty of friends there, anyway,' Tom said. 'As long as I don't meet up with Mammy. That would be hell, all right.'

And then, the memory of a lad tying twine between two trees flitted across Tom's mind and he felt an urgent need to tell his brother. He didn't know why – maybe the emotion of the day had got to him – but suddenly it was imperative that Joe knew it all.

'You are right though', he said, 'I will never make Heaven.'

'And you think I will?'

'No, Joe, I'm serious,' Tom said, aware that his heart was thumping in his breast.

'What is this, Tom?' Joe said, peering at him and seeing in the light from the moon just how agitated he was. 'This is just the beer talking, man. You are a bloody saint, you are, and most of the town acknowledge that.'

'I'm no saint.'

'Well, not many would put up with Mammy the way you did for bloody years.'

'Och, sure that was nothing,' Tom said dismissively. 'This is something I have thought of telling you for some time and tonight is as good a time as any.'

'Go on then.'

'I . . . I killed a man, Joe,' said Tom. 'Years ago.'

Joe stopped dead on the road and turned to face Tom. He felt as if all the blood had drained from his body, and he gave a nervous laugh and said, 'Come on, Tom, don't be daft, man. This has got to be the beer talking.'

'No it isn't,' Tom insisted. 'I was just thirteen at the time.' Tom went on to explain to his brother exactly what had happened that fateful February day over forty years before.

Joe didn't speak a word until he'd finished and then he said, 'I do understand how you felt, Tom. It must have been awful to see Aggie forced from her home that time, and the man get away scot-free.'

'It was when he started commiserating with Daddy after Mass,' Tom said. 'I felt such rage inside me.'

'But you didn't want to kill him?'

'D'you know, Joe, I think I probably did,' Tom said. 'I'm a mild-mannered man, too mild, many would say, and never before or since have I felt anger as I did that day. But when I tied the twine, I didn't intend to kill him. I wanted to hurt him, that was all.'

'And if he hadn't died, wouldn't it have been worse for everyone, as McAllister's wife told you.'

'Yes,' Tom said. 'She tried to stop me. But afterwards, when it was too late, she helped me and covered it up for me, so she was as involved as me, in a way.'

'You didn't kill the man, Tom,' Joe said. 'The fall from his horse did that.'

'That's splitting hairs, isn't it, Joe?' Tom said ruefully. 'I do know what I have done and that one day I will pay for it, but I will say the load has been lightened considerably by my telling you. And Mammy dying too. God, I haven't really got to grips with that yet and how different life will be from now on.'

'Different and better.'

'Oh, definitely better.'

'Will you go straight to Birmingham now?'

'I'd like to,' Tom said. 'I have dallied long enough, but we have two cows ready to calve and I doubt you would want to cope with that on your own.'

'Well, it is many years since I have done it.'

'I will stay, don't worry,' Tom said. 'I will write to Molly. She lived on the farm and knows about these sorts of things. She will understand I can't leave just now.'

Molly's twenty-first birthday came and went with Tom still in Ireland, and though everyone sent cards and all, he felt bad he wasn't there. But by the first week in March, both calves were a week old, fine and healthy, and by the end of the next week, with the spring planting out of the way too, Tom was ready for the off.

'I will send a telegram to Molly and will probably go up to the camp first,' Tom said to Joe. 'Then I can arrange to see her after work and probably meet this Mark she keeps on about.'

'Give him the once-over,' Joe said. 'See if he is good enough for our Molly.'

'I intend to,' Tom said. 'What that girl needs and deserves in her life is happiness.'

'I couldn't agree more,' Joe said.

'How do you feel about holding the fort for me while I am over in Birmingham?'

'Grand,' Joe said. 'I'll be fine.'

Tom nodded. 'I know that you are nearly

completely fit again, and Ben will be a fine help to you when he isn't at school, for all his tender years, but don't overdo it, for God's sake. I'll have to answer to Gloria then.'

Joe grinned. 'You would that, but don't worry, she will keep me in check. She is right fond of you, Tom. Can I tell her about this McAllister business?'

'Of course,' Tom said. 'There should be no secrets between a man and his wife. I envy you, Joe, for you have a fine wife and a son to be proud of.'

'I know how lucky I am,' Joe said. 'When you come as close to losing your life as I did, you don't take things for granted any more.'

Tom had never been further than Derry station before in the whole of his life and, what's more, he never had the slightest desire to go further. Much as he longed see Molly again, and meet Kevin too, and check that they were both all right, he didn't relish the journey.

He admitted this to Nellie when he sent the telegram to tell Molly of his intended arrival the following day.

'Aren't you the slightest bit excited?' Cathy asked.

'I will be glad enough to see Molly again and meet that young brother of hers,' Tom said, 'but you know I am just not the adventurous sort.'

'Give her our love,' Nellie said. 'Have you the letters we wrote packed away safe?'

'They're in the case already, along with two decent torches and a whole load of batteries because I know that is one thing hard to get in England at the moment,' Tom said.

'I thought they had to be shielded.'

'Aye, they have, but a bit of muslin tied on with string will be good enough, I think,' Tom said. 'Molly will advise me, I'm sure.'

'And so all that's left is for us to wish you Godspeed,' said Nellie.

'That's all.'

Ben threw his arms around Tom's neck and hugged him tight, realising suddenly how much he would miss him.

'Will you come back real quick, Uncle Tom?'

'I will, Ben,' Tom promised his nephew. 'I'll be back just as soon as can be.'

'Now let your uncle be on his way,' Gloria said, pulling Ben back. 'He can't afford to miss the train.'

'He won't,' Joe said. 'I'll see to that,' adding with a grin, 'me and the speedy old Dobbin, of course.'

'There's nothing wrong with that horse, I have told you,' Tom told Joe.

'Yeah, I know,' Joe said. 'He gets there at his own pace and in his own time even if his pace is two steps forward and one back. He hasn't a hurry bone in his body and if we are not away from here sharpish that train might well go screaming its way to Dun Laoghaire without you. Climb up here now and let's be off.'

Tom grinned at his brother, and climbed up beside him and they were on their way.

'Leaving here seems strange,' Tom said a little later, as the cart rattled down the road. 'Being away from the farm for one whole day seems completely alien.'

'I think that was one of the things I didn't like about farming,' Joe said. 'You are tied to it and can seldom have a day off, one whole day to go someplace else.'

'No, you can't,' Tom agreed. 'And that has never bothered me until now. Now that Molly is obviously settling in Birmingham I would like to see her sometimes. Between you and me, that wee girl stole away a piece of my heart.'

Joe laughed. 'Do you think you are telling me news? What you feel for Molly is written all over you, as plain as the nose on your face. But now that Mammy has gone, what's to stop Molly coming over here a time or two? When this war eventually draws to a close, it will be easier.'

'Aye, I suppose you're right,' Tom said. 'Worrying is part of my nature. I see problems where there are none.'

'That is living with Mammy for so long,' Joe said emphatically. 'She would have turned a lesser man than you completely bonkers, I think. So, all in all, you got away lightly.'

The station was ahead of them on the road then, and Tom felt his heart plummet. Joe saw the trepidation flooding his brother's face and said encouragingly, 'Come on, man. You'll be grand.'

'Course I will,' Tom said stoutly, but he knew if it wasn't for Molly waiting for him at the other end, he would have turned the horse round and headed back to the farm without hesitation.

Nothing more was said, and a few minutes later the horse clattered into the station yard and Joe secured it while Tom unloaded his bags. The train was in and panting like a wild beast that might take off again at any moment, and the two men hurried across the platform.

All the carriages had people in them and Joe helped Tom stow his stuff away on the racks above with everyone else's. Then he returned to the platform and Tom stood inside the train talking to him through the open window.

'Will you write when you have news?' he asked as the guards began slamming the doors.

'If you like,' Tom said, 'though there will hardly be time. I don't intend to stay away too long.'

'Stay as long as you need to,' Joe said. 'We'll keep things ticking over this end, don't worry.'

There wasn't time to say anything more, for there was a sudden sharp whistle and the train jerked forward. Tom waved to his brother as the train pulled out of the station. He was on his way.

Belfast docks couldn't be used by civilians any more. Not only had there been extensive damage from bombing raids in 1941 but also they were now a military base. From Derry, at that time, the train travelled down the country to the docks at Dun Laoghaire, just outside Dublin, and linked on the other side to the Welsh port of Holyhead.

It was a much longer journey than Derry to Belfast, and by the time Tom had gone a relatively short distance he decided that he liked trains. He had got over his initial anxiety that they were going far too fast and any moment the carriages would be flung off the rails, because none of his fellow passengers seemed the least bit concerned and he could bet they were more seasoned travellers than he.

In fact, he found them a very friendly bunch and he got on particularly well with two other fellows, brothers called Pat and Mick. They'd been born and raised in Donegal like himself, but they now both lived in Birmingham. Tom mentioned to them the niece who hailed from Birmingham.

'Where's she living?'

'Castle Bromwich. She works in the Naafi on the airfield and rents a house nearby from one of the airmen.'

'Fell on her feet then?'

'I hope so.'

'So, is this your first trip over?'

'It's really the first time I have ever left my home town. Everything is strange to me.'

'We were the same once,' Pat said. 'Stick with us and we'll see you right.'

Tom was glad of their help and advice, and the things they told him of the city and the wartime restrictions in place. It seemed in no time at all they were pulling into the docks at Dun Laoghaire.

The only boats Tom was familiar with were fishing boats. He had seen the ocean liner in Lough Foyle the time Joe had gone to the States, but that had been in the distance, and when he saw the mail boat looming up large in the water, he thought it the most amazing thing he had ever seen.

It had numerous decks and two funnels. RMS *Cambria* was printed on the side, and it was attached to the dock side with ropes as thick as a man's forearm, wrapped round concrete bollards. Tom felt ridiculously excited to be walking up the wooden gangplank, which listed slightly from side to side.

Mick, who had watched him with tolerant amusement, said, 'Let's hope you like it as well when we are out in the open sea.'

Tom was soon to find out.

The wind was fierce that day, and had whipped the waves into white-fringed rollers. The turbulence was hardly felt until the mail boat had moved out between the two piers, and then the waves broke against the sides of the boat in cascades of foam, the boat rolled slightly in the swell and Tom's stomach began to churn.

He wasn't actually sick, but he felt dreadful. 'A pint of Guinness is just the job for a bit of seasickness,' said Pat.

'Oh, I hardly think . . .'

'Well-known for settling stomachs,' Mick assured him.

The saloon bar stank to high heaven, the musty air filled with the smell of Guinness, cigarette smoke, body odour and vomit. Surprisingly the Guinness did make Tom feel a little better when he got it down him. Other men had drifted over to join them and Tom, who'd often found himself tongue-tied with strangers, meeting so few of them, found the beer had loosened his tongue sufficiently to join in with the rest. He forgot all about his sickness, and by the third pint began thoroughly to enjoy himself as he couldn't remember doing for a long time. He was quite sorry when the shores of Wales could be seen.

Pat and Mick took good care of Tom as the mail boat docked and the passengers disembarked, and he was grateful, for the beer had made him feel quite light-headed. Mick and Pat bundled him into one of the carriages on the waiting train.

Tom sat down with a sigh. 'Too many Guinnesses, maybe,' he said. 'Sorry.'

'What are you sorry for?' Mick said. 'You did no harm, and surely it was better than suffering seasickness?'

'It certainly was,' Tom said. 'I have seldom had such a good time.'

He remembered little of the journey after that though because he fell into a deep sleep and had to be shaken awake as the train approached New Street Station.

He was confused and disorientated at first. As he stepped onto the platform amongst the throngs of people, he noted the air was stale and smelled smoky. All around him people were chattering, laughing or shouting, porters with laden trolleys were warning people to 'Mind your backs' and the news vendors' shrill voices rose above it all. There was also the constant tramp of feet and the clatter of trains hurtling into the station, more noise than Tom had heard in his life. 'How do you stand it?' he asked Pat and Mick.

They were both mystified. 'Stand what?'

'This,' Tom said, spreading his hands expansively. 'The noise? Well, not just the noise, just about everything.'

Pat clapped Tom on the shoulder. 'Didn't we feel the very same when we first came over,' he said. 'You get used to it.'

'Where are they all going to, at all,' Tom said, 'all these hordes of people walking so determinedly with set and serious faces?'

Mick shrugged. 'Who knows or cares, Tom? See, that's the thing in a city: everyone minds their own business. Now let's get you sorted out. If you're making straight for the airfield at Castle Bromwich, and you haven't lodgings booked, it might be worth leaving your case in Left Luggage until you have a place to stay. You won't want to lug it around.'

'No, I won't,' Tom said. 'Where's that?

'We'll show you,' Pat said. 'And then show you where you can pick up a taxi.'

Outside, with the case safely deposited, Tom found things were worse. There was no clean air in Birmingham, he decided, for now he smelled petrol fumes and something sour, almost acrid, that hit the back of his throat. He could even taste it on his tongue. The streets were teeming with people of all shapes and sizes. The serious look on their faces and determined strides of them made it seem as though they had to get somewhere in a hurry.

But, added to the press of people on the pavements, was the traffic on the roads. Cars, buses, lorries and vans jostled with the carts and wagons pulled by huge horses with shaggy feet. And then, as they made their way to the taxi rank, a clanking swaying monster came careering towards them, to turn the corner. Tom saw with surprise it ran on rails set into the ground.

'It's a tram,' Mick said, seeing Tom's preoccupation with it. 'Best way to get about.'

'I don't know that I wouldn't be too feared to get into one of those.'

Pat laughed. 'That's another thing to get used to if you are here any length of time,' he said. 'Trams are much quicker than buses because they don't get snarled up in the traffic.'

'I'll bear it in mind,' Tom said.

'Anyway, here are the taxis now,' Mick said.

'You tell the driver you want Castle Bromwich Aerodrome and he will get you there in no time.'

Tom, with real regret, shook hands with the two men who had been so helpful to him and climbed into the taxi. He had never ever ridden in any sort of motor vehicle, and he enjoyed his first ride. It was made all the more pleasant by realising that every minute brought him closer to the time when he would see Molly again.

Tom wasn't allowed in the camp but the guard offered to fetch Molly when he said who he was. A few moments later, he saw her running towards the gate, holding hands with a pilot, and his heart nearly stopped for she looked so beautiful. Radiant, in fact.

'Uncle Tom,' she cried, and her smile lit up her entire face as she waited impatiently for the guard to open the gate. When she dropped the young man's hand and put her arms around Tom's neck and held him tight, his happiness was complete.

Then she introduced Mark Baxter. Tom appraised the man as he shook him warmly by the hand and said he was delighted to meet him. He was still in full flying gear and his eyes were glazed with fatigue, and Molly explained that he had had to land his plane in Cannock Chase and walk from there.

'It is a fair hike from here,' she said. 'I was told Mark had been shot down. Until a few minutes ago, I thought he was dead.' She gave a shudder as she remembered, and Mark put his arm around her and she leaned against him with a sigh. Tom knew that Molly had met her soul mate and his heart nearly burst with relief and joy.

When he eventually took his leave of Molly, he did something he had promised himself he would do as soon as he got to Birmingham, and that was to seek out Paul Simmons and beg his forgiveness. He had the address of his office from the letter Paul had sent him, but knowing he would never find it by himself he took one of those frightening trams that Molly had told him went straight into the city centre, and then showed the address to one of the taxi drivers grouped around New Street Station.

'Know where that is, all right, governor,' the taxi driver said, leaping out from the cab and opening the door for Tom. 'Hop in and I will get you there in two shakes of a lamb's tail.'

Less than half an hour later, Tom was standing in front of Paul Simmons and apologising for not looking after Molly properly.

'Sit down, please,' Paul said to the nervous man before him, and Tom sat on the chair one side of the desk and Paul faced him on the other side. He said straight out, 'I was far too hasty when I wrote that letter. Molly told me straight that you couldn't have stopped her if you had tried. She said there was no course open to her other than the one she took. And then for those dreadful things to happen to her . . . She was innocent of blame, a young and naïve girl, unaware that the people she met on the station that night that appeared so kind and friendly were so corrupt. She had no experience to draw on. It made me so angry that she had been abused in such a way.'

'Me too of course,' Tom said. 'We had no idea. Let's hope life will run a little smoother for Molly now. She seems very keen on Mark Baxter. Have you met him?'

'Oh, yes,' Paul said. 'Another fine man, and a brave one too. They are very much in love. You only have to see them together to realise that.'

'You think they will marry?'

'Almost certainly,' Paul said. 'And that is where I come in again.'

'Oh?'

'Ted would have paid for his daughter's wedding and would be proud to do so. I would like to do this for this young couple in his stead. Would they mind that, do you think?'

'I shouldn't think so, and certainly not if it is put to them like that,' Tom said. 'I am going over to see them both this evening. I will broach it, if you like.'

'I would be very grateful,' Paul said. 'And can I say something to you now?'

'Of course.'

'I know Molly had a rough time in Ireland,' Paul said. 'Not that she has given me a list of complaints or anything, but if she does say anything at all there is a sort of sadness lurking behind her eyes. Then there was that ridiculous subterfuge in sending her letters. But she has always spoken highly of you – more than highly – for it is obvious that she loves you very much and now that I have met you too, I can understand that.'

Tom's face was crimson and he got to his feet as he said gruffly, 'Ah, give over, man. You are embarrassing the life out of me. And now I will take up no more of your valuable time. I must in any case find lodgings for the next few days for it would not be seemly to stay with Molly.'

'Till we meet again, then,' Paul said, extending his hand. 'Let us hope it is sooner rather than later.'

TWENTY-SEVEN

Tom stayed in Birmingham almost a week and in that time, he had met everyone connected to Molly's life, from her old neighbour, Hilda, to her future in-laws the Baxters, especially Mark. Tom thought Kevin a grand fellow altogether and the two were soon the best of friends. Kevin wanted to know all about his new uncle, Joe, Aunt Gloria and his cousin, Ben, who was four years younger than he.

Tom had also met Will Baker, who had helped Molly escape her captors at great risk to himself and his family, and in doing so had saved her life. He had even been introduced to Terry, who owned the house that Molly was renting, who said that he was grateful to Molly for taking it on, preventing it from being requisitioned. 'Molly has looked after the house so well,' he told Tom, 'and Kevin has kept the garden in tiptop condition. Really, I can't thank them enough.'

'Don't be silly,' Molly said when she heard this.

'It is you who have done us the favour. Having this house and the job in the Naafi meant I could have Kevin living with me, which we both wanted.'

'I'll say,' Kevin said with feeling. 'All that time in the orphanage – I mean, they were all right and that, but all I wanted was for Molly to come and get me out.'

The words, spoken so wistfully, caused tears to sparkle behind Tom's eyes. He blinked them away rapidly. The time for tears was over now. Molly and Kevin were looking forward to a happy future and so must he.

'It relieves me greatly that you can count such wonderful people as these I have met as your friends,' he said that evening as he called to say goodbye. 'I can now rest easy that, with God's help, your life now will be on an even keel at long last.'

'I hope so, Uncle Tom,' Molly said. 'It will not be before time.'

'No, indeed it will not.'

'I'll miss you,' Molly said. 'It has been lovely seeing you every day.'

'I'll be back before you know it,' Tom said. 'Isn't the wedding planned for June? That being the case, you will be so busy arranging it, you won't have time to even notice I am not around.'

'But your train won't leave for hours yet,' Molly said. 'What will you do with yourself till then?'

'What I have been doing while you have been at work,' Tom said. 'Look around the place. Explore.'

Tom had indeed spent a lot of the time when Molly was tied up, exploring the city she had come from. He had been appalled by the bomb damage the city had suffered. Derry had got away lightly as only two parachute mines had landed there, killing thirteen people and demolishing five houses, but here, whole areas were laid waste. In the city centre there were huge gaps where shops had once stood, but even the residential areas around the city centre had taken a pounding.

The first time he had turned a corner to see a whole sea of rubble, he had stood and stared. He knew that the rubble represented streets and streets of houses, for the homes in that industrial city were pressed one against another. What had happened to the people? Where did they go to hide from such bombardment and how did they cope without their houses and possessions? They did as Gloria had, he imagined: camped out in church halls or other suitable places. Little wonder that Molly and Kevin's grandfather had died. Tom thought it was far more of a surprise that anyone was left alive at all.

In his sojourn around the city centre, he had found a pub on the outskirts that did delicious steak pies. Knowing of the rationing situation, he would eat little at Molly's and the pie slid down the throat beautifully, especially when accompanied by a pint of Guinness. He didn't ask at the pub either what animal the steak was from. Sometimes it was better not to know, though he guessed it was horse meat, which he had heard had been eaten in France for years.

As he neared the same pub again later, he realised that often what is quite a respectable pub by day, can turn into a fairly seedy one at night, and if he hadn't been so hungry he would have passed it by and sought food elsewhere. But, in the end, he decided to go in. It wasn't as if he intended spending the night there; a quick pint and a pie, and then it would be time to set out for New Street Station.

He couldn't wait to be home and he was thinking of all he had to tell them as he left the pub when, all of a sudden, he felt a tugging on his sleeve and a whining voice asked, 'D'you want some pleasure, kind sir?'

Tom felt the bile rise in his throat. He couldn't see anything of the woman for the blackout was complete, and he shook her off as one might a bothersome insect.

'Get away from me, you filthy trollop!'

But the woman was insistent because she was desperate. As she got older, it was becoming harder and harder to earn enough money. She blessed the blackout, though, because she knew that if many men were aware what she really looked like they would run a mile rather than lay a hand on her.

'Please, sir,' she begged, 'I'll make it good for you. I'll do anything you want me to.'

'What I want you to do for me,' said Tom grimly, 'is for you to get your filthy hands off my clothes and let me be on my way.'

At that moment, a courting couple, arm in arm, came around the corner. The man held a wavering, shielded torch, but as the couple were so totally absorbed in one another, that torch was spraying its feeble light every which way. For a split second only, it lit up Tom's face. The woman's hand dropped from Tom's and he felt rather than saw her take a step backwards.

Once before she had seen those eyes, and they had haunted her for years because they had been so full of deep sorrow. Now they were filled with disgust, but over forty years later they were the same eyes. She would stake money on it if she had any.

'Tom.'

The word was wrenched from her almost involuntarily, and it was barely audible. The couple had passed and they were alone again.

Tom said, 'What did you say?'

'Nothing.'

Tom reached through the dark and, finding the woman's arm, grasped it tight as he said, 'Yes, you did. You spoke my name. How did you know it?'

The woman sighed. The one thing she had dreaded had come to pass. Maybe she had best get it over and done. She had thought she was past hurt any more, but the repugnance she had glimpsed in Tom's face had cut her to the heart.

'Because,' said the woman, 'I am your sister Aggie.'

Her arm was released suddenly as Tom staggered

on the cobblestones of the alleyway. His senses were reeling with the news he could scarcely believe. With his whole mind and body screaming denial, he repeated, 'Aggie?'

Aggie heard the revulsion in his voice. 'Yes. Aggie.'

'But how have you come to this?'

'How long have you got?' Aggie asked. 'It's a long story and not one I wish to relate on the street. And,' she added bitterly, 'do you really want to hear it anyway? You have seen what I am, what I have become, and you are finding it hard to hide your disgust. Why don't you go back to your nice little respectable life, wherever it is, and forget this meeting has taken place?'

Tom was ashamed of himself when he realised that that was exactly what he wanted to do, but surely to God he was made of sterner stuff. This woman of the streets was his sister, for God's sake. He couldn't just walk away. He would miss the train, but that wouldn't matter. There would be another and he could send Joe a telegram in the morning and explain. So he faced Aggie and said, 'I do want to hear your story, but I don't know where to suggest we go, for I am only over here for a few days and I booked out of my lodgings this morning.'

Aggie gave a brittle little laugh. 'They wouldn't let the likes of me into respectable lodgings anyway,' she said. 'It will have to be my place, if you are determined?'

Tom nodded empthatically. 'I am.'

'Then before we go anywhere, will you go into the pub and buy me a bottle of gin?' Aggie asked.

'You won't disappear while I am in the pub?'

'Are you kidding?' Aggie said. 'I need a drink too much to go anywhere, but without a few gins inside me I can tell you nothing.'

'I will be right back,' Tom said. Once inside the pub he bought a bottle of whisky as well. He had a feeling that it was going to be a long night.

Aggie cheered considerably when Tom showed her the contents of the carrier bag the landlord had packed the bottles in. As she led the way, she glanced around nervously and said to Tom, 'If you can bear it, can you put your arm through mine and then they will think that you are a punter?'

'Who will?'

'Finch's men,' Aggie said. 'They watch me in case I should make a bid for freedom, though where do they imagine I would go if I did? There is nowhere I can go where they wouldn't find me and make me pay dearly. Mind you, it isn't so easy in the blackout to keep tabs on a person.'

Tom linked his arm through Aggie's, though with reluctance, and was glad of the concealing darkness. His head was teeming with questions. This whole set-up – what Aggie said, the way she lived – was beyond him, but he decided to ask nothing yet. He was certain that once inside, with a few gins to oil the wheels, as it were, Aggie would tell him all. Whether he could bear to hear it was another matter entirely.

He didn't see much of the area that Aggie led him through, nor the dilapidated house she said was hers. 'I'm on the first floor,' she said as they stepped into the hall. 'We don't put the light on because of the blackout, so follow me closely to prevent you breaking your neck on the stairs.'

Tom was glad to do just that because, although his eyes had adjusted to the darkness, he still could see very little, and so it wasn't until Aggie had lit the gaslight in her room that he saw her clearly for the first time. Her face was pasty white, her dark eyes were ringed with black, and her once magnificent hair was grey, lifeless and hung in lank, greasy strands around her face. More than merely thin, she was like skin and bone.

Tom's shock was apparent and Aggie gave a grim, tight little laugh and said, 'No oil painting, am I?'

'Aggie, I—'

'Leave it, Tom. I know what I am, none better. Sit down and I will get us a couple of glasses because I don't know about you, but I am gasping for a drink.'

Tom sat on one of the chairs in front of the hearth and looked around the room. It was long, and divided by a curtain that Aggie told him later separated the living area from the sleeping area. He had opened the two bottles so when Aggie came back from the small kitchenette with the glasses, he was able to pour a generous measure for them both. Aggie lifted her glass to her lips and downed it immediately, for her innards were crying out for it. Then she said with a sigh, 'Oh God, that was good. Pour me another, Tom, and I will tell you all that happened to me after I left the farm in 1901.'

Tom poured the drink, handed it to his sister and she began a tale of unbelievable sadness. He knew just how despairing and desperate she must have been to find that the only person that she knew of in that city, the one person who might help her, had disappeared.

Aggie told him of the prostitute Lily Henderson, who found her and ultimately saved her life. When she saw his lip curl, she cried, 'Don't look like that, Tom. I felt that way once, but all the prostitutes were kind to me. Lily was more than kind; she gave up her bed for weeks and tended me so carefully.'

'And the baby?'

'I lost it,' Aggie said. 'When I was recovered I knew I had to find a job, but there was nowhere respectable that would employ me without a reference. It was Alan Levingstone, Irish dancing and a nudge from Lily, saved me from the streets for years.'

'How come?' Tom asked and Aggie poured herself another drink before she told Tom all about the club.

'And did you just dance?'

'No,' Aggie said. 'I would like to spare you this, but it wouldn't be true, I also slept with men there.' She heard her brother's sharp intake of breath and burst out angrily, 'That's how it was. There wasn't a choice there for any of us. That's where I developed a taste for gin and opium.'

'You take opium?' Tom repeated in shock.

'We all do. Levingstone used to supply it,' Aggie said. 'It blurred the edges of what we had to do night after night.'

'That man took advantage of you,' Tom said. 'You were little more than a child.'

Aggie shrugged. 'Maybe he did,' she said, 'but at least he was kind to me in a world where I had experienced little kindness. There wasn't exactly a queue of people offering to help me, you know.'

'He forced his attentions on you.'

'No, he didn't, Tom,' Aggie said. 'I gave myself freely. Don't look like that. It was a different world, I was on my own in it, and I did what I had to do to survive.'

Tom was silent, thinking that that had been the type of future planned for Molly too, when she had first been abducted at the train station. Dear Christ! She had been an innocent victim and so had Aggie, but the thought that such things should happen first to his sister and then to his niece was shocking, horrifying.

'I'm sorry for judging you,' he said to Aggie. 'Please go on.'

Then Aggie told Tom how Levingstone had

wanted to marry her and she had welcomed it. 'I loved him, Tom, truly loved him, and he was handing me respectability: the one thing I wanted. I would have loved him for that alone, but it was more and much deeper than that.'

Tom heard the melancholy in her voice and asked gently, 'What happened?'

'Finch happened!' Aggie spat out, and though Tom saw the curl of Aggie's lip, as if she could hardly bear to say the name, he also saw fear in her eyes. 'You want to know about Finch,' she cried. 'I'll tell you about Finch.'

She told Tom of all the abuse she had suffered at Finch's hand from the first time he had attacked her and the many times after that, culminating in almost killing her in an alleyway just before her wedding day.

'Finch was furious that I was going to marry Alan,' Aggie said, 'because it meant I would never have to sleep with him or anyone but my husband ever again. That was probably why the attack, just before I was due to be married, was so violent.'

'This is monstrous,' Tom said. 'It causes me so much pain to hear this. You had suffered so much. This man you were to marry . . .'

'Knew nothing,' Aggie said. 'I was afraid of what he might do and so I said that I hadn't a clue who had attacked me. But he overheard Lily and me talking about it later and then he went after Finch, just as I knew he would. The following morning, in the early hours, Alan's body was found battered to death in one of the little alleyways in the Jewellery Quarter.'

'Aggie, I am so sorry,' Tom said, and the sincerity in his voice caused the tears to flood from Aggie's eyes. Tom put his arms around her and she sobbed as he remembered the last time he had held her it was to bid her farewell.

When she was a little calmer he poured her a drink before urging her to continue, and she turned sorrowful eyes to Tom and told him of the munitions works, another stab at respectability, of Polly and Jane, and her sister, Chris, who had been killed in the explosion, forcing them to find other employment at HP Sauce. And she told him of the death of Lily and the way that she was kidnapped in the street on her way home from work.

'I swore I would never work for Finch,' Aggie said fiercely, 'but in the end he won, as he said he would.'

'No, Aggie.'

'Ah, yes, Tom,' Aggie insisted. 'He has me so hooked on gin and opium, I truly can't do without them now.'

'Aggie,' said Tom, 'you are going to leave this life and I am going to do what I was unable to do as a thirteen-year-old boy, and that is look after you.'

'No, Tom.'

'Aggie, don't tell me you enjoy this life?'

'What do you think?' Aggie said. 'But I am not prepared to let you risk yours.'

'Aggie, I am not leaving you here.'

'Have you listened to one word I said about Alan and what happened to him?'

'I listened to every word you uttered,' Tom said, 'and many pierced me to the heart.'

'Finch will—'

'He will have no say in it.'

Aggie grabbed Tom's hands and looked deep into his eyes. 'Listen to me, for Christ's sake,' she cried in anguish. 'This man is brutal and vicious. He is completely heartless, enjoys inflicting pain and doesn't work to any of the rules of a civilised society.'

'I have bent some of those rules too,' Tom said. 'In fact the worst rule of all, because I have already killed a man.'

Aggie dropped Tom's hands and looked at him in horror, her eyes full of shock and disbelief. This was Tom, so gentle that their mother used to laugh at him. He would find it difficult to kill a fly, never mind a man.

'What are you saying, Tom?' she said. 'What nonsense is this? It can't be true.'

'It is, Aggie,' Tom said emphatically. 'I killed McAllister not long after you disappeared.'

'McAllister?' Aggie cried. 'Jesus, Tom, how I used to fantasise about doing just that.'

'Philomena said that I had done her and the world a favour because you weren't the first girl that he had taken down, nor would you have been the last.'

'Was Philomena in on it too?'

'No,' Tom said. 'She actually tried to stop me, but it was too late. Afterwards she helped me cover it up.'

'How did you do it?' Aggie asked and Tom told her. When he had finished she said, 'Well, I don't blame you in the slightest. Philomena was right. He did ruin my life. I am on the streets because of McAllister, and I hope and pray that something similar will happen to Finch one fine day. Only when that man is dead will I be able to breathe freely again.'

Tom had no intention of trying that trick with Finch. For what he put his sister through he wanted to beat him to pulp, and he would do that in a fair fight when he had no minders in attendance. However, Aggie was his first concern and so he said, 'Can I stay here tonight, Aggie? I'll take the settee.'

'You'll not be comfortable on that,' Aggie said. 'Take the bed. I'll have the settee.'

'You'll not,' Tom insisted. 'The settee or even the floor will be grand. I will fetch my case first thing tomorrow because I was booked on the night sailing, you see. I left my suitcase at the left luggage at New Street earlier today. Now I will need to find other lodgings to suit the two of us.'

'I can't leave here, Tom.'

'Let me worry about that. What time does that toad come around in the morning?'

'Anytime after ten.'

'And you have to give him money?'

Aggie gave a nod. Tom got out his wallet and peeled off three pound notes. 'Say I booked you for the evening. Is that enough?'

'I'll say it is,' Aggie said. 'I ask for ten bob now. Often they won't pay that much and I'm in no position to argue. I just take what they offer and it never amounts to three pounds for a night's work.'

'Are you watched all day?'

Aggie shook her head. 'I used to be, but now they think there is no need. With what they give me, I am usually out of it for the rest of the day anyway. Why?'

'Tomorrow you touch nothing,' Tom said. 'As soon as the coast is clear, you leave here and meet me in the library by the town hall.'

'How d'you know there is a library there?'

'I explored the town the day after I arrived,' Tom said. 'And when I saw it was a library I went in and started reading the papers. Did it a few times after that, and it is just about the safest place I can think for you to wait. I could put money on the fact that Finch isn't the literary type.' And then seeing Aggie biting her lip with agitation, he asked, 'Now what are you worrying about?'

'Tom, I am so frightened for both me and you,' Aggie said. 'I really don't think I can do this.'

'Yes, you can,' Tom said, grabbing her hands again and trying to inspire her with courage. 'Believe me, Finch knows nothing about me. He doesn't know that you have anywhere or anyone to run to. We have the element of surprise, don't you see? It will be the last thing that he will be expecting. Aggie, come on, I want you out of this place tomorrow. Now let us concern ourselves with practicalities. Have you a big bag of any sort?'

'I have a sailor's kitbag,' Aggie said. 'Early in the war, a young sailor spent the night with me. He had just left the ship and had his stuff with him in his kitbag and in the morning he forgot to take it with him. I put it in the wardrobe, expecting him to come back for it, but he didn't. I always wondered if he got into a heap of trouble because of it, but it's big enough to take everything I would want, if I tip his stuff out first.'

'Excellent. Fill it up,' Tom said, 'and be in the library as soon as you can. I hope to be there by half-past eleven at the very latest.'

'How do you know you will find us a safe place to live by that time?'

'I don't, though I will have a damned good try. But one thing I will promise and that is we will be far away from here by tomorrow evening. I have to send a telegram to Joe too, as soon as the post offices are open tomorrow, for he will be expecting me home.'

'Is Joe still on the farm then?' Aggie asked. 'Somehow, I thought he would be the one spreading his wings.'

'He did,' Tom said. 'He hasn't been that long back at the farm. A lot has happened to all of us since you left, Aggie.'

'Oh, tell me all,' Aggie said. 'This is what I have missed so much – hearing how you were all getting on.'

So Tom told her first of the death of Finn at the Battle of the Somme in 1916. Aggie was saddened by that, for she remembered the lovely little boy she had left at home. It seemed such a terrible and tragic waste. She was surprised though when Tom told her that Nuala had been allowed to take a job at the Carringtons' place, especially when she was of an age to be such a help to their mother.

Tom smiled. 'You are thinking about the upbringing you had. Nuala's was totally different. Mammy would let her do virtually nothing and so she got a job as nursemaid to the Carringtons' children. When the troubles were at their height the Carringtons fled to England and took Nuala with them. She was near Birmingham, she told us, in a place called Sutton Coldfield.'

'I have heard of it,' Aggie said. 'Some of the clients at the club came from there. Posh place, so I hear.'

'I imagine so if the Carringtons had a house there,' Tom said and went on, 'Just after Nuala left, Daddy developed a bad heart.'

'Daddy did?' Aggie said. 'I always thought that it would be Mammy, with the rages she used to get into.'

'Aye,' Tom said. 'We weren't allowed to write and tell Nuala in case it upset her. Some time later, when she met a man she wanted to marry she wrote and told them. And when Daddy read in the letter that the man was a Protestant, he dropped dead to the stone floor with the letter still in his hand.'

'Ah. Poor Daddy.'

'Aye, and poor Nuala too,' Tom said, 'for she was disowned from that point, as you were when you disappeared.'

'I expected it for me,' Aggie said, 'but Mammy was besotted by Nuala.'

'She blamed her for Daddy dying and absolutely hated her,' Tom said. 'Joe couldn't stand the atmosphere in the house and he went off the States.'

Tom went on to tell Aggie of Joe's marriage and son, his fluctuating fortunes in America, his role in the war in London and how he had at last returned to Ireland.

'He is nearly back to his old self now, and he is not the type of man to look down on his own sister. Joe will be delighted that I have found you. We have often wondered, and talked about you.'

Then he told Aggie about Nuala's children being orphaned.

'Nuala's death shocked me to the core, and I don't mind admitting I shed tears,' Tom said. 'Mammy wasn't shocked, though. She said she'd prayed for something to happen to Nuala for years.'

'God, she's a cold, hard woman.'

'Was,' Tom corrected. 'She died in January and

for weeks before her death she could neither move nor speak, but by then even I found it hard to feel sorry for her, because Molly came to live with us for five years and Mammy gave her hell, absolute hell. An awful lot happened to her before she was reunited with Kevin. One day she'll probably tell you all about it.'

'Tom,' Aggie said. 'What are you talking about? She won't want to see the likes of me.'

'Of course she will,' Tom said. 'And wait till you hear her tale. I am over here to see Molly and meet young Kevin, of course. They are living in Castle Bromwich and Molly is engaged to be married to a pilot. The wedding is in June, and by then you will be as fit and healthy as anyone else, and I will be proud to have you take my arm.'

Aggie shook her head. She didn't believe Tom for one minute, but her head was too addled to form the words to contradict him. But when he suggested that they both hit the sack because they had a big day ahead, she said, 'I doubt I will sleep with all this running around in my head.'

Tom smiled. 'I think you have drunk enough to ensure a good night's sleep,' he said, for he had noticed how often Aggie had filled her glass. He pulled her to her feet and, supporting her staggering form, helped her through the curtain to the makeshift bedroom where he sat her gently on the bed. 'Can you manage now?' he asked.

'Course I can, course I can,' Aggie said airily, waving her arms in the air in the manner of the very drunk. Tom smiled as he left her, knowing that she would have a head and a half in the morning and hoped she would remember the arrangements they had made for her escape.

When Tom saw Aggie waiting for him in the library, he was relieved, for he hadn't been sure that she would be brave enough to leave the man who still petrified the life out of her. He was late and it was almost half-past twelve. Despite the incongruous kitbag, he saw that she had made an effort to tidy herself up. Her face was not as white and pasty, and her eyes, though still black-rimmed, had more life in them. She had brushed her hair and put it up so that curls peeped out from under the very respectable navy hat that matched her coat. Even her boots were in good shape. Aggie saw Tom's eyes widen in surprise and approval.

'These were the things I had on when Finch's men got me,' she said, 'and since then they have hung in the wardrobe because Finch produces the trash I wear on the streets. I had almost forgotten I had them till I went in for the kitbag and saw them there. Mind you, they just hang on me now.'

'That's because you need feeding up,' Tom said, 'And talking of feeding up, we need a ration book so I am told. Have you got one?'

Aggie shook her head. 'I should have one – everyone should – but Finch used to give me the food he allows each day.'

'Well, that is a thing of the past,' Tom told her.

'Today we will register for a ration book each and an identity card too.'

'Here?'

'No, the town hall in Sutton Coldfield, where we are going to live for now. We have got a little two-bedroomed flat there. In fact, the less time we spend in Birmingham, the better I like it.'

'Me too.'

'Come on then.' Tom caught up her arm. 'We have to catch the Lichfield train from New Street Station. God, Aggie,' he said suddenly, 'you are trembling all over. Are you really that scared?'

'I am scared, all right,' Aggie replied, 'but much of the trembling is because I badly need a drink, or some opium, or both.'

'You know you must fight this, Aggie?'

'Of course I know,' Aggie snapped. 'But it is hard. Bloody hard, if you really want to know.'

Neither Aggie nor Tom was aware of just how hard it would be, and the trembling was just the tip of a very large iceberg.

TWENTY-EIGHT

Tom did not leave Aggie's side for four days. He couldn't have left her if he had wanted to, because she wasn't in her right mind at all. He had never seen anyone in such torment and he didn't ever want to see it again either.

The shakes were bad enough, it wasn't the odd shiver or even teeth chattering with cold or fear, this was Aggie's whole body trembling violently as if everything was loose inside and she would cry out against it. Worse than that, though, were the pains in her stomach, which would double her over, and she would groan and sometimes roll on the floor to try to gain some relief.

She was unable to sleep, and that meant that Tom had to go without as well. He managed light dozes at various times when Aggie nodded off through sheer exhaustion. He would rest in a chair in the living room, fearing that if he allowed himself to lie down properly he probably wouldn't wake for hours. His whole body and mind were so weary it was sometimes difficult to function, and he was becoming clumsy and slow.

He was heartily glad that he had insisted that first day on registering with a grocer and butcher, and collecting the rations for the two of them, for he hadn't been across the door since. Not that Aggie was eating enough to keep a bird alive. So when she began to vomit and have diarrhoea the second day he couldn't imagine where it was all coming from and could only assume that it was the muck and poison being cleared out of her system.

The hardest thing of all, though, was standing firm when Aggie would go through the cravings. Then he could barely recognise his sister as she begged and implored him to get her something, anything to help her. Sometimes she would approach him suggestively, promising he could take any delight he wanted if he would bring her some gin, and he would turn away in distaste, reminding himself that she didn't really know what she was saying. Other times she would scream at him or attack him, beating him with little fists that had no power in them, or she would cry in anguish with great gulping sobs that tore at Tom's heart. Sometimes she would even bang her head repeatedly against the wall.

If she would let him, Tom would gather her up in his arms, rock her and stroke her hair and tell her just how much she meant to him. He wasn't usually that good at standing firm and yet this time he had to, for Aggie's very survival depended upon him hardening his heart.

After the initial heart-wrenching four days, though Aggie was far from over her addictions, the vomiting and diarrhoea had eased and she was noticeably calmer. Tom was able to leave her for short periods to get the shopping in. By the time a week was up, Aggie was lucid enough for long enough to thank Tom for his support and for staying strong when she would have crumbled. Tom was embarrassed. No one had ever praised him for his strength of character before.

'That's all right, Aggie,' he said. 'I am just delighted that you are getting better.'

'I am not right well yet, Tom,' Aggie warned.

'I know that. I will be guided by you in this. You tell me how you are feeling and if I can help you in any way then I will,' he said, adding with a smile, 'As long as you don't ask me to bring you in a bottle of gin, or laudanum.'

Aggie sighed. 'No,' she said. 'But, oh God, Tom, you have no idea of the cravings. It's as if my innards are on fire. I feel that if I don't have something I will die. Even now, I am almost overcome at times, but I know I must fight it. I would have sold my soul in the beginning and, God knows, I had already surrendered my body.'

'Aggie, you have suffered so dreadfully since you were fifteen years old,' Tom said. 'I feel so sad about that and wish I could somehow get those years back for you.'

Aggie sighed. 'No one can do that.' Thanks to you, though, I will be able to enjoy the rest of my life. There is one blot that stops total happiness.'

'Let me guess. Tony Finch?'

Aggie nodded.

'I did feel bad letting him get away with all he has put you through,' Tom said. 'But my priority then was you. When you feel up to it we must have a talk about Finch, but don't worry, he has no way of tracing you here.'

'Tom, he has spies everywhere. Absolutely everywhere.'

'Then, my dear, he must be dealt with.'

That was what Aggie feared most. She cried, 'No, Tom.'

Tom covered Aggie's hands with his. 'This isn't something for you to fret over,' he said, looking into her agitated eyes.

'You know,' Aggie said, 'in the early days when I was so disgusted that I could hardly live with myself, I had a mad thought of contacting Polly Palmer. You remember I told you about Polly?'

'Wasn't that the woman you stayed with when you were working in the munitions?'

'That's right. I wasn't thinking straight. She was a lovely person, honest and sort of wholesome, and we got on so well, but she never knew the truth about my earlier life. Lily and I both said we had been in service. How could I land at her door, the state I was in then, gin-sodden and doped up to the eyeballs? If she didn't order me from the door, you can bet her husband would soon enough, and I wouldn't blame him either. Street women are unseen by decent members of society. Everyone knows they are there, but they don't expect to meet them, never mind mix with them and they certainly don't want them tainting their lives.'

'Was there no one you could confide in? No one who could help you?'

'Not a soul,' Aggie said. 'See, apart from Polly, Jane and the girls at work, I only knew prostitutes, and they were often in a similar boat. Jane knew what I was once, of course, but when she married she didn't let on to her husband what sort of club she worked at, she told me at Lily's funeral. She was living in Cheshire anyway, and though I got on with the girls at work I was never really friendly with them. I was always afraid of them finding out about my past and, anyway, I sort of didn't think I should make friends with these ordinary girls as if I was the same as them. With Polly it was different because we lived in her house, but even there we never spoke about the past. Poor Polly. I bet she often wondered what had happened to me. It was as if I disappeared into thin air.'

'You were so alone, so isolated.'

'It was better that I was,' Aggie said. 'In my clearer moments I knew that. Just suppose I had gone to Polly and she hadn't fainted from shock, and that she had seen past the drink, drugs and degradation and taken me into her home. The minute she did that, she would be at risk, and not just her, but her husband and children too. Finch would hunt me down and punish any that harboured me. And that is why I am so afraid for you.'

'I know,' Tom said. 'And believe me, there is no need. You are safe now.'

'I really want to believe that.'

'Try, Aggie,' Tom said. 'Don't let Finch destroy the rest of your life too. Now, if it's all right with you, I will go up to my bedroom and write a long letter to Joe, bringing him up to date with developments. He will be anxious because the telegram just said I had been unavoidably delayed and would write later.'

'Then write, certainly,' Aggie said. 'Are you writing to Nuala's daughter too? Molly, you called her?'

'Aye,' Tom said. 'But I shan't write to her yet. I want to keep you as a surprise.'

'A shock, you mean.'

'No,' Tom said, 'I had the right word. You will be a surprise to Molly and a very pleasant one at that.'

'You old flatterer, Tom,' Aggie said. 'You better get away to your bedroom before you embarrass the life out of me.'

'Now,' said Tom from the doorway, 'you sound like Molly.'

'I can't wait to meet her,' Aggie said wistfully.

'It won't be long.' Tom was confident. 'You are improving every day.'

*　　*　　*

Joe was astounded when he got Tom's letter. There were pages and pages of it. He read it all in silence and then turned to Gloria. 'God, this is almost unbelievable. Tom has found our oldest sister, Aggie. You mind I told you about her? She ran away from home at fifteen, after being raped and finding herself pregnant.'

'Sure I remember,' Gloria said. 'I was intrigued at the time.'

'Aye, and full of questions I couldn't answer,' Joe said with a grin. 'Anyway, it appears that the future that Molly escaped from, by the skin of her teeth, has been Aggie's lot for years.'

'Oh God, poor girl. How on earth did Tom find her?'

'He didn't,' Joe said. 'She found him. She actually propositioned him as he was leaving a pub.'

'God!' Gloria breathed. 'The chances of that happening must be incredible. I would be mortified by shame.'

'Tom said she was,' Joe said. 'Aggie was controlled by a man called Tony Finch, who got her hooked on drugs. I remember Aggie was always lovely. She never raised her voice or got in a temper. We all missed her terribly when she just disappeared and we weren't even allowed to talk about her afterwards, like she hadn't existed or something. It was stupid. Poor wee Finn was only five and he cried over her for days. And all the time Tom was carrying the burden of knowing where she had gone. He never forgot her.'

'Why don't you write to Tom and ask him what he intends to do about Finch, if anything at all?' Gloria suggested.

'I will,' Joe said. 'But answering an epistle of this length will take some thought.'

Tom's answer to Joe was that dealing with Finch was on the back burner. He would not forget about him, but his first priority had to be Aggie, and she was improving so much it did his heart good to look at her.

Her eyes were no longer bloodshot, there were no black rings around them and there was more colour in her cheeks. Her hair, now washed and brushed regularly, shone like silver, and she wore it in a sort of soft bun at the nape of her neck. Three weeks after Tom spirited Aggie away he took her to meet Molly.

'Molly won't know that I am even in Birmingham,' he told Aggie as they travelled on the train early that evening. 'I told Joe not to say, though he says she thinks it odd that I have not written. I had taken to writing fairly regularly.'

'She won't be cross at us just turning up like this?'

'No, not a bit of it,' Tom said. 'And she will be delighted by you.'

Molly was staggered with surprise at seeing her uncle at her door when she had imagined him back in Buncrana, and by his side a woman that she had never seen before. 'Uncle Tom!' she cried.

'What are you doing here?' She hugged him in delight. 'It's not that I am not pleased or anything but . . .'

'I never left,' Tom said. 'I met someone important to me and now I would like to introduce her to you.'

For a moment Molly imagined some sort of romantic entanglement until she turned and looked at the woman fully for the first time. She knew she had never met her and yet she seemed familiar somehow. Suddenly she realised the woman reminded her of an older version of her mother. Then Tom said, 'Molly, this is your Aunt Aggie.'

'Aunt Aggie?' Molly queried, her brow furrowed. Then she remembered her uncle telling her about his other sister. 'The girl who ran away,' she said.

Tom gave a chuckle. 'Aye, the very same. Now we have a lot to tell you and I don't intend to do that on the doorstep, so can we come in?'

'Oh, yes, of course,' Molly said, flinging the door open. 'Give me your coats or you won't feel the benefit. Then, Uncle Tom, if you lead the way to the living room . . . Kevin is in the kitchen, supposedly doing his homework, but he will be out as soon as he knows you're here. Paul Simmons is popping in later as well.'

'Why's that?' Tom asked.

'Oh, he's bringing some brochures of houses,' Molly said. 'Mark and I had intended to stay in Terry's house for the duration, but Paul said it would be wise to see if we can buy now rather than wait till after the war when everyone will be looking to do the same thing.'

'He is a very wise man, that Paul,' Tom said.

'I know,' Molly said. 'Anyway, that will be another pleased to see you.'

'I was going to see him anyway,' Tom said. 'It will save me a journey.'

Just then there was a whoop from the kitchen as Kevin recognised his uncle's voice, and the sound of a kitchen chair hitting the floor.

Molly commented wryly, 'That's the boyo breaking the place up to get to you,' and then Kevin was through the door and launching himself at his uncle. Molly went into the kitchen and began filling the kettle and Aggie followed her.

'You don't mind us landing on you like this?'

'No,' Molly said, 'I am delighted to meet you.'

'Tom has told me all about you – how you found your grandfather had died and your brother was in an orphanage,' Aggie told Molly kindly. 'I thought it terrible news for you to cope with on your own.'

'Of course that wasn't the only thing,' Molly said. 'I suppose that Uncle Tom has also told you what happened when I first arrived in Birmingham?'

Aggie shook her had. 'He said you had a story to tell, but wouldn't say anything more.'

'Well, as the whole of Birmingham eventually knew what happened to me, there is no point in keeping it from you,' Molly said. 'But instead of my telling it, I will let you read it because I have the cuttings from the newspapers upstairs.'

And so a little later Aggie sat on a chair in Molly's kitchen and learned just what had happened to her young niece when she had arrived at New Street Station. How brave of her to pick up the pieces of her life, and then to have to relive that dreadful time in a court room, telling perfect strangers all about it. What fortitude she had shown. She could easily have gone the way of her aunt. Suddenly it was too much for Aggie and she put her head in her hands and sobbed.

Molly put her arms around her, awkwardly at first, and more naturally as the woman continued to cry.

The doorbell rang and a few minutes later Kevin was at the kitchen door to say that Paul Simmons was there.

He regarded the tearful woman with under-standable curiosity. 'What's up?' he asked and when Molly signed for him to leave them, Aggie roused herself.

'No, it's all right,' she said. 'I am being foolish.'

Paul, following Kevin, saw a woman he had never seen before trying to compose herself and he withdrew a large snow-white hanky from his pocket and said, 'Would this help you?'

'Thank you,' said Aggie taking it.

Paul Simmons gave a start, for the woman's eyes were the same colour and shape as Molly's. In fact, she looked like an older version of her. This was explained a little later when Tom appeared. Seeing Aggie so upset, he put an arm around her shoulders, before saying to Paul, 'This is my older sister, Agnes.'

Paul didn't understand. Tom and Molly had talked a lot about the family and yet had made no mention of an Agnes.

Molly saw Paul's confusion and said, 'I have made the tea and it's spoiling. Shall we go back into the living room and maybe we can explain things to you?'

Paul gave a brief nod and took the tray from Molly's hands. As Kevin was about to follow, Molly stopped him.

'Not you, young man,' she said. 'You have homework to do.'

'Oh, Molly . . .'

'Don't "Oh Molly" me,' Molly said sharply. 'Get down to it.'

Tom smiled as a very disgruntled Kevin closed the kitchen door with a definite slam and Molly chided her uncle gently.

'You make him worse laughing at him.'

'He didn't see.'

'He probably did,' Molly said. 'You would be surprised what that boy sees and hears. Still, we didn't come out here to talk about Kevin.' She turned to Aggie. 'All Uncle Tom told me was that you ran away when you were fifteen. He didn't seem to know any more.'

563

'Oh, he knew much more than that,' Aggie said. 'He kept quiet to protect me, but you have shared your experiences with everyone and perhaps now is the time for you to hear my story.'

Aggie told it simply and directly, and Tom found it hurt even more to hear it for the second time. Molly listened with astonishment and thanked God that she had managed to escape before she had been sucked in completely, as her aunt had been.

Paul was astounded. Before the business with Molly he hadn't been aware that such things went on. He hadn't thought much about prostitution at all and had always thought it rather a crude and seedy way to go on. He seldom thought of the women who did this sort of thing for money as real people, and certainly not real women. Like Aggie had thought first, he imagined them to be the dregs of society, born into that sort of life, perhaps, and so knowing no better.

Then he had heard about Molly and been angered and upset at what she had endured. Now he heard of another naïve country girl, this one being forced to flee her home because of the consequences of a violent rape. It gave him an actual pain to watch Aggie's face as she relived her despair and desperation when she found the woman she had been sent to was no longer at the house.

He heard of the prostitutes who had been good to her, the Irish dancing, which had offered her a solution of sorts, of Alan Levingstone, who she had come to love dearly, and finally of Tony Finch. Paul burned with rage on hearing of the abuse she had suffered at his hands.

Aggie saw this. 'I wasn't the only one Finch was brutal with,' she said, 'although he really did seem to have it in for me. All the girls said so.'

'But why?'

Aggie shrugged. 'He was crazy and no one really understands him at all. But you know,' she said, 'leaving the abuse aside, the sex side of it used to affect me as much.'

The tears were brimming behind Aggie's eyes, which were like two pools of sadness in her bleached white face at the memories of that terrible time. Paul felt as if his heart was breaking.

'Do you want to stop?' he said. 'Is it too much for you?'

Aggie shook her head and almost whispered, 'I am mortified that I allowed men to use my body in any way they chose to. And now, telling it as it was shocks me to the core.'

'It shocks me too,' Paul said. 'Shocks me that you were driven to such measures.'

'I thought it was partly my own fault too,' Molly said. 'I couldn't believe I could have been so stupid. It was Paul who put me right.'

'I did,' Paul said to Aggie. 'As I would you, my dear. There is nothing that I have heard so far that could be deemed in any way your fault. The only shame I feel is that society allows such things to go on.'

'Well said,' Tom agreed. 'And, Aggie, there is no law in the land says that you have to tell us anything at all. If you don't want to say any more, then we will all understand.'

Aggie thought for a moment or two. 'No,' she decided, 'I have told you so much and now I will go on to the end and see what you think of me then.'

As Aggie continued, Paul went through a gamut of emotions – rage, shock and horror at the things Aggie had had to endure – and he often saw the anguish in her face and knew she was reliving it. And yet she never faltered or stopped, and the quiet calm way in which she recounted almost unspeakable cruelty made it even more distressing.

As her tale drew to a halt eventually, Paul said, 'This man Finch, where is he now?'

'I don't know,' Aggie said. 'All I am scared of is him catching up with me.'

'We need to go to the police,' Paul said. 'They will find him soon enough and if you tell them even half the things he has done to you . . .'

'No, Mr Simmons,' said Aggie. 'There will be no police.'

'What are you talking about?' Paul cried. 'We must have the police. The man cannot go unpunished.'

'Mr Simmons, the man is rich and influential, and has friends in the police,' Aggie said. 'He would deny everything and paint me as a scarlet woman, one mad for sex and all. He would be believed before me, a street woman. I would probably be the one in the dock and could easily find myself imprisoned. And I would betray all the other girls in the house who could easily find themselves in prison alongside me.'

'But this is monstrous.'

'Paul,' Tom said, 'we have to work with the system as it is, not as we would like it to be. Aggie is quite right.'

'So the man is to just get away with it?'

'He has so far,' Aggie said.

'The first thing to do is find out where he is,' Tom said. 'Then we can decide what action to take.'

'Leave that to me,' Paul said. 'And meanwhile, Miss Sullivan, why don't you return to Ireland? It would be safer for you.'

'I can never go back to Ireland,' Aggie said. 'They would never give over about what happened to me. No tale I fed them would suffice, even if I could think of one, and if I was to tell the truth, they might put two and two together and then Tom might be in big trouble.'

'Why?' Molly asked in bewilderment.

Aggie looked from Molly and Paul's puzzled faces to Tom's red one and realised that they didn't know about the business with McAllister. 'I'm sorry, Tom,' she said. 'Me and my big mouth.'

Tom shrugged. 'I didn't think you would ever need to know this,' he said, 'but today seems to be the day for confessions, so here goes.'

Paul and Molly were so engrossed in Tom's story as he described how he had caused the death of McAllister that none was aware of the click of the kitchen door, or Kevin coming into the room. He listened with open-mouthed astonishment.

Tom finished, '. . . and though I hadn't meant to kill him, I am not sorry. Aggie was not the first girl he violated and had he lived she wouldn't have been the last. Philomena knew that as well as me. When my time is up, I will let God be the judge of my actions.'

'Golly!' said Kevin.

Molly turned anger-filled eyes on him. 'Kevin, don't you creep into a room like that. What do you want anyway?'

'I didn't creep,' Kevin protested. 'I came to tell you I have finished my homework.'

'What did you hear?'

'I heard Uncle Tom say how he killed someone.'

'It is not something I am proud of, Kevin,' Tom said. 'And I suffered guilt for years. Still do, if the truth's told, and probably will until the day I die.'

'But he was a bad man. You said so.'

'Just because you consider a person bad is no reason to kill them.'

'Bet you wouldn't say that if he was a German,' Kevin said. 'People seem to have no trouble popping them off.'

'We are not talking about Germans, Kevin,' Molly said. 'And you do realise that you mustn't mention this to anyone or Uncle Tom will get into big trouble.'

'And not me alone,' Tom said.

'I won't tell anyone,' Kevin maintained. 'I ain't stupid.'

'I am serious, Kevin.'

'So am I,' Kevin said. 'Look, to prove it, I'll do summat you did to me years ago. You meant it then and I mean it now.' He licked his index finger and held it up. 'See it wet,' he said, and then rubbed it on his jersey. 'See it dry.' Then he drew his finger across his neck. 'Cut my throat if I tell a lie or tell another living soul what I heard in this room tonight.'

Molly smiled. When the two children were forced to part, she had promised they would be together again one day using the same childish words. However, as Kevin had said, she had meant those words when she said them, and this was his way of making a similar and sincere promise that Tom's secret was safe.

TWENTY-NINE

Four weeks later, a lot had changed. Tom had begun working in Paul's factory because his savings were considerably depleted. He felt he couldn't leave Aggie on her own, although Molly said she would look out for her and even offered her a room in the house. Tom knew, however, that Aggie felt safer being as far from Birmingham as possible. And he said as long as Joe was agreeable, he might as well stay in England until Molly's wedding, and then maybe look at the situation again.

Paul had also come up trumps in locating Finch. He had his address and his place of work, and had even found out that he went a lot to a club just off Broad Street in Birmingham called the Flamingo Club. He gave the information to Tom at work one day. He didn't ask what he intended doing with it. Tom was glad of this for he didn't want Paul to be involved, for, as far as he was concerned, it was family business. That night he wrote a long letter to Joe.

Aggie was alone in the flat that Monday morning in late April when there was a knock on the door. That had never happened before and she was almost too afraid to open it until she heard the visitor shout, 'Miss Sullivan, it's Paul Simmons.'

Aggie, alarmed that something had happened to her brother because Paul had never called on her before, opened the door hurriedly. 'What is it?' she cried. 'Is Tom all right?'

Paul was mystified. 'Yes, he's fine,' he said as he stepped into the hall.

'Then why are you here, Mr Simmons?' Aggie asked. Then, realising that sounded rude, she went on, 'It's not that you are not welcome or anything but . . .'

'I . . . I just wanted to see you.'

Aggie was completely nonplussed. 'Oh,' she said, and stood staring into Paul's deep eyes for a moment or two. 'Where are my manners? Come through to the kitchen and I will put the kettle on. You do want a cup of tea?'

'Yes . . . no. Oh, go on then,' Paul said, and Aggie laughed.

'I'd best not ask you a more involved question if you get so confused over whether you want tea or not.'

She led the way through to the kitchen and filled the kettle. Paul sat down at the kitchen table and watched her, his senses reeling. He didn't know what was the matter with him, but he had not been able to get Aggie out of his thoughts since

571

he had first met her. He had fought the attraction, for he had little experience with women. He thought, apart from money, he had little to offer, because he truly felt that he was ugly and dull, and he had a limp so pronounced his cars had to be adapted to enable him to drive them. But he had been so moved by the account of Aggie's life that he'd felt an almost overwhelming desire to enfold her in his arms and kiss the tears from her eyes. He had never had feelings like that before and they scared him rigid. It wasn't as if Aggie had given him any sort of encouragement, though she was always pleasant when they met.

He had thought he would get over it, but instead of getting easier, the feelings had grown stronger with each passing day, until he was now unable to sleep. In the end, he thought he had to see Aggie and ask her straight out how she felt about him. If she rejected him, as he fully expected, then he would have to deal with it, but not knowing was driving him crazy.

If Aggie was asked, if she allowed herself to think of any man that way, she would have said that she didn't think of Paul as ugly at all. His craggy face was interesting more than tradition-ally handsome, it was true, and his once fine head of black hair was now streaked with silver. His eyes, though, were beautiful, so very dark, deep and very expressive, and she liked his wide and generous mouth. More importantly, she knew him to be a kind man and a generous one too, because

Molly had told her of the things he had done for her and Kevin after the death of her parents.

In Aggie's book that was more important than looks, and he was anything but dull. Not that that mattered a jot to her, she told herself. At the end of the day, she wanted no truck with any man ever again.

She had made the tea and placed a cup before Paul, and still he hadn't spoken a word. Aggie hadn't known any way to break the uncomfortable silence. She had sat down opposite him, noting his brooding eyes and puckered brow, and she wondered what he was thinking so hard about.

'Penny for them, Mr Simmons?' she said.

'What?'

'Your thoughts,' Aggie said. 'I said, penny for them.'

'Sorry, my mind is on other things,' Paul admitted.

'Oh. Are they thoughts to share?'

Paul sighed. He was incredibly nervous now he was here and sitting opposite Aggie, but he had promised himself that he would speak out so he said, 'Yes, I think so.' And then without any lead in at all he said, 'What do you really think of me, Miss Sullivan?'

To say Aggie was surprised was an understatement. She looked at the man in amazement for a moment or two, then said, 'What an extraordinary question, Mr Simmons. I like you, of course.'

Paul's disappointment was apparent, though he

told himself it was the reaction he expected. 'Just like? Is that all?' he asked.

'Mr Simmons, what do you want me to say?'

'I want you to say what's in your heart,' Paul said. 'Could you do more than like me?'

'Mr Simmons, I barely know you.'

'All right then,' Paul said. 'Would you like to get to know me better?'

Aggie felt completely at sea, for she hadn't the least idea what Paul was on about. 'What are you saying, exactly?'

'You really want to know what I am saying?' Paul burst out. 'Then I'll tell you. Miss Sullivan, I am crazy about you. I have been able to think of nothing since I saw you that evening at Molly's, and when I listened to what you had endured it nearly broke my heart. I have never felt this way about anyone and though I have little experience of it, I think I love you, Miss Sullivan.'

'You must be crazy right enough,' Aggie said almost angrily. 'You know what I was. Dear God, I have had more men mauling and groping and having sex with my body than you have had hot dinners. If you have love to spare, then give it to someone more deserving than me. I am not worthy of any man's love and, what's more, I don't want it.'

'What are you saying?' Paul cried. 'Of course you are deserving. None of what happened to you was your fault. It was in the past and that doesn't matter to me.'

'Of course it matters,' Aggie snapped. 'The past shapes the people we are, the people we become. I was a whore, a street woman, and would lift my skirts for any who had the money to pay. That destroyed something inside me. It's like I am frozen. There is nothing there any more. If I was to encourage you in this fantasy, I could offer you nothing, and in time you would come to resent the life I had and the countless men who used and abused my body. This is a form of madness, but it will pass and then you will thank me.'

'No, I won't,' Paul said. 'I know that I was at the back of the queue when looks were given out, and I know my limp probably puts you off—'

'Your limp?' Aggie cried. 'What has your limp to do with anything? I have barely noticed it.'

'You must have.'

'All right then, let's say that it isn't important to me.'

'So why should the fact that you were forced into prostitution be important to me?' Paul asked.

'There is no comparison.'

Paul grasped Aggie's hands and said, 'Please, Miss Sullivan? All I am talking of is going to the pictures together or something. *Casablanca* is showing at the Odeon in Sutton Coldfield only a step away from here and it is supposed to be good.'

Aggie had a sudden memory of the times she had been to the pictures with Lily when they had worked together at the munitions and HP Sauce, and how much she had enjoyed those outings.

It was all so long ago, and in that other respectable period in her life, and she had a sudden longing to recapture those innocent pleasures. It wasn't all that far from home, after all.

Paul was looking at her almost fearfully and she realised that he almost expected her to refuse him. She felt sorry for him suddenly and suspected, for all his money, he was a very lonely man. Although she had her family around her now, she too often felt lonely. What harm would it do? So she smiled and said, 'All right, Mr Simmons. I think I would enjoy that. If we go as friends and nothing more.'

She saw Paul's hunched shoulders sag with relief. 'As friends, if that is how you want it,' he said, and his smile lit up his whole face.

Tom had a letter from Joe waiting for him that evening and he read it after he'd had his dinner. 'Joe wants to come for the weekend. Is that all right?' he said to Aggie.

'Oh, it's more than all right, Tom. I am dying to see him again. But who is looking after the farm?'

'Jack McEvoy,' Tom said. 'He offered to do it because he doesn't work weekends at the mill. Apparently, Joe won't be able to come over for the wedding, because there is no one to take charge of the place. Gloria and Ben are coming instead, so he is taking his chance to see you now.'

'I can hardly wait. He was eleven years old when I last saw him.'

'Aye,' Tom said. 'And one hell of a lot of water has gone under the bridge since.'

'D'know what time he is arriving?' Aggie asked.

'More or less,' Tom said. 'He's leaving after the milking on Friday morning and that means that he will be here in the afternoon, between say four and five. I mean, you know what the trains are like these days?'

'Yes, and if you complain about anything you are reminded that there is a war on,' Aggie said. 'As if that fact had slipped your mind.'

'It's all so much eyewash anyway,' Tom said. 'People say the trains were no better before.'

Aggie laughed. 'They probably weren't then,' she said. 'Depending what I can get on ration, I will try and make something that won't spoil if the meal has to be held back.'

'I'm sure you will manage,' Tom said. 'You can work miracles with those rations. After we've eaten, though, you'll not mind us going out for a few jars?'

That was where Aggie should have told Tom about Paul's visit and explain that she was going to the pictures with him on Friday night and so wouldn't be in herself. She was embarrassed, however, and instead she heard herself saying that she had no objection at all.

'You'll not be lonely on your own?' Tom asked.

'Goodness, Tom, I am not a child to be minded,' Aggie said. 'Go out and enjoy yourselves.'

Tom had no intention of enjoying himself that

weekend, and neither had Joe. When they met at the station, they didn't make straight for home but to the café on the platform where they discussed their plans for the evening.

'You sure you know where this club is?' Joe said to Tom as he put the mugs of hot sweet tea down before them.

'Aye,' Tom said, 'not the club exactly, but I know the general direction. I went more than once for a look while Molly was working. Anyway, Paul said his contact said the club was near the canal and all the side roads from Broad Street lead down to it, though some are blocked with bomb damage. I would say that it will be fairly easy to find, especially if we go in daylight.'

'That's another point, though, isn't it?' Joe said. 'There is too much daylight at the beginning of May.'

'I don't think they go to these places at half-past seven at night,' Tom said. 'Not if it keeps the same hours as the club Aggie was involved in. She said a lot of people wouldn't come in till most of the population were getting ready for bed and then stay until the early hours. All we have to do is be outside that Flamingo Club when the man arrives and nab him before he reaches it.'

'It's a bloody good job you found that picture of him,' Joe said.

'It was Aggie found it,' Tom said. 'Splashed all over the *Despatch* and the *Mail* were photos of him opening a rescue centre on the edge of the city for bombed-out families. Aggie very nearly passed out. As she said, what is an evil man like that doing getting involved in anything good and wholesome? Anyway, I had a good look at him then and cut a picture out later when Aggie wasn't looking. I tell you, he will be easy enough to spot. He is as bald as a coot, has big fat lips and eyes placed too close together. And now we best be making tracks before Aggie sends out a search party.'

Aggie was ecstatic to see her younger brother and she hugged him tight while tears ran down her face. She had never imagined in her wildest dreams that she would see any of her family again, and to have two of her brothers together and for them all to sit down to a meal was almost unbelievable to her. She looked from one to the other, her face one beam of happiness, almost too excited to eat the dinner that she had taken such trouble with.

Joe too was moved by the meeting. He looked at the sister he could barely remember and he realised that despite all that had happened to her, the old Aggie was still there. Kindness and a sort of goodness seemed to emanate from her and, like Tom, he mourned the lost years when his sister had been as good as dead to him. He vowed that night someone would pay dearly for that.

Tom and Joe found the Flamingo Club with ease. Joe was surprised by the scale of the bombing, though of course he had been well used to the Blitz in London. As Tom had said, some of the roads were blocked with fallen masonry, but when they went down Granville Street they found the club halfway down. It was all closed up, as they had half expected, and they wandered down to look at the canal.

'Nothing like the clean, bubbling streams of Buncrana,' Joe remarked, gazing at the torpid, brown, oil-slicked water.

'No,' Tom agreed. 'Molly said Birmingham is threaded with canals, and since the war began, they are more in use to transport stuff.'

'You have told me so much about Molly that I am dying to meet her,' Joe said.

'You will when this is over,' Tom said. 'Speaking of which—'

'No, Tom,' Joe said. 'We have been all through this. You avenged the rape of Aggie by killing McAllister. Now it is my turn.'

'You intend to kill Finch?'

'Not necessarily,' Joe said. 'I intend to beat him to pulp for what he has put my sister through. If he dies of those injuries, then I will not lose any sleep over it. It will be a fair fight too,' Joe went on. 'I don't want you to take part at all. This is between him and me.'

'Remember what happened to Levingstone.'

'Finch was sort of expecting Levingstone, wasn't he?' Joe said. 'This time the man will be totally unprepared.'

'All right then,' Tom said. 'Let us go and sink a pint or two. We can't hang about here for hours. Anyway, we could be spotted and maybe arouse suspicion, and we can't risk that.'

'All right, but no more than two pints,' Joe said. 'When I attack Finch, I want all my wits about me.'

And that was what they did, drawing out the second pint till the clock said almost ten o'clock. It was dusk as they positioned themselves close to the club, hidden from those arriving there by the concealing blackout.

Finch had no notion that he was in any danger. As he sat in the taxi that night, it still rankled that Aggie had got away from him and he concluded that she must have chucked herself in the Cut, as most people thought. Certainly he had had people searching for her day and night and they had all drawn a blank. He knew too how bad her cravings for gin and opium were and that had been enough to chain her to his side and do anything he demanded. Anyway, she had nowhere to run to, but he was furious that she had slipped out of his clutches and ended it herself.

So he was totally taken by surprise to be jumped on, just before he reached the door of the club. He was unable to struggle because his assailant's arm encircled him like a vice as he dragged him towards the towpath, and he was unable to make a sound because his mouth was covered so firmly he felt his teeth bruising his lips.

When Joe got Finch to the towpath, he threw

him to the ground with such force Finch had all the breath knocked from his body. He was also deeply afraid.

However, he had no time to reflect on his fear for Joe was on top of him, punching him from side to side till his head was reeling. Then he got to his feet and pulled Finch up with him. He parried Finch's flailing arms and his punches with ease and powered a punch to his abdomen.

'That is for Aggie,' he ground out.

'Aggie.' The name reverberated in Finch's brain. With a howl of rage he threw himself at Joe, but Joe hardly felt his desperate blows.

Tom watched the fight in the half-light, sometimes illuminated when the moon peeped from behind the clouds. He saw the power of Joe's fists and the desperation in Finch's inept efforts, both to lash out at Joe and protect himself.

Suddenly he saw Joe slam his fist extra hard into Finch and the man doubled over and groaned in pain. He was unable to protect himself from the next blow and he sank to his knees.

However, Finch's hands, which he had put out to try to save himself, had come in contact with a large chunk of wood on the ground. As he stumbled to his feet he had this in his hands.

'Look out!' Tom called to his brother, and Joe saw Finch circling him, the lump of wood held menacingly in front of him.

An evil smile played around his lips as he said

tauntingly, 'Come on, big boy. Let's see what you're made of now.'

Joe lunged at him and Finch hit Joe a powerful blow to the side of the head, which might have rendered many a man unconscious. Joe was momentarily stunned, and Finch, taking advantage of this, swung again to deliver a stinging blow to Joe's shoulder. Watching, Tom gasped as he saw Joe stagger a little. Joe's blood was really up, but he kept his head and when Finch raised the piece of wood again, he ducked beneath it, at the same time powering a punch into Finch's unprotected stomach. Finch fell to the ground and Joe was on top of him in seconds, grappling with him and wrenching the wood from his hands.

He looked at the man underneath him, who was whimpering with fear, and was tempted to clout him with the wood and put an end to him. Finch anticipated this and was putting his arms up, covering his face. However, Joe had said it had to be a fair fight and he threw the wood behind him, hearing the plop as it hit the water in the canal, just as Finch, seeing he was off guard for a second, caught him with a left hook that snapped his head back.

Joe, totally enraged now, went in for the kill. Lifting the man to his feet he snarled, 'Now fight, you slimy bastard,' as he pummelled the man with a volley of punches to his abdomen, so fast and furious that any counterattack from Finch was futile. Finch was tiring and gasping for air, but he knew he was fighting for his life and he kept the punches going, though Joe blocked most of them with his arm. And then a powerful right hook under Finch's chin, followed swiftly by a left, caused him to crumple to the ground in a heap. The heat, though, was still flowing through Joe and he aimed a kick at the unconscious form. When he lifted his foot again, Tom approached his brother.

'Hasn't he had enough?'

'Not while he breathes, no.'

'Joe.'

'Don't pretend that this is some decent human being that I am kicking the shit out of,' Joe said angrily. 'He is a brutal, filthy rat and rats deserve no mercy.'

'And you have given him none,' Tom said gently. 'But it's over now. Let's go home.'

Tom's words, soft though they were, penetrated Joe's brain and he shook his head to try to rid himself of the red mist that had surrounded him since he had first grabbed Finch.

'You all right?' Tom asked.

Joe nodded. 'I am now.' He looked at the unconscious man in a heap on the ground in front of him and said, 'Is he dead?'

Tom leaned down and felt for a pulse in Finch's neck. 'No. He is alive.' He had the sudden urge to put his hands around that scrawny neck and squeeze tight. He resisted that and got to his feet quickly. He had one man's blood on his conscience already. 'Come on,' he said. 'Let's get out of here quick.'

'Hush,' Joe said suddenly, and both men listened intently. The scraping, scratching sound that had alerted Joe came again. Both men moved towards the sound as quietly and quickly as possible, and though they had their torches ready, they didn't use them. They turned the corner of a bombed and now derelict factory and by the light of the moon saw a large rat sitting on a crate, cleaning its whiskers.

Tom's relief caused his limbs to shake slightly and Joe's was apparent in his voice as he said, 'Huh, aren't we the big men? Frightened of a bloody rat.'

'Aye,' Tom said, 'but let's away now. To hang about here is madness.'

They started up the road, but hadn't gone far when they heard a gigantic splash. Without a word they hurried back the way they had come. The towpath was completely deserted, running footsteps the only sound in the still of the night. There was no visible sign of anything or anyone, including the crumpled body of Finch.

Tom ran to the side of the canal, and in the light of the torch he played on the oil-slicked water he saw the crumpled body of Finch disappearing. 'Some one disliked that bastard as much as we did,' he said as his brother joined him.

'See anything?'

'Aye,' Tom said. 'I saw the slimy toad being sucked down under the water, and good riddance I say.'

'And me,' Joe said. 'Finch is no loss to the human race. Let's go and tell Aggie she can sleep easy in her bed now.'

Aggie had had a wonderful evening. Paul did nothing but hold her hand, which she found very comforting, and when he produced a bar of chocolate she was speechless with pleasure for she hadn't tasted it in years. The film too was magical, and she could not remember enjoying herself so much.

She hadn't been in long, and had just put the kettle on when Tom and Joe returned.

Aggie scrutinised Joe's face and said, 'Have you been fighting?

'Aye.'

'Oh, Joe,' Aggie cried in annoyance, 'what's the matter with you? Not five minutes in the country and you're fighting? And you're a right mess too. Come through to the kitchen and I will try and tidy you up.'

Joe followed her, sat obediently and watched Aggie pour water into a small bowl before saying, 'You haven't asked me who I have been fighting or why.'

'It doesn't interest me, that's why,' Aggie said shortly, dabbing at the lacerations on Joe's face with a soft damp cloth. 'I hate violence.'

'This time you won't,' Joe said confidently. 'It was Finch I fought with tonight.'

Aggie's hands were very still, but her voice shook as she said, 'Did you kill him?'

'No,' Joe said. 'I wanted to, but I didn't. I beat him, and badly, but he was alive when we left him on the towpath.'

'Then I am still in danger,' Aggie said, trembling at even the mention of the man's name.

'You're not, Aggie,' Tom said, from the doorway, 'because Finch is alive no more. Someone hated him as much as we did and heaved his unconscious body into the canal after we left. We went back and looked.'

Aggie could hardly believe it. 'He couldn't have stumbled away on his own?'

'We heard the splash and went back straight away,' Tom said. 'Someone took the opportunity to finish him off once and for all. I saw the last of him disappear beneath the water.'

'All the women who worked for him hated him,' Aggie said.

'Well, for them, and especially you, it's over,' Joe said. 'You are free of Finch and can go forward with your life now.'

Aggie felt the worry slide from between her shoulder blades as tears of blessed relief started in her eyes. She pulled her hands from Tom and covered her face as she sobbed. Tom and Joe looked at each other in consternation.

'Aggie,' Joe said uncertainly, 'I thought you would be pleased.'

Aggie looked up, and though the tears continued

to trickle down her cheeks, her face was lit up in a way the men had never seen before as she said, 'I am happy, you pair of eejits. God, don't men know anything?'

Aggie felt that her life started anew from that point, and Tom rejoiced with her as he realised she had been fear-ridden for most of her life. Now, of course, there was Paul in her life too, and the understanding they had that she had explained to the family. Everyone watched the tenuous relationship developing and hoped it would lead to something deeper, for they were both lovely people who deserved happiness.

Molly, though, knew what Aggie was afraid of, and one day she set out to visit her. Aggie was surprised to see Molly, but she was very fond of the girl and welcomed her warmly. They talked of inanities until Aggie had made the tea.

Then Molly said, 'How do you really feel about Paul, Aunt Aggie?'

Aggie smiled. 'He asked me that too and I will give you the same answer I gave him. I like him.'

'He loves you.'

'So he says.'

'He does,' Molly insisted. 'Anyone with half an eye could see it. It's in every line of his body, and especially in his eyes when he looks at you.' She saw that her aunt was uncomfortable and she said, 'You're not enjoying this, are you? It is embarrassing you even to talk about how Paul feels.'

'I am not used to it,' Aggie said. 'I was never encouraged to talk of feelings. I mean, most of what I used to feel for the punters was revulsion.'

'You said you loved the man who had the club – Levingstone, was it?'

Aggie sighed. 'I did, and when he died, God, it was terrible. I knew it was my fault in a way. I never felt that way for anyone again – never let myself, I suppose, if the truth is told. The pain of loss was too great too bear, and always at the back of my mind was Finch and his viciousness if I had become involved with anyone.'

'But he is gone now,' Molly said gently. 'You are free.'

Aggie shook her head. 'It's a habit I have got into over the years,' she said. 'It is too late for me.'

'I don't believe that for one minute,' Molly said. 'Tell me, do you stiffen up when Paul tries to put his arms around you?'

'He never puts his arms around me,' Aggie said. 'I stiffen just at the thought he might.'

'Does he kiss you?'

'Aye, on the cheek just.'

'What do you let him do?'

'Hold my hand,' Aggie said. 'Don't look at me like that, Molly. I am doing my best and Paul accepts this.'

'No, he doesn't.'

'Molly, he does. He understands.'

'Of course he understands,' Molly said. 'That's because he is a lovely man, but every man expects to do more than just hold hands with the woman he loves.'

'I can't.'

'You can,' Molly said. She took hold of her aunt's hand and said, 'I am not here to bully you, but to tell you I hear all you say and empathise with it. That's how I was with Mark, though I knew in my heart of hearts I loved him with everything in me. When I thought he was dead, my feelings sort of broke through that barrier and I was able to show my love for him fully. Finch, even from the grave, still has power over you. Break through it, Aunt Aggie, for if you do you will find a truly wonderful and fulfilling life on the other side.'

Long after Molly had left, Aggie sat and considered her words. Molly was the only one who could truly understand her, because she had been through a frightening experience too and reacted the same way. But, she had ridden above it, overcome her fears and trepidation and wanted the same for her aunt.

She examined her feelings for Paul. She honestly didn't know if she loved him or not. She had pushed that emotion so far down, she didn't know that it would ever surface again fully, but she admitted she felt something for Paul that she had not felt for any man since Levingstone. And Molly was right: now that Finch was no more, she was safe to love anyone she chose, safe to live her life in any way she wanted.

When Paul called for her that night, she greeted him in the hallway, for Tom was eating his dinner in the kitchen and she wanted a private moment with him. She knew he wouldn't make the first move as he would be wary of scaring her off, so as he removed his coat she steeled herself and put her arms tight around him.

Paul was taken aback and he dropped his coat to the floor. He took Aggie in his arms as he had longed to do almost since the first time he had seen her. 'Oh, Aggie,' he said longingly, using her name for the first time and she felt feelings coursing through her that she had thought were buried fathoms deep and she sighed in deep contentment. It was as if she had come home at last to where she belonged.

'Paul,' she said, and the name sounded strange on her lips, though she had called him Paul in her mind from the first.

'Yes, my darling?'

'I think, that is, I'm almost sure, that I love you.'

Paul was almost too choked to speak for a moment or two. Then he said gently, 'Aggie, you have made me the happiest man in the world.'

Aggie lifted her head and their eyes met. She saw the longing in Paul's eyes and knew that it must be mirrored in her own. Paul, overwhelmed with love, daringly kissed her gently and was surprised and incredibly pleased when she returned that kiss with passion.

They were unaware of Tom coming into the hall to greet Paul. He retreated rapidly to the kitchen.

'They were kissing?' Molly asked him when he told her what had happened, a few days later. 'Really kissing?'

'I'll say. Didn't see me in the hall, anyway. To tell you the truth, Molly, I don't think they'd have noticed if I had run through stark naked. They had eyes only for one another.'

'Oh, thank God,' Molly said fervently.

'I echo that,' Tom said. 'For they are two of the loveliest people to walk the earth, and if anyone deserves happiness in this life it is them two.'

Aggie could not remember a time when she had felt happier in her whole life. She wished she had known Nuala, for her children were delightful. She had drawn even closer to Molly, and Kevin was like a breath of fresh air. She remembered Lily saying to her that she was like the daughter she had never had, she herself felt the same about Nuala's children, and knew they loved her too, and both of them thought the world of Paul.

Molly was right. On the other side of fear was true happiness.

The Abbey in Erdington, the church that Molly and Kevin had once attended, was packed with family and friends all there to celebrate with Molly and Mark. Aggie, on Paul's arm, stopped for a moment in the foyer and looked at the sea of people. Aggie saw Kevin was sitting with Ben, whom he had immediately taken under his wing, Gloria beside the two of them. She also noted the very nervous groom at the front of the church. Mark's best man, sitting beside him, she saw was just as nervous as he was. She smiled when she saw one hand dive into the pocket of his suit, presumably to check that he still had the rings.

Paul, seeing Aggie's preoccupation, said, 'Full house?'

'Not half.'

'Are you ready?' he asked.

Aggie nodded, and Paul took her arm. Immediately *frissons* of excitement leaped inside her. Their eyes met and Aggie felt butterflies in her stomach. Her heart began to pound and she knew suddenly, in that split second, that she loved Paul Simmons totally and completely, and that her life without him would be no life at all. She had to tell him how she felt, for she knew now her future lay with this man.

She had no need to say anything, however, for it was written all over her face. Paul's heart leaped and he bent down and whispered, 'You are my own darling girl, and I love you so much. When we have this wedding done and dusted, shall we plan our own?'

Aggie felt as if her heart would burst and she couldn't trust herself to speak. She nodded, her smile nearly cutting her face in two. She knew when she married Paul her happiness would be complete.

ACKNOWLEDGEMENTS

I hope that you have enjoyed this book, which is the second about the Sullivan family. In a way, this book was easier to write than most from the research side, because I had already done a lot for the previous novel, *A Sister's Promise*, and the titles that would follow it, and so I knew quite a bit about the family who had their farm just outside Buncrana, in Northern Donegal.

In another way though, this book was more difficult because it spans forty years. The Uncle Tom we meet in *A Sister's Promise* is a cowed and downtrodden man, the only one left on the farm and totally under the thumb of his domineering mother. In *A Daughter's Secret* we find out why he has developed the way he has, and to establish that I needed to go back to his boyhood to an incident that happened then that shaped his life. This meant I was dealing with events at the turn of the century, and so I used *Donegal in Old Photograhs* by Sean Beattie and *Rekindling a Dying Heritage* by Evelyn Ruddy.

Tom's problems are linked to his older sister, Agnes. He is the only one aware of his sister's secret that causes her to steal away from her home in the dead of night, and he carries that burden throughout life too.

Writing over such a long period of years is something I had never done before, and I found it challenging as well as enjoyable. Helping me keep the balance of the book, so that it stands alone and doesn't intrude too much on *A Sister's Promise* or the book of Joe and Gloria that is to come, was my fantastic editor at HarperCollins, Susan Opie. This was compounded later by the efforts of Yvonne Holland, who suggested further amendments. Without these two people, the book would be a much poorer one and so especial thanks goes to them. I'd also like to thank my agent, Judith Murdoch, who started me thinking about this series in the first place and my new publicist, Kiera Godfrey. These are my wonderful support team.

My husband and family are also extremely important to me, and although we care greatly for each other they would have no hesitation in slapping me down if I should get above myself. Grandchildren in particular are tremendous levellers, and I have four of those.

However I thank first and foremost my lovely husband Denis, who has now taken over the website, as my son (who started it) is just too busy to continue; my eldest daughter Nikki, her husband Steve and her gorgeous children, Briony (my eldest and only granddaughter is sixteen this year) and Kynan (who has now reached double figures!). Then there is my son Simon, his wife Carol and their fantastic little boys, Jake, who will be nine this year and who this book is dedicated to, and six-year-old Theo, the youngest of them all. Last but by no means least, there are my two younger daughters Bethany and Tamsin, who have now moved out of the house into places of their own. Thank you all sincerely for your support, understanding and consideration when deadlines have to be met.

I would find life extremely difficult without my friends and I value them all, but I am extremely grateful to my dear friend Judith Kendal, who helps me more than she knows. I must also extend thanks to Judith Evans – now in charge of a chain of bookshops at Birmingham International Airport – who first introduced me to Peter Hawtin in the spring of 2001. I had just left Headline, after four books with them, Peter was then the Midlands Sales Director for HarperCollins, it was he who invited me to ask my agent to contact HarperCollins, with a view to joining their lists. I did just that and I signed my first contract with them in the autumn of that same year. Grateful thanks to you both. Without you, my life might have taken off in a different direction sltogether.

However it is you the readers who give a purpose to it all. You who buy and read the books are the reason that I go up into my study every day and pound away at the computer keys, and I love it when you write and tell me what you think after you have read a book. I extend immense gratitude to each and every one of you.

A Sister's Promise

Anne Bennett

Molly's life changes forever when her parents are killed in a horrific accident. Although her beloved grandfather wants to keep her and her little brother Kevin with him in Birmingham, the authorities decide it's best for the girl to live with her maternal grandmother on a farm in Donegal. So Molly is packed off to Biddy Sullivan, a hard, cruel woman who loves to bear a grudge.

Years of hardship follow and just as Molly begins to grow independent, war breaks out. She fears the worst for her grandfather – and what will become of Kevin? He's only ten. So the naïve country girl sets off for her home city, little guessing what perils are to befall her before she can discover her brother's fate...

'Anne Bennett draws on her own background to give emotional depth to an affecting story populated with rich, beautifully drawn characters' *Choice*

ISBN: 978 0 00 722602 3

Hettie of Hope Street

Annie Groves

A breathtaking tale of one girl's determination to trace her roots, find true love and succeed in a world where obstacles lurk around every corner.

Hettie is an orphan, taken in by Ellie Pride and her husband to their Preston home and treated as one of the family. But she has never felt she truly belonged.

On the cusp of womanhood, and in love with someone who she is not considered good enough for, she heads for the bright lights of Liverpool to find her fortune.

There, the only way to survive is working in the kitchens of a restaurant. Until, by chance, she is heard singing by the owner...

Whisked to London, Hettie is thrown into a theatrical and colourful world - but one with a dark and seedy side. It is a mad, dizzy, dangerous world and Hettie increasingly feels ill at ease. Thoughts of home and her lost love dominate her mind but she knows she cannot return to the fold.

Then tragedy strikes, and Hettie must decide between her heart and her head, her duty and her desire...

Praise for Annie Groves:

'An engrossing story.'

My Weekly

'Heartwrenching and uplifting in equal measure.'

Take a Break

ISBN-10: 0 00 714959 X